Proper
Charlie Cu

Alan M. Kent was born in St Austell, Cornwall and lectures in Literature for the Open University in South-West Britain. He is a prize-winning poet, novelist and dramatist. In 1998 he received a Doctorate for his work on Cornish and Anglo-Cornish Literature. He has written extensively on the literary and cultural history of Cornwall. His most recent titles include *Cousin Jack's Mouth-organ: Travels in Cornish America* (2004), *The Dreamt Sea: An Anthology of Anglo-Cornish Poetry 1928-2004* (2004), *Assassin of Grammar* (2005) and a new verse translation of the trilogy of Cornish mystery plays known as *Ordinalia* (2005).

To me ma, Marlyn Kent
fur puttin' up with the row.

Proper Job, Charlie Curnow!

Alan M. Kent

HALSGROVE

First published in Great Britain in 2005
Copyright © 2005 Alan M Kent

British Library Cataloguing-in-Publication Data.
A CIP record for this title is available from the British Library.

ISBN 1 84114 488 6

Halsgrove

Halsgrove House
Lower Moor Way
Tiverton, Devon EX16 6SS
Tel: 01884 243242
Fax: 01884 243325
email: sales@halsgrove.com
website: www.halsgrove.com

Printed and bound in Great Britain by
The Cromwell Press Ltd, Trowbridge

C harlie Curnow's all-time, top five, greatest, most significant rock recordings of the past forty years. If he was ever asked, this is what he'd say:

Led Zeppelin *IV*.

Nirvana *Nevermind*.

Metallica *The Black Album*.

Green Day *American Idiot*.

A toss up between Deep Purple *In Rock* and Hüsker Dü *Zen Arcade*.

The MTV interviewer wudn' even knaw who the hell Hüsker Dü were. Only the most influential US Punk band of all time. And if she asked what were his other earliest influences, he'd offer:

The Holman Climax Male Voice Choir.

Star Wars IV, *V* and *VI* (Okay – and *I*, *II* and *III*).

Camborne's Trevithick Day.

Skinner's Ale.

The Cornish poet, John Harris (1820-1884).

Maybe, he'd also add: His da – on how not t'do anything, and how t'fuck it all up.

And if the sexy-groovy-belly-button-pierced babe, sitting in the studio, overlooking New York's Times Square wanted to know where he found the inspiration for the finest rock recording of that year – the Brit and Grammy award-winning album 'Songs full of Bollocks', which was destined to spend longer on the chart than even Pink Floyd's 'Dark Side of the Moon', he knew what he'd say. He'd think of now, and say,

'Chrissie (she'd be called something like that), I base all my songs on the estate I grew up on back home in Cornwall. I got a lot of inspiration from the people there – and of course, Cornwall's ancient and romantic landscape... which these days, I don't get back to see often enough...'

* * * * *

'One t'Trelawny,' said Charlie to the *First* bus driver, slapping a quid-fifty on the tray.

'I dun't go there anymore on this route,' the driver announced. 'Not t' ASBO City least...'

'Wha'?'

'Thaas' the rule now, ever since some little fucker 'eaved a stone through me front window. See this do 'ee?'

The driver leant over an' showed Charlie a recent long and scary-looking scar on his right hand.

'A piece o'glass went clean through.'

'Fuck,' said Charlie.

'The Police 'eaved an anti-social behaviour order on 'un...'

'Jeez... Did 'um b'fuck?'

'I'll take 'ee t'Troon Chapel though,' the driver said, as if that were compensation for the inconvenience.

'A'right,' said Charlie. 'That'll do... Proper job...'

He found a seat and gazed up at the roof. There were adverts for *Pirate FM* bollocks and tourist shite like 'Inspirational Cornwall' and the Eden Project's 'Time of Gifts'. The Hoppa Bus rattled around Redruth station, past the Mining Exchange, and up Clinton Road. A mizzle had come down thick and the windows had steamed up. When the bus turned right past *Morrish's* fish 'n'chip house, and headed up Four Lanes, you cudn' see your hand in front your face – the mist was that thick boy. In the backseat of the bus were a few maids from the estate. They'd all just started secondary school, but were tarted up for their Saturday parade 'round Redruth – all fuckin' luminescent boob tubes (£2.99 down *Asda*), and blow-job lipstick. The five o'them looked like the Spice Girls or some manufactured girl group from another fuckin' mutant universe.

'Yew Charlie!' one o'them shouted. 'Mel'll give yer cock a suck if you want.'

The maids all collapsed inta' laughter.

'Ah, you'm a'right,' Charlie said, turning 'round. 'You'n try givin' head t'that one though, if your gob's big enough!'

He pointed to the huge, granite Bassett memorial that topped Carn Brea. The phallic-like structure disappeared in and out of the mist.

The maids liked Charlie. He was a'right, not like most o'the boys back on the estate. All of 'um in the back row would get

Proper Job, Charlie Curnow!

off wid 'un if they had half the chance. So what, if he was eighteen? 'Ee was quicker than duckshit, and never talked like 'ee had the world hold by its asshole. Thaas' what they liked about 'un. They took photos of him on their mobiles, an' texted them to their mates over Pengegan.

'I'll give 'un a try dreckly,' shouted Mel.

'Like fuck y'will,' said Charlie. 'You'd be in some state maid, if you had t'run your tongue 'round the rim o'that...'

While the maids giggled – one or two giving him evils – Charlie looked at his purchases – the new Green Day album, a copy of any decent rock fan's weekly bible – *Kerrang!*, and *The West Briton* newspaper. Like most people up Trelawny, he was on the dole. All the work in Cornwall was shite – either selling fuckin' ice creams t'cunts down Portreath, or else bagging groceries for second-home owners in *Sainsburys*. Still, every fucker was the same up Trelawny – even his faather had no work now that South Crofty tin mine was finished. And then there was all that bollocks on the television about social cohesion and shite in Cornwall. Switch on *BBC Radio Cornwall*, and some knobber from Objective One be there goin' on about the 'county' had entered a new phase of prosperity. Where the fuck was that?

He viewed the CD. He'd got it at *John Olivers*, like he did most Saturdays. There wudn' much he didn' knaw about rock music. Most o'the kids on the estate weren't inta' rock though. They liked what his sister called 'techner' or 'gabber', DJs and dancefloor shite. Then he remembered last summer, when some Trelawny boys organised an illegal rave over Chycarn farm. The music wasn't so bad he thought. He even had time for some of that industrial stuff. Still, Charlie held the CD with real care. He'd wait 'til he was back home 'til he'd take off the cellophane an' play the disc.

The Hoppa stopped at Four Lanes. An old boy got on, an' sat before him. Charlie took out *The West Briton*. He'd long since given up lookin' for work in there, but always scanned the gig guide to see whas' on. It was the paper's headline that caught his attention though: DEAD MAN FOUND AT SHAFT USED HEROIN.

'Whisht innit?' said the old boy, seeing the front page.

''Es,' said Charlie. 'Happens though...'

'Knaw 'un did 'ee?'

9

'Yeah – I knawed of 'un, the twat...' Charlie said.

Charlie didn' need t'read the rest o'the story. He'd knawed it for over a week. 'Twas Chrissie Williams they'd found out Condurrow on the Sunday morning. They'd gone school together. Amongst all the other fly-tipped crap, some walkers on the mineral tramways route had found his body, with needles an' shite next to him. They reckoned he'd overdosed. The story on the estate was that the heroin had originally come from some Scouser fucks over Newquay. There was a real trade route up the M5, M6 and M62.

'Poor bugger,' theorised the old boy. 'Only twenty-one wudn' a?'

''Twas only a matter o'time,' Charlie said. 'You knaw what 'tis like...'

Chrissie's story had shocked the rest o'Cornwall, but on the estate, no one was that bothered. They'd seen what was happenin' at No.23 for months. No cunt intervened though. Even the police didn' intervene. The council had the place boarded up within days and then 'eaved out all o'Chrissie's gear. The sofa was the first thing t'go from the lawn, but the fridge stayed until yesterday. *Rentokil* 'ud be 'round next week, then some other poor fucker 'ud be movin' in. Thaas' the way 'twas. Social services dumped all their shite on Trelawny. Well, in some ways, it was easier really; rather than put 'em anywhere else. Least this way, it would contain 'em all.

'You live up Trelawny then?' asked the old boy.

''Es, lived there all me life,' Charlie replied.

'Many drugs up there then?' the old boy asked – like 'twas something you only found up the line.

The bus came to a halt outside Troon Methodist Chapel. Charlie got up.

'Only one or two,' he said, winking to the old boy, and headed towards the door.

'Cheers,' Charlie said to the driver, and stepped down to the pavement. The maids in the back followed 'un off and they all headed for the turning inta' Trelawny.

From here, the estate didn' look too bad. In the 1970s of course, it had been cheap land – only a few older shafts to seal. His father had told Charlie they were built in six months. It was in the 90s that the shite first started happenin'. He could remember it when he was a tacker – the older kids using the estate as a fuckin' banger-racing track. Then there were the air-gun attacks on the women coming back from Harvest Festival at the chapel. Then there was the time when a few boys torched a jam sandwich, but made sure they had the tyres clean off, before they blawed 'un.

So Kerrier District Council had them painted up in pinks an' pastel colours to improve the ambience o'the place. They spent some money modernising the estate, making it safer to walk through. Every fucker knew 'twas a waste o'time. 'Twudn' long before people put up barbed wire along their walls. That was their way o'telling the Council what they thought o'their environmental improvement scheme. So thaas' what Trelawny looked like now – like the fuckin' mutant offspring o'somewhere like Mousehole. The only thing good about it was that everyone was Cornish who lived there. No fucker from up the line would ever dream o'living in somewhere like 'ut. 'Twas an Emmet-free zone boy.

Charlie's place was on the far side o'the estate – near the old Trelawny United Mine. The maids and he split up, but before they went up the steps, Mel reminded him o'their party later. She was on her mobile, texting some poor fucker from Chacewater.

'Make sure y'come mind! Me mother'll be out. Bring some booze n'all…'

'A'right,' Charlie said, 'I'll be there.'

He headed 'round the corner and found the usual scene. There was a scramble ramp set up in the middle o'the road on five breeze blocks, an' some tackers were out jumpin' it.

'Out the way y'cunt,' shouted one o'them to Charlie, as he moved too close to the run-up.

Elsewhere was the usual proliferation of dog shit, burnt tarmac, rubbish and broken fences. A pair o'tits from an old copy o'*Men Only* blew across the drive an' the tackers chased it. In the air was the permanent smell o'blow. A tacker'd been caught with a joint last week in the primary school. Apparently 'ee was lighting up a spliff in the bogs.

Inside of one of the houses some cunt was playin' a Country and Western record. The mist was gettin' thicker. Disappearing out o'sight was the ruined chimney of Condurrow. Charlie thought o'Chrissie Williams, but the recollection was only momentary, and not sympathetic. He was a fuckin' asshole of the first order. He'd got what he deserved. Buyin' gear off an emmet, an' you were askin' fur trouble.

There was no one in. There wasn't much these days. His faather, havin' lost his job when the mine shut, had moved out. He and his mother had been goin' fur'n for months before – always fuckin' rowin', so it was perhaps for the best. He'd gone an' shacked up with some woman over Scorrier. She was a few years younger an' a pain in the ass. His ma had hurt like hell over it, but she wudn' show it, not t'him or his sister Jessie.

In the kitchen, he threw a *McCain* frozen pizza inta' the oven for his tea and settled to listen to the new CD. In seconds, the first track pumped out of his da's stereo in the living-room. He grabbed the remote t'see what was happenin' on MTV, and watched it with the sound down. His da always had the graphic equaliser adjusted wrong, so he played with the levels until the sonics felt right. He cudn' resist a blast o'air-guitar as he strolled out to check on the pizza. Yes – 'ee was that fucking sad. He pressed the volume up button on the remote. The room shook. The crappy little jugs emblazoned with St Ives that his grandmother had given them, wobbled, since they stood next to the left-hand speaker.

He was no longer in Trelawny. He was onstage at the Los Angeles Bowl, fifteen thousand rabid fans before him. Americans still love their rock. They still have a bit o'taste in terms of music. He put his foot on the side of the chair, knocking off his Cornwall rugby jersey that was there drying as he did so. It was his stage monitor, and this was his solo. The guitar cranked out so well, it seemed even to lift the mist outside his house. He wielded so many riffs out that he nearly forgot where he was: in a shite-hole right at the arse-end of Britain.

Oblivious, he failed to notice the back-door open. It wasn't an unusual scene that his ma and sister observed, but it didn' prevent his ma from saying, 'Oi – y'silly shit! Your pizza's burnin', an' turn down that bleddy row for God's sake.'

Startled still, Charlie grabbed the remote control an' paused the CD.

'Where of 'ee been?' he asked.

'Oh – Camborne, then *Tesco*,' his ma said.

Proper Job, Charlie Curnow!

'Whaas' this rubbish?' Jess asked Charlie, picking up the new CD case.

'Green Day – a class band...'

'Shite, if y'ask me,' said Jess.

Like she knew.

Charlie resisted arguing with his sister. He was through all that crap. He knew what he wanted.

'Here's yer pizza,' shouted his ma while she unpacked the groceries.

He looked at his ma – Sally Curnow. She'd had it fuckin' hard, an' not just of late either. She worked hard for shite money. Monday t'Thursday she had worked over Pool Market, selling fake flowers. Then she had cleaned for a woman up Mount Hawke for a while. Now, she had a job on the check-out down *Do-It-All*. She was still different than the other Trelawny mothers though. She still had it somehow. The others had fuckin' given up long ago. If only his stupid bastard of a da would realise it.

What a life though? She been born over Lanner, an' met his da at the *Talk of the West* club – when that was where the action was in Cornwall.

''Ee was some 'andsome back then you,' she had said a while ago.

No one spoke about 'un much since he'd moved out though. Charlie only saw 'un over Troon AFC club – where he sometimes went drinking. That was it really though – his ma was stuck here, like countless others. Housed here when it was cuttin' edge, like it was something to be proud of. And what did she have now? Satellite television an' her fuckin' *Poldark* DVDs.

'I almost called you Ross,' she'd said, 'an' yer sister Demelza...'

'Lovely,' his sister said, glad that events had turned out otherwise.

'I prefer Charles,' Charlie said.

'That was yer stupid father's choice,' his ma said.

'Oh,' said Charlie as he manipulated another slice of the pizza into his mouth. At the same time, he pressed the eject button on the player and it spat out his new CD. He would listen to it upstairs whilst his sister an' mother settled down to watch the usual Saturday night's shite television – *Pop Idol*,

Alan M. Kent

Ant an' Dec knob around for an Hour, an' *Stars in their sad fuckin' Eyes.*

Upstairs, was where he kept his guitar and amp. It was a Gibson copy – nothun' special. He made sure it was locked away in a cupboard each night. You never knew who was goin' t'break in – an' if it wudn' bolted down they'd fuckin' have it. They weren't havin' this though. His own CD player was inferior to his das, but his collection was more impressive. He took care of his music – didn' leave the CDs lyin' 'round outside of their cases t'be scratched, like his sister did.

He unlocked the cupboard an' took out his guitar, placing the strap over his neck. He'd tuned it that morning, so it should be fine. Next, he slipped out the Green Day CD and put it into the player. In the window he saw his reflection and grimmaced his face, so he looked harder. The music swirled around his bedroom. He strummed along, tryin' t'make sense of the new riffs. Outside, it was dark. Despite it being January an' the weather cold enough t'freeze the balls off a brass monkey, the tackers were still outside, jumpin' the ramp an' swearin' like troopers.

He knew if he didn' get a band together soon, he'd go the same way as Chrissie. Gettin' heroin in Cornwall was easy as fuck. He didn' live in a place with a history o'smugglin' fur nothun'. There were nightly missions down Newlyn – well, there were no fuckin' fish – so 'twas either that or have their trawlers decommissioned.

The lights of the television mast over between Carnkie an' Four Lanes throbbed in time with the music. Between there and here was Condurrow mine, where Chrissie had died. Still, that was last weekend. He had the rest o'the CD and a party that evening t'look forward to.

* * * * *

The Wine Mine was a shithole. It sold cheap alcohol though an' thaas' why it was packed on Saturday nights with boys and maids from Trelawny. The shopkeeper hated the cunts from up there. They were all fuckin' scroungers as far as he was concerned, fuckin' nutters an' druggies who should be locked up. He tolerated them because just one party on the estate meant he he'd have to re-stock the next week. In the air was a smell of

Proper Job, Charlie Curnow!

sweet perfume the maids had got off some bloke down Pool Market. The boys all stank of aftershave – an' this, combined with the greasy salt 'n' vinegar of the chip house – made for a smell Charlie knew to be Saturday night.

Outside, there was a bit o'blow on the air. A cop car went past ASBO City just to show they were watching. They wudn' interfere though. They knew better. See, Trelawny sort of policed itself. It was anarchic yeah, desperate yeah, an' poor as fuck, but there was a line. It was like Picard in *Star Trek: The Next Generation*. Cross it an' y'were dead. Everyone knew that sooner or later, the Scouse cunt who'd sold Chrissie the shit he'd overdosed on, wudn' be 'round there much longer. Most people hoped he'd gone already. The last dealer like that had had a Stanley screwdriver shoved up his nose.

It was good when it was like this. Charlie knew most o'the buggers down there. In and out an Escort or a Vauxhall Nova'd pull up an' someone would be in there who y'knew. Then little kids'd be down there too, hanging out an' learnin' t'roll joints n'that, what was in and what was out, an' who got beat up last week. Else, they were returnin' DVDs to the *Hollywood* video store next door.

The party at Mel's place started at nine. Most o'the estate would be down the football club beforehand. No one went in the Trelawny pub, even though it was nearer the estate. That was where all the posh cunts went of a Saturday night – all they from over Treslothan way and from Boscean Close. They were the fuckers who complained when a few o'the boys vandalised the Troon village sign. They'd added 'Your' to the sign which read 'Welcome to Troon'.

'They are fuckin' welcome to it,' said Yak.

'It's meant to have an apostrophe on it, y'twat – an' a extra 'e',' said Neil.

'Wha'?'

'You spelt it wrong,' said Neil.

'Eh?'

'Oh – never mind y'cunt. Just get in another round,' said Neil.

Yak moved to the bar and plopped down a twenty pound note.

'Six pints of Skinners,' he said to the barman, who knew the

Alan M. Kent

routine when the Trelawny crowd came in. By the time he'd poured the second three, they'd have downed the first lot.

'Filthy fuckers! Drunken bastards!' he muttered to the bar-maid on his left.

Charlie recognised the chaos at the club. He'd been drinking here since he was eleven, when older boys tipped vodka in his coke. No fucker knew. No fucker really cared either. Thaas' what he liked about it.

On the club's tiny stage were a band called 'Route A30'. They were right cunts. They looked like Simon and Garfunkel, only with mullets.

''Es – two men an' a drum machine...' said Neil.

'Goodeveningtoyouallhereat...TroonAFC...Here'soneofourfa vouritesongs; a song by The Eagles called 'Lyin' Eyes'...'

'One two, one two three four... YOU CAN'T HIDE YOUR LYIN' EYES...'

'Bollocks,' said Neil.

'AND YOUR SMILE IS A THIN DISGUISE...'

'Shite,' said Yak. 'The music here's always crap... Why can't they have something decent for a change?'

It was a conversation they'd had before.

By now, the place was packed. The extractor fans were on full, an' it was four deep to the bar.

'Where else can y'drink ten pints for just over twenty quid though?' Charlie asked.

'No fuckin' where I s'pose,' answered Neil.

Neil Davey and Charlie had known each other since primary school. He lived on Trelawny as well. He came from a musical family. His father once worked for *Holmans* – the rock drilling crowd – an' he used t'sing in the Holman Climax male voice choir.

'That always sounds like a fuckin' mass orgasm t'me man,' said Yak.

Yak had another name, but nobody called him by it. T'Charlie an' Neil, he'd always been known as Yak, since the early days of secondary school. He was always a hairy fucker, so people reckoned he was as hairy as a yak. The name had stuck. These days he had his long hair tied back and a small goatee. Yak was like Charlie an' Neil – on the dole.

'Got me kit back together again,' Yak said in the group's

Proper Job, Charlie Curnow!

interval, droppin' a fifty pence piece into the jukebox and making a selection. 'I'm gettin' more lessons too – from the drummer who used t'be in Hawkwind.'

'In Hawkwind?' asked Charlie.

''Es...'

'Idn' that all fuckin' synths, naked dancers an' weird shit?' Charlie said.

'Not only that though is it?' said Yak. 'They were fuckin' pioneers really. Anyway, how are you gettin' on? You mastered that Nirvana music book I gave you?'

Charlie shook his head.

'Not yet,' he said. 'I'm on 'un though.'

'Thaas' better,' said Yak loudly, as the Garfunkel of the band tried to gain access to the bar. From the jukebox out blasted Black Sabbath; Ozzy Osbourne's vocals rebounding 'round the club.

'FINISHED WITH MY WOMAN 'CAUSE SHE COULDN'T HELP ME WITH MY MIND...'

'Sabbath are the dog's bollocks boy.'

'Shame Ozzy's fuckin' lost the plot with that stupid show with his missus...'

'Ay – landlord, turn the fuckin' jukebox up!' Yak shouted, 'An' six more pints while you're about it...'

'Piss off,' said the barman, as he refilled their glasses.

'Time t'syphon me python anyway,' said Yak and headed off to the gents. Neil and Charlie joined him. When they'd all slashed, Neil leant against the condom machine.

'See her out there – Ally Juleffe – she's mine tonight. Imagine it...'

They'd all gone t'school with Ally Juleffe.

'She's got tits that are out o'this world,' said Yak.

'She's a big maid,' said Charlie. 'You think you'n get it on with her do 'ee?'

'Definitely. See her now look – the way she d'look at me...' said Neil.

''Ent she seeing matey from down Beacon though – whasisname – Markie Phillips? He's a right hard bastard mind. He used t'play rugby for 'Druth.'

'Your cock's doin' all the thinkin' these days,' said Charlie.

'So?' said Neil, inserting a quid inta' the machine. 'If she's up for it, then I am.'

Back in the bar, 'Paranoid' had finished and Ian Gillan was spouting the opening lines of 'Smoke on the Water'.

'WE ALL CAME DOWN TO MONTREAUX ON THE LAKE GENEVA SHORELINE...' – only to have the plug pulled on the jukebox, as the band was about to start again, back on stage.

'Okay,' the lead singer announced nervously, 'We can see you like a bit of rock here in Troon. Here's a song called *Eye of the Tiger*.'

'Christ almighty,' said Charlie.

NA, NA NA NA, NA NA NAAAAH. 'RISING UP, BACK ON THE STREET...'

'Look,' said Neil. 'Ally's leaving... she's off t'the party. Here we go...'

Neil was gone. Yak an' Charlie finished his pint for him.

'We'll be there in a minute...'

The Football club had emptied a little now, as more people from the estate headed to Mel's place. Hers was No.15 – bang in the middle of the estate. There was frost in the air and the moon had come up over Carn Brea. That didn' stop couples from gettin' it on outside though. Shaggin' was the thing on Saturday nights. Fucking was the best thing when there was fuck all else to do.

* * * * *

Mel's party was heavin'. All the alcohol that people had purchased down *The Wine Mine* was now piled on her ma's dining room table, and Mel herself was in the kitchen, pouring all kinds of shite inta' a bucket t'make a punch. Blow was being skinned-up all over the place, and a few boys had already spewed outside. On the CD was some 70s' compilation, so every cunt was up doin' Abba impersonations, or else pogoing 'round to the Sex Pistols.

'This is a right fuckin' lash-up,' said Yak. 'They've got no taste. I'll see if they've got any Led Zep...'

Yak marched over to the CDs an' found only Mel's ma's albums.

'Robson an' fuckin' Jerome... *Millennium Party Mix 2000*...'

Mel an' the other maids were back in the dining room now. She was pissed-up and had trouble heaving the punch onto the table. Charlie gave her some assistance.

Proper Job, Charlie Curnow!

'A'right Mel? Do 'ee want a hand?'

''Es, proper,' she said. 'Glad you could make it Charlie...'

'Wudn' miss one of your piss-ups,' said Charlie.

' Me neither,' said Yak, 'though yer music's crap...'

Some twat had turned up the CD player and Charlie knew the party could prob'bly be heard all the way down Camborne Hill. Somebody 'ud bound t' complain – an' then the coppers 'ud be forced to have a word. People were texting other friends to turn up there.

The three o'them started work on the bottles of Skinners on the table. They revisited the conversation they'd had earlier that night.

'But Charlie, it's no fuckin' good. Cornwall's just a shit-hole man,' said Yak. 'Full a'fuckin emmets in summer – an' then nothun' in winter. An' how many bands have made it from Cornwall eh?'

'*Thirteen Senses*,' said Charlie. 'Their album *The Invitation* is good... They're from Truro.

'Roger Taylor in *Queen*. He's from Truro too,' deadpanned Neil.

'I mean Cornwall's the fuckin' backyard o'nowhere idn' it? It's not fuckin' Liverpool, or Glasgow or Manchester. There's no fuckin' music industry here. The clubs are all dance shit and no one gives a toss.'

'The bass player in *Big Country*. He's got a studio up Lan'son,' offered Neil. 'They was big once – I seen 'um on *Top of the Pops 2*.'

'And us like – livin' here in Trelawny. I mean it's hard fur people in Cornwall to be proud o'who they are, 'cause no fucker on tv has a Cornish accent. You'n be fuckin' Irish, or Scottish, or Scouse or fuckin' Geordie – an' everyone thinks you'm cool, but if y'speak like we, no fucker wants t'knaw 'ee,' theorised Yak.

''Ee's right,' said Neil. 'Up the line they think we all have straw 'angin' out o'our mouths an' spend the days makin' clotted fuckin' cream.'

'You knaw yer music Charlie,' said Yak. 'You can't name me one Cornish band thaas' ever made it...'

'There's *The Mechanics*,' said Charlie.

'The who?' asked Neil.

''Es, I knaw,' said Yak. 'Yer' right – they fuckers from over mid-Cornwall. They played down the Penmare a while back. Got Al Hodge on vocals. They toured with Leo Sayer...'

'Leo 'Afro' Sayer?' said Neil.

''Es – the 'You make me feel like dancing' bloke,' said Charlie.

'Fuckin' fame that is idn' it! Tourin' with Leo Sayer,' said Yak sarcastically. 'I mean the world's yer fuckin' oyster after tourin' with 'ee.'

'There wus *Rootjoose*,' said Charlie. 'Y'knaw – they made it into the charts.'

''Es – surfing dudes with perms an' hats,' said Yak. 'I saw 'em. They're crap...'

'Na, they 'ent,' said Charlie.

'Pull plenty o'maids though,' said Neil.

''Es – typical surfin' cunts,' said Yak.

'There's Graham Bath,' offered Charlie.

'Who?' said Yak and Neil simultaneously.

'He used t'be in Paul Di'Anno's *Killers*.'

'Paul Di'Anno was the lead singer on the first two Iron Maiden albums,' said Charlie.

'Well, fuck me – what talent we have – the Leo Sayer band, a bunch o'surfin' wankers an' some bloke who played with the ex-singer of Iron Maiden.'

'We could do it,' said Charlie, casual-like. 'I mean we could fuckin' do it...'

'Us? You mean us three?'

'Why not?' said Charlie. 'We're as good as anyone else – an' we're better than all of those. An' if there's no fuckin' scene in Cornwall, we'll make the fuckin' scene.'

That was one thing Yak and Neil admired about Charlie. The cunt was on the dole like them, but he had bollocks – or like he was goin' t'take the world hold by the bollocks. They watched Charlie like he was a fuckin' saint who'd just crossed the Atlantic – an' ended up convertin' the locals. Their bottles o'Skinners became holy wells in front o'them.

'Thaas' all we need t'do – we'll create the scene,' said Charlie. 'No fucker'll stop us.'

'So what sound will yer band have?' questioned Neil.

'You know what sound...' said Charlie. 'It'll be pure fuckin' rock, comin' from the blues – like in all the best bands – Free,

Proper Job, Charlie Curnow!

Led Zeppelin, Bad Company. I tell 'ee boys, there's nothun' like pure rock. Y'knaw it yourselves... But then, let's keep it punky too... the right attitude an' that...'

''Es – a'right Charlie, but there's something missing,' said Neil.

'We'll need a bass player,' said Yak.

'Yeah – an' some bastard t'mix the sound n'shit,' said Neil.

'Yeah – an' some cunt t'make us *hors d'oeuvres* an' wash me cacks before the gig...' pleaded Yak.

'We'll have the bass player an' the rest o'it... I promise you,' said Charlie. 'Mark my words – we'll be back after a world tour t'play a week o'home-coming gigs at the Hall for Cornwall...'

'Giss on with 'ee!' said Yak, but he had no real reason to doubt Charlie's words. He passed two more bottles over to Charlie and Neil, then opened a third for himself. He looked at the party – and saw some thirty-six-year-old ex-con gettin' off with one o'Mel's friends. He had his hands on her tiny tits. He was that pissed he didn' even knaw she was only in Year Seven at school.

'I'm with 'ee Charlie,' said Yak, then he turned and shouted, 'Fuckin' paedophile!' across the room.

It didn't matter. No one heard him.

Ally an' Neil had managed to mingle by now, an' Neil tried to remain calm.

'See that fucker,' said Charlie t'Yak. 'He's goin' t'get his head kicked in.'

The two of them knew that Ally's boyfriend Markie Phillips had just been released from Exeter prison a week before. He'd done two years for GBH after he bungled a garage robbery over Tuckingmill. Some poor security firm cunt had taken a real beating. He wudn' work for the rest of his life.

'If Ally's here,' said Yak the prophet, 'then Markie's around somewhere nearby. We'd better save the bugger...'

They went over to Ally and Neil. Ally was a good-lookin' maid a'right. She'd been in the year below them at school – but 'twas true – she had a fuckin' body t'die for. Neil was attracted to her like she was the bleddy Mermaid o'Zennor. She was a siren sure 'nough – an' Neil cudn' resist her.

'A'right Ally?' said Charlie. 'How be doin'?'

'Oh, hi Charlie,' said Ally, sucking down a mouthful of

punch. She was pissed-up, an' all over Neil. Neil's eyes were glazed like he'd just won three million on the lottery.

'Dun't bother,' said Yak. 'Whatever we say idn' goin' t'make naw difference. 'Ee's besotted with her. 'Ee has been for ages like.'

While Neil was gettin' it on with Ally, the party was gettin' wilder. The crowd had spread inta' the back-garden, an' a few o'the boys decided it would be fun to set fire to some of the rubbish on the grass from the last party Mel had thrown.

'Fuckin' assholes!' said Yak.

Then, once they'd started the fire, they 'eaved on anything they could find. On went a couple o'old Metro seats, all the rubbish from the kitchen an' any other crap lying about. For some o'they, that meant takin' down next door's fence an' 'eavin' that on as well. Next thing Charlie heard was them all shouting, 'Burn motherfucker!' an' jumpin' across the flames.

'Fuckin' dickheads,' went Yak.

Charlie knew that fire could sometimes be a constructive thing on Trelawny. Last autumn, when they found out old bloke Masters across the way, had been inviting little kids in for sweeties, a petrol bomb went through his living room window. He got out, but he'd never live on the estate again. His house was still boarded up.

Ally an' Neil were nowhere t'be seen. Charlie had a good guess that they were upstairs in Mel's mother's room.

'They'll be shaggin',' said Yak with an air of romance. 'Good job the fucker bought condoms down the club – 'ee might even manage to put one on...'

Charlie went upstairs for a piss. There were bodies on the landing from those already mullered. The bathroom was already coated with puke. He took a slash with the seat still down. He didn' bother to flush it – it hardly seemed worth the effort. Passing Mel's ma's bedroom door, he stopped for a second to listen, but the stereo downstairs was on so loud that he cudn' hear anything inside. He'd leave them to it.

In the garden, the fire was gettin' out of hand. Mel had sobered up a bit an' some boy had one o'the chairs from the kitchen about to 'eave that on the fire as well. Charlie made a move to sort it out, but Yak advised him to remain where he was – halfway up the stairs – like a fuckin' muppet.

Proper Job, Charlie Curnow!

That was when Markie Phillips arrived.

'Cunt!' said Yak under his breath.

'A'right boys,' said Markie to them.

The moment Markie entered, the boy with the chair had dropped it. He knew Markie would have a word. The fire was still raging outside though – an' now the tree over next door's fence was catchin' fire on the flames.

'Good fire idn' a?' went Markie.

'Idn' bad is a?' said Charlie.

'Seen Ally have 'ee? She said she was comin'.'

'Na, I 'ebm seen her Markie. She was up the club earlier though...'

Charlie looked up the stairs to see if there was any sign of them.

'She must a gone home earlier,' suggested Yak.

Markie ignored him, an' helped himself to the remnants of a bottle of *Cripple Cock* cider.

'Whaas' that noise?' asked Charlie.

'Eh?' said Yak. Then he heard it. A siren was comin' up Newton Road.

'Police idn' it?' said Markie.

No one confirmed his suggestion. They knew the police siren all too well. He should a' done as well. Obviously, two years on the inside was long enough fur'n t'forget.

'Na,' shouted one o'those standin' on the front lawn. ''Tis the fuckin' fire brigade.'

'Mel?' shouted Yak, 'I think you'd better come out here.'

Everyone at the party picked their way through the debris an' stood in front of the house. The Camborne fire engine pulled onto the courtyard. No fucker on the estate had been sleepin', but lights came on all over the place. Before the vehicle had even stopped, a fireman – all kitted up – leapt down from the cab.

'Had a report of a fire up here,' he said. 'Who's the owner of the property?'

Everyone looked at Mel. She looked her age – twelve. No one answered.

'Out the back,' said one of her friends.

In seconds, a hose had been run through the house and the pump of the engine had started up.

'I want everyone out o'the house,' said the fire-chief. 'Anyone upstairs?'

'Fuck,' said Yak.

'No one,' said Charlie.

The fire in the back-garden was out in a matter of seconds. A huge, steaming black patch was all that was left o'it – on Mel's ma's lawn. Next door's tree was half-blackened.

The light in Mel's ma's room came on. Neil stuck his head out of the window and saw everyone outside; the fire brigade moving 'round the estate.

'Whaas' on?' he shouted.

'Whaas' it fuckin' look like?' Yak shouted back. 'The fuckin' garden was on fire!'

'Nice one,' said Charlie t'Yak.

Within seconds, Neil was downstairs. Ally was following him. Neil had only his cacks on, an' Ally just a towel, which she could barely keep in place, her body bursting out all over the shop. Moast o'the boys got in a good eyeful.

Charlie tried to warn him.

'Markie's here y'twat! Go back up!'

Neil was havin' none o'it. He'd seen enough fires on Trelawny to know what they could do.

'If 'ee sees you've been shaggin' Ally, he'll fuckin' kill 'ee,' said Charlie. 'Go out the back!'

It was too late though. Markie was a cunt, but he wudn' stupid. He saw what was goin' on, and went slamming through the hallway to the staircase.

'Y'bastard! You're fuckin' dead!' said Markie. He pushed over Ally at the same time. Neil went inta' the garden, and over the wall. Next door had a set of Rottweilers an' they went fuckin' apeshit. Before Markie was over that fence, Neil was over the next. He had a choice now. He could go back an' face Markie – an' end up for a fortnight in intensive care in Treliske or he could risk jumpin' No.16's barbed wire.

In the end, thaas' what 'ee did. The fucker's cacks got all teared t'lerrups – so much so he had to leave 'um behind.

Markie came back over the fence like 'ee was ready t'rip anyone's head off who spoke to 'un. Most people knew it was time to head home. The fire-chief had already bollocked them all for being irresponsible.

Proper Job, Charlie Curnow!

'Nothun' new up here though is it?' he'd said, and told Mel he'd be reportin' it t'Social Services. Then, it would mean bugger all to her. There were far worse things that could happen up there. Mel cried, but she'd seen enough o'life to know the fireman's words wudn' affect her very much. Their social worker 'ud have a word thaas' all – a young bastard from up the line with a degree in Psychology or some bollocks. That sort o'help was fuck-all squared t'be honest.

So now, Neil was around the estate somewhere, bollock-naked with no keys to get in at home. It was gettin' cold now.

'Leave the daft fucker,' said Yak. 'Let 'un freeze his knob off...'

Ally had got dressed by now an' she an' Markie were havin' words. Well, 'twudn' really words – 'twas more a kind of huge fuckin' row – out on the front lawn.

'Markie... listen...' said Ally, but Charlie had seen it all before. He'd slap her 'round a bit back home. She wudn' be workin' up *Do-It-All* tomorra'. She'd have it fuckin' done to her tonight.

Charlie helped Mel to clean-up a bit. Her ma 'ud be back on Sunday night. She'd been clubbing herself down Penzance, on the *Pernod* an' blacks, so she wudn' be too worried about the mess. Mel had told her she'd be havin' a few friends over. She didn' tell her that meant the whole fuckin' estate you.

'Fuck them for mates,' said Charlie, but he knew Mel's position. You had to have parties like this. It was like a kind of initiation into the tribe of Trelawny. With the last of the hoses rolled up, Charlie decided that he too, had to head back home.

'You'll be okay,' he said to Mel.

Charlie picked his way through the bikes and dilleys that had been left outside by the tackers and made his way home. It had been a helleva' night, but at least he'd put the idea of the band into the minds of Yak an' Neil. Maybe that night, they'd stumble into bed an' consider it. Maybe life didn' have t'be like it was on Trelawny. But then maybe for the Cornish, thaas' all they could expect – more decades o'fuckin ignorance and more fuckin' emmets. The bottles of Skinners were beginning to kick in now. He knew he'd have t'drink a couple o'pints o'water to prevent Sunday's hangover. He opened the back-door, dropped down his keys and Neil's gear he had collected, then put his mouth under the tap. No one was up.

As he turned off the kitchen light, there was a tap on the door. Outside was Neil – naked, aside from a fertiliser sack, wrapped 'round his waist.

'I knaw yer knob's small,' said Charlie, 'but fertiliser won't make 'un grow any bigger... Only Ally Juleffe seems t'make 'un grow...'

'Ha fuckin' ha – very fuckin' funny,' said Neil. 'Let us in will 'ee? I'm freezin' me bollocks off out here.'

Charlie tried to hand him his clothes.

'Wha'?'

'Put 'em on, then you'n go home...'

'No way. I've got to crash here. I 'ent goin' 'round the estate no more. Markie'll be lookin' fur me.'

'Y'sad bastard,' said Charlie. 'I'spose you'd better crash here then.'

'Thanks,' said Neil, droppin' the sack, and wandering naked inta' Charlie's ma's living room. 'I owe you one, Charlie Curnow.'

'Just practise your guitar,' said Charlie. 'Thaas' all...'

* * * * *

On Sundays, Charlie's ideal day was to remain in bed for most o'the morning, go for a walk somewhere in the afternoon, then in the evenin' grab a take-away at the *New Bengali* an' come back an' watch a DVD. This Sunday would be different though. For one thing, there was Neil downstairs, crashed out on the sofa. For another, he'd arranged to meet with his da. The first part – he'd still get in though. Charlie reached out of bed, and from the floor, grabbed the latest issue of *Kerrang!*. You could read all the other mags – *Q* an' *NME* an' that, an' *Select* an' *Classic Rock*, but none of them dealt with rock the way *Kerrang!* did. It was an ass name for the mag, describing as it did, the sound comin' from an electric guitar. But still, it featured everything y'needed t'know about rock. Therefore, for Charlie, it was essential reading. This issue was a special on old school hardcore punk (Minor Threat, Black Flag, Sick of it All and Bad Brains). Metallica, Mastodon, Muse, Rammstein, Feeder, Ash and The Deftones were also featured. He'd even bought all the back issues from one o'Yak's older brothers. He had Issue One – with Angus Young of AC/DC in a typically metallic pose on it – and now it was framed above his bed on the wall.

No cunts toured Cornwall these days. A few years ago – he could just remember the Cornwall Coliseum – a great aircraft hanger of a building down on Crinnis beach up St Austell. They had some good bands down there, but then Cornwall was too fuckin' far. So now y'had t'travel t'Plymouth to see anyone half-fuckin'-decent, but the Pavilions was all sanitised – like goin' to the opera or something – not seeing a decent band. The sound was shit there as well. It was too clean, too nice. The Hall for Cornwall was a'right, but they never attracted the really big bands – 'twas too small. These days the bigger bands did a few warm-up gigs there, or else 'twas tribute bands and musicals.

The Coliseum was different. It was dirty, sweaty – every cunt packed in together. He liked the smell o'it. It was just like every-thing else though – all the good stuff went up the line, like all the good jobs. Yak's brother had worked for South West Water in Truro, 'til everything shifted up to Exeter. Same with Neil's ma – she used t'work down Lelant at the St Ivel dairy. Then they moved that. The bastards still called it 'Cornish butter' – even though 'twas made up the line somewhere.

He scanned the pages of *Kerrang!* He knew what kind of a rock band was needed for the millennium. 'Es, they'd be a com-bination of all the best elements of rock bands from the last forty years. They'd have the songs of Zeppelin, the bottom end of Sabbath, the melody of Purple an' the attitude of Nirvana an' Green Day. They'd be fuckin' unstoppable, an' they'd be from Cornwall. Cornwall 'ud be the new Seattle, or Orange County. It was about fuckin' time.

* * * * *

Charlie heard a noise outside his window. He looked out, but soon drew the curtain back when he saw it was Mrs Williams next door goin' chapel. Sunday morning was usually when the estate was at its quietest. Every other cunt was either hungover, drugged-up, or in the cells down Camborne Police station. The exception was Neil – who was crashed out on Charlie's ma's sofa in the middle of the living room. When Charlie came down, his ma an' sister were up, an' *Pirate FM* was blazing, but Neil wasn't moving.

'Good party?' asked Jess loudly.

'Wha'?' said Charlie, tipping coffee into a mug.

'Was it any good – Mel's party? Neil looked like 'ee 'ad a good time.'

''Es – it wudn' bad,' said Charlie with typically Cornish understatement.

'Make 'iss mind,' said his ma. 'Yer faather's comin' 'round today t'pick 'ee up. He phoned laas' night from over *London Inn*.'

'What for?' asked Charlie.

'I dunnaw. You'll have to ask 'un – an' Charlie, can y'remove your friend from the living room? I've got work t'do...'

'A'right – 'ee'll be up in a minute.'

Charlie sat down on the chair opposite the sofa, an' Neil began to emerge from the blanket an' cushions. Like a lot o'the houses on the estate, they had that air of dampness to them; especially in the morning, and when each of them spoke, y'could see their breath.

'Ah fuck,' said Neil. 'What time is it?'

'Twenty to...'

'Twenty to wha'?'

'Twelve.'

'Shit – I gotta' meet Ally at half-past.'

Charlie could hardly believe what he'd just said.

'Y'nearly got your head kicked in laas' night by the fuckin' beast o'Bodmin Moor – an' now yer seein' his maid again... Y'got fuckin' shit for brains Neil.'

'She wants t'see me... Any coffee goin'?' wondered Neil. 'I need some caffeine...'

'I'll get 'ee some...'

Neil swung his legs over an' sat upright. His legs were bruised an' cut from the chase over the back walls an' fences laas' night. He scratched his bollocks, but then realised Charlie's sister was watchin'. Charlie came back with a coffee an' plonked it before him.

'S'where 'ee meeting her?' he asked.

'Over Trelawny mine...'

'Yer a fuckin right romancer 'ent 'ee... Be just like fuckin' *Poldark* – with the bleddy fly-tippin' an' *Tesco's* trolleys...'

Proper Job, Charlie Curnow!

'It was her suggestion...' pleaded Neil.

''Es – well, take 'un easy,' said Charlie, 'an' stop scratchin' yer bollocks under the blanket...'

'Any toast goin'?'

'Yeah – I'll get 'ee some...'

Charlie threw down two slices of droopy *Londis* white bread an' put them on the grill. *Pirate FM* was givin' out its usual dosage of news. For Cornwall, that normally meant hearing how many more jobs had been lost. This time the report had mixed blessings.

'D'y'hear that?' shouted in Charlie to Neil. 'They're goin' t'close Camborne Police station's custody centre – centralising it in Plymouth... The bastards can't control us – they gotta' go east o'the Tamar... an' then have raids on Trelawny...'

Then there was a report about the Eden Project in St Blazey. They'd got another lottery grant fur phase two. *Roach Foods* were also planning on opening a new bacon-boning factory in Bodmin. There'd be thirty new jobs. The way 'twas yapped about on the radio, you'd think some fucker had found the Holy Grail.

Charlie came back in, t'see if Neil was gettin' dressed.

'Thaas' it though idn' it? What does Cornwall get – a fuckin' huge tree museum for emmets t'visit, an' a bacon factory. Lovely idn' a?' he said as he pulled his sweatshirt over his head.

'Thaas' why we've gotta' do it,' said Charlie.

'Wha'?'

'Form a band... between us... Look, I'm gonna' find us somewhere t'rehearse... proper like...'

'Yeah – like yer bedroom...'

'Naw – rehearsal space. Like real groups have...'

'When?'

'Next week...'

Neil had finished dressing.

'Are you up for it?' asked Charlie. 'Yak is.'

Neil's eyes swivelled to the kitchen.

'Is me toast ready?'

Disappointed at Neil's lack of enthusiasm, Charlie went out an' threw his toast onto a plate, an' smeared butter over it.

'I want 'ee t'be the guitarist,' Charlie explained, trying a different tack.

Alan M. Kent

"Course I'm in,' said Neil, 'if it'll mean I'll get t'shag more maids...'

Charlie had ticks mentally placed against his drummer and guitarist. He saw himself on vocals and the band's major lyricist. All they needed now was someone on bass. He watched Neil shove down his toast an' knock back the coffee.

'You're a star in the makin',' said Charlie.

'I've a shag in the makin' too,' said Neil. 'I'd better get over mine...'

As he was about to leave, there was a knock on the backdoor. Charlie recognised the figure behind the safety glass.

'See 'ee later,' said Neil. 'A'right Mr Curnow?'

'A'right da,' said Charlie.

His faather stood next to their dustbins in the bright winter sunshine. He looked humble, like he was the kid from next door askin' for his ball back. Charlie recognised his own features in his da. The same dark Cornish skin, the same black hair, the same strong torso – borne from generations of wielding pick-axes an' shovels underground. He had the same piercing eyes as well – deep as Dolcoath – an' darker than the cows' eyes in the fields up Croft Common. His da's eyes were duller these days though, yet around the folds of skin under them, Charlie reckoned he could still see tin dust. It made his face glitter – like he was fuckin' Marc Bolan – but his da had long since had his days of shimmering in the eyes of his ma.

'Is yer mother in?' he asked.

'Yeah...'

'How is she?'

'The usual,' answered Charlie, 'Y'knaw...'

His faather nodded.

'How's Jessie?'

Charlie didn' need t'answer. His sister came out to greet their faather.

'Da,' she said. 'How are you?'

'I'm okay maid. I'm okay...'

Charlie looked at 'un. 'Course he was fuckin' okay, he said to himself. He was shacked up with some twenty-three year old from Redruth – name o'Karen Retallack. 'Twas money that split he and their mother up though. Sometimes, it even looked like the two of 'um might have another crack at 'ut, but then other

Proper Job, Charlie Curnow!

times, like today, it looked like fuckin' World War Three was imminent.

'If thaas' yer faather, tell 'un he d'owe me fifty-five quid for the house insurance...' his ma shouted down from the top of the stairs.

His da heard. Charlie didn' have t'tell 'un.

Outside the Troon mist was beginning t'burn off, and a few tackers were out kickin' a ball around, pretendin' they were in the *Premier League* – all *Match o'the Day* commentaries an' that. Y'could see the mine stacks across the Great Flat Lode. Charlie thought o'Neil an' Ally out there,

'Y'ready t'go then?' asked his da.

''Es – I'll just get me coat...'

By the time he'd turned off the radio, his sister was doin' her usual plea for him to come back home. All Charlie caught was, 'I can't Jess... not yet... Not when...'

His da stopped when Charlie joined them.

'I'll see y'soon.'

It would have been good if his faather could have kissed his daughter. It wudn' goin' t'happen though. His da wudn' like that. His da wudn' like it when he was at home, an' they were growin' up, so 'ee wudn' goin' t'be like it now. His faather was a right cunt really. This goin' out on a Sunday afternoon was his da's suggestion.

'It'll be a bit o'male-bondin' like,' his da had said on the phone, like he was on fuckin' *Richard and Judy*.

The only thing they seem to still have in common these days was music. Thaas' where Charlie had got it from. His da had a fuckin' ace LP collection – stuff from the 70s mostly. He had a lot of crap – y'knaw, like the fuckin' Doobie Brothers n' Chicago, but then he had other stuff no fucker had ever heard of – like Focus, Mountain an' Iron Butterfly. Then there was his fine collection of Jethro Tull, Uriah Heep and Aerosmith. They got in his Capri and drove off. He had Rainbow's *Rising* in the stereo. No cunt ever listened to it these days but 'twas good stuff. Charlie felt his hangover beginning to disappear.

The rest o'the estate were beginning to emerge now. A few boys were puttin' in a new gear box inta' a knackered XR3i, an' the tackers were 'eavin' up a rope into a tree in the park t'make a new swing. You could tell someone'd be hung there next

Alan M. Kent

week, an' be rushed inta' Treslike. There was no sign o'life at Mel's place.

'I gotta' go up Pool Market,' said his da.

There was a line in *Star Wars: Episode IV, A New Hope* that reminded Charlie of Pool Market. It was the moment when Luke Skywalker and Obi-Wan Kenobi observe for the first time – the city of Mos Eisley – an' Obi Wan says that it's a wretched hive of scum an' villainy. That was Pool Market – the Mos Eisley o' Camborne an' Redruth.

The voice of Ronnie James Dio was blaring out as his da swung the Capri left up inta' Troon village: 'I DON'T WANT TO GO. SOMETHING TELLS ME NO, NO, NO, NO. THE TRACES IN THE SAND, THE LINES INSIDE MY HAND, YOU CAN GO, GO, GO. BEWARE OF A PLACE... A SMILE ON THE BRIGHT SIDE...'

'Stop!' said Charlie.

The fag his da was rollin' fell onta' the floor of the car as he jammed on the brakes.

'I wanna' speak to someone,' Charlie said.

Chapel was finishing. The few has-beens and never-weres were walking out from the door. Sunday usually allowed them to walk home in peace, without little cheeky cunts 'eavin' stuff at 'um.

Charlie recognised his next-door neighbour.

'Mrs Williams...' he shouted.

She was too busy talking about a Sankey evening over Portreath.

'Mrs Williams,' he said again. She turned around.

'Would it be possible to use the chapel hall next week?' Charlie asked.

'Wha' me 'andsome?' she said.

'We've formed a group an' we need somewhere to rehearse... I thought you could help us...'

'Want the hall do 'ee?' she asked. 'You'n pick up the key from me – when you want 'un, but Thursday's cleanin' an' when me an' Mrs Steadman d'change the flowers...'

'Thanks,' said Charlie.

'Now listen... Dun't 'ee think I'm silly mind. Naw drink, nor drugs – the last time we had any youngsters use the place, 'twas vandalised terrible...'

Proper Job, Charlie Curnow!

Charlie didn' need reminding. A few twats on the estate had put on a Youth Club disco, but it went wrong when some little cunt started playin' the organ. Next thing they knew, someone had 'eaved the collection boxes through the stained glass windows. The harmony between Methodism an' Trelawny's youth had been forever broken that day – not that it had ever been brilliant t'begin with. A preacher'd complained when Neil'd whacked 'The Number of the Beast' by Iron Maiden on the Youth Club CD player.

Mrs Williams scrutinised Charlie's da. She knew he'd left home.

'I used t'knaw your faather Tommy, when he worked over Tolcarne...'

'Yeah?' said his his da. 'I thought you might...'

Charlie sensed a tale comin' out.

'I'll pick up the key sometime this week...'

He got back inta' the Capri. Mrs Williams went on her Methodee way.

'First time I've seen you have anything t'do with chapel,' said his da. 'Not since tea-treat when you was about six.'

'Oh 'tidn' nothun' really t'do with chapel,' said Charlie, ''tis more t'do with rock 'n' roll.'

His da had finished rolling a new fag now, an' was just lighting it up. He put the Golden Virginia sachet in his pocket, let down the hand-brake and sped off. Charlie looked back at the chapel.

'That place'll be rock 'n'roll history one day,' said Charlie. 'Tourists won't go t'*Flambards* or *Land's End*, they'll come here...'

''Es,' said his da, 'an' fuckin' pigs'll fly...'

John Wesley, thought Charlie. Thank fuck fur'n.

* * * * *

Pool Market: Cornwall's wretched hive of scum and villainy. They had come down the drag from Carnkie, and over the railway bridge into Pool. Charlie saw the 'Free Cornwall' graffiti that had been sprawled over the bridge ever since he could remember, and then on the horizon, South Crofty's silent headgear. Still ripe for transformation by some fuckwits from the

Alan M. Kent

Regional Development Agency. The market sat between these two things, next to *Homeworld* – an upmarket furniture store – where his ma looked, but bought nothun' – and the *Do-It-All* store where she worked. The market was full o'shit. All fuckin' cement piskies y'could stick in yer garden an' bootlegged Cornwall rugby jerseys. It stank of gone-off meat and pet food. It was cheap though – an' so thaas' why the Cornish shopped there.

His da was after some cheap parts for his car. He'd find it there if he looked hard enough. They parked the Capri in the *Homeworld* section and walked over, avoiding the middle-class fuckers from St Ives, there, to buy shelving for their studios and second homes. There wudn' no *Ikea* in Cornwall, so they had to fuckin' make do. They headed past the regulation doughnut and candy-floss stalls into the market. The cold air stayed within the market hall, and even though it was meant to be indoors, the traders clutched coffees and bacon rolls like they were life-support systems. A lot of people from the estate were there – buying all the shit on offer. The place was heavin' with fat women in leggings an' squalling kids, tugging at their mother's denim duffle-coats. There were sports stalls which sold rip-off trainers and shops carryin' 'Britney Spears' an' 'Jordan' posters. There was shit like that all over the place. Everyone was on their mobiles talking bollocks.

'Fuckin' wrong day t'come up here,' said his da.

'Any day's the wrong day fur this place,' Charlie said. 'I'll check out the CDs.'

There were a couple o'stalls that sold music in the market. The first, was tucked in between the hippy shop and the place that did wood signs fur your house. It was run by a sweaty bastard who specialised in Country and Western tapes an' shite like Celtic classics – which only ever had Irish songs on 'em. None o'they cunts ever seem to have heard of Cornwall. He had a whole New Age section as well, with albums called bollocks like 'The Druid' an' 'Awakenings'.

'How much fur this?' asked Charlie, pickin' up a second-hand Thin Lizzy compilation on CD.

'A fiver,' the sweaty bastard said.

'Take four will 'ee?' asked Charlie.

'It's a fiver...'

Proper Job, Charlie Curnow!

'Your loss,' said Charlie.

Charlie knew what stuff was worth. He'd get it cheaper else-where. Else, he'd download the fucker, and 'eave it onta' his iPod.

'Can 'ee change the fuckin' record for chrissakes?' asked Charlie. 'All y'ever play in here is fuckin' country. I mean I knaw this is the West Country an' that, but honestly, we 'ent that far fuckin' west...'

'Bollocks,' said the sweatster. 'People d'like it here.'

'Then they're fuckin' as mad as y'are,' said Charlie under his breath. 'Fuckin' line-dancin' shit...'

Outside, it looked like they were goin' t'have a drop a rain. It wudn' stoppin' some kid he knew from the estate from takin' a piss in a drain outside, or from more o'Camborne an' Redruth's dole queue arriving t'spend their Jobseeker's Allowance. His da had spotted a few o'his mates from Crofty an' they were reminiscing over what it used t'be like. Pasties. Yap. Shift Captains. Yap. Price o'tin. Yap. Big tits calender in the crowst hut. Yap. Charlie had no time fur all o'that. He went past the cushion stall and around to the café and paperback book exchange. Next to the book exchange was the second-hand music stall. It had been there years, but a new boy was running it. He had a lot of rarities an' picture discs pinned up on the wall behind, an' a box o'bootlegged live concerts on CD.

'Any good are 'um?' Charlie asked.

'Live album quality,' said the boy behind the counter. 'Recorded a lot of 'em meself...'

Charlie picked up a bootleg by new and critically-rated prog-gers The Mars Volta, an' asked him to play it.

The racket shock up all the old fuckers passing the stalls.

'Not bad,' said Charlie. 'How much?'

'Six quid each.'

Charlie saw one o'his cards on the counter. It read, 'Micky T – Music Dealer and DJ' with an address in Scorrier.

'I've seen you,' said the boy Micky, 'down the dole office...'

'This yer young business grant then?' asked Charlie jokingly.

'Fuck that,' said Micky smiling, 'I'd lose me dole then wudn' I?'

'Yer own fuckin' black economy then...' said Charlie.

Alan M. Kent

'Got t'be done 'ennit?'

'Are 'ee a DJ then?'

''Es – make a bit that way y'knaw. I do a few nights up Newquay an' that – but I'm hopin' for somethin' at the Penventon soon...'

'What d'y'do?'

'Anything really – what they want – depends who's payin' if y'knaw what I mean... I got me own decks an' sound system like... Y'inta' DJ-ing then?'

'Naw – 'fraid not,' said Charlie. 'I'm more inta' rock... I like all that industrial stuff though – y'knaw Nine inch Nails, Fear Factory an' some o'the dance metal – The Prodigy an' that...'

'Y'got a band then?' asked Micky.

'Not yet,' said Charlie, 'but I'm gettin' there.'

'I'm offerin' me services...' said Micky. 'All bands these days have a DJ as well... as yer standard set-up...'

'Thanks... but I dun't think so,' said Charlie. 'I'm thinkin' along more traditional lines like... a bit punky still though...'

'Suit yourself,' said Micky. 'Your loss... but take me card anyway. Do 'ee want that disc or no?'

Charlie picked up the CD and handed him six quid. He also slipped one o'Micky's cards into his pocket, noticing his full address. United Downs was all he had t'read. The area was as notorious as Trelawny for trouble – only there, it wudn' an estate, it was a collection of what the newspapers called New Age Travellers.

'Fuckin' travellers with business cards...' Charlie said. 'Whatever fuckin' next? Websites an' BMWs?'

'I'll see y'round,' said Micky, moving to a new customer.

'Prob'ly,' said Charlie.

When he found his da again, he was at the car parts stall, negotiating the price of a new carburettor for his prized Capri. His hands were already full of new plugs and leads.

'Cheaper n'fuck up here,' whispered Tommy to his son. 'I'd pay double fur this lot down *Halfords* or somewhere.'

Charlie looked around. That was it really. Living in Cornwall at the start of the third millennium was a battle of wits. It was about outwitting the dole, outwitting the emmets – any cunt really. The struggle to earn a living from the land, or the sea, or under the ground was about outwitting the elements, an' to

Proper Job, Charlie Curnow!

survive, you had t'be cunning as fuck. Charlie's idea was to continue this noble tradition of Cornwall.

'Y'ready?' asked his da. 'I've got all I want...'

'I've finished,' said Charlie.

Feeling hungry, they picked up two pasties from one of the stalls, an' pounded across the car park to the Capri. The pasties went down well.

'Do 'ee fancy a drink?' said his da. 'We'n go up Carnkie fur a pint...'

'Na, you'm a'right da,' Charlie said. 'I had bellyful laas' night t'be honest with 'ee... I'm still shakin' that off...'

'Let's go up Carn Brea then...' he suggested, casual-like.

Charlie didn' mind. He went there walkin' a lot anyway, an' given that it was a dry winter's day, the view wudn' be bad either.

'I'll need t'change the sparks when I get back,' his da announced as they drove back up Carnkie. 'The bugger idn' accelerating like 'ee should...'

They pulled into the pot-holed lane that led to the top of the Carn. The collective effect of the holes and his faather's shit drivin' made for a rough ride to the car park. By night, the Carn was frequented by kids in Novas and Corsas who went up there to smoke dope, or for a quick shag, but on Sundays, families went up there to climb over the huge piled boulders. On a day like today, y'could almost see as far west as the Scillies an' up t'Brown Willy on Bodmin Moor.

Charlie's da rolled another fag an' stuck it in his mouth. He wound down his window to toss out a match, then exhaled. The smoke blew eastwards to where the castle stood. These days it was a restaurant – though they never seemed t'be very busy – not like the *McDonalds'* restaurant down in Pool, which was always packed with divorced weekend fathers treating their barely-seen kids to Happy Meals.

'You'n forget it all up here,' said his da. 'All the crap goin' on down there...'

Charlie looked to see the sprawling mass o'Camborne an' Redruth below. He viewed the old mining ground and the new industrial estates; in the distance, the Atlantic Ocean an' Newquay's hotels.

'I wish...' said his faather, 'I wish... things were different...

Remember when we used t'bring 'ee up here when y'were a tacker... an' you used t'sit in the seats in the stones...'

Charlie hated his da when he was like this. Being sentimental didn' suit the cunt, especially when he knew some nights his mother 'ud squal her eyes out over 'un. But then he was suddenly quoting some poems, as he flicked ash into the Carn's breeze.

'Thou art full of the Eternal, and His voice is heard among the Druid temples of Carn Brea...' orated his da.

'Whaas' that?' Charlie asked.

'A poem.'

'I knaw that. We did 'ut at school I think. Who wrote 'un?'

'Man by the name o'John Harris – born back Bolenowe way. I dun't knaw any more o'it than that – but I learnt that from a chap over Crofty who had it on his locker. Beauty idn' a? That captures it up here fur me... I reckon years ago – they'd come up here t'escape what 'twas like underground. Now I d'reckon they just do it for whaas' above ground...'

Charlie looked at his da. Whatever people thought of 'un – and twudn' much – he was right about some things. 'Twas that side of 'un his mother still liked. 'Twas sad that she cudn' fuckin' stand the rest o' 'un these days.

'Still, I'll have me redundancy come through soon...'

'What are 'ee goin' t'do with that?' asked Charlie.

'Dunnaw yet... but I got an idea or two in mind. I'll be spendin' it wisely though – not like the other boys, pissin' it up 'gainst the wall down *The Rose Cottage*, or goin' on some fuckin' cruise. Na, I shall,' he said with some degree of pride, 'be re-investing in the beleaguered Cornish economy.'

He sounded like some knobber from Objective One.

'Y'should put it inta' my band,' said Charlie.

'Yer band!? Like fuck I will,' said his da. 'Gaa! Y'can't even plaay, tell 'bout form a fuckin' band... That wudn' earn 'ee any money...'

The car went silent. Money was the fuckin' root of all evil.

'You'll see,' said Charlie.

'So will you,' said his da.

He threw his fag out of the window and wound it up.

'I'd better get back to Karen... I've got to work on the car as well...'

Proper Job, Charlie Curnow!

'A'right,' said Charlie. 'You'll drop me back though?'

''Course I will,' said his da.

He spun the car 'round and they went down the lane like his da was in the Cornish section of the RAC Rally. The druid temples of Carn Brea were once again at peace.

* * * * *

Monday mornings always sucked. Every fortnight they sucked even more. Charlie had to go sign on in Camborne. It always seemed t'be pissing down with rain, an' the people behind the Jobseeker's desks were bastards. Charlie'd been on the dole for nearly six months now after he'd chucked in college.

'It's about time, Mr Curnow, we signed you up for Job Club...' said the Jobseeker's officer. 'Let me just check your Jobseeker's record on your Jobseeker's form.'

The officer's hands whizzed over the Jobseeker's keypad of his Jobseeker's terminal. Charlie knew what he'd put down. It didn' stop the officer repeatin' it.

'It says you are seeking employment in either tourism, mining or music... Quite a diverse field Mr Curnow... Maybe we should be a little more specific about the job you are seeking...'

The Jobseeker Charlie had heard about Job Club. Neil had been on it a while back. The only reason that people found jobs within six weeks, was because after all the shit y'had to sit through, y'd take anything. Suckin' tramps' knobs down Camborne bus station was gainful employment, rather than attendin' the Job Club seminars. Besides, there were so many fuckin' types o'seminars y'could attend – that there was a fuckin' whole industry based on the unemployed. One cunt even opened a café between the Job Centre and where they held Job Club. Camborne, man, was the fuckin' university of unemployment, an' most o'Trelawny estate had fuckin' Ph.Ds in Dole Office studies.

'Have you completed any work since you last signed?' the officer asked in the usual monotone.

'Nope,' Charlie said.

'Sign here.'

Charlie completed the form and dated his signature. Other poor bastards were still havin' t'wait, standin' there, lookin' t'find work, with their ticket in hand for the next available offi-cer. It was as if you were buying cheese at *Tesco*.

'Like the lottery idn' a?' said Charlie on the way out.

''Zactly the same,' said one old boy he'd seen every time he signed on. 'Same chances o'winnin' an' all.'

But Charlie was fed up with losin'. Despite the shit his faather had given 'un, he'd get the band off the ground. He wudn' goin' to naw Job Club – not if he could help it. Besides, he'd asked about a business grant for young people. The dole'd give it to 'un – if he filled in the application. They needed to get together an' rehearse. That was the job on this week. Somehow, he had to motivate the cunts – or they'd do the same as every other week: blast fuckin' blobs on a computer screen or else vegetate in front of a DVD.

Then there was still the problem o'the missing bass player. There was no one on the estate who could play either – who might even consider swapping – an' start playin' bass. He'd have to put an advertisement in *The West Briton* an' see who responded. After rehearsals, they'd need the gigs. And publici-ty. It 'ud have t'be classy as well, Charlie knew that. Professional from the outset – else it wudn' worth bothering. He thought of all the arse-end bands he'd seen play in the pubs and clubs locally. None of 'em were good enough because they weren't fuckin' hungry enough. Success was fuckin' free Skinners all night, the chance of a shag, an' a bit of a laugh. That wudn' good enough anymore.

Charlie reckoned he was cleverer than all of them. He had strategies for success. He knew the stages – what to do at each point – when to support, when not to – all the bollocks of the music industry he'd read up on. He knew it inside-out and ass-'bout-face. They'd conquer the world he told himself. They'd be on the cover of *Kerrang!*. They'd be on MTV. They'd sell out the NEC. He even had the songs written.

He was thinking all o'this as he walked up Cross Street from Commercial Square. Generally, he had a gake in the music shop window there, to see if there was anything o'interest. Mostly, they sold fancy organs for old boys – with built-in rhythms, so they could practise shit like 'Lamorna' and 'Little Lize'. There were a few pieces o'modern gear tucked in the back, but he didn' go in. He had fuck-all money on 'un anyway. Most musicians locally, traded their gear in the free advertising newspapers – or else in the exchange shop in Trelowarren Street. All o'that would need to be investigated. As well as the worry of a lack o'a bass player, somehow they also had to get hold of a PA system. 'Eaving that around without a car or van, was also a major problem.

He reached the mini roundabout between Cross and Trevenson Street, where the statue of Richard Trevithick stood. The inventor was positioned so he stared up Trevu Road. He would have to be as inventive as Camborne's most famous son, if he was t'get what he wanted.

At home, he used his mother's Barclaycard to take out an advert in *The West Briton*. The girl at the other end took his details.

'Under what heading do you wish the advertisement to be placed?' she said, her cockney accent grating against his ears; his Cornish one grating against hers.

'Musicians wanted,' Charlie said.

'The only category is Music,' she said.

'That'll have to do,' said Charlie.

'And the wording?' she asked.

'Innovative Cornish rock band require bass player,' Charlie said instantly. He'd rehearsed it in his mind a few hundred times. 'Influences: Zep, Nirvana, N.I.R.V.A.N.A., Green Day. Phone 01209 270073.'

'*The West Briton's* advertising sectionthanksyouforyourcall. Wewishyousucesswithyouradvertisement...'

Charlie put down the phone and made a cup of coffee. He pressed 'play' on the remote. Led Zep *IV* burst out.

* * * * *

There was absolutely fuck-all response to the advertisement.

'Wha' – not one fuckin' call?' asked Yak.

'Nothun',' said Charlie.

'It did go in though, didn' it?' asked Neil.

''Course it fuckin' did. Look...'

Charlie showed Neil the advert.

'I like that,' said Neil. 'Innovative. Sounds good dudn' it?'

'Fuckin' would if somebody called us,' said Charlie. 'Anyway, I've got the keys to the chapel hall...'

Alan M. Kent

Various bits of musical instruments were being loaded from vans and cars into the yard of the chapel. It had taken all o'the previous week and the weekend, to get Yak, Neil an' Charlie in the same place for a rehearsal. Mrs Williams had given Charlie shit – she'd been expectin' 'un all o'laas' week, an' then 'ee didn' turn up. Charlie had to apologise before she'd give him the keys.

'Just don't fuckin' damage anything,' said Charlie, as he opened the door.

The place stank of tea, biscuits and Methodist dust.

'Jesus,' said Neil. 'What a hovel...'

'All the greatest bands start in hovels,' said Charlie. 'Shut yer moaning an'get your gear inside.'

Yak's drums took a little longer to set up than they'd thought. One o'the connecting pins had been damaged in transit, and had to be held in position with a bit o'gaffa tape.

''Tis prop'ly fucked now,' said Yak. 'I'll need a replacement...'

'A'right Yak – we'll get it... but you all knaw what today's about. It's about forming a proper band. It's about kicking our fuckin' asses an' about checkin' what we can do and wha' we can't do. It's about our attitude for now and the future...'

'Hear of 'un,' said Neil. 'He thinks he's fuckin' Kurt Cobain – a poet of his generation...'

'Ah fuck off you party... Look, I just want to know we're all in this together...'

''Course,' said Yak. 'One an' all 'ennit?'

'Let's tune up then,' said Neil.

That took longer than any o'them expected. It was gone eleven by the time they felt they were in tune. Yak was doin' his nut.

'Yeah, sorry Yak. It wun't take us as long next time...' offered Neil. 'It's got to be right though – else we may as well give up...'

'Free? 'All Right Now'?' said Charlie.

The three of them got into position. It was no longer Troon Chapel hall. It was somewhere else – far away from Trelawny.

'1, 2, 3, 4,' shouted Charlie.

DUH, DA DUH. 'THERE SHE STOOD...'

The sound ricocheted around the chapel. It sounded good.

AAALLL RIGHT NOW... BABY, IT'S ALL RIGHT NOW...'

Proper Job, Charlie Curnow!

Then it came to the section where the bass played the melody. The song collapsed.

'Where've 'ee gone?' asked Charlie.

'Nowhere – there's no music for us here though – it's only bass,' said Neil.

'O'course,' said Charlie. 'Shit... let's just edit that. Just bridge to the next verse.'

'A'right,' said Yak.

'1, 2, 3, 4,' began Charlie.

DUH, DA DUH...

This time it was better. They made it to the end of the track. It was a crap rendition – that didn' stop the three o'them from feelin' good though.

'Shit-hot,' said Neil.

''Twudn' bad,' said Charlie, 'We'n do better though...'

They played it again, but Neil completely ballsed up the solo an' stopped.

'Me fuckin' hands are too cold,' he said.

'You've been out shaggin' in colder conditions than this,' shouted Yak. 'What're 'ee moanin' about?'

They played the song again.

'It's a'right now,' joked Yak.

'Naw – not yet,' said Charlie. 'It's improvin' – we're all improvin'. We got to have more energy in there though...'

'Technically, it's good though,' said Neil.

''Es, technically, it's fine,' said Charlie, 'but 'tis no good. Live rock music's not about being technical, it's about the pauses and the cock-ups; it's those slight differences... thaas' why those who improvise'll always be bigger fuckin' stars than those who learn stuff parrot-fashion. Look at Jimmy Page – or Hendrix – they two never played the same solo twice... Thaas' where their greatness lay...'

It was nearly six o'clock before they decided to call it a day. Charlie was pleased. Step One had finally been taken.

'Back here tomorra',' he said. 'Nine o'clock sharp... so don't get too pissed-up tonight.'

'You're a stupid fucker an' knaw mistake Curnow,' said Neil.

'Worried you'll be knackered for all your shaggin'?' chipped in Yak.

'Ah, y'should knaw me better than that...' Neil replied. 'I'n

Alan M. Kent

ready any time o'the day or night.'

'Thaas' 'cause 'ee has t'be,' said Yak, 'in case Markie catches 'un on the job!'

'Let's keep our private lives separate eh boys?' suggested Charlie on the way out o'the chapel. 'Y'knaw 'tis fur the best. Just go home an' learn they riffs Neil...'

Charlie crossed the road with the others. Yak had left his kit in the hall, but Neil an' Charlie had decided to take their guitars home.

'Are you party buskers?' asked two little cheeky cunts on their way back over. 'Play us a song...'

'Fuck off,' said Yak to them.

'Fuckin' hippies,' shouted the kids back.

'It reminds 'ee, that does,' said Yak, 'of why I fuckin' entered rock 'n' roll – t'escape little shits like that...'

They went their separate ways across the courtyard. Charlie glanced over at Mels. He hadn't seen her for over a week. He felt he must pop in an' see how she was, the poor maid.

When he got in, his ma had tea on, an, was watchin' the BBC news between fryin' eggs.

'How did it go then?' she asked.

'A'right... progress has been made up the ladder of rock...' said Charlie with complete confidence.

'Have y'heard?' asked his ma. 'They took Mel inta' care this week. I only just found out meself. Her mother's on the game... over Redruth. Whatever is 'ut like? The poor maid... an' see this here look, more bad news for Cornwall. The Labour crowd are shuttin' more hospitals down here...'

Charlie had barely taken in the news about Mel an' her mother, when his ma spoke again.

'There's two messages on the answerphone as well. One from yer shithead of a faather an' another from some maid from over Truro. Dun't get 'em now – yer tea's nearnly ready...'

* * * * *

Still eatin' the last o'a bowl o'Angel Delight, Charlie listened to the two messages on the answerphone. The first, from his faather, was a drunken garble about how much he still loved his ma, and if things were different, how they would still be

44

together. In all, a pile of bollocks. The second was – at last – a response to the advertisement in *The West Briton*. She was from Truro. Her name was Beverly Bennetts, an' she played bass guitar.

'Fuck!' Charlie said t'himself. 'A fuckin' female bass player...'

Charlie considered the novelty of it. Singers – yes. Drummers – yes. He thought of 'the artist formerly known as Prince'. But bass players. He could only think of D'Arcy out o'the Smashing Pumpkins, an' then he wudn' sure whether she played bass or guitar. The only down-side was that she lived in Truro – that could a' been John o'Groats for them at the moment, as none of 'um had any transport.

He looked at his watch. It was half-past six. He'd usually watch *The Simpsons* on Sky this time o'night, but now, there were other priorities. If his da didn' get too pissed-up tonight, he'd get him to drive them over t'Truro in the morning to meet their potential bass player. First, he'd need to phone her. He took out his mobile.

Charlie carefully dialled the number. A posh woman answered. She sounded like she was sucking a pebble off Portreath beach.

'Hello, the Bennetts' residence.'

'A – a'right,' said Charlie. 'Can I speak to Beverly please?'

'May I ask who's calling?'

'Yeah, it's... a... Charlie Curnow, lead vocalist with the innovative Cornish rock band.'

'I'll just get her...'

Charlie heard the noise of dishes being washed in the background. Then footsteps came to the phone.

'Hello,' came Beverly's voice. 'You got my message then?'

'Yeah – I'm Charlie Curnow. I'm sort of organising the band. Y'play bass then?'

'Yes. I've been playing for about five years now.'

'Who are your influences?' asked Charlie. It was an important question.

'Oh – anyone really... Avril Lavaigne's cool... Alanis Morissette...'

Charlie's heart sunk. Not the answers he wanted.

'Whatever's in the charts...'

Definitely not the answer he wanted. There was a grim

silence on the phone-line. Charlie tried another line.

'What players d'y'most admire?'

This time, Beverly was more thoughtful.

'Oh – I really like Jeff Ament out o'Pearl Jam. I'm into King Crimson as well, so I like Adrian Belew... a lot of the progressive stuff... But Mike Dirnt's cool too...'

Fuck. She knew her stuff.

'Really?' said Charlie. 'Look, can we meet up sometime. Is tomorra' any good?'

'Tomorrow's fine. I've got nothing on.'

'Have y'got any transport?' asked Charlie.

'Not really,' she said. 'I'm learning to drive – but only in me dad's car.'

'Me da'll bring us 'round to your place if y'like. Is that okay?'

Charlie instantly regretted the first statement: Innovative rock band that relied on his da – the most fuckin' unreliable cunt ever. But then, he told himself, she didn' have any transport either.

'Where d'y'live?' asked Charlie.

She gave him directions – Malpas in Truro. It sounded posh. Charlie wondered what she'd think o'three unemployed losers from Trelawny estate. She'd prob'ly show them the fuckin' door an' then set the hounds on 'um.

'What time?' negotiated Charlie.

'About ten or something,' she said.

'I look forward to meeting you,' Charlie said, like 'ee was setting up the fuckin'-mega-contract of all time.

'Me too,' said Beverly.

As soon as he'd put the receiver down, he had to take in a deep breath of air. Right now, Charlie didn' even care what she was like. They needed a bass player – an' she'd do. So much for fuckers queuing up to be in the band – an' them sittin' there havin' to listen to a thousand Yngwie Malmsteens – or any other bollocks.

He licked the Angel Delight from the bowl an' phoned his da. His mobile wudn' switched on. He'd have t'try his lover.

'Redruth 482487,' came a voice.

It was Karen – the brazen hussy (thaas' what his ma called her), who his da was humpin'.

'Is me da there?' asked Charlie.

Proper Job, Charlie Curnow!

'O – hello Charlie,' said Karen. 'Naw, he's not here. He's gone up the club.'

Charlie heard her draw hard on her cigarette. She shouted somethin' at one o'her tackers.

'Right,' said Charlie. 'Look, can y'tell him I phoned. I need t'get hold of 'un fairly quick.'

'Yeah – no problem m'andsome!'

M'andsome! How fuckin' old was she? Only retired women had the right to call Charlie that. It was a problem though – his da 'ud be downin' the first o'his twelve pints by now, up the *Miners and Mechanics Institute*. At eight o'clock he'd shoot a few games of pool, and by nine, he'd be stickin' a clear tenner in the bandit an' winnin' fuck-all.

He'd need t'contact Neil an' Yak as well. That 'ud be okay. A quick ring to their ma's – and they'd be ready to leave widn' in the mornin'. Yak was in anyway, so he told him to make sure Neil was there – an' that he wudn' out for an early mornin' shag with Ally.

Next, he phoned *Institute*. Clarence, the barman, was deaf as fuck, from two many cunts bawling orders of Hicks Special Draught at 'un.

'*Miners and Mechanics Institute*,' came his voice.

What bollocks that was, thought Charlie. No cunt mined and any mechanics being done were in fuckin' outhouses with no questions asked.

'Is Tommy Curnow there?' asked Charlie.

'Tommy Curnow?' confirmed Clare.

''Es, me faather...'

'I'll have a look..,'

That was a laugh. Charlie knew his faather 'ud be propin' up the far end of the bar, beneath the photograph of the 1963 Redruth Rugby side. Charlie heard the call go out, an' some twat singin' in the background.

'Hello,' came his da's voice.

'Da – I need y't'take me inta' Truro tomorra' mornin'. Can y'do it?'

''Spect so,' said his da. 'Why, whaas' on?'

'I'm meetin' with a bass player...'

'Yeah, I'n do it fur 'ee,' said his da. 'What time?'

''Bout quarter past nine,' said Charlie, 'so dun't drink too much.'

'Here,' said his da, 'd'ee' get me phone message?'

'Yeah,' said Charlie.

'What did yur mother say?'

Charlie decided t'be honest.

'She wudn' too impressed.'

'Well...' said his da. 'Least I tried...'

'Yeah – I knaw,' said Charlie.

'Listen,' said his da, 'y'knaw this band you'm on upon. I reckon Clare 'ud give 'ee a gig here...'

'Wha'? At the *Institute*?' Charlie was incredulous. 'Playin' old fuckers who'd rather be playin' bingo or euchre...'

'Well, he's keen on tryin' t'bring in a few more youngsters... See, he's booked the Great Gonzo, but y'knaw what he's like... Clare d'need somethin' else. You party could have a crack if y'like...'

Charlie had seen the Great Gonzo. He was an old fucker by the name o'Hedley Kent. Used t'tell jokes, sing songs like 'The Laughing Policeman' and 'Old McDonald' an' do breakdancin'. The general opinion was he was so fuckin' appallingly bad, he was actually good.

'You'll do it then,' said his da. 'I'll tell Clare...'

''Ang on da,' protested Charlie.

'Anyway – I'll pick 'ee up tomorra' mornin', so you'n get inta' Truro. See 'gin.'

'Proper job,' said Charlie, but his da was already gone.

Jesus, he said to hisself. Megastardom beckons: support to the Great Gonzo – Redruth club entertainer *par excellence*. But then, he thought: they had their first gig – and they might have a bass player. Things were lookin' up.

His sister entered the kitchen. She had her clubbing gear on – an' plugged in her curling tongs.

'Where you off?' asked Charlie.

'Down *Twilight*,' said Jess. 'We're goin' *Rose Cottage* first though...'

By *Twilight*, Jess meant the *Twilight Zone* at the *Penventon Hotel*. It was the only decent nightclub locally, and it was found at one of the posher hotels in Redruth. Charlie considered the place shit – it was full o'cunts who all looked like they'd just stepped out a' *Burtons'* window display, and who all drank bottled lagers. They'd dance to fuck all except the

Proper Job, Charlie Curnow!

Stereophonics or Oasis, an' then act like real cunts on the dance-floor. He an' Yak had felt like deckin' a few o'them last time they went.

The only time y'went was when you'd had a skinful an'one o'yer mates suggested it. There were fireman's poles in there – an' all the boys stood around them waitin' for some hammered maid t'have a go, so they could have a gake up her fanny. Friday night was even sadder. For a start, it was free for maids to get in, but then anyone who was either divorced, separated, or even fuckin' happily married, would go there to pull. Friday – it was full o'blokes in their forties who reckoned they still had it – sweaty, fat fuckers from place like St Day and Stithians who had fuck all else t'do. There'd been a run lately of drugs busts inside the place – shit like Tranx, Benzos, Temazies and Diazes. Last time Charlie'd been there, the coppers had been handing out leaflets 'bout rohypnol. There'd been a spate of date rapes hadn' there.

His sister loved it though. To her, it meant freedom from Trelawny for a few hours, for her to forget about her college course in hairdressin' an' party it up. She'd drink a few pints o'lager an' then move onta rum n'blacks. By eleven, she'd be shakin' her ass an' wigglin' her tits at the boys, hoping for a dream date. She an' her crowd were always oglin' surfin' boys, but only a few o'they ever went t'*Twilight*.

'What you doin' tonight?' she asked Charlie.

'Nothun' much,' said Charlie. 'Stayin' in – an' watchin' the telly I 'spect.'

'Be warned,' she said. 'Mum's in a bad mood... she was tellin' me upstairs just now... about dad an' that...'

'Fuck,' said Charlie.

'Yeah – she's in their... ah... her room...'

A horn honked outside.

'Thaas' me taxi. See ya.'

Jess grabbed her handbag and went out. The house became very still, and silent. Y'cud still smell her perfume. Jess wudn' be back until the small hours, an' he prob'ly wudn' see her for much o'Saturday. Charlie hoped she'd find a boy who'd treat her right. She'd been out with some right shits from the estate recently.

In the fridge was a lone can of Newcastle brown ale. Charlie opened it and lounged on the sofa. He whacked on MTV, an' watched a video with the sound down. It turned out t'be a special on Mötley Crüe. Hair metal boys. Their bass player, Nikki Sixx, was clinically dead for a bit after a session on smack. They kick-started the fucker's heart with a shot of adrenaline.

He listened upstairs. It was silent.

'Ma,' Charlie shouted up the stairs. 'You a'right?'

He heard his mother's voice say something in her bedroom. Charlie climbed the stairs. Mötley Crüe was still blasting out.

'Ma,' he said again.

'It's a'right Charlie,' his ma said. 'I'm a'right really...'

But she wudn'. Her face was all red. She'd been squalin'.

'I've decided,' she said snivelling, 'me an' yer faather are gettin' a divorce...'

Charlie sat on the bed and comforted his mother. He found a box of tissues on the bedside cabinet and gave her a couple. She wiped away some of the tears.

'It's a'right ma,' said Charlie. 'It's a'right...'

* * * * *

The chaos and squalor of Charlie's own home contrasted richly with that which they found at Beverly's the next morning. Fortunately, Charlie's da hadn't been so pissed-up the night before that he hadn't forgot to pick them up. Unfortunately, in the front seat of the Capri was Karen, so Charlie, Neil and Yak had to bundle up in the back. Though his father had been late, they soon made up time on the A30. His da was still a bit o'a speed king when it came down to it, so they were there on time.

Beverly lived near the *BBC Radio Cornwall* building on the road down to Malpas.

'Posh here ennit?' offered his faather, as they pulled into the drive o'the address she'd given Charlie.

That was it though. Truro, these days, was posh. It was where any fucker in Cornwall who was rich, went to shop. The streets were full a'cunts wearing barbour jackets an' brown corduroy trousers, an' the women all looked haughty, like they needed a night out on the piss down Troon Football Club to lighten them up. It was full a'clothing stores no fucker could afford t'buy anything in, an' other shops selling bollocks you

Proper Job, Charlie Curnow!

didn' need. As far as Charlie was concerned, there were only three good things about it – *Solo Music*, where he'd generally buy an album, *Truro Bookshop* – where they'd get any obscure book he wanted, an' the *Fleamarket* in the Hall for Cornwall – where y'could buy anything else y'wanted – bar sex. All the posh cunts o' Truro – those who worked at County Hall, an' along Lemon Street – they shopped at *Sainsburys*. Other cunts had t'make do with the *Co-Op* and *Tesco*. That was the way 'twas.

'We'm off up *MFI*,' said his da. 'What time d'y'want pickin' up? Give us a ring on me mobile...'

'You'm a'right da,' said Charlie. 'We'll get the bus back, wun't us boys?'

Neil an' Yak grunted in agreement.

'Hope she's good,' said his da, as he let them out o'the back-seat.

'Hope she'n play,' said Charlie.

His da got back in, an' the Capri sped down the drive, blasting out Rainbow. A few fuckers out pruning their roses expressed their concerns to each other about today's youth, oblivious to the fact that 'twas a fuckin' forty year old.

Beverly's place looked rich as fuck. There was a pond with a fountain in the front garden, an' in the drive was a brand new Freelander 4x4.

'En't short of a bob or two are 'um,' stated Neil.

They looked at themselves critically. Yak tied his hair back into a ponytail. Neil tucked his shirt in. Even Charlie looked at the state of his jeans (they had holes in the knees) an' wished he'd worn something else.

'She 'ent goin' t'play with the likes o'us is she,' said Yak, 'especially when she finds out where we'n from...'

'Shut up,' said Charlie, pressing the doorbell.

Yak's view altered when she opened the door. She was grungily dressed – chunky New Rock boots an' a flowery print dress. Her hair was long an' in braids. She had a ring through the left side of her nose an' a bunch of Celtic design jewellery. She looked a complete babe – like the Iseult in a picture they had up in 'Druth school.

'You Beverly?' asked Charlie.

'Yeah – most people call me Bev though,' she said.

Alan M. Kent

Charlie looked at Neil and Yak. It was like the fuckers had turned to stone. Charlie introduced them.

'So this is the band then?' Bev asked.

'Yes – this is ov' 'un,' said Charlie sheepishly. He corrected his normal language to, '- this is it...'

'You'd better come in,' Bev said. 'My folks are out shopping – so we can turn it up – if you know what I mean...'

'Cool,' said Neil.

'I tried to form a band up Truro College,' she said, 'but no one was interested. D'y'want a coffee?'

They did.

'I mean, I'm doin' A-Levels n'stuff – an' my parents want me to go to University, but I'm not into it at all really.'

'Where did y'go t'school?' asked Yak.

'Truro High School for Girls. How about you?'

''Druth comp,' answered Yak.

'Do any of you go to college?' asked Bev.

'I used to,' said Charlie, 'but it didn' offer what I wanted...'

'Me neither,' said Neil. That was a laugh. He'd gone right on the dole after he'd walked out of the school gates.

Yak said, 'I did a day release, on a training scheme at *Holmans*, but they run out a' money after the first year... They had me back for a bit, then the whole place went under...'

What a fuckin' talented bunch, Charlie thought to himself. At this rate, she was bound to say no.

'So what do you called yourselves?' asked Bev as she dealt out spoonfuls of coffee.

'What d'y'mean?' asked Charlie.

'What's the band called?'

'Nothun' yet.'

'You haven't got a name?!'

'Naw, not yet,' said Charlie. 'We're in no hurry though. It'll come along when it's good and ready...'

She poured hot water into the coffee, and they helped themselves to milk and sugar. Charlie didn't normally take any sugar – but today, well today he spooned it in.

'So, d'y'want t'hear me play?'

''Es,' said Yak, 'proper – whenever you'm ready...'

'My gear's in the lounge. Come on through...'

The three o'them followed Bev though the expanse of the

Proper Job, Charlie Curnow!

house. Her mother had classy paintings of Cornwall on the walls – all very St Ives – not like his ma's ocean scenes or crap pictures of Padstow on hardboard.

'I dun't care how bad she is,' whispered Yak to Charlie. 'She's fuckin' a'right. She 'ent stuck up like other maids I've met from Truro.'

'Let's hear her play,' said Charlie, even though he was already in agreement with Yak.

When they got into the lounge, they could barely believe their eyes. She had a Marshall cabinet, a Peavy amp and a Fender Bass all set up ready to go. Proped next to the Fender was a fretless bass.

'Fuckin' hell,' said Neil quietly. 'Puts our gear t'shame.'

'Ready?' said Bev.

The three of them sat on the sofa and watched. Bev placed her coffee on the table before them, then manoeuvred the bass guitar over her head. She plugged in the lead to the radio mike on the strap, and switched on her amplifier. It buzzed to life, and she adjusted the output.

'Any requests?' she asked.

'No – whatever,' said Charlie.

'"NIB" – Black Sabbath,' Bev said.

BUMM BUMM BUMM BUMM, BA BA BA, BUMM BUMM BUMM.

Charlie, Neil and Yak were pinned back by the sound. They felt it in their feet, in their legs and in their chest cavity. It was brilliant. She smiled and played the rest of the song. Charlie mumbled a few of the words.

'My name is Lucifer please take my hand...'

BA BA BA, BUMM BUMM BUMM, BA BA BA BUMM BA.

At the end of the song, Bev slapped the thick strings like they were cotton threads. She wudn' gazing at her feet either. She played it with style – like she meant it – like the noise was coming from her own soul. She moved the bass up an' down like the way real rock stars do it. There was a scarf tied to the strap and Charlie, who couldn' help it, had an instant boner. He tried to style 'un in a direction so Bev wudn' notice.

'Shit,' she said when she'd finished. 'I messed up that last section...'

'Sounded good t'me,' said Yak, 'Y'can't beat Geezer Butler's bass work...'

'Needs drums though,' Bev said. 'What d'y'think?'

'Excellent,' said Neil.

'Spot on,' said Yak.

'What else can y'do?' asked Charlie. He was impressed as fuck, but 'ee wudn' lettin' on, not just yet anyway.

'Try this...' she said.

It was 'American Idiot' by Green Day, and it kicked even harder.

'Shit hot,' said Neil.

'Yeah,' said Yak, like he was listenin' t'Jazz or something.

Charlie could resist no longer.

'Look's like you're in,' he said.

'Really?' asked Bev.

'Definitely,' confirmed Charlie.

Bev's audition had lasted all o'ten minutes. She played some Muse then some Marilyn Manson. Charlie looked at the others in amazement. They all knew it was goin to take slightly longer for them – an' Trelawny – t'audition for her. Charlie just hoped her love of rock 'n' roll was greater than her love o'all the the shit she might have t'deal with.

'When can 'ee come down to Camborne?' asked Neil.

'Whenever...' she began, beaming.

'Have y'been t'Troon before?' wondered Yak.

'No – I haven't I'm afraid...'

'Thaas' a'right,' said Charlie cool as mustard. 'We'll show you the ropes... Our estate... our area... it's very rock 'n'roll...'

'What are you doin' this afternoon?' she asked.

Yak nearly fell over. No maid ever asked cunts like them questions like that.

'Dunnaw,' said Yak, the fuckin' anus that he was.

'Hanging out in Truro I s'pause,' said Charlie – cool still – 'You know how 'tis...'

'Can I hang out with you guys?' Bev asked.

Charlie smiled. This was rock 'n'roll, he thought to himself. It was happenin'.

'Sure,' he said. 'We're a band now...'

'Fuckin' right,' said Yak.

'Ay – an' mind yer fuckin' swearin' Yak,' said Neil.

Proper Job, Charlie Curnow!

* * * * *

They left Bev's house and walked up past *BBC Radio Cornwall*. The traffic was bad. Sometimes, it felt like every bleddy car in Cornwall had t'drive through Truro to get anywhere else. Thaas' the cunts in the Planning department fur 'ee.

'Here they come, walking down the street, get the funniest looks from everyone we meet...' Neil sang.

He had them walking like The Monkees, and singing in the underpass over to Lemon Quay. Bev, Neil and Yak were talking technical. They headed over to *Modern Music* on Kenwyn Street, and were soon inside, looking at new gear. Trace Elliot. Marsball. Sonor. Pearl. Jackson. Gibson. Boss. Aria. Zildjian. The language of rock 'n' roll. Charlie was elsewhere. He could see the back of their debut album for EMI – their pictures all moody and mean-looking. Then their names – in classy lettering:

Vocals / guitar – Charlie Curnow
Lead guitar – Neil Davey
Bass guitar – Bev Bennetts
Drums / Percussion – Yak
Yak?

Fuck, he thought. Yak needed a new name – a proper name like – but it would come. He hoped a name for the band would come too. After all, the chance of a first gig was in the bag. The pasty he bought for dinner that Saturday tasted good; very fuckin' good indeed. He looked over at the other members. They were nothun' really – two wankers from Trelawny estate – an' a posh maid from Truro. But Charlie could see greatness in them. They were fuckin' great, and they were in a band.

'See these,' he said to the others while they looked at the albums in *Woolworths*. 'That'll be us... very soon.'

Most cunts said shit like that for a laugh, as a wind-up, to have y'on. Not Charlie though. The way he said it was so convincing, he didn' leave ya any room t'doubt it.

'It will happen,' Charlie said.

'Dun't be a tosser,' said Yak, but from the way Charlie looked, selling out the Reading Festival was only a few drum-rolls away.

Y'mean it dun't 'ee?' said Yak.

Alan M. Kent

'I've never been more sure,' said Charlie. He checked the Hall for Cornwall to see that it was free in four years time for their home-coming gigs, after their hugely successful Japanese tour.

* * * * *

On the way back from Truro, they were all sure of one thing – they needed jobs. They needed proper jobs to buy better equipment – an' so they didn' look right twats in front of Bev. It was the wrong time o'the year t'be looking for work in Cornwall though. All the fuckin' hotels were shut down after the Christmas Party season and there was nothun' goin' down on the coast. You had all these tourist bosses saying how the shoulder season was extending an' that, but it made no difference on most Cornish people. The only fuckers who seemed t'benefit were they crowd who were from up the line t'begin with – cunts up Padstow – sellin' fuckin' fish fur fifty quid a go, or else others who ran wanky painting holidays down St Ives. In summer the tourist industry barely touched Camborne an' Redruth, so in winter, 'twas piss poor.

'Nothun' goin' boy,' was the answer y'expected t'get.

There was nothun' on.

Each of them were resigned t' this as the Hoppa bus wound its way past Truro College towards the A30. On the horizon could be seen the windfarm out near Three Burrows and westwards, the mass of Carn Brea. A mizzle was blawin' in from the Atlantic, an' the top of the Carn was negotiating with the weather to stay in view. All the way down to their turn-off could be seen haunting mine stacks. Not that long ago – every cunt from 'round there would a' been deep in the ground, hacking at the bloody rock fur tin or copper. They were good at it too. Cunts from Cornwall opening up nearnly every mining operation 'round the world. These days, no fucker put Cornwall on the map.

The bus pulled up Tolvadden Road and Crofty came into view. He remembered the time recently when it was closin'. Y'had every cunt standin' outside then with placards an' fuckin' loudhailers, thinkin' they could do something. Nationalist cunts wearing fuckin' kilts, shoutin', 'Kernow bys

Proper Job, Charlie Curnow!

Vykken!, and all that bollocks. Fuckers who reckoned they were more Cornish than you were. His da said they were a'right – least they'd turned up an' tried t'support the mine. They were still wankers though.

At the traffic lights, the bus turned down into Tuckingmill and moved past the tiny rows of ex-miners' cottages that lined the street. From the chip house upwards, they'd put in traffic-calming measures, so the Hoppa swerved all over the fuckin' place, an' Yak an' Neil were jolted out o'their dozing state.

'Like fuckin' Brands Hatch this is,' said Yak as they pulled past the bright neon sign of the *Kernow Aquarium Centre*.

It was getting dark now and Camborne was beginning to sparkle in the mist.

'Y'seeing Ally t'night then?' Charlie asked Neil.

'Dunnaw,' he said. 'Depends...'

''Es, depends on whether the fuckin' Terminator's anywhere near 'ee...'

'I'n handle 'un,' said Neil.

'Like fuck y'can,' said Charlie.

At *Tescos* some women got on who lived up Trelawny. They looked old before their time, with fuckin' screamin' kids and handfuls of *Tesco Value* product shopping. It looked like they'd fuckin' given up. Charlie could understand why.

'Thaas' you an' Ally there...' he said.

'Wha'?' said Neil.

'I just fuckin' hope you'm bagged up when you'm over mine givin' her one, else you'll be down here with yer own chield...'

'Dun't 'ee worry,' said Neil. 'I always take precautions...'

The bus sped down Wesley Street, past the Methodist Chapel and into Centenary Street. Somewhere inside, the Cornish were pretendin' they were elsewhere, pretendin' half the shops in Treloworren weren't boarded up and piss-stained from those caught short waking home from *Tyacks Hotel*, pretendin' that the government gave a fuck about 'em, an' hopin' they might come up on the lottery.

Let that not be me, thought Charlie to himself. He wondered if Neil and Yak thought the same.

'Monday,' said Yak, 'we should all go down the dole...'

'Wha' d'y'mean?' said Charlie.

'Look for jobs...' said Yak. 'It's got t'be done.'

Alan M. Kent

*   *   *   *   *

Monday morning froze their bollocks off. They were down the dole by quarter to nine, an' the three of them stood outside like they were waitin' for a concert, rather than waitin' for the cunt o'a manager Gary Yelland, t'open the doors. Aside from their meeting with Bev, it had been a shit weekend. There had been no party on the estate, but there had been a fight in No.11 over a hash deal. The coppers had turned up, but time they got there, all the boys had scarpered over Bolenowe Moor – an' there was no way – tracker dogs or not – that they was goin' over there on a February night. They could fuckin' smoke their blow for all they cared. His sister was in a good mood though. She'd met some new boy down *Twilight*, so fur once, she went to College with a smile on her face. He hadn't heard from his da. Presumably he was at Karen's, fixing up some crap piece of *MFI* furniture that 'ud fall down within the week. His ma was just his ma – same as she'd been for a few months now.

'You boys are keen,' said Gary 'I've got a job and you cunts haven't' Yelland.

The wanker even gave his watch a glance t'check that he wudn' opening the dole office two seconds earlier than he had to, t'let in shit from Trelawny.

When the door bar slid back, the three o'them rushed in.

'Like the January sales this – ay, Mr Yelland,' quipped Yak.

This time, they'd scan the boards hard. They were full o'crap jobs, which they tried t'make sound better than they really were. When it came down to it, most o'them were either daffodil picking, selling double-glazing or else cleaning fur the rich. Real jobs didn' exist.

'Mr Yelland,' said Charlie. 'Have y'got one of them 'Young Enterprise' grant applications?'

'What?' said Yelland.

'Y'knaw – the 'New Deal' forms which encourage unemployed youth t'get off their asses, and get aid for a business venture of their own choosing...'

'They don't include dope dealing,' said Yelland, the bastard.

'Naw, I'm serious,' pleaded Charlie.

'Okay,' said Yelland. 'Sit down an' tell me...'

Proper Job, Charlie Curnow!

'Four of us,' explained Charlie, 'we've formed a band. I'm kind of their manager and lead singer. We're goin' t' go fur it. See if we can make it...'

'A pop band?' asked Yelland.

'Well... rock actually,' said Charlie.

'Here's the form. You'll have to fill in all the sections... I warn y'though, they aren't likely t'give hand-outs for somethin' like that...'

'I'n try though – can't I?' stated Charlie.

'Why not?' said Yelland. 'People'll try anything 'round here...'

Yelland started shaking again. He did that from time t'time. It was the stress o'workin' there. Too many cunts took out their frustration on him, like it was his fault they were unemployed. Like he said once, he couldn't help it if the price o'tin was piss poor.

'Whaas' that?' asked Neil.

'A business proposition,' said Charlie. 'Y'found anything...?'

'Something,' said Neil. 'They're sortin' out an interview for me...'

'Yak?'

''Es – I dunnaw if 'tis worth tryin' – but they'm havin' a look for me...'

'I gotta' go t'the bank,' said Charlie.

'The bank?'

'Yep – I need t'see someone there,' said Charlie. 'Look, I'll meet you party tonight. Half-six over the chapel... Y'knaw Bev's comin' dun't 'ee?'

'A'right,' said Neil. 'Dun't worry. We'll be there...'

'Good luck,' Charlie said to them both.

He stepped outside. The morning was still cold, but he strode across Commercial Square to *Lloyds Bank*, where his mate Kelvin worked. Kelvin lived up Beacon, the next village inta' Camborne from Troon. They'd gone t'school together. Kelvin had done a'right for hisself – or so Charlie's ma thought. She was always fuckin' remindin' him of it, at least. Kelvin worked at the bank. He'd been there almost two years, an' was now their small business adviser. The role was like selling sand in the Sahara. There was nothun' t'do.

'I'd like t'see yur small business adviser,' said Charlie to the pretty girl on the enquiries desk.

Alan M. Kent

She looked Charlie over. He had on his normal jeans, a lumber shirt, an' a pair of Doc Martins. He should o'had on a suit, but Christ, he told himself, this was rock 'n' roll. Besides, the only suit he had, he'd worn to his gran's funeral when he was fourteen, an' then the trouser bottoms came up to his knees.

Kelvin came out from behind the locking door. Sure, he had on his fuckin' bank clerk clobber, but he was still the same little bastard who'd bricked up the science teacher's Mini on the last day o'school, an' flogged the wheels over Chalkie White's scrapyard.

'Mr Curnow?' joked Kelvin. 'What can I do for you?'

'I need your help, mate,' said Charlie. 'Have y'got a few minutes?'

'No problem,' said Kelvin. 'If you'd like t'step inta' the room to the left of you.'

It was one o'they places where suits sort out mortgages an' that.

'Whaas' on?' asked Kelvin.

'I've got this look – a 'New Deal' form from the dole. Y'knaw I've been on about forming a band – serious like – well, there could be some money fur us...'

'Let me have a look,' said Kelvin.

He scanned the form. There was a lot about projected income and projected expenditure. Long and short term planning.

'It's like a grant application,' said Kelvin. 'I do 'um all the time with people... piece o'piss...'

'Right on,' said Charlie.

Kelvin took off his jacket an' Charlie moved his chair 'round.

'I want a credit on yer first album mind,' said Kelvin, 'when yur radio-friendly unit shifters...'

'Of course,' said Charlie, cool as fuck.

* * * * *

It took moast o'the mornin' t'complete the form. Charlie could hardly believe how Kelvin had just conjured some figures out of the air.

'Easy,' said Kelvin. 'You're just playin' the funding game... just like all they wankers on Objective One.'

Proper Job, Charlie Curnow!

'Cheers,' said Charlie.

Kelvin went back around the counter and became respectable again. It looked piss boring there – but at least some o'the maids who were clerks, weren't bad looking.

'There 'ee is,' said Charlie t'Yelland. 'All complete...'

'Really?' went a surprised Yelland. 'All of it?'

'Yes – no problem,' said Charlie. 'I told 'ee I was serious about the band...'

'Well, yer application should take a fortnight to process, and we will write to you to inform you whether your application has been successful.'

'Excellent,' said Charlie. 'An' can you give me the details on this job please?'

'Certainly,' said Yelland. 'Ha... y're really goin' fur this...'

''Es, why not?' asked Charlie. 'It sounds a'right...'

'I'll see if the position is still vacant...'

* * * * *

Charlie got back home late. He'd have to gulp down his tea if he was t'make it over chapel for the rehearsal on time. He'd been all the way down t'Hayle in the afternoon for an interview at the *Haven Holiday Park*. It wasn't what he wanted, but what could you do? A job was a job.

'Dun't go in the living room,' his ma said.

'Why not?'

'Your sister's in there with her new boyfriend...' his ma whispered.

'I've got to,' said Charlie. 'I need me gear for the rehearsal...'

'Just leave them a minute. They're havin' their tea. He's a vegetarian...'

She said it as if it was Jess' fifth birthday party.

His ma stood under her photo of Freddie Mercury an' the picture of Botallack Mine his da had mounted above it. A plateful of microwaved chips and beans was between him and her.

'Here,' she said. 'Eat 'um out here...'

Charlie relented. He barely had time to shovel in the first mouthful of food an' tell her about his new job, before his sister came in carryin' two empty plates.

'A'right?' she said nonchalantly to her brother.

Alan M. Kent

'Fine,' said Charlie. 'I need t'get me gear in a minute...'

'Whaas' fur afters?' asked Jessie.

'Angel Delight,' said their ma.

Charlie had really wanted to have a bit of a shave and a shower before the rehearsal, but that wudn' goin' t'happen.

'You'n go through,' said Jess. 'Micky an' I dun't mind...'

He went through to the living room, still clutchin' his plate-ful of food.

'A'right mate?' said a voice on the sofa.

Charlie peered across the room.

'D'y'knaw me brother?' asked Jess.

'Yeah, 'course I do. He was up market a few weekends ago...'

Charlie recognised him now. It was Micky T, the traveller DJ.

'I got that gig at the *Twilight*,' he said. 'Thaas' how I came t'meet yer sister like...'

Fuckin' rave shite, thought Charlie. Now he was goin' out with his sister.

'How's that Mars Volta bootleg then?' he asked.

'A'right,' said Charlie. 'Drops out a bit on the last tracks though...'

'Really?' said Micky, tryin' t'ingratiate himself. 'I'll see if I'n get 'ee another...'

'Micky's the new DJ on Friday nights,' said Jess.

'Spot on,' deadpanned Charlie. 'Look, I've gotta go... I need t'get over chapel....'

'His band,' his sister explained, 'they rehearse there...'

'Rock 'n' roll preachers eh?' joked Micky.

'Not really,' said Charlie.

He was up the stairs by now – and had grabbed all his gear. He still had to lug the stuff over the estate, an' negotiate the fuckin' little tackers, who'd try to touch his guitar.

'I'n give y'a lift if y'like,' said Micky. 'It's no problem...'

'Na – y'a'right,' said Charlie proudly. 'It's no distance...'

Truth was, Charlie didn' like the cunt. He was too full a'him-self. Too much of a cocky bastard for his liking. Not that he said anything anti-Cornish or anything, it was just his way. His da knew the type. They sort, always seemed t'be squarin' up at 'ee like a bottle o'piss.

'Idn' a' lovely?' said his sister, cuddlin' 'un, as if he were a Teddy Bear she'd bought in *Clinton Cards*.

Proper Job, Charlie Curnow!

Charlie tipped the rest of his chips inta' his mouth an' struggled out the front door.

'Fuck, fuck,' he said t'hisself. He was late.

* * * * *

When he got t' the Chapel, the other three were outside. Bev's dad was just arranging what time he'd come to pick her up. He looked even more concerned when Charlie arrived.

'Are you going to be alright?' her father asked quietly.

'Dad!' she bawled at him. 'I'll be fine – honest...'

Her father eyed Charlie up – like he was on drugs – an' was about t'offer his precious daughter a shot.

'Y'found it then?' asked Charlie.

'Yes,' said Bev, 'it was a good map.'

'A'right boys,' said Charlie. 'How d'ee get on today?'

'A'right,' said Yak. 'I got a job down Barripper way...'

'What doin'?'

'Pickin' fuckin' daffodils...'

'Yeah?' said Charlie. 'Y'want t'be careful there – the juice can give 'ee a skin disorder. I seen some'ut about it on telly...'

'They give 'ee gloves n'that,' said Yak. "Me fuckin' back's aching though... I've only done an af'ernoon's work...'

Charlie opened up the hall.

'Nice,' said Bev.

'One day, they'll flock here,' said Charlie, 'like that bridge in Newport, in Wales, where Kurt proposed to Courtney Love...

Charlie was off on one again.

'How about you Neil?' asked Bev.

'Shelf-stacking,' he said, 'down *Tesco*.'

'Right on,' said Charlie. 'We'm in the money...'

'How 'bout you?' asked Neil.

'Yeah... I got something,' Charlie said. 'Down *Haven Holiday Park*, over Gwithian way...'

'What doin'?'

'Freddy Bear,' Charlie said.

'Wha'?'

'Freddy Bear,' he repeated. 'I dress up in Bear outfit all day an' walk around the camp – givin' out sweets n'shit...'

Alan M. Kent

'Fuckin' hell,' said Yak. 'Is there any cunt down there this time o'year?'

''Course,' said Charlie. 'Extended season these days ennit?'

'You, in a bear suit,' said Bev. She collapsed in laughter. Yak an' Neil joined in.

'Shut-up y'tossers,' said Charlie. 'It's a proper fuckin' job a'right...'

'Right on boy,' said Yak. 'Let's set up the *bear* necessities for the rehearsal..."

'Oooh, the *bear*-faced cheek of 'ut,' said Neil.

'Fuck off,' said Charlie. 'Anyway, I've some other news. Y'knaw that new deal form I picked up. Well, me an' Kelv filled it in, an' I handed it back t'Yelland... it might mean we get some money fur settin' up the band.'

'That's great,' said Bev.

'Beauty,' said Yak.

'Anyway, let's get on...' Charlie said. 'We have t'practise. Remember, we've got a gig comin' up soon over *Institute*...'

* * * * *

The rehearsal was better now that Bev was there. Yak an' Neil didn' ass around as much. They took it more seriously. Perhaps she intimidated them – or maybe they got serious about it themselves. Either way, it worked. With Bev's bass playing, the rhythm section really started locking in. Yak improved because he wanted to match her. Neil took more care over what he was playing. Their sound widened out. It was the usual rock covers t'begin with. Thaas' what they'd be playin' at the *Institute* – songs from off their jukebox – the rock music people danced to if they were pissed-up enough – music for all the air guitarists over there.

'Zeppelin?' asked Neil.

'Yeah – do it,'said Bev,

It had to be 'Rock and Roll'.

Neil kicked in with the opening riff.

'IT'S BEEN A LONG TIME SINCE I'VE ROCK AND ROLLED...'

Charlie's vocals powered around the hall. In his mind, it wasn't Troon Chapel, but Wembley Stadium. Bev watched him. She admired that boy. He put everything into it.

'LONELY, LONELY, LONELY, LONELY, LONELY, LONELY TIME...'

Yak's drumsticks crashed down and ended the song.

'Mr John Bonham,' congratulated Bev. 'That was good...'

'Good,' said Charlie. 'We'n make it better though... it needs something...'

'Like what?' asked Neil.

'More balls,' said Bev.

'Yeah – sort of... like the 'vibe' of it, is missing... like we know it too well... Led Zep didn' worry if it wasn't perfect... that was all part of it. Every time they played it, it was different to the last... 'cause they knew each other's playing so well...' said Charlie. 'We need t'be like that...'

'Tight, but loose,' said Yak.

'Yeah – thaas' it,' said Charlie. 'You've put yur finger on it 'zactly... all the best bands were tight, but loose...'

They ran through it again.

Neil stopped playin' mid-way through.

'That was too fuckin' loose,' he said.

He was right. No one was together at all. It was a complete shambles.

'Again,' shouted Charlie. '1, 2, 3, 4...'

DA NA, DA NA.

'IT'S BEEN A LONG TIME, SINCE I ROCK N'ROLLED...'

DA NA, DA NA.

'IT'S BEEN A LONG TIME, SINCE I DID THE STROLL...'

DA NA, DA NA.

'CARRY ME BACK, CARRY ME BACK...BABY WHERE I COME FROM'

Charlie turned around. This time they were groovin'. He hoped Neil could keep focused on the solo an' not collapse inta' laughter. Bev looked serious, rockin' her bass from side to side; he watched her fingers move along the frets, her nails painted black. She was a fuckin' star. Yak hit the kit so hard, y'could prob'ly hear o' 'un up Carnmenellis.

When they'd finished, they were all beaming.

'Lovely,' said Charlie. 'Thaas' it...'

The feelin' was fuckin' fantastic. The band actually seemed t'be comin' together.

'Remember,' said Charlie, 'Cornwall used t'be fuckin' called

Alan M. Kent

West Barbary n' people from up the line reckoned we was fuckin' savages. Thaas' it though – we're modern savages... it's got t'be that intense... it's gotta' reflect where we're from. Led Zep didn' write songs like that sittin' by fuckin' mountain streams, they did it because they were pissed off – because they had something t'say... we've gotta be the same... an' we will...'

'Thaas' right...' came a voice from the back o'the hall. 'It's soundin' good... very good...'

'Fuck,' said Charlie. It was Micky T. With him, was his sister.

'Real savage,' Micky said, like he was takin' the piss.

Charlie introduced him to the band. They soon made the connection between him and the *Twilight*.

'This 'ent your sort o'scene really then,' stated Yak.

'I dunnaw,' said Micky, 'I listen to a lot of rock. I use a lot of samples like. I'm inta' Nine Inch Nails stuff an' that...'

'Me too,' said Charlie. 'Like I said though, the band's more traditional rock though...'

'Yeah – but no one's inta' that now though, are they?' he said. 'Post-rave an' rap an'that. Everyone'll make their own music in the future...'

'What d'y'mean?' asked Neil.

'Technology. The technology's there... Old-style rock and punk has had its day hasn't it? An' CDs – I mean they'll be gone soon. We'll just be downloading it all...'

Charlie took off his guitar, an' sat down on his amp. He took a swig of water from a glass he'd found in the chapel hall kitchen. Who did this cunt think he was anyway? – comin' in here an' lecturing the band he'd formed. His band.

'Faith No More an' the Red Hot Chili Peppers – I mean they transformed rock didn' they? – combining it with the dance scene...'

Micky sensed that they cudn' give a toss about what he was saying. It was Charlie who knew music. All that altered in the next forty seconds though.

'I've got a van,' Micky said, 'an' I've got lights, mixing gear an' a PA. It's yours if y'want it...'

Micky lit up a fag.

'Honest... I'd like t'see y'use it. All it's doin' now is sitting there back United Downs...'

Proper Job, Charlie Curnow!

'What d'y'reckon Charlie?' said Bev.

'We should go fur it,' said Neil, not wishing t'look a fuckin' gift horse in the mouth.

Charlie had to concede. The band was a democracy – an' they needed everything Micky was offering.

'A'right,' said Charlie.

'Magic,' said Micky an' gave Jess a kiss. 'I'n put some samples in if y'like...'

'Fuck off,' said Charlie smiling. 'Yur a'right on that...'

The door opened. It was Bev's dad peering in. His little girl stood there next to a crustie, three cunts from Trelawny an' Charlie's sister – who with all her make-up on – looked like she'd been toutin' fur business.

'Ready to go home now love?'

'Yes – we've finished now haven't we?'

'Yes,' said Charlie. 'We're finished.'

* * * * *

It was half-term. That meant trouble. On Trelawny, it wasn't the teenagers who were the problem. They were out over the mines doin' drugs or shaggin'. Some o'them would have gone down *Do-It-All*, an' be on with bags o'Evostick, comin' in an' tellin' their mas they all had bad colds. Y'had fuckwits goin' inta' schools an' that. Charlie could remember when his school's Police Liaison Officer came, an' he passed 'round various substances they should be wary of, in jars, with the lids sealed down. Most o'the kids in the classroom knew more about them than he did. That was it with Cornwall as well. Most people think all the drug problems are in the cities. That was fuckin' bullshit. When y'live in a smugglin' culture, what d'y'fuckin' expect?

Na – the real problem were the fuckin' little cunts – the primary school kids who threw stones at 'ee as soon as look at 'ee. Right little hard bastards. But that was it really – their muthers and faathers were all out workin' – payin' off whatever fuckin' crap they had on higher purchase or their lastest satellite and widescreen television system, n' not worryin' about what their kids were up to, on the estate.

'Y'should be home watchin' the fuckin' *Teletubbies*...' Charlie

Alan M. Kent

said t'one kid who aimed t'stick a steel bar through the spokes of his bike as he was cyclin' t'work.

'Fuck off y'cunt!' said the tacker.

It was seven in the mornin' an' the hyperactive fuckers were out around the estate already. It was like they never slept. That week, the problem had been with the air rifles again. Two o'the fuckers had already gone inta' Treliske with pellets in their asses an' what they'd been rehearsin' – a few o'them had been up in one o'the trees in the park shootin' at pedestrians – an' then later, the police.

Charlie eyed them carefully as he cycled past. He cudn' see a rifle anywhere, though the evidence of one in operation surrounded him. The speedbump signs had been shot t'fuck, an' a few of the cars along the ring road o'the estate had dents in them. No doubt the Trelawny Residents Group 'ud have somethin' t'say. They were well-meanin' fuckers – his ma had attended the first few meetin's – but they cudn' alter things. Y'needed President Bush t'do that – an' even 'ee wudn' a match t'this fuckin' crowd.

Dodging the last o'the tackers, Charlie pulled out o'the estate, an' headed for Beacon. He remembered laas' night. The rehearsal had been good – but he resented Micky T being onboard. Then again, he needed him. Micky had every fucking thing he didn' have. He had t'deal with him though. Christ, he was shaggin' his sister. The band was gettin' professional though – it was movin' forward. The next stage was t'decide on a name, on an image, on their look. After that, they'd start writin' their own songs an' gradually introduce them inta' the set.

He checked his rucksack to be sure his notebook was with him. He'd played around before, but since Christmas, he'd been seriously writin' songs an' notin' down ideas when they came to him. He'd read an interview about Trent Reznor – described by *Time* magazine – as one of the hundred most influential people in America; an' about how he did the same thing. That was the model in rock 'n' roll, Charlie told himself. It was to survive, an' still be half-decent. It was no good goin' down the pan after the first album – like Guns n'Roses – or else dyin' young. He knew it that was the rock-star thing t'do, t'end up like John Bonham, or Bon Scott, or Jim Morrison, or Sid Vicious, or Kurt Cobain, – or any other cunt with talent, who'd kicked the bucket earlier

Proper Job, Charlie Curnow!

than they should – y'ended up in the hall of fame – but it was-
n't fur him. To last, was important. T'make a career out o'it, had
t'be the goal. 'Ee wanted t'be a survivor; not a casualty.

It wasn't too windy that morning, so he'd go down the A30.
Sometimes the wind would come in from the Atlantic so
strongly, that y'could barely turn the pedals. Today, it was
calmer, reflecting the milder February they'd had. He passed
under a bridge with 'Free Kernow' daubed on it, tryin' t'avoid
the earliest richo tourists with their BMWs an' caravans. Half an
hour later, he was dealin' with tackers again in the fuckin'
Haven Holiday Park. At least the cunts weren't shootin' 'un, but
they were still pullin' at the sleeves of his Freddy Bear suit, an'
accidentally hittin' 'un in the bollocks. He was givin' out sweets
an' prizes to the kids while their parents slept an' wondered
why they'd decided on a week in drizzle-filled Cornwall.

The Holiday-Park manager was a'right really, even though
'ee was from up the line. He had a view that the Cornish were
all fuckin' yokels – which was about an incorrect a view of a
group o'people as fuckin' possible, but the pay an' conditions
didn' seem too bad – at least the first day he was there anyway.
This mornin' he told Charlie it was the kids' day out, a time,
when the camp took all the tackers off their parents – so they
could relax. Freddy 'ud be goin' with 'um – over *Merlin's Magic
Land*.

'Shit,' said Freddy Bear. 'Wearing this bollocks on the fuckin'
dodgems an' paddle boats...'

'You'll be alight saahnn,' said the manager.

Charlie looked outside the office at the heavin' mass o'childhood. He knew the power o'tackers.

* * * * *

The bastards had been a'right t'begin with. They'd covered 'un
n sticky shite from sweets an' peered inta' his face with cheese
'n' onion crisp breaths. But that was a'right. Even the seven-
teenth ride on the haunted train 'round Camelot was fine, but
then a few a' the Yellowcoats had told 'un t'get on these fuckin'
power boats. They were rubber rings with engines. If y'didn'
drive 'em right, y'just spun in a circle. O'course, some o'the
tackers cudn' resist splashin' 'un – but worse than that, they all

69

Alan M. Kent

fuckin' piled on 'un at one point, an' tipped Freddy Bear inta' the tank full a'water.

'Poor Freddy,' said one o' the sarky Yellowcoats.

'Give us a fuckin' hand out,' said Freddy.

He was drenched. The hair on the suit made him look like a drowned rat. He had t'take the headpiece off because it was filled with water, an' it was near drowning of 'un.

'The kids loved it,' said the Yellowcoat.

'Good fur they,' said Charlie.

* * * * *

He spent most o'the afternoon in the drying room o'the camp, standin' in only his cacks – with the suit an' his clothes hangin' over a heater.

'The bastards,' he kept sayin' to hisself. 'The bastards...'

Charlie wondered how Yak an' Neil were gettin' on in their respective jobs. Then he thought o'Bev, dashin' around the academic corridors o'Truro College, talkin' t'fuckers way cooler than he could ever be – an' then o'Micky – prob'ly out United Downs, skinning up, an' tryin' t'prevent Kerrier District Council from movin' on his van. He was sure he could keep the band together – but he'd have t'be more careful. Yak an' Neil were workin' hard for shite all – they'd need some relaxation and recuperation. Bev would need times on her studies if she wasn't t'get shite off her parents, an' Micky, he'd want time with his sister. It 'ud need careful balancing.

A woman walked inta' the dryin' room. She gave a little shriek. She didn' expect t'find a boy sat there in his fuckin' cacks at three in the afternoon.

'A'right?' said Charlie. 'Just dryin' Freddy's suit...'

She looked Charlie like ee'd just escaped from a mental unit an' backed out the door. He laughed to himself. He hadn't escaped from Trelawny yet, but it was in hand; it was very much in hand.

* * * * *

Micky was putting his muscle t'good use an' loading in gear. The cunt kept his t-shirt sleeves rolled up all night at the rehearsal. His arms always looked healthy an' tanned. Charlie looked at his own arms. They were milk-bottle white – with a few dark hairs protruding. He needed to get more tanned. Some hope o'that in his Freddy Bear suit. It was only February, but even Yak was lookin' good from his days out in the sun down Barripper.

Aside from their collective image, the stage set was lookin' fuckin' brilliant that night. Micky'd been there since four o'clock with Jess. They'd got the key off Mrs Williams an' they set up everything on the stage. It seemed only a while ago that Charlie was up here playin' one o'the three kings in the School Nativity. Now, they had a production. Micky had speakers an' monitors set up, all connected back to a mixing desk. It looked like something y'd see photographed in black an' white in the back of a U2 tour programme. He had lights in as well.

'This is the fuckin' business,' said Yak, as he dodged bits o'lead stuck down with gaffa tape, and manoeuvred his kit into position.

Bev moved a pile o'Methodist Society hymn books an' set up her bass cabinet.

Even Charlie admitted it looked excellent. He stood up an' grabbed the mike.

'One a – two a – smeg ma...' he voiced.

The sound was better as well. He picked up the mike stand an' twirled it like he was Roger fuckin' Daltrey, then crouched down as if he was Freddie Mercury. To his left, stood Bev – tunin' her bass. On his right, Neil – sat on a chapel chair – an' bashing out some riffs. He turned around. Yak was at his kit – shirt off already – and bangin' the fuck out o'his bass drum. Then he spied something else.

'Whaas' that?' he shouted t'Micky an' pointed to left o'the kit.

'Me decks an' a synth,' said Micky.

'Wha'?'

'Me decks an' the industrial department,' said Micky confidently.

''Er 'ee hopin' t'use that are 'ee?' shouted Charlie.

'Reckon so,' said Micky. 'You'll thank me when yur contractually obliged t'do a remix album... Y'knaw, like Linkin Park...'

Alan M. Kent

'It sounds cool,' said Jess, who was makin' coffees in the chapel hall's kitchen.

'Just let me show you what I'n do,' said Micky. 'If y'dun't like it, I'll fuck off out o'it...'

Before they rehearsed prop'ly, they sat down for the coffees Jess had made. There was a pool of light comin' in from the west window, an' they sat there on a couple of old benches.

'Heard y'went for a swim today!' joked Bev t'Charlie.

Charlie laughed.

''Es, all part o'the fun o'being a children's entertainer... Anyway, how are all y'jobs doin'?'

'A'right,' said Neil. 'I can't make it tomorra' though. I'm on a late turn – I dun't finish 'til nine...'

'It'll have t'be Thursday then – for the next rehearsal... Y'can still practise on yer own though...'

'I'm a'right with that,' said Yak. 'Me back's better now...'

'Bev?' asked Charlie.

'Yeah – no problem,' she said.

'Micky?'

''Course – whenever y'need me,' he said.

'Y'knaw me da's set up that gig fur us – Saturday after next – over *Institute*, well, we need t'be ready fur it – but then we're goin' t'need more gigs – so each of 'ee needs t'get out there an' find us some. We need a name an' all...'

'What, fur the *Institute* gig?' asked Yak.

'Well... maybe not,' said Charlie,' but the time is right now... Can 'ee all have a think?'

Outside, the sun was goin' down.

'Ready t'rock?' asked Neil.

''Course,' said Micky. 'Let's do it...'

* * * * *

T'begin with, there were the usual fuckin' balls ups an' shite, but once they got inta' the swing o'it, they sounded good. Each o'them knew they were gettin' better. Charlie's voice wudn' up t'much tonight though. He blamed it on his experience in the pool. More coffee – an' at the suggestion o'Yak – a couple of Marlborough 100s – did little t'improve it. It was the rock classics set again, but Charlie had brought along the music to

'Come as You Are' by Nirvana, so they had a crack at that as well.

'The fuckers up *Institute*'ll love that,' said Yak.

'TURN IT DOWN PUULEASSE,' he said, imitating Clare – the barman.

'We'll have t'make sure they knaw what t'expect,' said Charlie.

'Definitely,' said Neil. 'Else they'll fuckin' walk out...'

'We need t'let everyone knaw we're playin',' said Yak.

'Yeah – we need t'get all our mates along...' said Bev.

'I bet yur friends'll love *Institute*,' said Yak. 'Sad old fuckers leering over y'friends an' tryin' t'chat 'um up.'

'They can deal with that,' Bev retorted.

'Habm' they got some sort o'sensor up there?' questioned Neil.

'Wha' d'y'mean?'

'There's red box above the stage. It measures the decibels so the music isn't too loud. If it gets too loud, the fuckin' thing cuts the power...'

'Shit,' said Yak. 'We'll need t'sort that out...'

'I'll talk t'me da,' said Charlie.

As it was, Charlie had t'concede that Micky's input inta' the band sounded a'right. For now, he just added in samples an' a bit of synthesiser when they sound needed somethin'. It sounded bigger, and gave the songs more power. Charlie was beginning t'see how he could be useful. He might even attract a few more fuckers t'see them – if they thought he had any kind o'input.

They went through the set again, but Charlie's voice was gettin' fucked.

'You party can come in on the choruses as well, if y'want,' he said exasperated.

'Wha', harmonies like...?' went Yak.

''Es – y'knaw – Queen-style...'

'It's worth a try,' said Bev.

Micky boosted the mike outputs an' ran back t'be on stage. Jessie stood behind the mixing desk. Micky shouted at her, to move up one o'the channels. She looked fuckin' lost. Charlie gazed at his sister.

'Five rows in,' said Micky. 'Push it forwards...'

She was a hairdresser, Charlie realised. She'd always been like this. He remembered the time Father Christmas has brought him a Scalextrix an' his sister had stepped on one o'the cars on Boxing Day. She cudn' find the right channel. Micky ran back from the stage t'the desk.

'Easy see. This one...'

'Oh right,' went Jess, like she'd really been enlightened.

'A'right,' said Micky. 'Let's do it again...'

Charlie looked at his sister as he spat out the vocals. He knew her limitations, but he also knew her talents.

* * * * *

They needed a name.

Charlie thought of all the cool names in rock an' tried t'identify what was cool about them. Led Zeppelin, he thought. Easy – it was the 'pel' in Zeppelin. It sounded good. Nirvana. That was easy. It was an 'in' word. U2. Easy – an America spy plane, but also involving 'you too'. The Prodigy. Yes – good that. The Prodigal Son.

'Leatherhead,' said Yak. 'How 'bout that?'

Shite. Sounded like somewhere in Surrey.

'Omega.'

Shite. Sounded like a planet off *Dr Who*.

'Trelawny.'

Shite. Too Cornish, and definitely shite.

'Treason.'

'Fuck off,' said Charlie. 'That sounds like an early 80s' metal band from Wolverhampton.'

'One of them trendy Punk bands with a number after it? Y'knaw Blink 182 or Sum 41?

'Naw... Thaas' naw good...'

'Celtic something...?'

Shite.

'Some band called their album 'Praze-an-Beeble',' offered Neil.

Praze-an-Beeble was a village between Camborne an' Helston. It sounded weird.

'Thas' 'cause they have shit fur brains,' said Charlie. 'And 'cause it's Cornish...'

'Servant,' suggested Bev.

Proper Job, Charlie Curnow!

Better.

'It's like we serve them what they want,' she said.

Charlie had to hand it to her. She was a smart maid, was Bev. It wasn't right though. It was too harsh somehow, too industrial or something.

By now, Yak an' Neil had lost it.

'Split Beaver,' they sniggered.

Fuck off.

Charlie hadn't said a lot. The best he'd heard was from Bev. The rest o'the band's suggestions were toss. He'd need to offer his own idea. He'd come up with it in the dryin' room o'the Holiday Park.

'I reckon we should be called *Balance*,' he said.

'*Balance*?' questioned Neil. 'Why?'

'I just think it's a cool word,' Charlie said. He had other reasons, but he was keepin' them t'hisself.

'I like that,' said Bev. 'It's got a good environmental theme – like keeping everything in balance, in harmony sort of ...'

'It sounds like a fuckin' slimmin' aid,' said Yak. 'Like a new brand of Ryvita...'

'Or summin' out o' *Star Wars*...'

'*Balance* – Live at the *Miners and Mechanics Institute*, Redfuckin'-ruth...' went Neil, like the name was in blue neon lettering somewhere.

'I like it,' said Micky, rolling a huge joint. 'It's got the right feel...'

'It's bollocks I reckon,' said Yak.

''Es,' said Micky. 'Thaas' 'cause you want it t'sound like something like Def Leppard – or some crap like that...'

'I reckon it's okay,' said Neil, who'd offered bugger all t'begin with anyway.

'Bev?' asked Charlie.

'Yeah – it's cool. It's growin' on me...'

Four were for it. Only Yak was against. He was outvoted.

'Get the beers in Yak,' said Neil. 'You're the fuckin' drummer in *Balance*...'

Yak hurled some abuse at the rest o'them.

'Y'cunts,' he said. 'Y'lucky t'have me...'

He handed over a tenner to the barman at Beacon Inn an' brought back a round of Skinners.

Alan M. Kent

'T'*Balance*,' he said, raisin' his glass. The rest o'the band put their glasses in, and drank.

It was happenin' Charlie told hisself. It was happenin'.

* * * * *

Charlie needed a computer geek. He needed a computer geek because he wanted some posters printed up t'advertise the *Institute* gig. Kelvin 'ud do it. He spent all his money on computer gear for his bedroom down Beacon. It was the only way really t'escape the reality o'what he could see from his window: Trelawny estate and the wastelands of Camborne. Instead, he spent most o'his Saturdays zappin' fuckin' zombies on some other computer-generated wasteland from the safety o'his room. That mornin', it was so foggy, y'could barely see his da's outhouse.

Kelvin's house was posh. They had all the right stuff from *Homeworld* – leather-look sofas, lots of lights an' cushions, all matchin', with coordinating accessories. Y'cudn' hear next door havin' a fuckin' row either, or have yer ass shot off by some tacker outside in the street. Beacon, man, half a mile down the road, was like another world, 'twas that different.

Kelvin's ma had opened the door. She was good lookin' fur her age. Y'knaw the way some women never lose their looks. They're old, but they're still beautiful, still fanciable. You'd-give-her-one-if-you-were-her-age-sort-o'-thing. Not one bit like half the women up Trelawny. He'd heard the same thing about his ma though – the way blokes talked about her over Football Club.

Then again, he didn' think o' her in that fuckin' twisted kind of way.

Kelv's ma was a'right though.

'Kelvin's upstairs,' his ma had said, 'on his computer...'

What a surprise.

Charlie pushed the bedroom door open.

'A'right Kelv.'

'A'right,' said Kelvin. 'Here, have a look at this lot...'

He pointed the mouse at the screen icon an' clicked. The cursor scanned lines down the screen t'show a naked maid, her hands on her inner thighs, her fingers exposing her labia.

Proper Job, Charlie Curnow!

'Not bad,' said Charlie.

'The wonder of the internet,' said Kelvin. 'I'll show 'ee sum Bakkuke facials in a minute...'

'An' I thought it was all about business solutions...'

'I'n give 'un a close-up if y'like...' said Kelvin.

'Na, yer a'right,' said Charlie, gettin' t'the point. 'Look, I need another favour. Can y'do me some posters for our first gig...'

'No probs.'

'I've got a photo. Can y'scan it in?'

'Sure. Let's have a look...'

Charlie handed him a black an' white o'them. Everyone in the photo was tryin' t'look hard. He placed it on his scanner, and worked his way around the keyboard. Kelv's room was filled with downloaded CDs, MP3 players and other bits of dead computer equipment. Kelv's bedroom was the kind of place where computers went to die. It was Kelv who sorted Charlie out his iPod. Charlie'd had a computer, but the bugger'd developed a virus from somewhere. Accordin' t'Kelv, it was some powerful variant trojan caught off his messaging. Charlie didn' knaw what the fuck 'ee was on about half the time.

'Ha... what a right bunch a'tossers,' Kelvin said. He knew them from school. 'Who's the maid though?'

'Bev,' said Charlie. 'She's from Truro...'

'Nice,' went Kelvin. 'She's a'right idn' she...'

Charlie didn' answer. Instead, he gave Kelvin his specifications for the poster. On the bottom, he only wanted the words 'On' and 'At', so they could write in the dates and places of any future gigs.

'D'y'want any fancy lettering?' asked Kelvin.

Charlie was sure on this.

'Naw – nothun'. Just keep it simple...'

He'd read-up on this. All the design stuff could come later, when they had a record deal.

'I'n make it speckled – like that – if y'like...'

Kelvin manoeuvred the mouse. The black of *Balance* was flecked with white.

'Yeah, okay,' said Charlie. 'Thaas' good...'

'How big can y'print it out?'

'Only A4,' said Kelvin. 'It's a laser though, so you'll get good quality when y'blow it up.'

Alan M. Kent

After they'd proofed it, Kelvin printed out a final copy. The printer whirred, and the sheet slid into Charlie's hands.

'Beauty,' said Charlie. 'Cheers Kelvin... you'll be there next Saturday wun't 'ee? – if y'oun leave that internet porn alone...'

'Sure,' went Kelvin. 'Wudn' miss it fur the world...'

* * * * *

Charlie pressed the stop button on his iPod. The Jane's Addiction album he was listening to, clicked off.

'Hi ya,' said Mel.

'You're back then,' Charlie said.

He caught his breath from the ride up t'Trelawny from Beacon.

'I was worried about you,' said Charlie.

'I was a'right,' said Mel. 'They had me in care... me mum's back now though...'

'Really? Thaas' great...'

'Is it? She's a stupid slag...'

Charlie cudn' respond. Mel was right. Her mother was a stupid slag. Her daughter had grown street-wise because o'it.

'Y'goin' back t'school on Monday?' asked Charlie.

''Spect so. It's one o'the conditions o'me being back here...'

'Sure. It'll be okay... Anyway, d'y'knaw anyone over *Institute*?'

'Why? Whaas' on?'

'We are. Me band's playin' there next Saturday...'

'Yer band?'

'We formed it while you were gone...'

'I'll try t'go... Can y'get in if yer under eighteen?'

''Spect so,' said Charlie. 'Just be careful...'

Mel knew Charlie's advice was good. She'd have t'keep in order: no booze, no fags, no dope, no men.

'Thaas' brilliant Charlie... Look, I'd better go. Me ma's expectin' me...'

Charlie watched her walk back across the estate. He feared for her, an' the shit she had t'deal with. It was a downward spiral fur maids like her. It was like he'd known ones like Mel all his life – an' sometimes, there was bugger all he could do. He just hoped he wudn' be the one t'find her body.

Proper Job, Charlie Curnow!

* * * * *

His ma had the tea on when he got back. She was boobed-up in the middle o'the kitchen under a fuckin' hair-dryer. Her sister was practicing her perming technique on their ma. Jess had an exam next week.

'This *Vidal Sassoon* now is it?' went Charlie.

'Leave her go,' said his ma.

'Yeah – fuck off...' said his sister.

Micky was in the living room. It was like he'd moved in of late. His van was in their back drive, an' his sleepin' bag was sprawled out behind the sofa. He had a can o'lager in his hand, and with the other, he was rollin' joints fur later on.

'Get it done?' he asked of Charlie.

Yeah, look...'

Charlie showed him the poster Kelvin had assembled for him.

'Smart,' was Micky's response.

He went to his jacket and pulled out a CD.

'Here,' said Micky. 'I listened t'that Mars Volta an' – you were right – it was a bit shit at the end. This one's fine – I checked it out...'

'Cheers,' said Charlie at the unexpected replacement. 'Do y'fancy a trip down town?'

'What for?'

'T'get this copied...'

Micky nodded. He downed the last o'his lager. Charlie looked at 'un.

'I've only had one...'

'We're off t'do some copying...' Charlie announced t'his ma an' sister. His ma and her newly-curled hair emerged from beneath the plastic dome.

'We're copyin' this...'

Charlie showed his ma the poster.

'Who are *Balance*?' she asked.

'Thaas' their band,' announced Jess before Charlie could get a word in. He glared at her. Charlie had had plans for his sister. He thought she'd jump at the chance o'being the band's stylist. Turned out, she wudn' interested at all.

'Y'knaw – have a look at those...' he'd said to her, showing her a bunch o'trendy pictures of Metallica an' U2. Charlie knew his plan wudn' work, when she came back an' said, 'They all look like a bunch o'gays t'me...'

Charlie had blamed it on her limited world view and chalked it up as experience.

Now, she was interrupting his first fuckin' moment of glory, showin' his ma that he could get off his ass an' do something.

'Very nice,' his ma said, 'like it was a skirt in a *Freeman's* catalogue...'

'Fuckin' crustie bastard,' shouted one o'the tackers at Micky as they stepped outside.

'Piss off,' shouted back Micky, turnin' t' Charlie. 'Such a fuckin' welcomin' place here ennit?'

Charlie laughed. Micky started up the van and it shuddered down their drive an' onta' the road 'round the estate.

'We'll need some wallpaper paste, an' a brush an' all,' said Charlie.

'What for?'

'Tonight,' said Charlie. 'We're goin' on a poster campaign.'

* * * * *

Before Charlie an' Micky could head out in the small hours, they had t'take his da home. He'd been over Football Club t'begin with, spendin' more o'his Crofty redundancy money on booze an' gettin' thoroughly fuckin' canned. He came over t'the estate 'round midnight t'sing songs an' serenade his ma, the stupid cunt.

'Twas like the balcony scene in *Romeo and Juliet,* you.

At first, his ma just ignored it, then she fuckin' opened up the bathroom window, filled a bucket with cold water, an' tipped it over her husband outside. The fucker only stopped singin' fur a second. Charlie tried his best.

'Da, you're wakin' everyone up?'

'They should like my singin'... Why can't I sing?'

'You'n sing down the Karaoke da, but not this time o'night...'

'But I still love y' mooother,' he slurred.

Next thing, his da staggered over t'the drain in the road. He

Proper Job, Charlie Curnow!

bent over an' groaned. Spew emptied out of his mouth.

'Go home will 'ee Tommy! I dun't want 'ee 'round here...' bawled his ma from the bathroom window.

When his da had finished, he could barely stand. Charlie an' Micky manhandled his da inta' the back o'the van an' put him in the recovery position.

'If he spews again,' said Micky, 'he'n clean it up himself...'

'Right,' said Charlie. 'Let's just get the fucker home...'

* * * * *

Karen was fuckin' jumpin'.

'Where's a been?'

She grilled Charlie.

'Over the club...'

'The fucker! 'Ee idn' comin' in here in that state...'

Charlie scanned the caravan estate at Scorrier. Beside a couple o'mobile homes across the way, some Alsatian dogs barked at the noise.

'I'm a'right honest...' pleaded Charlie's da.

'Sounds like it,' said Micky.

Tommy was now singin' 'Up Camborne 'ill, Comin; Down' like he was fuckin' Tom Jones Live at Las Vegas.

'I 'AD 'ER, I 'AD 'ER I DID...' he sung.

'Shut the fuck up,' said Karen, shakin' 'un. 'You'll have me thrown off this site...'

'Look,' said Charlie. 'You've gotta' let 'un in – or else he'll be out here all night...'

His words worked. She opened the door an' Micky an' Charlie 'eaved his da in. A few o'Karen's kids were up now an' stood at their bedroom door in their pyjamas an' holding cuddly toys.

'Is' a'right,' said Karen to them. 'Tommy's just had a bit too much beer...'

That was the problem though. His da had always had a bit too much beer.

'How the fuck did I turn out as well as I did, I do not know,' said Charlie as they headed back to the van. On the air, they could hear the sound o'his da being bollocked again.

'Is yur da a sadist or somethun'?' asked Micky. 'I thought

being bollocked by one woman was bad enough... but yur da's got two...'

'He was always inta' free love an' that,' said Charlie. 'Come on, we've got a lot o'posterin' t'do...'

* * * * *

Y'always did it at night. Charlie'd read about 'ut. Otherwise someone was bound t'bollock 'ee. The only thing y'had t'be careful of, were the late-night coppers – lookin' out fur drink-drivers or people pissing on the steps o'the chapel on their way home from *Twilight*.

They did a good job though. Charlie had two hundred copied, an' now there were five left. They'd even had t'go back t'Troon t'mix up some new paste.

'Like fuckin' Saatchi an' Saatchi ennit?' went Micky.

Any space on the urban landscape o'Camborne had a *Balance* poster on it. Boarded-up places had more on them. They'd dec-orated one shop at the top end o' Trelowarren. Cross Street an' College Street they'd fuckin' plastered. By four o'clock, they were workin' on Pool, an' by six, they'd finished Redruth.

'Some cunts 'ud better show up,' said Micky.

'They will,' went Charlie, yawning.

He pulled out a camera from his coat pocket, an' snapped a green traffic light box that had *Balance* posters all over it.

'Whaas' that fur?' asked Micky.

'For posterity,' said Charlie. 'One day, someone'll be needing this kind o' material for our biography...'

'Come on,' said Micky. 'Let's get back an' get some sleep...'

They passed a few o'the winos bundled up in Rowe's fruit cartons, an' Blewett's pasty crates. They drove back across the world's first post-industrial landscape. It was also the first land-scape of *Balance*, an' those fuckers awake enough t'buy a Sunday paper, would have somethun' else t'read aside from the shite in the *News o' the World*.

* * * * *

It took the Great Gonzo just twenty minutes to set up his gear, an' he was now ensconced in one the *Institute's* corners with a

Proper Job, Charlie Curnow!

pasty supper an' a pint of St Austell Mild. It had taken *Balance* most o'the day to be anywhere near ready. Charlie's da had got the key for them at eleven, so they could get into the *Institute*, and according to Micky's tight-ship, check the sound properly. There had been a lot to do. Micky had trekked over Truro first of all, to pick up Bev – her parents were away for the weekend seeing friends up in Exeter – an' then cram all o'Yak's drumkit in the back. What with all o'Micky's usual gear, an' all o'Yak's and Bev's, it was like movin' house.

'Jesus,' said Yak, 'all this t'play beneath that old duffer.'

'Dun't knock it,' said Neil. 'The fucker even has two CDs out... more than we have.'

Charlie had asked the jukebox t'be turned off. It took a while, because some bloke had put in a quid's worth an' wanted t'hear Gary Glitter. Finally, when Clare found the right switch on the wall, they could soundcheck. They'd had a run-through a bit earlier when Charlie's da had walked in. He looked like he was still pissed-up from the previous weekend.

'Sorry about tha',' he went. 'I appreciate you party takin' us home an' tha'...'

'I'm just thankful y'didn' puke in the back o'me van,' said Micky.

His da tried to offer more personal thanks t'Charlie.

'I'm grateful boy, honest...'

Charlie had heard it before.

'Just tell us what it sounds like da,' said Charlie.

Outside, the Paddington t'Penzance 125 was just passin' through. The glasses on the tables shook as the train rumbled past Miners Row. *Balance* went into 'All Right Now' followed by their rendition of 'Come as You Are'. Charlie's da barely moved. At the end, Charlie shouted, 'What d'y'think?'

'Bit fuckin' loud idn' a?' said his da.

Charlie looked around. Everyone shrugged. Bev made a movement to turn down her bass output.

'Really?' said Charlie.

'Yeah,' went his da. 'Clare wun't have it that loud y'knaw. He wun't be able t'hear what people're orderin' over the bar.'

'He's gettin' us fur free,' quipped Neil.

'Anyway, that sensor thing'll cut the power if 'ee get too loud...' said his da.

Alan M. Kent

'What sensor thing?' said Micky, smiling. 'I just altered a few wires...'

'Dun't worry da,' said Charlie. 'We'll keep it low – so it idn' too loud...'

They smiled about this as they went through their proper soundcheck. This time, it was Sabbath's 'Nativity in Black'. It was a fuckin' suitable song for both the occasion an' venue. *Institute* – everyone called it that – was more important than the rest o'the watering holes in Redruth. For one thing, it had taken on the temperance of Methodism an' won – movin' from snooker an' billiards t' karaoke an' pints o'vodka an' *Red Bull*. For another, beer was about seventy-five pence cheaper there than anywhere else in Redruth – an' that was as good a reason as any, t'drink there. Y'didn' really go fur atmosphere – it was all brown Formica tables, an' stained wood from *Trago Mills*. The walls were dotted with pictures of mines from years ago an' Great Wes'ern Railway locomotives. Though there were several fans, the ceiling was stained brown from fag smoke. Old maids who'd seen better days, sat on the bar stalls drinkin' rum n'cokes, moanin' on.

This part o'the evenin' was full o'old men. Y'knaw – blokes who wear their fuckin' trousers over their nipples, an' who've got nothun' else t'do but talk about the lottery, or their fuckin' view on Tony Blair and the war on Iraq, an' then see how long it takes fur them t'drink a bottle o'brown ale. Later, y'd get the younger couples in – boys an' maids gettin' ready fur a night o'dancin' an' shaggin'. They'd come here – the blokes all wearin' Calvin Klein aftershave imitations an' the maids in crop tops. Then there were the really sad fuckers – people who'd got married, an' had dumped their sprogs on someone fur the night, an' were out fur a night down *Institute*. The women all had short perms an' if they felt a bit darin' – a split skirt; the blokes were all fuckin' beer bellies hangin' over their chinos. Added t'this were the usual mixture of losers, winos, mental cases an' weird fuckers who y'could find in any club in Cornwall.

That was the good thing about *Institute* though. Y'had none o'the fuckin' Cornish Tourist Trail shit littering the bar, or any false fuckin' mock agricultural implements attached t'the ceiling. Y'didn' have fuckin' rhubarb an' custard, Strawberry or Scotch Whisky flavoured condoms available. It was plain Durex

Proper Job, Charlie Curnow!

– for plain fuckin' shaggin' down the station platform afterwards.

Charlie noticed this as he took a piss in the gents. His piss swirled the few fag ends at the bottom of the urinal. Somehow, rock 'n' roll was very real now. This wudn' *Kerrang!* or MTV – it was them playing live, in Redruth. Comin' out o'the bog, he eyed the punters at the other end o'the room. There weren't that many in yet – but then, it was still early. At the mixing desk, sat Micky. How exactly he proposed t'mix their sound an' be on-stage, Charlie didn' knaw. That was one thing yet t'be sorted. Another, was how his sister would get on workin' their lights. It wudn' difficult, but this was Jess. All she had t'do was flick on an' off two switches – one way meant reddish lights, the other way meant blue lights. It was that fuckin' advanced.

Some twat had switched on the jukebox again. Celine Dion was wailing. Charlie hoped his own voice would hold out. He stood in the middle o'the dance floor. Yak an' Neil were grunting and groaning, and moving the pool table t'the right o'the stage. The stage production wudn' brilliant. A set o' 'anging pool cues on stage left, an' then a dartboard hung just above Bev's amp.

'You okay?' he asked her.

'Fine,' she said.

'What d'y'reckon t'this place?'

'It's fun,' she said, ' the people are really friendly...'

'Yeah?'

'Yeah – I've just been bought a drink at the bar... see...'

She pointed across the room. It was Clifford Mellow – one o'the biggest fuckin' head-cases goin'.

'D'y'know him?' asked Bev.

'Everyone knaws him,' said Charlie.

He left it at that. Cliff was a real fuckin' beauty. He was dafter than a carrot half-scraped. Now, he was sat on a bar stool, shovelling tomato sauce flavour crisps in his face, an' eyeing up Bev. He had sideburns like a Victorian patriarch, an' lived up a farm near Carnkie. Y'heard all sorts about 'un. There was all the usual stuff – 'bout how someone had caught 'un shaggin' a goat, an' havin' a wank in *Dorothy Perkins*. Then there was the weird stuff as well – about how he spent all his wages on lottery tickets an' lived on animal feed fur the rest o'the week.

Alan M. Kent

'They say he's got Mad Cow Disease – y'knaw Creutzfeldt Jakob disease...' said Charlie.

'Well, he's coming over now,' said Bev, turning to tidy up the leads beneath her feet.

'O shit,' said Charlie.

Cliff walked like a man on a mission, like he had a purpose. He had the arrogance of twenty thousand Cornishmen who knew the reason why. Charlie tried a last minute escape. He peered across the dancefloor hopin' someone from Trelawny had walked in. Too fuckin' late.

'Been workin' down the Tate Gallery t'day,' announced Cliff, like he was Terry fuckin' Frost, 'fittin' drains... cementin' of 'um in...'

'Really?' said Bev, beginning now to understand Charlie's reservations.

Thaas' it Cliff. Maids really like t'be chatted up with a conversation about drains. 'Ee'd be on his usual in a minute – 'er eyes were like spanners. They made 'is nuts tighten.

'Right Charlie...' said Cliff. 'Y'playin' t'night are ee?'

'Yeah – doin' a few songs like...'

'Proper. Proper,' said Cliff. 'Do any AC/DC do 'ee?'

'Na – none tonight Cliff,' said Charlie. 'Might do some in the future though...'

'Nice maid this Bev 'ent she?' Cliff asserted. 'Like her nose-ring. I got a bull up farm like that...'

Bev laughed at his pathetic attempt at a joke.

'Cliff maate...' said Charlie. 'We'm ready t'go on...'

Nothun' stopped the cunt.

'Got another drink for 'ee,' he said t'Bev. 'Here, how old d'ee think I are?'

Bev looked at him like she was the fuckin' final contestant on a daytime television game show, about t'win the star prize – a romantic weekend with Clifford.

'Twenty-eight,' she guessed.

Cliff looked fuckin' amazed t'bits.

'You'm some smart maid,' he said. 'You'm spot on...'

Bev wasn't really. Charlie told her how old he was behind Cliff's back.

She was temporarily rescued by Clare's right-hand man up the club – a bloke named Brian Morcombe. Brian was a maate

Proper Job, Charlie Curnow!

of Charlie's da. They used t'go drinkin' together out St Agnes. Brian was a'right, but he was a bit of a Country an' Wes'ern fan. Y'knaw, he wore fuckin' stetsons an' cowboy boots, an' did a bit o'line dancin' on Tuesday nights. He was Cornish, but he spoke like the cunt had been born west o'the Mississippi, rather than west o'the Hayle river. Brian himself put it down t'the fact that his granfer had worked as a miner in the Upper Peninsula of Michigan, USA in the 1920s; others put it down to the fact that he was a twat who liked dressing up. He went up to the microphone, stumbling over speakers an' leads.

'Clare – can 'ee switch the lights on off at the door? We'm on down here. Cheers y'all...'

The lights went down. Everyone checked their gear. Charlie asked if they were all okay. He looked down. The set lists were all stuck in place. As Brian was speakin', a few more people started t'arrive, payin' their quid on the door fur a night's entertainment.

'Ah – good evenin' ladies an' gentlemen o'the *Miners and Mechanics Institute*, Redruth. Got a superb night's entertainment for you on Saturday night. First of all, can I remind you that next week it is karaoke with the 'Karaoke King' from Tuckingmill – an' also about tonight's draw – for the Cornwall Air Ambulance...'

'Get on with 'ut y'cunt,' said Yak from behind the kit, his torso already naked from the chest up.

Neil played a few hammer-ons. Yak did a few fills. Bev checked her machine head.

'Tonight, live later at nine-thirty pm, we have the return o'the greatest comedian this side of Scorrier – one Hedley Kent – alias the Great Gonzo... but first, a bit o'live rock music with...'

He turned away from the mike.

'Whaas' yer name again?'

'*Balance*,' said Bev.

'... a band formed over Trelawny...'

Charlie saw a few sniggers in the crowd.

'...name o'*BALANCE*...'

Brian did his game-show ending, like it was the London Palladium an' walked off, bendin' down, like anyone really gave a toss whether they could see the band or not.

Alan M. Kent

This was it, Charlie told hisself. He swung around. Attack mode. He'd slay any cunt who doubted. His vocals 'ud pin 'um t'the far wall. He belted out the count in.

'1, 2, a 1, 2, 3, 44444...'

NA NA, NA NA, NUM NUM NUM, NA NA NA NA.

'THERE SHE STOOD, ACROSS THE STREET... SMILING FROM HER HEAD DOWN TO HER FEET...'

Charlie didn' look at the rest o'the band. In fact, he didn' give a shit about them. If they fucked up now, it was their fault, not his. He was just tryin' t'be as focused as he could. He just hoped they were as well.

'ALL RIGHT NOW, BABY IT'S ALL RIGHT NOW...'

Then he realised he had his eyes closed. He hadn't been looking out there at all. During the instrumental section – Bev's bit – he tried t'move t'make eye contact. It was like his feet were embedded in concrete. Then he made out Cliff bangin' his head near the bandit. He looked over at the Mixing desk. Micky was givin' a thumbs up. Jess's expression was blank – but her fingers were movin' – flicking the lights up an' down. The adrenaline inside made him shake – it was like he cudn' control the notes. A couple o'lines came out flat. He hoped they were buried somewhere deep in the overall mix.

More drinkers were arriving – some o'the younger ones. He saw a hand wave. Mel had made it. Then he saw the unmistakable whispy hair of his da come in. He stood at the back, stock still – not sure what the fuck t'do. If his boy was crap, they'd blame him. But it wasn't crap. Sure, there were loads of fluffs, loads of cock-ups, even in the first song – but it wudn' bad. Charlie had seen a lot fuckin' worse on this very stage.

He went fur the Paul Rodgers sold-my-soul-for-rock-n'-roll style ending.

'IT'S ALLLLRIGHT NOOOWWWWW... YEAH.'

Yak's drums kicked, an' the song finished. The ending was a bit crap, so the audience didn' 'zactly knaw when the song had finished. A few fuckers clapped, but Charlie didn' want t'knaw. He was already inta' the opening lines of 'Rock and Roll.'

Y'cudn' go wrong with Led Zep. It was like bread an' butter to most o'them packed inside the club. Even if they hadn't heard the original, or had no idea who Jimmy Page was, they still knew the track from a hundred other bands.

Proper Job, Charlie Curnow!

'Dance if y'like,' Charlie said between verses. It sounded naff, like it was ballroom dancing or somethun'. He needed t'say, 'Get yer mutherfuckin' asses out here now, an' boogie t'y'-drop'. That would come, he hoped. Right now, it was enough to remember the chord changes an' sing at the same time. Micky had run around the back o'the pool table an' had now joined them on stage. He was throwin' in a few samples here an' there – makin' their version o'it crunch along a bit more. A few more heads were bangin', an' a few more feet were tapping back the other end.

It was true. Most o'the clubs were hard fuckin' crowds. On television, they always talk about comedians doin' the Northern clubs. They fuckers should play t'crowds in clubs in Cornwall. It was like most stuff with the Cornish – they knew quick if they liked it or not. Y'didn' get a second chance, an' it had t'deliver right away. It had t'hit deep or else 'twudn worth the effort. Charlie tried to key inta' the soul of his people.

'CARRY ME BACK, CARRY ME BACK...'

He looked over towards the bar. Clare was glarin' back. The drills down Wheal Jane had taken away half his hearin' – so he was strugglin t'hear the orders for pints of Skinners, diet cokes an' bacardi an' lemonades. Tough, Charlie thought. You've got t'have power in a rock band, or else 'tidn worth botherin'.

'Rock and roll' came to a tighter finish. They were more focused, an' hadn't let the track ramble to an ending.

Charlie turned around an' raised his thumb. Neil, Micky and Bev were smiling. Yak was covered in sweat. They looked at him like he needed to talk to the audience.

'Good evening Redruth,' said Charlie. 'We're *Balance* and its good t'be here...'

'Shite,' shouted a joker from the audience. It was one o'the boys from up Trelawny. The fuckers were being ironic, he hoped.

'A song from Nirvana...'

BUM BUM BUMP PA, BUM BUMP thudded Bev's bass. Cliff was watchin' her like she was a rock goddess – Suzi Quatro – Courtney Love – or Stevie Nicks or somebody.

Meantime, out in the wastelands, more beer was being downed. Kelvin was in now, an' he was standin' next to Mel. Some students from the College came in. Charlie wondered if they'd seen the posters. They were into it right away. Gradually, the old boys got up an' wandered in next door, where even older fuckers sat an' played dominoes and euchre.

'NIB' came next. Then, a cover of the Red Hot Chili Pepper's version of Stevie Wonder's 'Higher Ground'. At last, a few o'the boys got up an' had a jump around. Between snatches of verses, Charlie joined them pogoing on the dancefloor. Brian Morcombe had to remind them not to dance with bottle out there. That was a laugh. They nearly scat the cunt flyin' as he told them the club rules. A bit o'drink got spilt – but there was no trouble. Micky's scratchin' over the top o'it had definitely worked.

'Kickin'!' one student said, as they finished the cover.

There was a slight break. Neil had a problem.

'Me fuckin' top string's gone...'

'Wha'?' said Charlie.

A piece o'wire hung down from Neil's guitar.

'Swap,' Charlie went, takin' off his Gibson copy an' handin' it to Neil.

'You'll be a'right... You give me yours... I only need it fur rhythm...'

Neil's face was incredulous. He hoped he could play Charlie's guitar like this. They'd done it a few times in the past – in each other's homes, strumming along t'some CD, but now? Live at the fuckin' *Institute*?

'See – multi-talented an' multi-instrumentalists...' yipped up Charlie t'the audience.

It was the right moment t'introduce the band. Bev got the biggest cheer. Y'didn' see too many maids like that doing the *Institute* – especially ones yielding a Fender bass. Yak did a few fills on his bit. Some cunts called out fur a drum solo – but they weren't gettin' it. Yak an' Charlie had agreed – *Balance* weren't Mötley Crüe. Neil was next: he didn' do a wanky faster-than-you-are solo; just some simple harmonics. Then it was Micky. Most o'the crowd knawed he lived at United Downs. He was a'right though. Micky did some samples, an' they cheered an' whistled.

Whistlin', in fact, was a bit of a taboo in the club. The fuckers on the committee had tried t'ban it at one stage, t'no avail. It only made those watchin' shout, 'Whistle! Whistle!' in appreciation o'anything decent an' t'wind the committee up one stage further. The cunts on the committee ended that rule no sooner than it was brought in.

Brian was an experienced MC. He chose his moment carefully – the same ducking down – so everyone could see his builder's ass.

'Y'need t'turn it down a bit boys,' he pleaded, not knawing Micky had fixed the sensor. 'Clare can't hear the orders up on the bar...'

'We've only got a couple o'songs left,' said Neil,

'We'd appreciate it,' went Brian, aiming fur a final try, an' sayin' it like there wudn' be any more free pints o'Skinners if they didn'.

Charlie's voice needed more lubrication.

'Cliff,' he said, bendin' down toward 'un, 'get us some more drinks will 'ee?'

Charlie handed him a tenner in case they weren't free any more. He went back to the mike.

'A song called 'American Idiot'... We'd like to dedicate this to George Bush...'

He introduced it like he as playin' New York's *Radio City*. The song crunched along. The pogo-ers an' any other fuckers who had enough drugs or drink to not give a toss, went our an' danced. Y'needed stupid cunts like that t'get everyone else dancin'. A few old-style mullet-haired metalheads started air-guitaring. The Great Gonzo went for a piss. In corners of *Institute*, people rolled joints and lit up. The committee fuckers just thought it was a new flavour o'fags. In the bog, someone was prob'ly shootin' up. *Institute* didn' give a toss though, as long as there was a bit o'profit in it.

Charlie was workin' up a good sweat himself. It was awkward playing Neil's guitar an' his fingers had to go a set o'strings downwards. But he was still belting out the lyrics. His voice felt good from the pint that Cliff brought back for him. The fucker moved about like he was a full-time roadie. He did the same with all the bands that played there. It gave 'un somethun' t'do – t'make 'un feel important. T'make 'un feel like he wudn' just a cunt from up Carnkie.

More bodies were entering the club. Charlie's voice stayed good – even when Markie Phillips an' Ally walked in. He didn'

Alan M. Kent

even look at Neil. Mel an' Kelvin were out dancing now, an' a few more of the thirty-somethings tried to look cool. Thaas' what y'needed, Charlie thought to himself: mass appeal. Even Clare's missus was out there – goin' on seventy – but still shakin' her tits. She could only step from side to side, but hell, thought Charlie, free yer mind, an' yer ass will follow.

'Last song time,' said Charlie. 'A bit of T-Rex...'

T-Rex – one o'the most underrated bands o'all time. Fuckin' classic.

'GET IN ON, BANG A GONG...'

They were rocking now. Neil was pulling shapes, an' Bev was swinging her bass like she meant to kill. Charlie knew it looked good. He even had a few fuckers come up an' sing the chorus. They were tone deaf – but it didn' matter. The Great Gonzo came back from the bog doin' up the zip o'his trousers. Charlie enjoyed the pissed-off look on his face that said, 'I wish these fuckers would stop, so I'n get on with it.'

His da gave him the thumbs up. It was unusual for him not t'be dancin' at this stage. It was on another night like this, that he'd grabbed Karen an' they'd slow danced t' 'Nights in White Satin'. That was before Karen an' his ma had framed up fur a fight along Bassett Street.

That wudn' Charlie's immediate concern though. More worryingly, every one dancing, had lined up on the sides of the dancefloor, an' were clappin' at someone aside from the band. It was that mad fucker Clifford, doing his striptease act. If he got pissed enough, he'd do it – it didn' matter how early it was in the evenin'. The band just kept playin' – it was like the 'Get it On' twelve inch extended dance mix or somethun'.

The cunt was doin' tiss-tosses now up an' down the floor, to much applause. Nobody was buyin' drinks now. Then he took his lumberjack shirt off. He was hairy and fat; the flab peelin' out over his belt. A few o'the maids 'ad 'un on – an' made out like he was a Chippendale or somethun'. Next thing, he had his belt off an' was passing it between his crotch like a real fuckin' twat. Even the Great Gonzo was watchin', letting his St Austell Mild go warm.

It wudn' 'zactly what any of them had in mind for a successful gig – them being upstaged by this prick. After he'd whipped his back a few times – he strode down to Bev – an' tried t'get her interested. She laughed so much she forgot she was playin'. It didn' matter. No one cared. Bev was havin' none of Cliff's intentions though, however honourable they may have been.

Ally had joined the dancers now, Charlie noticed. She looked good – always did. She had long legs, an' a pair o'tits that put Carn Brea t'shame. No wonder Neil fuckin' worshipped her like she was a goddess. She was always a good laugh as well. Some o'the maids had egged her on t'take off Cliff's trousers. The twat he was, he let her do it.

Balance were still churnin' out the music. Charlie's fingers were aching. He knew Neil's must be sore as well.

'CLIFF MELLOW... GET IT ON, BANG A GONG,' Charlie improvised.

Cliff stood there with his jeans 'round his ankles an' fuckin' wearin' a hideous pair of brown an' orange Y-fronts.

Ally an' her friends were pissin' themselves with laughter. So was the rest o'the club. There was a limit though. Cliff had too much o'the Methodist in him t'counteract the probable score of Jack Daniels he'd had earlier. Soon, he bowed, grabbed his jeans an' headed for the bog.

'Round of applause for Cliff,' said Charlie.

The audience obliged.

Brian Morcombe was there to his left, ready t'take the mike from him.

'There y'go ladies and gentlemen. Boy Cliff there, gettin' it on. And a round o'applause for *Balance*, providin' the sound-track... We'll have a break o'ten minutes for the Weekly draw, an' then I'll hand you over t'the star himself – the Great Gonzo...'

The lights buzzed back on.

'Not bad...' said Brian.

'Packed this place fur 'ee,' said Neil.

'Another gig then?' went Charlie.

'I'll have t'discuss it with the committee first...'

Brian walked off like he was re-entering a saloon.

'What a prick!' said Neil.

'An' sayin' we're the fuckin' soundtrack...' said Charlie.

It took Bev an' Micky t'calm the pair o'them down.

'It's alright,' she said. 'They enjoyed themselves... they'll remember us for that... honestly...'

She put her hand on Charlie's shoulder.

'Bev's right,' said Micky. 'That was fuckin' high energy... not bad for a first gig...'

Charlie eventually smiled an' wiped the sweat off his face and arms. He downed the last of the Skinners he'd had on stage. It was warm, but the beer slid down his throat nicely.

'Y'got a friend there,' said Micky, pointin t' Cliff an' nudging Bev.

'Yeah – remind me t'ask about your friends next time Charlie.'

'I didn' knaw he was goin' t'take a shine t'you,' argued Charlie.

They began to sort out their gear, whilst Brian conducted the draw.

'First prize tonight – a family pass for *Flambards Theme Park*...'

'Fuck,' said Yak. 'Did y'see that?'

'Wha'?'

'Neil an' Ally look...'

While Markie was up the other end o'the *Institute*, orderin' up another round of Hick's Special Draught, Ally 'ud given Neil the come-on. That was scary. Hicks Special Draught (or HSD) was known locally as Head Skull Death. That was what Neil was heading for.

'Rock star now then,' Yak an' Charlie heard her say.

'I'll be yer groupie,' she teased.

'Y'could fuckin' stand on his tongue,' said Yak. 'He's droolin' that much...'

'Neil,' shouted Micky. 'Give us a hand...'

'Yeah,' said Bev. 'I need y't'sort out some leads...'

'Shall I ring fur an ambulance now?' said Yak.

Ally had her arm 'round Neil's waist.

The way Markie responded wasn't yer usual Markie response. Normally, he'd have decked the cunt in seconds, with his right hook. The story went that Markie had done a bit o'Cornish wrasslin' in his time, as well as playin' fur 'Druth. He could handle himself. In fact, as he lunged across the room at Neil, Charlie could even see him as band security for *Balance*. He had that don't-even'think-y'-can-try-it Gorilla kind of look, that the most successful professional Security wore most seasons. This time, Markie separated them an' just pushed Neil inta' the bog.

A few boys piled in after them t'see what would happen an' obviously t'have a geek at the fight.

Brian and Clare were oblivious to these events. They were too caught up with who had the ticket for the bottles of *Sparbräu* and the *Mint Matchmakers*. As it turned out, his da had the numbers – the jammy cunt.

Markie was soon out. He looked like he'd done whatever needed doing.

Cliff was next out.

'Bri – y'd better have a look in here. That cunt just knocked the piss-pot off the wall...'

He wudn' wrong. Water was streamin' out o'the bogs an' inta' the hallway. The other boys were soon out o'the bog. They didn' wunt t'get the blame. Neil wudn' no where t'be seen. Ally an' the rest o'the band ran in. Neil was a'right. Markie hadn't scat 'un one. He'd just roughed 'un up a bit, an' then, accordin' t'Ally, 'He's taken out his sexual frustration an' inadequacies on the urinal...'

The piss-pot was smashed inta' about six pieces on the floor. Bits o'yellow deodorisers covered the tiles.

'He's hurt me fuckin' hand,' said Neil.

Only Charlie an' Bev realised what that meant – that it might stop him from playing guitar. Bri Morcombe rushed in – as if he knew anything about plumbing.

'We've turned off the stopcock,' he said.

He did know somethun' at least. The water stopped pouring out of the pipes.'Last bleddy rock group we'll have in here,' he said. 'Always more trouble than they'm worth...'

'It wudn' our fault...' pleaded Charlie.

Brian was havin' none o'it. He was already makin' his way t'the stage t'introduce the Great Gonzo. Once the entertainment was back on, things would calm down. His introduction was short. The Gonzo took t'the stage t'applause that was bordering on the ecstatic. It was all part o'the piss-take. The Gonz was so crap, he was good. He doin' the first song o'his set – 'The Laughing Policeman' – as they helped Neil out through the *Institute*.

Charlie's da was havin' a word with Brian.

"'Tis the boy Phillips y'need t'be talkin' to... 'Ee's a bleddy animal sure 'nough...'

Markie was long gone though.

Outside, on the steps o'the club, they looked over Neil more closely. There was a bruise coming out near his eye – Markie had hit him one after all.

'D'y'need t'go inta' Treliske?' asked Yak. 'With yer hand like...'

'Yeah – you should get it checked out,' said Bev.

'I'll take 'un in,' said Micky. 'No problem...'

They helped Neil inta' Micky's van.

'What the fuck are you like?' asked Charlie. He could only laugh.

'Dunnaw,' Neil said. 'I s'pose this is rock 'n' roll ennit?'

Just then, Ally came out. Her hair was a mess.

'Hold on,' she said. 'I'm comin' too... I'm so sorry Neil...'

She clambered up inta' the van, showing more leg than she really wanted. Well, t'be honest, it was more ass than leg.

'Fuckin' hell,' said Yak, under his breath.

As Micky's van pulled away, a twenty-four hour plumber pulled up outside the club.

'It's in there,' Yak said to the bloke behind the wheel.

'Jesus,' said Charlie. 'Striptease, fights, rock, sad fuckin' nutters... what more d'y'want?'

Bev didn' answer. Charlie was concerned that Bev might have had enough already – that they were a crowd o'losers.

'D'y'see that?' said Yak. 'Yer mate Kelvin man – gettin' off with Mel – I didn' knaw he was a fuckin' child-molester like...'

'I dun't 'spect he knaws either,' said Charlie. 'Y'goin' back in?'

''Course,' said Yak. 'Wudn' miss the headliner – he'll be doin' his breakdancing in a minute...'

Yak disappeared through the door. He was left standin' there with Bev an'a plumber.

'Say if you've had enough,' said Charlie. 'I'm used t'all o'this...'

Bev smiled at him. He could see why Cliff had fancied the ass off her.

'I wouldn't have missed it for the world,' she said.

Charlie was silent. Y'could just hear the Gonz reeling off one

Proper Job, Charlie Curnow!

o'his jokes. The laughter from inside was too appreciative – it must o'been a really sad bit of humour.

'You've done well Charlie Curnow,' she said. 'Come on – let me buy you a drink somewhere...'

She pulled him by the arm.

'For once... Charlie Curnow...' Bev said softly, 'Forget the band... forget the *Institute*... forget Neil... forget the estate...'

'Okay,' Charlie said, finally relenting.

'Now, where – aside from *Institute* – is it good t'go in Redruth?'

'Any o'the roads out,' joked Charlie.

Truth was, he had a plan. They walked past the Station, by the old Mining Exchange, and up Clinton Road.

'Where are we goin'?' asked Bev.

'In here,' said Charlie, walkin' past a sign painted with medieval-looking woman, wearing a red gown.

'Like red Ruth do 'ee?'

'She looks like she rocks,' said Bev.

They walked up the path an inta' the converted chapel.

'What's this? she asked again.

'*The Meadery*,' said Charlie. 'I have a need o'some mead...'

* * * * *

Food at *The Meadery* was dear. Well, it wudn' *Morrish's* fish 'n'chip house fur nothun'. The Meadery was like a lot of the others in Cornwall. Y'd normally find them in converted chapels. They'd rip out all the seats and replace them with alcove tables lit by candles. On the walls, were all kinds of Arthurian tack – pictures o'Merlin and Lancelot – an' other bollocks like that. The waitresses all wore old-fashioned bal-maiden type o'clothes an' were supposed t'be bare-footed serving wenches. None o'them did. Redruth in February was far too cold fur any o'that. Charlie didn' blame them. The sort o'music they played was Clannad an' Enya, so the place was all ethereal. Anyone eatin' their chicken-in-a-basket was meant t'think the Age of Chivalry had never ended.

Then, of course, there was the mead; primarily the reason that Charlie an' a few o'the boys from Trelawny had been in there before. Y'could buy bottles of mead in *Tescos* these days.

It came in all kinds of flavours and it was great t'put in punches, i.e. it made y'think y'd downed three or four bottles o'wine – even though y'd just had a few glasses o'it. The other thing about it was that it was meant t'make y'feel horny -thaas' why all the menus called it the Honeymoon drink.

Charlie explained all this t'Bev, as the waitress showed them to a table upstairs. As it turned out, Bev was more used to eatin' in places like *Pierros* an' *Bustopher Jones* in Truro – places Charlie had only looked in the window, an' then gone down for a cheap curry. She'd been t'Rick Stein's as well, up Padstow.

'Haven't y'got t'book six months in advance or something?' asked Charlie. 'I saw it on *Holiday* on BBC1.'

'Only for the restaurant,' said Bev. 'We went to the Bistro...'

'All the same,' laughed Charlie, 'I'd be starvin' if I had t'wait that long fur a table. I'd eat elsewhere...'

'Here is good...' offered Bev.

After they'd ordered food, and a carafe of mead, Charlie found Bev in reflective mood.

'It was good tonight – you know that don't you? I mean, I know there was all that rubbish with Neil... but the vibe of it just felt right... I mean, I know you want the big-time an' that, but if it all fell down tomorrow, it would still have been brilliant...'

Charlie was playing with the wax of the candle, pulling off strips and re-melting them again.

'You're right,' said Charlie smiling, 'an' I knaw what you mean... but you knaw me as well... I mean, we both live in Cornwall right, but look at where you live an' look at where I live. If this dudn' work – I mean, if we dun't make it any further than the *Miners and Mechanics Institute* – then I've got bugger all. I'll be back on the estate, with nothun' better t'do than get pissed-up every Friday night, shacked-up with some girl an' renting DVDs from *Londis*...'

'I understand.'

'See, I dun't want t'end up like me dick-head of a da – in his forties, an' wishin' his life away, or washin' his life away with beer an' fags... I mean, you've seen the estate – thaas' the reason they do the heroin – thaas' why my maate Chrissie Williams went. He wanted more outta' life – but 'ee was never goin' t'get it...'

Proper Job, Charlie Curnow!

'Everyone escapes from reality,' said Bev. 'I know I do... People find their own way o' doing it though...'

'Ow!' said Charlie, letting the wax burn a little too long, and burnin' the tip o'his finger.

'Careful,' said Bev. 'We can't afford t'have the rhythm guitarist out as well...'

Charlie stuck his finger inta' one o'the finger bowls.

'They're fur washin' your hands anyway. Y'dun't get a knife an' fork...'

When he'd taken it out, Bev passed him a serviette to wipe off the water.

'How did y'learn t'play?' asked Bev.

'Guitar?'

'Yeah...'

'I had a few lessons at school. One of those peripatetic teachers come in to our comp every week. Meant I could miss a Science lesson. Me ma had t'pay for it – it was the best thing she'd ever done for me. An' then, well, y'knaw – we just jammed. Played in me bedroom, practised – stood in front o'the mirror an' that...'

'What – singin' into the hairbrush microphone?'

'All o'that,' said Charlie laughing. 'I still do! And you...?'

'Got forced into it. My parents are fairly musical. My mother plays the violin. Dad taught me a lot of the chords an' things when I was still at primary school, then I played at school...'

'Not like our place,' Charlie went. 'All the Trelawny crowd let loose in the music room... pandemonium you. The teacher wudn' let anyone near any decent instruments. All we had were maracas an' those tube things y'play with a ruler...'

'O – I remember those...'

'I want one o'they cowbells fur on-stage as well. I like the sound they make...'

Their food arrived. They hadn't ordered that much. They'd both gone for the garlic mushrooms and chips.

'I need t'work a few more weeks an' then I should be able t'buy some new gear. Some o'our mikes are really dodgy...' Charlie said between mouthfuls.

'I know. I had t'keep tapping that thing Micky gave me...'

'Anyway,' said Charlie raisin' his glass o'mead. 'A toast – t'*Balance* an' future gigs...'

Alan M. Kent

'To *Balance* and future gigs...'

She watched this boy, Charlie Curnow. Charles Curnow. She said it over and over again in her mind. Charles Curnow. He didn't seem like a Charles. When she'd met him, she didn't know what t'think. Was he a trendy grunger from over Camborne – or was he a scruffy layabout? Her dad had been worried. She'd try to reassure him that Charlie was alright. He was certainly different. In another age, he'd have been inventing steam engines, or discovering lodes of copper, or smuggling whisky in from the coast. Now, he was making modern rock music an' after world domination of the album charts. She hadn't met anyone like him. All the lads at Truro College were there – not really because they wanted to be there – but just because it was the thing t'do. It was safe and neat, without risk, without chance. Most o'them were sexist gits as well. What had made Charlie like he was? She asked herself this, as she ate.

'Are 'ee a'right?' he asked. 'You'm not eatin'...'

Bev checked herself. He was right. She wasn't concentrating on what she was doing. She speared a couple more mushrooms and chewed on their succulence.

It definitely wasn't his dad, she said to herself. But then, she rethought it. Perhaps it was his dad. Perhaps, that's exactly what his dad had taught him: how to cope, how to deal with the shit life threw at you. Perhaps it was only his dad. Perhaps it was what he'd seen, what Trelawny had made him feel about the world, what learnin' of his mate dying of a heroin overdose at twenty-one had done to him. What all the other stuff he'd dealt with meant. Suddenly, her life was very secure and neat.

'More mead?' asked Charlie, not waiting for an answer, but just pourin' more of the Strawberry sweetness inta' her glass.

'Thanks.'

Charlie wondered what was wrong with her. He'd been havin' his own thoughts while they ate. That he fancied her, was common enough knowledge with the others. Neil an' Yak had ribbed 'un about it at the first rehearsal. He thought it through a bit though. Y'had to. That was the problem with most people back home – they thought with their genitalia before their brain. That was why the Child Support Agency had s'many difficulties sortin' out who the fuck was who's faather on the estate. As he saw 'ut, there were two problems – first, there was what Charlie labelled the socio-economic one: she was rich – he was poor as fuck. Secondly, there was the line-up problem. If they went out, an' it all went wrong – one of them would walk. Line-up stability was essential. Fans hated it when core members left. Y'only had t'look at the rock history books. Could he take the chance? He didn' even knaw if she wanted to go out with him. He might have been readin' it all wrong t'begin with.

'You'll move away from Cornwall then?' Bev asked.

'We'll have to, I 'spect. I want t'alter that though... London's got all the labels an' record companies – but all y'have t'do is make Cornwall the scene t'be involved with...'

'You reckon that'll happen,' she said sarcastically.

'It already is. Cornwall is fuckin' youth culture central... It's still a good place t'be young in... Look at Newquay or Falmouth... all we got t'do is mobilise it...'

'So y'think we should play Newquay and Falmouth next?'

'No – not yet.'

Charlie was adamant on this.

'We're not ready. All we are right now... is a good cover's band. We'll need our own material before we start doing that...'

'So – what next?'

'We need more gigs – more pubs an' clubs. If they pay, then all the better... I want t'do *The London Inn* next,' Charlie said, wiping his mouth with a serviette. 'It's our audience in there...'

Bev had heard about *The London Inn*. It was one o'the original coaching inns of Cornwall, bang in the middle of Redruth. *The London*, as everyone seemed to call it, had been re-named, and re-fitted. First of all, its modern-day crowd – all the bikers, goths an' dopeheads of the area – had gone to another pub down the road, but gradually they'd reconquered it again. Neil an' Yak had talked about them having bands back there.

'I'm up for it,' Bev said.

'Everyone's got to work at it,' said Charlie. 'We've got t'find venues to play...'

Charlie downed the last drop o'mead in his glass. He sat back on the bench and watched Bev eat. He wasn't usually bad at comin' out with the right thing t'say, but right then, it was like the two o'them were miles apart. After the soundcheck, the gig, the strip, the fight, the silence seemed awful and unforgiving.

Alan M. Kent

At times like this, y'realise how fuckin' noisy most o'modern life is, an' how stillness unnerves 'ee like nothun' else.

Both o'them wanted t'talk about how Neil might be over Treliske, to end the silence – or say somethin' naff about the food or atmosphere. But sometimes, y'have t'put your cards on the table an' bugger the consequences.

'So, life-changin' moment Charlie, me an' you – am I readin' it right? Are we an... item – or don't you go out with band members?'

She moved her hands onto his, and leaned in over the candle.

This was romance, Charlie told himself. Like a scene out o'his ma's fuckin' DVDs. He'd go with it – he cudn' stop hisself even if he'd wanted to. He should a said, 'Miss Bennetts, I've hoped for your affections for weeks.' It came out Trelawny-style.

'Y'knaw I've fancied the ass off 'ee fur weeks...'

This was history. Biographers would be writin' up this moment. Only the official biography would contain his exact words though. An' though it came out in the language o'Trelawny, the action was very different. If someone said that at Mel's party, that was enough t'start shaggin' in the middle of the living room. Not this with Bev though. Nothun' like 'ut. Y'didn' even need t'kiss because y'knew that would come soon enough. So now, y'just wanted t'savour this moment. It was delicious an' decadent enough.

'You're shakin',' Bev said.

Led Zep's 'Thank you' came inta' his head.

'I know what you were thinkin' about,' she said.

Whooah – she mind-read him.

'You're thinkin about the band – an' if you and I didn' work – and what would happen...'

Charlie nodded.

'I'd be professional about it,' Bev said.

'Yeah?'

'And I know you would be...'

'I hope so.'

'There's no problem then...'

'None.'

They both savoured this moment; the only part of their bodies touchin' were their hands. Charlie felt the tips of her fingers – the skin was harder there from pushing down her bass strings.

Proper Job, Charlie Curnow!

She ran her fingers along his palms, where earlier, he'd gripped the microphone.

'What is it like,' said Bev, 'when I have t'fight off the attentions o'two men?'

'How d'y'mean?' asked Charlie.

'You... and your friend Clifford...'

In all the romance, Charlie had forgotten about that fuckin' nutter.

'I had t'settle for second-best,' went Bev, t'wind him up.

'We'd better go,' said Charlie. 'If we're quick, we'n catch the last o'the Great Gonzo.'

Charlie paid, an' they walked back down Clinton Road an' under the railway bridge. They hadn't let go of each other's hands.

* * * * *

The twenty-four hour plumber's van was still outside o'*Institute*. Inside, the Gonz was comin' t'the climax o'his set. Y'd never believe y'd see grown adults applaud such shit. The Gonz had a fuckin' Michael Jackson tape on – with a wig on his head – doin' moonwalkin' an' breakdancin' in the middle of the *Institute* dancefloor. Jess was still there, sat in a corner next t'the fag machine an' chattin' to a few o'her mates.

'Is da still here?' Charlie asked her.

'Na – 'ee went 'bout twenty minutes ago...'

'Where's a gone?'

'I think 'ee was off down *Twilight*...'

'Fuck,' said Charlie.

'Where did y'two sneak off then?' a voice said knowingly.

It was Yak, beered up an' enjoyin' the success o'his first gig. 'Took you two long enough didn' 'ut?'

The plumber tried t'dodge the Gonz as he staggered back t'his organ. The cunt had drunk too much Mild. His accent was s'strong y'could hardly make 'un out.

'Look's like they fixed the bog,' said Yak. 'We was all goin' in the women's... 'Twas 'anging in there you...'

'EMPTY YER GLASSES PUULEASE!' yelled Clare from the bar, flickin' on an' off the lights t'remind anyone shoutin' louder than he was.

Alan M. Kent

At the bar, it was silly time. A few o'the boys were on triple vodkas an' tryin' t'empty the optics.

'*Matchmaker*?' asked Yak. 'Y'da gave 'um t'me...'

Charlie ate one o'the chocolate sticks.

It was as if the Meadery had been a kind of Paradise, an' now they'd been expelled to the Hell that was *Institute*. Institutionalised more like.

Charlie fed Bev one of the minty sticks.

'Any news on Neil?' she asked.

''Ebn' heard anything,' said Yak.

'DRINK UP PUULEASE,' went Clare again, almost in Charlie's earhole.

People were beginning t'mill around outside now. Clare already had his mop an' bucket ready for the vodka boys. It was a certainty they'd pebble-dash the steps on the way out. The Gonz had collapsed in a chair.

'See that fucker,' went Yak. 'He's onta a winner. Brian picks 'un up, brings 'un here, feeds 'un a pasty supper, has free beer, gets t'act like a twat all night, an' then they take 'un home again... Now, that, is success...'

Other people were ready for more. They were phonin' for taxis t'take 'um down *Twilight* for the second half o'the evenin'. A few o'them told Charlie the band had been a'right. Listenable, one cunt had said. Then, that was the way o'the Cornish – always understate everything. The real highs o'life were better then. Outside a couple o'Kernow Kabs had pulled up. They knew their trade well – knew their clientele's needs. Some o'the drivers even had sick-bags for the passengers travellin' from the *Miners and Mechanics Institute* to the *Penventon Hotel*. Charlie knew the smells: the driver's b.o. an' the danglin' *Feu Orange*. Then there were the furry seat covers an' the crackle o'the radio: 'Car t'Illogan Highway fur *Twilight*'. Thank fuck he wudn' goin' there he thought.

When the last o'the clubbers had left, an' when Clare had got the bulk o'glasses behind the bar, Charlie, Yak an' Bev started to pack away all of their gear. Jess was there as well, but she had a strop on because Mickey wudn' back from Treliske yet, an' she'd hoped t'go clubbing as well. It was a problem fur the others as well – how the hell would they get their gear back tonight? They might have t'be nice t'Clare – who might let

Proper Job, Charlie Curnow!

them pick it up in the mornin'.

''Twas still too bleddy loud,' said Brian, tappin' the decibel sensor.

The Gonz had already packed away his organ, an' was now waitin' fur Brian t'take 'un home.

'We're a'right fur a bit en't us?' asked Yak.

'Yeah,' said Clare, 'I'll be an hour or so yet, cleanin' up...'

'Never have 'ut again,' said Brian stoically.

'Wha'?'

'Bands like your's. Som'un about 'ut – causes trouble. Attracts the wrong sort o'crowd.'

What? Free and Led Zeppelin covers? If y'were twenty when their first albums came out, y'were almost fifty now. Radical as fuck weren't they?

Yak coughed a 'bullshit'.

'So, it's definite...' enquired Charlie. 'Y'wun't have us back?'

'I've told 'ee already,' said Brian. 'I'll tell yer faather as well... we dun't want 'ut up here.'

'Your loss,' said Charlie.

They carried on coiling up leads an' loadin' out amps.

'I bet Lars Ulrich never had t'do this,' moaned Yak.

''Ee did once,' said Charlie, 'an' one day, y'won't have to...'

'I need a shower,' said Yak.

'Not yet y'don't,' said Bev. 'Get shifting!'

It was comin' on for half-twelve when Micky got back. Jess stopped being moody, an' carried out some o'the improvised lighting desk. Neil was with them; his hand bandaged.

'It's badly bruised,' he stated. 'No playin' fur a while...'

'A while? How long's a while?'

'Fortnight.'

'Jesus.'

'We've no other gigs anyway,' said Neil. 'It idn' a problem.'

Ally was cuddlin' up t'the twat. If it wudn' fur her, they wudn' have the problem.

'No wankin' fur you then,' offered Yak, t'lighten things up.

'Piss off!'

'Come on,' said Bev. 'Let's get finished... me dad's here look...'

Her faather's car stopped some distance away – like he really didn' want t'get involved with any o'this lot.

Alan M. Kent

Considering they'd had all day to load in an' sort everything out, it wudn' too bad t'have all the gear loaded out in an hour.

'Breaking down the production – thaas' what real bands called it...'

'Shut up y'cunt,' said Micky. 'Jus' get on with it...'

Charlie an' Bev went inside to check they hadn't forgotten anything. The stale smoke and smell of the dregs of a score of empty pints of Skinners made everything delicious and decadent again. In a minute or so, they'd be separated.

'You've done well Charlie Curnow,' she said.

'And you.'

They kissed.

Clare was movin' broken bits o'urinal out of the gents.

'Filthy fuckers!' he was mumbling.

That kiss was a long one.

It was like they were two tackers on the estate: I'll show you mine, if you show me yours. For Bev, this moment was t'be the end of any safety she'd ever known. She was goin' out with a lad from Trelawny Estate, and she fuckin' loved it. Fur Charlie, this moment was t'be the inspiration for a thousand songs.

* * * * *

Despite the late night, Micky was up early t'get his stall set up over Pool Market. He had moved now, an' had his sleeping bag laid out on the floor in Jess' room. As if, Charlie thought. He'd heard them shaggin' a couple o'nights ago.

He had out the *Cornwall and Plymouth Yellow Pages*, and was set up by the phone, with a diary, a pen and a cup of coffee. MTV was on – with the sound down. His mission was to find *Balance* more gigs. He dialled the first number he'd found.

A woman answered.

'Hello, *The Brea Inn*...'

'I wondered if you'd be interested in bookin' some live music,' said Charlie, posh as fuck.

'What sort of music?'

'Classic rock music,' went Charlie.

The woman on the other end of the phone shouted to someone in the pub. It sounded like she was speaking to the landlord.

Proper Job, Charlie Curnow!

'No, I don't think so... We only have folk nights...'

'Okay.'

He wasn't happy. What was rock if wudn' the folk music of the people. Why did fuckin' *Wrigley's* chewing gum choose 'All Right Now' if they weren't appealing t'the soul of the nation? He'd accidentally been t'one of the folk nights up Brea – a load o'cunts with fiddles an' crowdy crawns – bodhran-like drums, all drinkin' real ale an' moaning about alcopops an' the death of the traditional brewing industry. None o'them were Cornish – they were all fuckers who'd 'downshifted' from up the line, seekin' a more spiritually-fulfilled lifestyle. There were fuckers like that all over the place these days – openin' crystal shops or more fuckin' potteries. *Balance* were well out of it.

Charlie tried another.

'*Bassett Arms*,' came a man's voice.

'Do y'book bands?'

'Yeah – we have bands – every fortnight. Fifty quid...'

'Spot on.'

'Got a date in December,' said the man. 'Saturday the fifteenth...'

Fuckin' December, thought Charlie. That seemed a decade away.

'Haven't y'got anything sooner?'

'Nothun' boy – 'tis all booked up before then...'

'We'll do it,' Charlie said. He had no choice.

'What sort of music are 'ee?'

'Rock.'

'Thaas' a'right,' he said. 'They like a bit o'that here... Do bit o'Quo do 'ee?'

'The band's called *Balance*.'

Charlie pencilled in the date. Saturday fifteenth of December, *The Bassett Arms*, Pool. It wudn' 'zactly the *Camden Underworld* or the *Marquee*, but they cudn' be choosy. Charlie gave the landlord his phone number.

'Thanks for the booking.'

'No problem boy. Cheers...'

Charlie put the receiver down and keyed in another number. Someone answered.

'*Trevithick Arms*?'

'Not any more,' said the barmaid. 'We're *Macnamaras*...'

Charlie knew the score. They'd turned a good old Cornish pub inta' an Irish theme bar. Fuckin' pictures of James Joyce an' old tin Guinness signs – someone had made laas' week.

'D'y'have bands?'

Charlie knew the Trevithick had a damp backroom for local boys, who might have a crack at a bit o'music.

'Yeah,' she said, 'but the manager's on holiday... Can y'phone back late next week?'

'Sure.'

Jesus, he'd only phoned three places and he felt knackered.

He found the number for *Tyacks Hotel*. *Tyacks* was one o'the largest pubs in Camborne. A few years ago, they'd had loads o'bands. Nights there were legendary on the estate. These days, they were a bit more upmarket though – fuckin' sofas an' books on shelves everywhere.

'*The Tyacks Hotel*. How may I help?'

Fuck. Charlie didn' knaw people in Cornwall could be that polite. He put on his own airs an' graces, and changed tack to management.

'I represent a band called *Balance*. I wondered whether you might be interested in booking them?'

'I expect so,' the woman said. 'Hold on – I'll just get the diary...'

She dropped the phone.

Come on, Charlie thought. He tried to telepathically communicate with her, as if he were Obi-Wan Kenobi dealing with the stormtroopers in Mos Eisley..

'We've got a cancellation if you're interested,' she said. 'I need someone t'do the lunchtime set on Trevithick Day...'

'Really?'

'What sort of stuff do y'play?'

'Kind of classic rock,' said Charlie. A bit o' Free, bit o'Led Zep...'

'It's not tha' thrash or punk or anything is it?'

'No – nothun' like that...'

'Can I take a contact number?'

Charlie gave her his ma's number.

'You'll bring in some posters for us t'put up...'

'Sure.'

'Okay – you are booked for twelve o'clock on April 20th. Thanks.'

Proper Job, Charlie Curnow!

Charlie was made-up. *Balance* were playin' on Trevithick Day. It 'ud be a good gig. Camborne would be packed with people. *Tyacks* prob'ly sold more beer that day than over the whole o'Christmas.

Thinkin' things were lookin' up, he phoned some others.

'Hello. *Miner's Arms*.'

'Do y'book bands?'

'No.'

Cunt.

'Good morning. Is that *The Railway Inn*?'

'Yes, how can I help?'

'I represent *Balance* – a popular music group...'

'We don't book bands.'

Wanker.

'Hello – yeah?'

'Is that *The Vyvyan Arms*?'

'Yeah...'

'Do you book music?'

'Yeah discos an' Karaoke an' that...'

'No bands?'

'No – they're not worth it. Sorry...'

Bitch.

Charlie had Cornwall's hottest fuckin' property in contemporary music at his finger-tips an' they'd rather book some crap like the High Energy Roadshow. He had no choice but to extend the net. He'd move through all the Football Clubs, all the Rugby Clubs, all the Institutes, all the Working Men's Clubs (what a fuckin' irony that was in Camborne an' Redruth), an' the Holiday Parks. After that, he'd go even wider, an' try to find gigs in Helston, Hayle, Penzance and Truro. Fuck, he'd even try the places in Cornwall's Bermuda Triangle – St Day, Stithians an' Lanner. Phonin' 'round was not the way t'do it though. Instead, he'd send out flyers – provide them with the image – then get them to phone him back. Any fuckers who didn' book in bands could bin them instantly. Those who wanted Cornwall's hottest property could phone his ma's.

The other thing they needed was publicity, but future articles in *Q* an' *Kerrang!* were a long fuckin' way off. They cudn' even consider fanzines or anything yet – the reality was that they were just a covers band until they started writing their

Alan M. Kent

own material. Charlie flicked through the local paper. A lot o'people seemed to have tribute bands these days. He scanned the gig listing – *By Jovi* had played St Agnes, then there was *Limehouse Lizzy* down Penzance. He blamed it all on *Björn Again* and *The Bootleg Beatles*. The newspaper gave him an idea though. Kelvin knew Sam Polglase – the bloke who wrote the music column and reviewed albums. Charlie rarely agreed with his reviews – but Polglase might give 'um a feature. It was worth a try.

By the time, he'd got off the phone with Kelvin, his ma was out o'bed. She looking fuckin' 'anging.

'How did it go?' she asked.

'Good,' said Charlie. 'It was a good first gig...'

His mother looked fur her fags.

'Get paid?'

'No...'

'I thought yer faather said y'would... being a lying bastard again was a?'

She shoved a *Silk Cut* into her mouth, and clicked her lighter.

'Not much good if y'dun't get paid is 'ut?' she said, exhaling.

'We'll get paid soon enough...'

'Was that fucker down there laas' night?'

She meant her husband; Charlie's da.

'Yeah, he was there. Da really enjoyed it...'

'That bitch there?'

She meant Karen.

'Na – she wudn' there. He was on his own...'

She left it at that. Charlie was glad. Every time he did anything with his da, he got this fuckin' grillin' afterwards. He didn' tell her about *Twilight*. She'd go through the fuckin' roof.

His mobile rang. It was a welcome break from the interrogation.

'Charlie – it's me...'

Bev was up as well.

'How y'feeling?'

'A'right. You?'

'I'm fine. Look, can I come 'round... I'd like t'see you...'

Charlie looked at his ma's place.

Like his ma, it was 'anging. There was crap everywhere. He wanted t'see her though. He wished he had a car, so he could pick her up instead.

'Brilliant,' he said. 'When can y'come over?'

'I'll be over about two-ish...'

'See ya then...'

'Okay... bye...'

'Who was that?' asked his ma.

'Bev. She's comin' over...'

'What, to rehearse?'

'Na, t'see me...'

That shut his ma up.

As Charlie took a shower, his sister was gettin' up. She was in a good mood again. She and his ma 'ud prob'ly go down market that afternoon – and then later on, Micky'd prob'ly take her to the cinema over Redruth. As he lived there most o'the time now, Charlie had got more used to 'un, but even though, he had the PA an' that, it didn' mean he had t'like the cunt.

Charlie wanted t'look the part today. He dressed up a bit, an' slung on some o'his da's *Calvin Klein* rip-off aftershave. It stung like buggery, but least he smelt good. He'd even planned where they should walk – out over Bolenowe Moor, to see the stone circle up Nine Maidens. His ma an' sister left about one-ish, so that meant he could whack on the debut album by *The Darkness* an' play it so loud they could hear it over the recreation ground. Charlie checked the weather. It was overcast, but didn' look like it would rain.

He smiled t'hisself about Kelvin an' Mel. Kelvin had only found out Mel was still at school down the shelter on Redruth station.

'I thought she was about seventeen,' Kelvin had pleaded.

'I bet. She certainly acts it...'

'I cudn' believe it, man. She was drinkin' the *Bacardi* an' cokes I was buyin' her...'

Charlie smiled over Kelvin's innocence. Mel had done all o'that an' worse. There was a story goin' 'round that her da – who'd done a few years up Dartmoor Prison – was now back on the scene. He'd spent Friday night hittin' Mel's ma around the place.

Charlie decided not to tell Kelvin this.

'What did y'do then?'

'Well, we was gettin' on 'ut like – an' she comes out with that – that she's only twelve... I ordered her a taxi home...'

'Y're a gent Kelvin...'

He hoped Kelvin could fix up that interview. The band needed it.

Justin Hawkins' voice gave out emotive sounds from a larynx of stone, which Charlie tried to imitate. He was in the kitchen when Bev arrived – actin' the twat – air-guitaring as if he were Pagey himself.

'Havin' fun?' said Bev through the window.

Charlie opened the door.

Of all the fucking naff things he could say he went, 'Like your gear.'

Bev laughed. She was wearing a surf-style frock an' Doc Martins. Over that, she had a long leather coat. That was one o'the things Charlie liked most about her. She dressed like she doin' a cover for *Rolling Stone*. She had that Alanis Morissette look.

'I've got us two gigs.'

'When?'

'The first one's a'right – it's at *Tyacks Hotel* in Camborne – on Trevithick Day...'

'Trevithick Day?'

Truro maid, see. Didn' knaw much about the steam pioneer.

'It's a festival. Lot o'old blokes have all their traction engines on display. Everyone else gets drunk an' has a good time... it's late April... then there's one in December, at the Bassett Arms in Pool...'

'You're booking far ahead then?'

'Didn' have a choice. Thaas' the only date he had free... Beggars can't be choosers...'

All of this had to be shouted, because *The Darkness* were still blasting out through the stereo. As he went to turn it off, the phone rang. Charlie gestured to Bev, for her to pick it up.

'Hello, the Curnow residence...'

'Who's tha'?' came a voice.

'Beverly.'

'Beverly. Have I got a wrong number or no?'

'Can I ask who's speaking?'

'Yeah – it's Tommy Curnow... Is me wife there?'

'It's your dad,' Bev shouted over to Charlie.

He grabbed the phone.

Proper Job, Charlie Curnow!

'Wozon da?'

'Who's she then?'

'Y'knaw – Bev – she's the bass player in the band.'

'Aw 'es. I knaw now... Here, good night laas' night wudn' a?'

'Dunnaw da – I didn' go down *Twilight*... Hope y'didn' get off with anyone else...'

'Naw, naw – nothun' like that boy. Look, I've got a surprise fur 'ee tonight. 'Tis a one off, an' I want you t'go...'

'What is it?'

'Can't say that can I? I'll pick 'ee up 'bout seven...'

His da's enthusiasm was great. It was one o' his few redeeming features.

'Can Bev come?'

''Course she can. 'Course she can boy. She'll love it...'

'You're invited as well,' Charlie motioned to Bev.

'Bev can go – if we take her back home.'

'A'right, no problem boy. Back Truro ennit? See later on...'

'See gin...'

'What is it?' asked Bev.

'I dunnaw – he's like this sometimes. Knawin' 'ee, it'll be a talk on fuckin'-mine-engines-I-have-known, over the School o'Mines...'

'I don't mind,' said Bev. 'It'll be good t'get t'know your family better...'

Charlie didn' say anything. Her not knawin' his fuckin' nutcase of a family would perhaps be better.

* * * * *

It would take about an hour to reach Nine Maidens. They walked across the courtyard o'the estate an' past the *Metro Stop* garage; then up Fore Street towards the *Londis*. No one was about. *Ursula's Hair Fashions* was closed an' *The Trelawny Arms* was dead. It was a typical winter Sunday in Troon. Come t'think of it, Summer Sundays wudn' a pile different. At the *Londis*, they turned left an' headed up onto the Common, past Magor Avenue an' Boscean Close. Magor was almost as bad as Trelawny. They didn' have quite the number of fuckin' rusty fridges or matresses in their front gardens there; least thaas' what Charlie joked to Bev.

The two o'them enjoyed the fresh air. It was good t'inhale the wind up on the Common instead o'stale cigarette smoke. Charlie could still taste the *Institute* inside his mouth – even though he'd cleaned his teeth four times that morning.

'D'y'tell your da you're seeing me?'

'Na – not yet.'

'He must be pissed-off drivin' 'ee down here all the time...'

'He's okay about it. I've got me test soon, so he won't have to do it much longer...'

'You're not tellin' me he's pleased t'have y'come down here though... I mean, hardly a week goes by when *Radio Cornwall* aren't down here – reportin' on some new problem... Me ma was fillin' in this survey laas' week – from the Council – on how they intend t'regenerate the estate...'

'You should be proud o'where you come from... I mean I know I'm not from the estate, but it's got something about it. The right attitude... I can't explain it.'

Charlie grinned.

'Perhaps you're right.'

They walked on, down inta' Bolenowe valley, an' up past Carn Moor. This was the old stomping ground of John Harris – the poet his da was always goin' on about. The stone circle itself was in a field on the Helston Road. Well, it was hardly a stone circle t'be honest. Only nine o'the stones were left, to make one semi-circle. The rest had been decimated by the farm buildings and the hedge to them left of them.

'Sad ennit? Old boys years ago would use the stones fur fencin' posts an' that...'

'I suppose they didn' know their archaeological importance then...'

They wove in and out of the remaining stones.

'They're still cool though,' said Bev. 'D'y'come up here a lot?'

'Na – not any more. Used to though. My parents used t'bring us up here for picnics... y'knaw when it was different...'

'Must've been fun...'

'Yeah – it wudn' bad...'

'These stones must have seen a lot of sights through the centuries...'

'And now us,' went Charlie.

He sat with his back against one of the stones facin' westwards. Bev sat next to him and lay back. Charlie wrapped his arms 'round her waist. Very softly, he kissed the back of her neck. She shivered in the breeze an' Charlie felt the goosebumps on her arms.

'I like the way you kiss me Charlie Curnow...'

It wudn' like Charlie t'blush, but he did. He'd never been this close to a girl before. Sure, he'd had a few slow dances an' that, down the Football club, fondled their asses like, an' walked a few maids home. But this bass player – this woman who gave *Balance* their bottom end – she'd hit him hard – made him feel breathless, made him forget his global domination o'rock.

'Come on – kiss me some more,' she said.

She turned around. She placed her tongue with his, and pushed him harder against the stone. Bits o'moss an' lichen attached themselves t'Charlie's jacket, an' soon they were oblivious. Her hands found their way inside his shirt. They were fuckin' cold – so it tickled a bit – then, soon, he was inside her frock as well.

Charlie was tryin' t'be careful. He didn' want t'go too far with her – that was, unless she wanted him to. When at last, they broke, their lips felt numb with the force of the kissin'.

'I like that,' said Bev.

'I didn' want t'bruise you,' went Charlie, like a twat.

'Don't worry...'

They went at it again.

When they come up fur air again, Bev nibbled his ear.

'Nice kissin' Charlie Curnow,' she whispered.

So this was it. He had the rock 'n' roll. He was near t'gettin' the sex. On the way back t'Troon, he wondered when the drugs would come in.

* * * * *

Not at where his da had decided t'take them at least. Or perhaps even he had even seen enough o'drugs already – what with Chrissie's death. He certainly wudn' find any down Centenary Chapel in Camborne. That was where Charlie's da wanted t'take them.

'Wha'? You goin' chapel? You're fuckin' kiddin' 'ent 'ee?'

Alan M. Kent

Charlie went to his da.

'Naw I'm not,' said his da. 'The Holman Climax Male voice choir are singin' tonight...'

'I though a bit o'fuckin' rave over *Twilight* was more your scene – an' chattin' up twenty-one year olds...'

His da shook his head an' looked like his son was totally misreading him. Tommy tried a new approach.

'So you call yourself a singer do 'ee? Well, you 'ent seen or heard no singin' like these boys. I tell ee – 'tis proper 'andsome. You could learn a lot from 'um – an' I'n introduce 'ee t'Jimmy Pengelly as well...'

'Who's 'ee?'

''Ee's their musical director... Got some voice on 'un you...'

Normally, Charlie's ma would be peerin' out at her husband from behind her nets. She wudn' there tonight. She'd gone Bingo over Football Club. Micky an' Jess were inside. He'd done okay up the market, an' was takin' his sister out for an Italian.

'Idn'a a Crustie?' asked his da. 'A fuckin' Crustie takin' me maid out fur Italian meals! Whatever fuckin' next?'

'You, takin' us, t'see this choir,' quipped Charlie.

'Come on,' said Bev. 'It'll be a'right – I've never seen a male voice choir...'

They got inta' his da's Capri. The back seat was full o'fuckin' kiddie's toys from Karen's sprogs.

'She let 'ee in laas' night then?' asked Charlie as they headed past the rec.

''Es – why shudn' she?' his da went. 'Karen knaw she can trust me... Here, I won a tenner on the lottery laas' night...'

Charlie looked embarrassed at Bev. Sometimes he wished he could fuckin' strangle his da. A bigger twat, he hadn't met. The problem was everyone liked 'un. He was always good fur a laugh – t'anyone outside their household anyway.

'Clare's not havin' us back again up *Institute*...'

'Naw – 'ee's a'right is Clare. I'll have a word. He d'just get pissed-off when 'tis too loud. Dun't worry boy – I'll fix up another gig fur 'ee there...'

Charlie tried tellin' his da that they were a'right fur another gig there, but he wudn' having any o'it.

'All the bleddy money I spend in there an' all...' he went.

His da parked the car in the *Tesco's* car park, an' they wan-

Proper Job, Charlie Curnow!

dered down to the Chapel. It was a cream-coloured giant of a building, with an imposing façade o'four pillars. The preacher was welcomin' in all those attendin'.

'A'right boy,' his da said to 'un.

'Good evenin' Tommy,' went the preacher, a man with a glass eye.

'He lost that down in Cook's Shaft in 1970,' went his da. 'A bleddy hole he was chargin' with an iron rod exploded...'

'Lead, kindly Light, amid the encircling gloom... Keep thou my feet: I do not see. The distant scene – one step enough for me,' Charlie read on a plaque inside the chapel.

'J. H. Newman,' said his da. 'He wrote some lovely hymns – my faather used t'sing 'um all the time...'

It seemed like there was no one under forty in the congregation. Most o'the seats were filled with little old women with tight perms and creaky voices. Up in the choir o'the chapel stood the boys from Holman Climax, grey hair brillcremed down and blazered up, full o'Cornish pride.

'Best choir goin',' said his da t'Bev. 'Can't beat 'um. Do 'ee knaw they've only ever 'ad three musical directors?'

What the fuck did he knaw, Charlie thought t'hisself.

'Testament t'the fine men o'this area,' his da went.

'What do they see in it?' Charlie asked Bev.

'I don't know – probably a sense of unity... of carrying on what's always been done here. Like the band really...'

Charlie was surprised by that last bit. That shut 'un up. His da carried on chitterin' away though, like there wudn' no tomorra'. Charlie then watched the Reverend walk down the aisle. There was a prayer everyone mumbled along to, an' then he introduced James Pengelly – the present musical director.

He'd gone school with Charlie's da's da – up Beacon Infants.

'Good evening ladies and gentlemen. Welcome to Camborne's Centenary Chapel and the Holman Climax male voice choir's night of classic Cornish songs. We will begin tonight with 'Lamorna'.'

He snapped his baton in the air an' looked over at the pianist. Then the choir was away, singin' in unison an' belting out the lyrics. Some o'them even had smiles on their faces, like they were enjoyin' it, like the song – even though it was quirky – really moved them. Charlie was beginning t'understand it now.

By the time they came to 'The White Rose', Charlie understood what musicians meant when the talked about 'diverse an' disparate influences' – like the way Metallica had started t'experiment with Country an' Western. The songs weren't that special. The lyrics were crap – but none o'that mattered. It was the way the music moved people. He watched the old women in the congregation. He watched the way the music lit up their eyes. It wasn't Wembley Stadium, it wudn' even the *Miners an' Mechanics Institute*, but t'them, Jimmy Pengelly was fuckin' rock 'n' roll in its purest form. He was their fuckin' Elvis Presley.

'They're really good singers aren't they?' commented Bev. 'The sound is so full...'

By the time they did 'Goin' up Camborne 'ill, comin' down', Charlie had been blown away. The last time he'd felt that way was when he an' Neil travelled t'Bristol t'see Bob Mould out o'Hüsker Dü. It was that good you. He watched the choir. There were blokes up there pushin' eighty – half o' 'um had spent most o'their workin' lives down some shaft or makin' drilling gear over Holman's factory. This music had kept them going – given them the will t'carry on.

'We've got to make music that moves people this way,' said Charlie. 'My songs are goin' t'do that...'

They stood for 'Trelawny'. Charlie an' his da had sung it enough times up *Institute*. Bev had heard o'it. She didn' knaw all the words though.

'What do 'ee reckon then Beverly?' said his da.

He was calling her Beverly now.

'Oh – they're excellent,' she said.

'See...' his da said, lookin' at Charlie, like Charlie was an ignoramus.

There was tea an' biscuits afterwards. The tea tasted shit – it was weak as fuck – an' rang o'everything Charlie hated 'bout Methodism.

'I'll introduce 'ee t'Jimmy,' said his da. 'Y'both bein' singers like...

'Jesus,' said Charlie. 'It's like the twat's on acid or somethun'...'

'Y'knaw me boy Jimmy, dunnee?'

'A'right,' said Jimmy, stuffin' a rich tea biscuit inta' his

Proper Job, Charlie Curnow!

mouth. 'Do a bit o' singin' I hear? We'n do with a few more youngsters in the choir... we 'ent goin' t'be around forever are us Tommy?'

Jesus, his da was only in his forties. Mind you, sometimes the way he acted made 'un look like he was fuckin' senile.

'Not my scene,' said Charlie. 'I'm inta' rock music...'

'You'n sing proper then?' challenged Jimmy.

'What do 'ee mean?'

'You've had lessons then...?'

'Naw – nothun' like that...'

'Well boy, you ought to, else you'n damage yer voice...'

Charlie looked at 'un in disbelief.

'Thaas' true,' said his da. 'Told 'ee Jimmy d'knaw all 'bout 'ut.'

'Tell 'ee what,' said Jimmy. 'Faather's got me number. You come over an' I'll coach 'ee a bit...'

'Na – you'm a'right. Y'dun't knaw any o'the stuff we d'sing...'

'Dun' matter,' deadpanned Jimmy. 'Dun' matter. 'Tis your voice that counts. Dun' matter if 'tis 'Camborne 'ill' or *The Beatles*...'

Charlie looked even more concerned now. This old boy's idea of modern rock was *The fuckin' Beatles*.

'You give me a ring,' said Jimmy Pengelly.

'Yes – you should Charlie,' said Bev.

She gave him a look.

'A'right,' he said, but the fact was, he'd done it t'just end this conversation more than anything else.

'Make sure you do,' said Jimmy, an' he was off, being grabbed by a couple o' his permed, blue-rinse groupies.

'Told 'ee didn' I?' went his da. 'Told 'ee 'eed sort 'ee out...'

'Y'ready t'leave da? We gotta' take Bev back t'Truro yet...'

As he let them into his Capri, his da looked out over Holman's factory and their yard. A load o'plant equipment was still ready t'be transported t'the world's mines, even though the place was closing down.

'Y'knaw,' his da said, ' if Jimmy didn' work there, 'ee could a been the Cornish Pavarotti...'

Charlie said nothun'. He was just glad *Holmans* hadn't made Jimmy redundant forty years earlier.

Alan M. Kent

* * * * *

Charlie was on MTV again. He'd just helped review the singles with some has-been like Elton John. There 'ud be a lot o'fans outside: too many really for security to deal with. Nevertheless, he'd slap a few hands, autograph a few posters and programmes, and take time to chat to some individuals. He would never let down his fans. And sure, the band would progress – they'd have to, to keep their vitality, but they'd keep their intrinsic sound. With their first album, they'd conquer Britain and Europe, then they'd do a support tour of the States, blowing away the headliner. Their second album – always a difficult one – would eventually break them in the States and the Far East, though the recording of it might take six months longer than they'd anticipated. The World Tour would take all year, so there'd be a fan's only album o'b-sides an' remixes t'follow. There might be a live video then as well – interspersed with the band talkin'. Hell, the web page would be set up an' the band could go on-line an' talk to their fans.

They'd need a break then. Charlie and Bev might take a fortnight in the Caribbean – then return to Cornwall t'write songs. They might even do a few low-key club dates – an' somethun' at the Hall for Cornwall, just t'keep their hands in. The third album though – would be their killer – their multi-platinum contribution to the future of rock music; the sort of album that turns rock 'n' roll inside out an' upside down – an' reinvents it for the next decade. Thaas' the sort o'album they'd have to deliver then. Once it was out, they could do the stadiums, the big festivals an' travel to South American for 'Rock in Rio', India and Australia. For such gigs, they'd probably fly in on a helicopter to the concert, an' then be whisked away in a limousine at the end of it.

Charlie would always make sure they had ego-ramps an' platforms out in the crowd though – he'd still want t'be in touch with those watchin'. Between all o'this – they might do a film soundtrack album, or perform at some Charity events – campaigning for the rights of indigenous people, or for the release o'political prisoners. They'd pioneer a new phase of music – a whole new downloadin' generation. Sony or

Proper Job, Charlie Curnow!

Nintendo would approach them to do the first interactive music/game release. Yes, they'd push back boundaries.

Next, would come the live album. It 'ud be a two disc affair, Charlie reckoned – warts n'all. No fuckin' overdubs. It 'ud be better than Thin Lizzy's *Live and Dangerous* or Deep Purple's *Made in Japan* – in Charlie's view, two of the best live albums ever made. The first disc would be their heavier music; the second a kind of unplugged acoustic set. It 'ud be one of the best live recordings of all time. That would give them time t'write their next album, though they'd try not to spend too long in the studio. Playing live was what they liked the most.

An' sure, there 'ud be the usual range of arguments, fuck-ups, scandals with Yak an' Neil an' all-girl bands, bust-ups with paparazzi, hotel-wreckings, television-throwings and difficulties with local authorities, but all o'that would be worth it, for the set o'platinum discs on their walls, and Brit and Grammy statues on the mantelpiece. An' Cornwall would be the coolest fuckin' place on the planet...

All o'this took Charlie about ten seconds t'imagine while he lay in bed on Monday morning. He'd thought about it and dreamt about it s'many times that it already seemed t'be a reality. All he had t'do was meet it at the right points along the way. A lot o'bands talked all that bollocks – Charlie had met a hundred o'them – but none o'them had planned it the way he did.

His alarm started buzzing. It jolted 'un back from the fantasy MTV studio to his fuckin' heap o'a bedroom, an' the fact that he had t'go back t'work again. His sister was already up – though these days she rarely need t'catch the College bus, as Micky would give her a lift, before heading back t'United Downs. All their gear was still in Micky's van. The plan was to rehearse on Tuesday night. Charlie'd make sure Neil was there, even if his injury wudn' allow 'un t'play.

Overall, things were lookin' up. He an' Bev were definitely an item, the first gig had actually gone okay – an' he'd been inspired to write moving music – by, of all people, the Holman Climax male voice choir. Charlie weighed it up. There were a couple o'downsides – his da. That was fuckin' obvious. He hardly needed t'think it – an' then, there was Jimmy Pengelly – the Cornish Pavarotti. He'd promised he'd ring the cunt.

Alan M. Kent

'Charlie – make 'iss,' shouted his ma. 'Get yer ass out o'bed...'

She was right. Time was goin' on. If he didn' shift his ass soon, 'ee'd be late fur work. A different group o'kids each Monday. He hoped these fuckers wudn' be as bad as the last crowd.

Downstairs, there was a letter fur 'un. It was the response to his grant application for the band. He could tell by the logo on the envelope. He jammed his finger inta' where it was sealed and tore it open. Any sort o'confidence he'd placed in Gary Yelland had been wildly mistaken.

'Dear Mr Curnow,' he read. 'Thank you for your application for 'New Deal' grant assistance with your proposal. However, on this occasion we regret to inform you that your funding application has been unsuccessful...'

'Aaa fuck,' said Charlie.

'Wha'?' said Micky, who lightin' his mornin' fag.

'They turned down me fucking grant application t'fund the band...'

'What d'y'expect? They see fuckin' rock band an' they think yer goin' t'blow it all on booze an' drugs... They just want y't'find a proper job, settin' up a window cleanin' round or something like that. They 'ent interested in us...'

Dejectedly, Charlie went for a shit in the outside bog. It was a place of peace in troubled times. It seemed like he'd been in there a lot recently. He took the letter with 'un an' sat down an' read it through again. It went on t'say how they would welcome another application at some time in the future. No reasons were given though as t'why they'd been turned down. It wudn' Kelvin's fault either. He'd gone over it with a fine-tooth comb. Shagger of twelve year olds he might be, but he knew his financial stuff.

Sometimes, it seemed like if yer address had Cornwall on it, the fuckers in charge anywhere, automatically seemed t'think y'were okay t'begin with. As if y'were fuckin' happy livin' in those fuckers' holiday destinations an' the highest fuckin' unemployment statistics in Britain. In their fuckin view, Cornwall was alway sunny, had kids playin' in rockpools an' makin' sandcastles. Every cunt walked around smilin' an' happy t'live in social deprivation.

Proper Job, Charlie Curnow!

He flushed the toilet an' went back inside for some toast and a cup of coffee. Within minutes though, he was on his bike, an' on his way down to the Holiday Park.

* * * * *

The shite at the beginning o'the day didn' really disappear. All the kids he was lookin' after on Freddy Bear's fuckin' Teddy Bear's picnic, were real little shits. Y'knaw, four year olds with fuckin' attitudes who treated Charlie like he was a punch-bag. Charlie reckoned it might have been safer t'go a few rounds with Markie Phillips than this crowd.

Sittin' with Bev up Nine Maidens seemed a long time ago now, She'd be back in Truro College t'day with her mates – back doin' her English, Art an' French A Levels. Last night, she'd said how she'd really enjoyed the choir. Charlie's da was a good laugh as well. She said he spoke to her like she was an adult – different to her parents. Charlie didn' tell his da tha'. Tha' 'ud only make 'un worse than ever...

It was amazin' how much he thought about the cunt while he was working at the Holiday Park. He reckoned it was because he met a lot o'the mothers an' faathers who brought their kids along. His da had given 'un somethun'. He'd definitely helped him get inta' rock – especially with the albums he'd bought when he was Charlie's age. He'd even bought 'un a *Take That* tape when Charlie was in primary school an' he used t'sing along t'it on his Fisher Price cassette player.

His da had had it hard though. All the da's here – they were from the South East; all fuckin' estate agents an' accountants. His da – he tried to grow up an' follow all the done things – go down the mine – like his da – but by the time he'd left school, the Cornish economy was already in the shits – and in the late '90s, it was about t'get worse. There were loads o'his generation on the fuckin' dole – workin' the black economy – repairin' cars here, doin' a bit o'building there – cash in hand. Y'had t'do it to survive.

In the afternoons, Freddy Bear's work was easier. Basically, he just had t'escort them t'the playing area an' supervise them. Occasionally, that meant puttin' a plaster on a grazed knee – or just speaking to them like he was in a fuckin' *Walt Disney* film.

Alan M. Kent

Between this, an' pushin' the roundabout, Charlie found he had a bit o'time t'write.

He had an A4 pad tucked in his ruck-sack an' if an idea came, he'd just jot it down. Sometimes, he'd get phrases – things people had said – that were poignant or funny. Other times it would just be the words. Laas' week he'd noted down enough t'have more or less a set o'completed lyrics. What he needed was a dictaphone, so he could record some of the melodies with the words. They'd come inta' his head in the weirdest places, an' he didn' want t'forget them.

He enjoyed the process. He wanted words that would move people – make them think; not the usual 'baby, baby' shit a lot o'rock bands wrote. Charlie knew the place o'the latter – it could work, but all the best songs – what made them, were the lyrics. They could be simple – but they had to create emotion in people – move them in either a joyous or sad way. Ideally, y'wanted a mixture of the two. All the best rock songs, the really fuckin' huge songs had a fuckin' irrisistable combination o'melody an' lyrics. If he could find that – do that with *Balance* – the world was their fuckin' oyster. Bein' turned down for a shitty grant wudn' stop them.

The other things Charlie resolved t'do was t'send out flyers. It 'ud cost them a bit, but it was a more efficient way o'contacting venues. They'd be able t'put together more of a tour that way. He'd see Kelvin for the design, then have Yak an' Bev do the envelopes. Neil could lick the stamps or somethun'.

On the way home that night, he popped inta' *WH Smith* an' bought a bargain pack o'envelopes an' some more stamps. It cost 'un nearnly thirty quid. Necessary expense, he told hisself as he headed up Trevu Road. Rock 'n' roll was never just about music – oh no – it was always beyond music. Music wudn' even the half o'it.

* * * * *

Micky T was havin' problems of his own that day. Charlie was later to learn that after he'd dropped Jess off at Cornwall College, he headed back t'Camborne, signed on, and then went over t'United Downs. His idea was t'see if anyone knew o'any gigs or festivals where *Balance* might be able to perform.

Proper Job, Charlie Curnow!

United Downs was straight out a' T.S. Eliot's fuckin' 'Wasteland'. In the nineteenth century, the area around there – an' in Gwennap Parish had been one o'the most densely populated areas o'fuckin' Europe – let alone Cornwall. Every fucker had been crammed in to search for tin an' copper in the rock below. Now, the place was full o'sealed shafts, ruined buildings, fly-tipping an' a traveller colony. People called 'um 'New Age' but there was nothun' really 'New Age' about his crowd, as far as Micky knew. It was the fuckin' economics o' it that made them live there. If y'wanted New fuckin' Age – all y'had t'do was head down t'Penwith. That was where the joss sticks, crystals, reverse polarities and druids were.

When Micky got there, the road in had been blocked by a load o'council workers an' police. It had taken fuckin' years, but finally, the Council had got the legislative power t'remove the travellers off the Downs. Problem was, Micky's fuckin' caravan an' bender tent were still in there. A few o'his mates were already in their buses an' campers an' movin' on – t'fuck knaws where.

The High Sheriff of Cornwall was givin' it stick with a loud-hailer.

'Move off the property within the next two hours – or you will be forcibly evicted...'

Why they had t'do this, Micky didn' knaw. No cunt could build on the land – else their living room 'ud end up seven hundred feet down a hole. No one wanted it for anything. It wudn' like they were on the coast – where tourists might be offended. An' then there was a lot o'shit written about how the travellers were all from up the line. That was bollocks an' all – three quarters o'the cunts at United Downs were Cornish t'begin with.

A copper came over t'Micky. He knew 'un – he was a constable name o' Combellack.

'Got stuff in there 'ave 'ee?' the copper asked.

'Yeah – me bender an' caravan...'

'Better get it out – or it'll be trashed tomorrow...'

Combellack got Micky beyond the cordon around the site. He hooked up his caravan t'the towhook on his van, and packed away the tent. Things were serious. The coppers had fuckin' full body armour on, and carried batons. Micky knew, on this occasion, it would be best to comply. His van and caravan wound over the Downs, scating bits o'gorse out on the way. He headed past the ruined count-house, where they'd had a good few parties, and emerged through the cordon at the main gate.

'Fuckers,' he yelled at the police.

They ignored the dreadlocked loser.

He gave the Council workers the middle finger. Half o'they cunts 'ud be dancin' t'his music down the *Twilight* on Friday nights.

Micky had no where else t'go – except the Curnow's place. He headed up towards t'the Four Lances road, an' went 'round the back o'Carn Brea.

'Bastards! Bastards!' he mouthed over an' over again.

He went past the tall Cornish hedges on the Helston road, then turned in for Troon.

When Charlie got back from work, there was a multi-coloured caravan parked in the back-garden. Charlie's ma called it 'the drive', but the reality o'it had been the place where his da had sat his un-MOTed and uninsured 'classic' Capri for six months beforehand. He'd knocked the rear wall down t'get it in. Charlie put his bicycle in the shed an' viewed the various rainbows an' cosmic signs adornin' this huge fuckin' green caravan.

Micky stood at the back-door.

'Whaas' on?' asked Charlie. The 'fuckin' Glastonbury festival happenin' here this year is it?'

'Sorry Charlie,' said Micky. 'They've evicted us off the site. If I didn' go – the police would ha' trashed it...'

'It'll still get trashed 'round here. The fuckers'll be unable t'resist it... Y'might as well put a great sign on it – sayin' 'Free t'vandalise'.'

'I'll chance it,' said Micky.

'You'll fuckin' chance with me ma as well. She'll do her fuckin' nut... There'll be no more shaggin' me sister...'

'Shit,' said Micky.

'An' you'd best move yer van as well,' said Charlie. 'It's still got the band's gear inside hasn't 'ut?'

Charlie told him it 'ud need t'be more secure or the next thing they'd know was they'd be payin' for it all over again down Camborne's Pawnbrokin' shop.

Proper Job, Charlie Curnow!

'They'll spray yer van as well,' Charlie said, for that had been the latest craze. Some daft fuckin' art teacher down Camborne school had shown 'um some New York graffiti art. Next thing – every fuckin' wall, car an' fuckin four year old, who would stay still enough for more than ten seconds – had been fuckin' tagged. It was the teenagers' efforts to push along the Trelawny regeneration scheme.

'Can y'have a word with y'ma?' went Micky fondling his caravan, like it was the last time he'd see the fuckin' wreck.

'I'll try,' said Charlie, rueing the day he'd spoken t'the cunt down Pool Market.

'Spot on, Charlie Curnow!' went Micky. 'I knew y'wudn' let me down.'

* * * * *

On Tuesday night, Charlie was givin' everyone the run down about the gigs that had been booked, an' about his plan with the flyers. He'd been down t'Kelvin's an' got them printed out.

'All we need t'do it t'put them in envelopes an' address them,' he went. 'I've got the *Yellow Pages*...'

Neil was there with Ally. He still cudn' play – but his hand was gettin' better. It looked like Ally had made her mind up. She'd left Markie Phillips for good. That, at least, was a weight off Charlie's mind.

Then he told them about the grant being turned down.

'Thaas' Gary fuckin' Yelland's fault,' said Yak. 'I 'spect the cunt told 'um t'turn us down...'

'It dudn' matter,' said Charlie. 'That wun't stop us – but like we agreed, we're all goin' t'need t'contribute money to gettin' us some new gear. Our mikes are fuckin' crap really...'

No one was particularly happy at puttin' their beer money inta' the band, but they realised it had t'be done.

'I know we've only done one gig,' said Charlie, 'but we've gotta' start writin' our own songs next. It's important if we're goin' t'move beyond the fuckin' Institutes o'this world...'

They knew Charlie was right. Each o'them had blank looks though. None o'them had ever written a song.

'It might take a while,' said Charlie, 'but we'en do it... We just have t'think about what makes good rock music...'

Micky was quiet tonight. Normally, he'd have contradicted everything Charlie 'ud say – but tonight, he was just thankful. It had took a while on Monday – an' breakfast on Tuesday, t'convince Charlie's ma that leavin' his caravan there, was a good thing. Charlie's main argument was for his ma t'think o'it as a kind o'mobile extension t'the house. Eventually, it had worked, but his ma had gone 'round the fuckin' houses 'til she agreed. Her main objection, it seemed, was that it reminded her every day, through the kitchen window, that her 'bastard o'a husband' was shacked up with a younger woman, in a caravan. Charlie had sweet-talked her though.

It was meant t'be a rehearsal, but the reality was that there was little point in playin'. Neil, Ally an' Yak had a production line set up, whilst Charlie an' Bev talked about songwriting. He showed her his note-book.

''Scuse the handwriting,' he said, 'but it's hard holding a biro with bear hands on...'

She read through the scribbles.

'They're good,' she said. 'Very moving...'

It was what Charlie wanted t'hear.

'I reckon we could come up with some good songs – between us,' said Bev. 'I can write some of the music if you like...'

Yak came over.

'What are 'ee like?' he joked. 'Can't 'ee leave one another alone for ten seconds... Y'knaw we need more gigs. Well, this bloke I knaw – down Baripper – he's a Cornish speaker. They got some kind o'social evenin' goin' on down his barn... They want a band... an'they'll pay...'

Charlie had come across that lot before. They had what they called 'Yeth an Werins' in pubs, where they sat 'round an' lamented lost olde worlde Cornwall.

'Yeah,' said Charlie, 'fuckin' middle-class beardie-weirdies with fuck-all else t'do but argue over spellings o'place-names...'

'They want us on March 5th – St Piran's Day... What d'y'reck-on?'

'A'right,' said Charlie. 'Long as they dun't expect us t'sing in Cornish or anything...'

St Piran's Day sealed it for Charlie. No cunt outside Cornwall had heard o'it. Y'never saw it in diaries or on calendars, but every year it was gettin' bigger. It was meant t'celebrate

Proper Job, Charlie Curnow!

Cornwall's patron saint. The reality was, it was just another good opportunity for a piss-up.

'D'y'hear that?' said Charlie. 'Yak's got s a gig over Baripper on March 5th... Y'd better get yer hand mended Neil...'

'Lovely, said Neil, lickin' another stamp, like Gene Simmons outta' Kiss.

* * * * *

The phone went.

Charlie was upstairs readin' in bed. He was hopin' Jess or Micky would pick it up, but they were out in the caravan – sortin' out all the stuff that had fallen over in the journey. His ma had gone t'Bingo over Redruth.

'Hello,' Charlie went.

He heard the sound o'coins being shoved inta' the slot.

'That Charlie?' went a voice. It was his da.

'Where you to?'

'Over *Institute*...'

The cunt was pissed-up again. Aside from the rehearsal, Tuesday had been a shitty day. It was prob'ly about t'get even more shit.

'I was thinkin',' said his da, slurring his words badly. 'Y'knaw your band...'

'Yeah.'

'Well, y'knaw the redundancy money...'

'Yeah – that you've pissed up against the wall...'

'...how about if I invested it in yer band boy?'

The fucker was definitely pissed. He'd never come up with that if he was sober.

'Na – you'm a'right da. Honest... y'need t'invest it...'

'It would be an... an... an... investment, an' then I could be yer manager like...'

Fuck, his da thought he was fuckin' Peter Grant, Rod Smallwood or Robert Stigwood.

'I could get gigs for 'ee, an' y'give me ten percent o'what you earn...' he was going.

'Honest da – we dun't need a manager yet...'

'Well, think about 'ut. Yer mother there?'

'Na – she's at Bingo...'

'Oh... well, see 'gin then boy...'

'See ya da.'

Rock n'roll – the most dangerous profession in the world. Charlie contemplated how dangerous it would be t'have his da on board. It scared the fuckin' living daylights out of 'un.

* * * * *

'*London Inn*, Redruth.

Crown Inn, Helston.

Plume o'Feathers, Pool.

Lanner Inn, Lanner.

Heathcoat Social Club, Pool.

Whitbread Social Club, Redruth...'

'Thaas' a real fuckin' tour,' went Yak. 'Spot on Charlie.'

Charlie was reading out a list o'places where he'd got gigs for the band. The flyer t'response ratio was piss poor t'be honest, but at least some gigs were comin' in.

'One more,' Charlie went, ' – *Hayle Conservative Club*...'

'Jesus,' said Neil. 'I bet we'll go down well there... When we walk in the blue rinses and green-fuckin'-wellie-brigade'll walk straight out...'

'Their loss,' said Charlie. 'Thaas' the gigs anyway...'

'Do we get paid?' asked Bev.

'Yep – all the pubs'll give us fifty quid fur the night – the clubs only pay what they take on the door...'

'Looks like somebody'll be fly-posting again,' shouted Micky from the front, crunching down the gears as they went 'round the corner by Pendarves Wood.

'Take 'un steady fur fuck's sake,' shouted Neil, as his equipment almost fell on 'un. 'You'll injure me other hand in a minute...'

Micky didn' take much notice. If he could run police cordons around United Downs, he could drive them down Baripper. The evenings were a bit lighter now, an' shadows from the trees fell on those sittin' – or rather holdin' on fur their lives – in the back o'Micky's van.

'The cunt thinks he's Michael-fuckin'-Schumacher,' went Neil.

Charlie was aware they'd only had Tuesday night t'practise – an' that had been without Neil. Tonight, might be a good night

Proper Job, Charlie Curnow!

fur fuck-ups. He decided to mention his conversations at the Job Centre earlier that morning.

'I seen Yelland,' he announced. ''Ee reckoned he had nothun' t'do with us gettin' turned down that grant...'

'I bet,' went Yak. 'He hates the sight o' us lot...'

'Then I said to 'un like... that we were hopin' fur a few gigs. D'y'knaw what he said?... That we'd need t'make sure we declare any fuckin' earnin's.'

'What – like a bag o'pork scratchin's an' a Scotch Whisky condom,' laughed Neil.

'He'll laugh on the other side o'his face one day,' said Yak.

Charlie overall, was pleased with Yak's progress. Over the last month, he'd been transformed from a dope-smoking, beer-drinking idiot to a dope-smoking, beer-drinking serious rock star. Before, he'd hung out a lot with Chrissie Williams an' his crowd. But now, it was like he'd seen the light. Perhaps it was all the fuckin' flower-pickin' he did. Yak had seen that the band was a way o'moving forward an' could eventually be a way o'life. Maybe Chrissie's death had given 'un the shake-up he needed. Then again, he still knew the Scousers who'd sold Chrissie the bad shit. Crack cocaine was the latest thing in ASBO City. Cheaper n' fuck these days apparently. Easy t'smoak too – all y'needed was a pipe.

Charlie's more immediate concerns were with Neil. Sometimes, he didn' even seem t'care – like he'd rather be down *Tescos* on three-fifty an hour, stackin' fuckin' Value Baked Beans – an' having Ally lick his earlobe, like she was doing now.

Micky stopped the van in a lay-by.

'Where the fuck is this place?'

They looked out the window. They were in Baripper.

'It's on a farm just outside... Carry on a bit,' said Yak.

Charlie looked to his left where Bev was sitting. She'd had a tough week. There had been a lot o'work to be completed for college – an' her parents had been puttin' on the pressure. Charlie knew she'd had the University application forms out – an' was decidin' where she might want to go. Least these days there was University College Falmouth. Maybe she'd consider that. He'd tried talkin' about it to her over the phone, but it was a no go area. She'd given him the silent treatment over it. Her parents were probably givin' her shit over the company she kept as well. In bed at night, he could hear them saying, 'Why do you want to spend your time with those boys?' and 'Surely, there are nicer boys up the College'. It was that kind o'a fuckin' deal. He knew it. The good thing was that Bev gave all o'that the two-fingered salute. Charlie had t'make sure she kept giving it. He gave her a kiss an' she held his hand tightly.

Micky was slowing down.

'This it?' he asked.

Charlie crouched up an' looked out the front.

'Yeah,' said Yak. 'See where the cars are...'

They pulled in to a converted farmhouse.

'It's in the barn,' said Yak. 'I said I'd meet Wella here...'

'Wella?' went Micky.

''Es – it's Cornish for William...' Yak said.

'Like fuck,' said Micky.

* * * * *

'This is one worse than *Institute*,' went Neil.

He wudn' far wrong.

The stage – if y'could call it that – was a corner o'the barn with a few extension leads thrown in. There were hay bales around the place fur people t'sit on.

'They expectin' fuckin' Garth Brooks are they?' asked Micky, loadin' in his decks an' samplers.

The bar was a table with a few cans o' warm lager thrown on it.

'No fuckin' expense spared,' laughed Yak.

After Wella had given them the obligatory 'I can speak Cornish, but you cunts can't' introduction, he showed them the sockets and told them they'd be on around eight.

'Can 'ee make out what they'm sayin'?' asked Ally.

'All I can hear is every cunt goin' 'Da lowr'. Da lowr this. Da lowr that...'

'Let's just do the gig,' Charlie went.

He did look around the barn though. Every cunt in there looked like they were ready t'launch Scud missiles at the fuckin' Tamar Bridge. Most o'them were good ole' boys an' maids – but a lot o'them didn' knaw much about places like Trelawny. They were full o'devolution an' the problems o'Devonwall, an' kept

on about cunts like Athelstan an' Angov, but none o'the fuckers knew Cornwall they way Charlie did. He just hoped they
wudn' think he was too much o'a cunt just because he didn'
knaw much Cornish.

They were gettin' better at setting up. At the *Institute*, it had
taken them nearly all day. Down Baripper, it took just under an
hour, to have all the gear loaded in – an t'do a soundcheck.

More people arrived, carryin' fuckin' quiches an' garlic
bread. Some twat draped their PA speakers in Cornish flags.

'It'll muffle the low end frequencies,' went Micky.

'So what,' went the boy who did it.

'Da lowr,' went Micky, shruggin' his shoulders.

He came over.

'An' I thought all the wankers o'the world were t'be found
over yer da's *Institute*...'

'Let's just do the gig,' Charlie repeated.

He looked across the stage. Neil was practising. He'd
removed the bandage from his sprain an' was aimin' to warm
up. His chunky riffage boomed out of the PA an' caused everything in Cornish t'be spoken twice.

Charlie grabbed one o'the Cornish speakers.

'How d'y say 'Good evening – we're *Balance*'?'

The boy looked at Charlie like he was half-gone. First o'all,
he had t'switch his brain back t'English.

'Y' say Gorthugher da – thaas' 'Good evening'.'

'Gor-thuukker daaa,' went Charlie. It sounded unnatual as
fuck.

'We are *Balance* is '*Balance* on ni'.'

'*Balance* on ni,' went Charlie, manipulating his lips 'round
the sounds.

Bev laughed as he said it over and over again.

'Thanks,' went Charlie.

'Da lowr,' said the language boy.

Come eight o'clock, all of *Balance* were ready t'go. They'd
stood 'round for long enough t'eat plenty o'quiche an' garlic
bread, an' drink plenty o'warm Skinners. The place wudn' 'zactly heavin' with people. The only good thing was they wudn'
have t'deal with any fights or strip artists.

A beardie-weirdie introduced them an' Charlie went up t'the
mike as others put on their instruments.

Alan M. Kent

'Gor-thuukker daaa' he went. '*Balance* on ni.'

The audience seemed t'like that. A few o'the fuckers would prob'ly have one or two things t'say about his pronunciation, but Charlie didn' worry. He thought o'it as good practice when they'd do their first European tour. They were sure t'play places like Poland an' Norway. Iceland was trendy too.

Balance slammed through their set as usual; the same order o'songs as at the *Institute*. It was harder to get the audience motivated though. At the *Institute*, people were so hammered, that by the first song, they were ready t'dance. Here, they were more reserved.

'Y'can come down the front if y'like,' went Charlie.

'Tidn' no good,' went Yak. 'All o'our songs are in English...'

They had a break at nine, an' then played a second half. This time, a few more people tapped their feet. Charlie tried again.

'I'm feeling lonely down here...'

No fucker moved. Presumably, they were still plottin' the revolution, an' marchin' up t'Blackheath next Tuesday.

They didn' bother with an encore. No one really seemed t'care. Besides, Neil had told Charlie his hand was beginning to throb.

'You've been a great audience,' Charlie said, like he was live at the Budokan, an' drainin' up every last ounce o'enthusiasm he had in 'un.

'Y'win some, y'lose some,' said Micky.

Charlie started packing up.

'Let's not do a gig like this again,' he shouted over t'Yak.

'Sorry,' said Yak. 'I thought they'd go a bit fuckin' crazier...'

'The fuckin' Troon Women's Institute would've have been more wild,' went Charlie.

'This idn' like you,' Bev said to Charlie. 'I mean, normally, you're saying how it doesn't matter – as long as we play well an' people still enjoy us. You should hear yourself.'

Charlie was quiet. He was annoyed because he was up for it, an' the audience hadn't been.

'You don't always have t'go crazy t'enjoy rock,' said Bev. 'You told me that on the way up to Nine Maidens...'

'Maybe,' said Charlie, unconvinced of his own words.

He began to disconnect the PA. leads, an' fold down his microphone stand. Charlie stayed in a strop until most o'the gear had been nearly tucked away in Micky's van. A lot o'the language people had gone home – the revolution planned and sorted.

''Twas a lash-up,' went Charlie t'Yak.

Yak felt bad. Charlie had wanted more gigs an' Yak had got them one. No, it wudn' Hammersmith Odeon, but it was a gig. The boy Wella came out o'the barn.

'Nos da,' he said.

'Nos fuckin' da,' went Micky.

'Everyone really enjoyed the gig,' went Wella. 'Excellent band. Anyway Yak, here's what we promised... I'll see 'ee Monday.'

Wella handed over an envelope t'Yak.

They all got inta' the van, an' opened it up.

'How much?' asked Bev.

Yak pulled out a handful o'money.

'Hundred and fifty quid...'

'Whaa'?' said everyone.

'Told 'ee,' said Yak. 'Worth doin' then wudn' a Charlie?'

Charlie had t'fuckin' eat his words. He'd learnt a lesson, all his *Kerrang!s* could never have taught 'un. No matter how good they were, not everyone was goin' t'think they were the saviours o'rock. Crap gigs were crap gigs – but if they paid, then all was fuckin' well in the world.

'I'll be down the dole Monday,' joked Yak, 't'declare our earnin's t'Yelland...'

Charlie smiled an' rolled up the twenty pound note Yak had given out t'all the members o'the band.

'Nice one Yak,' said Charlie appreciatively.

* * * * *

'Like Bodie an' Doyle ennit? CI5 – *The Professionals*...'

Charlie's da was explaining why he liked Capris. It was Saturday morning, an' they were at Pool Car Auction. He was hopin' t'trade in his old model for a newer one.

'Go fur something different...' said Charlie, pointin' to a Sierra that wudn' in bad nick.

'Well... as y'wun't let me be yer fuckin' band's manager, I thought I'd go a little more upmarket...'

Alan M. Kent

Upmarket meant a fuckin' reputable dealer in Charlie's mind – not the fuckin; shifty-eyed deals goin' on in this place. 'Twas full o'clock-fixed, fuckin' heaps o' automobile shit. It seemed t'be where every fuckin' bad motor this side o'Truro seemed t'end up. Charlie reckoned half the cars there were ringed or stolen.

'Ought t'go up the line really,' said his da. 'Always get a good deal up the line. Go west, an' the rubbish I've seen – two thousand fur stuff y'could get in Devon fur half that price...'

This was somethun' his da always said when it came t'cars. Charlie put it down t'the fact that the Cornish were tighter than a duck's asshole when it came t'money – but up the line, they were good at finding faults (which may, or may not even exist in the cars), an' gettin' the price down.

'I'm after a 2.0 or a 1.6 laser really,' went his da, scanning the pages o'*Auto Trader* magazine. 'Preferably an '86 or '87...'

All the cars the auction had in were a lot earlier than that. Several o'them Charlie would be seeing up the estate soon.

They carried on up the rows o'cars. There were a lot o'wankers about with briefcases an' mobile phones, as if they were goin' t'make their fortune here. A lot o'them looked oddly at Charlie's da. Well, he did look a fuckin' sight. For one thing, his eyes were bloodshot from the St Piran's Day promotion on HSD they'd had up *Institute*, an' for another, he was togged up in his rugby-watchin' uniform. Most people wore a fuckin' scarf – or a black an' gold jersey. Not his da; that was too fuckin' normal. Na, 'ee had on a fuckin' black an' gold jester hat with a stupid-lookin' woollen chough sown on the side o'it. His ma had made it a few years ago when they'd all travelled up t'Twickenham, t'see Cornwall win the County Championships. The chough had seen better days.

His da was near-runnin' up the next aisle, almost knockin' inta' a few wing mirrors in the process.

'Charlie,' he shouted. 'Look at this...'

Charlie moved up the line towards his da. His da read the gen.

'...'86. C reg. 11 months MOT. 4 months tax. 5 speed. Burgundy. 5 good tyres. Beauty idn' a?'

His da went 'round the body work, tappin' it with his hand. 'Solid.'

Proper Job, Charlie Curnow!

'Bit o'rust on the seal here,' went Charlie.

'Thaas' nothun',' his da said. 'Shallus bid furn'?'

Charlie didn' answer.

He was thinkin' o'Bev at home, workin' on her coursework. Did she think he was an asshole from laas' night? He cudn' get away from that thought all morning.

'Fuck,' went his da, near the front wheel arch on the driver's side.

'Whaas' up?'

'Look at this...'

Charlie bent down. His da's hand had disappeared. A scattering o'corroded metal lay on the floor.

'Went clean through...' said his da. 'See, 'tis all filled in here. Bleddy patch-up job... crap ennit?'

He could o'told his da tha' before they'd even walked in the auction.

'Problem?' went one o'the salesmen.

'Nope... nothun' wrong,' went his da, standin' with his foot on the pile o'rust. 'Y'got some lovely cars in boy...'

If there was one thing Charlie had inherited from his da, was an innate ability t'bullshit under pressure. His da's bullshitting skills had been why he an' his ma had been together for twenty years. It was only of late, that they'd gone all t'wry, in that context. Elsewhere, he was as sharp as ever.

'Let's go,' his da said, when the salesman went back t'his office. He carefully kicked the rust under the car.

* * * * *

The day before being St Piran's Day, and then Saturday bein' the Rugby Quarter-Finals, Redruth was in fuckin' high spirits. Even the poor homeless sods had scrawled 'Good Luck Cornwall' on their fuckin' bits o'cardboard they'd taken from out the back o'the market. Every shop had a scarf in the window, or a mascot with black an' gold on it. Vendors sold merchandise in the street, an' assholes in kilts an' tartans were stompin' 'round the streets. 'Twas a like a kind o'carnival in black an' gold – an' even the old women in the pasty shops were fuckin' up fur it. The pubs always did good business. On days like this, y'could believe every fucker worked, an'

Cornwall was the centre o'the universe. The coppers were out
in full force an' all. Boy Truscott – a bloke his da knew from
Four Lanes – was all dressed up in his Special Constable gear,
an' they had police cones everywhere.

"Tidn normally like this is 'ut Trus?' went his da, biting inta'
a steak pasty.

'Na,' said Truscott. 'The Duke of Edinburgh's here today...'

'Is a be buggered?'

Why that fucker wanted t'come down an' stand on the terraces o'Redruth Rugby ground in March, was beyond Charlie.
Perhaps the fucker was as mad as the rest o'the Cornish.

By three o'clock the ground was chocker-block you. A few
silly fuckers from Hampshire had come down. Charlie felt sorry
for them, surrounded by the black an' gold monster that was
the Cornish fans. Yak an' Neil would already be there, prob'ly
well-tanked-up on beer from *The London Inn*, an' spendin' the
fruits o'last night's labour. By half-three they'd be caught short
an' have t'piss on the terraces. Urine an' beer were the two
smells Charlie associated with rugby. Trelawny had its own
section at the ground, down by Hellfire Corner. It was kind
o'demarked by one o'the fast-food kiosks an' a broken down bit
o'fence, where over the years, anyone who was anyone, had
scribbled a bit o'graffiti. It was like a home from home.

Charlie an' his da soon found the rest o'the Trelawny mob,
an' got ready t'watch the precedings. A presentation was bein'
made by the Duke of Edinburgh. It was some bollocks that no
fucker in the crowd really understood, or was interested in. The
police kept a close eye on the crowd.

'Piss off back up the line t' Charles and Camilla,' one old boy
shouted t'the Duke o'Edinburgh.

That got everyone in the right mood.

Y'gave Hampshire a few cheers in an' out – because y'felt
sorry fur the cunts – havin' t'come all the way t'Cornwall, play
in fog an' rain – an' be at the mercy o' the Cornish crowds. That
was it though really. Hampshire prob'ly had a lot o'things. The
fuckers had no pride though. That was what made the Cornish
team, an' their supporters different. Even his fuckin' da an' his
stupid hat an' chough showed that pride.

In the scrums, everyone was shouting for the Cornish boys
t'heave as hard as they fucking could. That was the other things

about it. Y'went t'listen t' the crowd shouting. Y'went t'watch people's faces an' t'hear old boys hurl abuse at the ref. The technique o'Cornish rugby was also good. Y'never let the opposition ball get further than the Cornish fly-half. Hampshire kept aiming fur tries from their threequarter move, but the Cornish always closed them down. By half-time, the Cornish were sixteen-three up. Come second-half, the Hampshire tackling was even slower. Cornwall was pushin' more an' more cross the gain line – with good crisp rucks an' mauls. 'Twas easy you. Hampshire didn' have a hope in hell. Got on t'be twenty-one-three after a cheeky Nancekivell try.

'The back row's the business,' said Charlie's da. 'See Tommy Bassett you...'

''Eave it up you Janners,' shouted Charlie t' Dean Shipton on the pitch.

T'be honest, what with Hampshire just about stamped underfoot, there were more interestin' things t'do in the crowd. Yak an' Neil had started a drunken Mexican wave that was spreading over t'the east stand, an' Charlie tapped forwards a blow-up doll that someone had let loose over the Cornish crowd. A lot o'the boys were beered up good an' proper by now, as the ref blew the final whistle. Cornwall had demolished Hampshire, an' were through t'the Semi-Finals.

'Get ready fur Twickenham,' went his da, shouting, 'CORN-WALL, CORN-WALL, CORN-WALL...'

Fuckers were shoutin' an' clappin' all the way out o'the ground an' back inta' Redruth. A few piles o'spew marked their direction. The chip-houses an' kebab shops were doin' good business along Green Lane, an' the pubs prepared for the evening onslaught. Win or lose, the landlords had noticed, it made no difference 'bout the amount o'alcohol consumed. Y'either celebrated or drowned yer sorrows.

'Oggie! Oggie! Oggie!' shouted his da goin' up Fore Street.

'Oi! Oi! Oi!' came the response.

The heavin' mass was ready t'get fuckin' slaughtered.

* * * * *

Yak, Neil an' Charlie were spoutin' bullshit, the way y'do when you're so fuckin' pissed y'can hardly point y'todger at the porcelain. After a good session in *The London*, the three o'them had caught a taxi back from Redruth. Charlie's da had come back too. The stupid fucker had gone upstairs, an' had crashed on what was now – his ma's bed.

They'd covered the fuckin' ins an' outs o'Cornish rugby for the past few hours, an' explained t'each other what Hampshire would need t'do next time – if they were t'have a hope. 'Course, if the three o'they had been playin', the victory would have been even more o'a landslide than it already was.

When the beer had begun t'wear off, Yak had proposed a visit t'*The Wine Mine*, t'pick up some more cans an' finish the job o'creatin' one fuckin' beauty o'a hangover. The conversation moved t'songwritin' an' guitarists, t'what the ideal rock band should have. Outside, some cunt was drivin' 'round an' 'round the estate, with his fuckin' car stereo thumping. Charlie's house was absorbin' the dark rhythms o'drum an' bass that rattled the front windows from what seemed like a mile away. The thuds kicked in like their hangover was a'ready startin'.

Charlie was on a music jag. There was no stoppin' the cunt.

'Y'need the aural equivalent o'shagging in the gutter after a night on tequila. Lo-fi primitivism with swaggering fat riffs. Y'got t'be punkoid an' wired, but with the body-shaking stomp... Y'need that Keith Richards-cool-as-fuckness, coupled with rhythm and melody...'

'Y'do,' went Neil, 'but y'want that an' powerchords, with hip-hop dynamics. You've got t'be cool, funky – always keepin' it on the edge. I like that atonal feel as well...'

'Who are yer top ten guitarists then?' asked Charlie. 'I mean, who are the fuckers who changed the face o'music?'

Neil had a good think whilst he supped a mouthful o'Skinners. Then came the run-down.

'Jimmy Page, Kurt Cobain, Tony Iommi, Jimi Hendrix, Eddie Van Halen, Brian May, Angus Young...'

He paused after the eighth.

'Then, I'd have t'say Ritchie Blackmore, an' Tom Morello...'

'All old fuckers – most o'them are...' went Charlie.

'Who would you add then?'

'Have t'be Stone Gossard,' went Charlie, 'an' then there's Bob Mould, an' The Edge... I mean Tom Morello – 'ee's good an' that – but 'ee idn' in the same class as Bob Mould an' The Edge for fuckin' inspired bits o'music...'

Neil didn' argue. He knew Charlie 'ud always have the knowledge on what was cool, an' what wasn't. He was kind o'inta' the meat an' two veg world o'rock. Charlie was inta' fuckin' obscure stuff no other cunt had even heard of. It didn' matter though. In fact, even Neil knew it gave the band good dynamics.

By the time the next bottles o'Skinners had gone down, the three o'them were in the mood for some songwriting. Songwriting? Well, it was more like seeing if they could wake Charlie's da from his stupor upstairs. They fetched in their guitars and amps from Micky's van an' loaded it inta' the living room.

'Where is the cunt?' asked Yak as he lifted out Neil's amp from the depths o' the van.

'Gone *Twilight* I 'spect,' went Charlie, 'with me sister...'

Inside, Neil an' Charlie plugged in, an' Yak set a tape rolling. A lot o'bands had drunken an' drugged up jams an' recorded the results.

'I mean, look at Hendrix,' went Yak. 'Y'ent tellin' me he wudn' on somethun' when he recorded all o'his stuff...'

Charlie gazed at the fretboard. He knew he was pissed up bad. Still, this wudn' hurt. They might be able t'knock somethun' out. When they were sober again, they might even have the riffs t'a couple a songs. If other cunts could do it, then they could.

'Try this,' went Neil. He played a riff he'd been working on.

Charlie watched his fingers, then repeated it.

'Not bad,' said Neil, 'I reckon we might do somethun' with that...'

'It's got a good funky feel t'it... Play it with more swagger...'

Neil stood up, an' gave it stick.

'Nice,' said Yak.

Neil kicked ass.

'Put it down on tape?' asked Yak.

'Go on then...'

Charlie was one step ahead o'them. He was diggin' 'round in his rucksack for some o'the lyrics he'd been jotting down. He'd bought himself a dictaphone too. Maybe Neil's riff might suit them – or maybe he could write some words around it. All he needed was a chorus t'begin with – one huge fuck-off of a chorus – t'move people the way the Holman Climax choir could.

'Play around with it,' Charlie went. 'See what you can do. Have y'got any other sections o'the song? An' Yak – see if y'can think o'the beat...'

They assed around fur about half an hour; Neil puttin' down variations on a theme, an' Charlie drunkenly shoutin' whatever words he could find in his notebook, t'complement it – or others he just improvised. Yak had tried t'work out a few rhythms. He borrowed a piece o'paper t'write down his ideas.

Yak played some o'the dictaphone tape back. It sounded like the very worst bit o'recording history ever made – a lot o'drunken cunts shoutin' an' randomly playin' anything that came inta' their heads.

'Na – hold on,' went Charlie t'Yak. 'Play that bit again. Rewind it about ten seconds...'

Yak hit the button an' the tape buzzed back.

'Stop,' went Charlie t'Yak. 'Play it from there...'

The living room o'Charlie's ma's house, on the Trelawny Estate, in Troon, near Camborne, in Cornwall – went quiet – an' listened. Somewhere, in the gurgling mix o'Yak's recording, an' their drunken laughter, a song was screamin' out t'them. The song was still strugglin' in the primordial soup that was their idea o'songwriting – but a song was there nevertheless. Its riff rocked like a bastard, an' Charlie's words would pull more heartstrings than Valentine's Night over *Twilight*.

Charlie looked over at Neil's hands clutchin' a celebratory bottle o'Skinners. Those hands stacked tins o'beans by day, they fondled Ally whenever possible, an' they'd just devised one helleva' fuckin' rock song.

'We'n do it,' went Charlie. 'I fuckin' knew it...'

''Andsome,' said Neil, a huge smile over his face.

Yak rolled a joint, an' lit it up. After sucking deep on it, he passed it over t'Neil an' Charlie. Charlie usually only did one kind o'substance abuse – alcohol. Tonight, he'd do another. He took a long drag o'the joint an' dreamed privately o'the future. Then, he passed it over t'Neil. Neil shoved it in his mouth, an' pogoed 'round the room.

Proper Job, Charlie Curnow!

'The Lord be blessed,' went Charlie, 'that Cornwall's a nation o'fuckin air guitarists...'

Yak whacked on AC/DC's 'Back in Black' on the stereo, an' the three o'them went fur it.

Charlie didn' hear the back-door key go in, an' they barely even noticed when the kitchen light flickered on.

'What the hell d'y'think yer doin'?' came a voice that easily drowned out the riffs o'Angus Young. It was Charlie's ma – back from *Do-It-All*. She'd been doin' a stocktake, an' earnin' some overtime. She was in a bad mood.

Charlie could understand why. There were leads, guitars an' amplifiers set up all over the living room. They were knee-deep in beer cans an' empty bottles. They were pissed an' Yak had a joint in his hand. Yak put the joint out.

'A'right Mrs Curnow? Been workin' 'ave 'ee?'

He was a cheeky cunt like that. You cudn' help but like 'un.

Charlie's ma recognised what was goin' on.

'Cornwall win did 'um?'

That seemed fuckin' hours ago somehow.

The potential wrath they might suffer from Charlie's ma suddenly seemed insignificant, when Charlie though o'what his ma would find in her bedroom. His da – as far as he knew – was still up there – definitely crashed out with his fuckin' stupid hat on. They'd be lucky, if he hadn't pebble-dashed the bedspread, or left a coatin' o'spew 'round the toilet rim. Charlie could feel hisself goin' white with worry. If she found his da upstairs lying on the bed – an' 'ee out with some brazen hussy – 'twould make the Iraq War look like a game o'euchre up Football Club. He wondered whether she'd go fur his neck or his bollocks first. The mood she was in – he reckoned the bollocks.

'I'm goin' up t'get changed,' his ma went, 'an' by the time I come back down, I want all o'this lot sorted out...'

She pointed t'the rock 'n'roll chaos.

'If it idn' a traveller in my back-garden, 'tis you lot...'

Neil an' Yak looked sheepish. Rock stars they may have been. Charlie's ma could bring 'um back down t'size.

Charlie did his best t'keep his ma downstairs, but she wudn' have any. She even sussed there was a problem.

'Fuck,' went Charlie.

Alan M. Kent

The three o'them anticipated the row. It was like waitin' fur a bomb t'explode.

A head appeared at the kitchen window. It was Charlie's da. He gestured fur them t'come out the back.

'What y'doing da?'

'I climbed out o'the window... I could hear yer mother's voice...'

Charlie looked up. The bedroom window was still open; the curtain flappin' in the breeze. His da must a been mad t'have climbed down that way. The only route was t'hold onta the drain-pipe, an' then jump about a metre an' a half across t'the shed. He then had t'jump off the shed.

'I went 'round next door,' said his da. 'Good job their fuckin' dog didn' hear me...'

They heard the window shut above them. She'd be wantin' an explanation.

'I straightened up the bed an' everything,' said his da. 'I s'pause I'd best be off... I'll get a lift off someone over Football Club. 'Ere boy – I'm still interested in being yer manager mind...'

'What did a say?' asked Neil.

'Never mind,' said Charlie.

He grabbed a bin bag an' started clearin' up the living room. Yak an' Neil loaded their gear inta' Micky's van, then decided it was time to head home themselves. Charlie's ma didn' have much t'say. She just supervised the clean-up, even making sure the ash-trays were wiped out. Between this, Charlie had a chance t'dash upstairs an' check fur spew. There was nothun'. His da mustn't have moved onta' the vodka over *London*.

'See ya,' went Yak an' Neil, an' the two o'them staggered out inta' the Trelawny night. One big bastard o'a hangover was what they could expect. But still, Cornwall had won, they'd got royally fuckin' hammered, an' they'd written a song. *Balance* wudn' just be a cover's band from now on.

Charlie's ma was sittin' down watchin' the repeats o'*Coronation Street* on ITV2.

'Yer faather was here earlier wudn' a?' she said matter-of-factly.

'Na,' went Charlie. 'He went back t'Karen's after the London...'

144

Proper Job, Charlie Curnow!

'Did a now?'

Charlie knew he was in trouble.

'Why d'y'say that?'

Charlie tried t'stay cool. It was hard. He was tired, he was pissed an' he just wanted t'go t'bed.

'I found these,' his ma said, holding up a pair o'shoes. Charlie peered at them. He saw where the left toe curled – the place where his da had injured his foot playing goalkeeper fur Troon in 1985, an' where the heels were worn down from the umpteenth raves he went to down *Twilight*. They were old an' battered – an' his da's.

'He forgot t'take 'um with 'un when 'ee left,' said his ma.

'Y'saw the window then?'

'Cudn' help but see 'ut.'

Charlie left his ma t'watch *Coronation Street* an' he went t'bed. These days, she didn' cry. In his ma's dreams, she just went t'other places. Charlie dreamed o'winnin the Ivor Novello songwriting award for services t'rock music. In the morning, his da's shoes would be on the kitchen table.

* * * * *

He was thinkin' o'Bev, when he pulled back the curtain o'his room an' opened the window. He needed somethin' attractive an' sweet-smellin' t'think of. His face looked like a welder's bench down *Holmans*, an' the room smelt o'farts an' beer breath. It was as if a hard-rock drill was goin' inta' his skull – the hangover was that bad. He consoled himself with the fact that half o'Redruth an' Camborne 'ud be feelin' the same way. 'Twould even have a detrimental effect on the black economy o'Cornwall – no cunt 'ud be up, earnin' a bit o'cash in hand. Y'could write-off Sundays after rugby as a day o'fuckin *Alka-Seltzer* or hair o'the dog.

When his eyes adjusted t'the light, he saw a cop car outside their row. That in itself was nothun' unusual. The hours between nine o'clock on Saturday an' twelve o'clock on Sunday morning normally brought a sprinklin' of they up onto the estate.

There were four o'the fuckers there this mornin' though, an' an ambulance. Hangover or not, he needed t'find out what was on. No one had moved his da's shoes when he got downstairs. Micky, Jess an' his ma were out in the back-garden, havin' a gake at what was happenin'. There were coppers all over the old Trelawny Mine.

'Some kids,' went Micky, 'doin' glue. They've taken one away... 'ee wudn' lookin' very good. Bleedin' nose an' sores an' that. They're lookin' fur the other fucker now...'

'Mrs Trudgeon's boy,' went his ma. 'Y'knaw – Anthony...'

Charlie knew of 'un. He was one o'the hardest little fuckers on the estate. He'd have a go at most things if they came his way. Glue wudn' the half o'it. The more Charlie thought about 'ut, the little cunt was lucky t'have lived this long.

'Someone said they'd been doin' lighter fuel...' went his sister.

No one had cared t'stop them though.

They watched a few social workers arrive. Charlie knew their faces. They were a'right really. Fuckin' twenty-five year olds with degrees in bollocks like Media Studies and Sociology, who'd moved t'Cornwall for a 'challenge'. They'd expected sun, sea an' surf. They got shite, smack, crack an' social deprivation, spendin' their time between Poverty Hearings an' lookin' for youths seekin' any fuckin' escape from what surrounded them.

It took 'um until one o'clock t'bring back boy Trudge.

'It looked bad,' Micky said. He's seen enough cases in his time up United Downs. When 'ee said it was bad, y'knew he wudn' kidding.

On reflection, it turned out t'be a pisser o'a day really. Charlie's hangover lasted most o'the afternoon. He could just about handle watchin' some black an' white film on BBC2, an' drinkin' black coffee. His ma was in a mood still. His da's shoes hadn't moved. He wondered how his da would explain that one t'Karen.

T'top it all, Neil phoned up. He wanted t'meet Charlie over the recreation ground.

'Over rec?' joked Charlie. 'Y'doin' a deal or something...?'

'Na – just see me there...'

He sounded downbeat, like it wudn' just the hangover.

Charlie pulled on a pair o'boots an' flipped the television off. The coppers were still outside. A few of 'um were havin' a yap with Trelawny residents about what had happened. It turned out the two boys were 'stable' in Treliske. Trudgeon had a fuckin' collapsed lung though. 'Twudn' long before the fuckers from *Westcountry Television* 'ud get hold of 'ut – an' be down on the estate again. The time before last – when it was Chrisse out there – some o'the tackers had 'eaved rocks at their van. Charlie had a secret hope they might do it again.

Neil was sat on a bench in the corner o'the rec. The area was always 'anging. There were chip papers, a shopping trolley an' all kinds o'crap around the play area. On the old conker tree, wherein generations o'Trelawny shags had been carved inta' the bark, a rope swing had been tied – an the blue binder twine blew in the afternoon breeze. Neil was scratchin' at the green paint o'the bench.

'How's yer head?' went Charlie.

'Bad,' came the response.

'Y'heard about the kids?'

'Yeah – shits idn' 'um...'

'So whaas' on? Why the fuckin' James Bond-style meeting?'

'Nothun' like that...'

Neil paused.

'Laas' night was great wudn' it? I've been workin' on more...'

'Really?' went Charlie. 'Get 'em on tape mind...'

'The band's goin' somewhere idn' it Charlie?'

'I fuckin' hope so...'

Neil paused again.

'I dun't knaw if I'n go on with 'ut...'

'Dun't be s'fuckin stupid...' went Charlie.

'Na look, I seen Ally this morning. She's pregnant... She d'reckon 'tis mine...'

'Didn't 'ee use they Scotch Whisky condoms then?' joked Charlie.

'I think one o'the fuckers ripped...'

'She keepin' it then?'

'She wants to,' said Neil, the Keith Richards-cool-as-fuckness slipping from his face.

'Does her ma know?'

'Not yet.... She only told me this mornin'...'

Charlie looked across t'the estate. His eyes followed the *Westcountry Television* van as it rounded the ring road.

Alan M. Kent

'Fuckin' lash-up ennit?' went Neil.

'Na,' said Charlie. 'You'll be a'right. Look at how many kids most fuckers have round here. They'm a'right idn 'um?'

Neil nodded uncertainly. He was still in shock. He didn' knaw his todger could change fate.

'Dun't even think o'leavin' the band...' went Charlie, walkin' back across the football pitch. 'Okay?'

Neil put his head in his hands.

'Get home y'bugger – an' write some more music...' was Charlie's parting shot.

He put his hands in his pockets an' kept his head down in the wind. A fog was creepin' in – one o'those pea-soupers y'only get in Cornwall, that last fur days an' made 'ee think y'lived in a raincloud. The air was gettin' clammy an' moist.

It was a lash-up Charlie though. What made girls like Ally – want t'be up the duff – s'fuckin' young? What made his fuckin' mate be such a twat not t'be more careful? It cudn' be love, could it? Na – it was instinct – a kind o'instinct y'only got from years o'living on the estate. When y'could fuck, y'had kids. Charlie hoped for one thing – that Neil's sprog wudn' grow-up knowing his da could've made 'ut. He hoped it wudn' see its da still doing covers down the *Institute* on Saturday nights.

* * * * *

The band reconvened on Tuesday night. They were doin' an interview with the main local newspaper's music correspondent – Sam Polglase. The fucker was late. He'd got lost in the fog. Kelvin had arranged it all. Troon Methodist Chapel looked the last place on earth he wanted t'be seen in.

'So, this is where it's happening?' he said, looking up at the cobwebbed ceiling. He had a tape-recorder an' pad an' asked the questions like he'd met a thousands bands before – all hopin' t'make it, but never would.

'Who are your influences?'

Charlie told 'un.

'What d'y'reckon o'the current state of rock music?'

Easy. Charlie gave 'un the sort o'comprehensive answer the fucker had never come across.

Proper Job, Charlie Curnow!

'So, d'y'reckon there's a Cornish scene then?' the fucker asked, laughing.

Bev put 'un right. Charlie chipped in too. "Course there was a fuckin' scene. Where had he been the last few years?'

'Y'got any songs written?'

Charlie an' Neil gave 'un some titles, even though they didn' really have the songs.

'How would you describe your sound?'

Neil remembered last Saturday. He put the right kind o'adjectives Polglase's way.

'Really?'

'Fuckin' right,' went Yak.

'Where are y'playing?'

Bev gave 'un the list o'prospective dates.

'Y'got a demo?'

Not yet, Charlie explained. They were biding their time. He'd get a copy when it was ready.

Polglase looked down his list o'questions. He looked at *Balance* – another article on another bunch o'Cornish no-hopers. He had a job interview at *NME* next week. He'd review and interview real bands then, not fuckers like this, in cold chapel halls on Tuesday nights.

'D'y'want a photo t'go in?'

Why not, Charlie reckoned. It wudn'do them any harm.

'Where?'

Polglase looked 'round the hall. Perhaps he was right; it was a fuckin' hovel. He hoped this was the last o'these band features he'd have t'do. See this fuckin' crowd from Trelawny. No hope o'even playin' *The Pirate* down Falmouth, tell 'about anything beyond that.

Bev, who had a bit of an idea about image, suggested that the best feature o'the chapel hall was the ceiling.

'Y'should take the photo from below,' she said. 'Can y'lie on the floor – and then we'll gather around... You can get in the rafters in the ceiling then...'

Polglase wudn' happy about it (he'd get his trousers dirty), but in the end, he complied with Bev's wishes.

Yak was fartin' like a steer, so it was hard t'look mean an' moody. Charlie looked down at Polglase. He could do his job standin' on his head. The fucker thought he knew everything.

He didn' knaw much at all.

'It'll be in this Thursday,' went Polglase. 'Your gigs'll be high-lighted an' all...'

They thanked Polglase. It felt like he'd only been there fur five minutes. Then it turned out he had.

'Blame the pressures o'journalism,' went Micky.

'Anyway,' went Charlie. 'I want your party t'hear this song that me, Neil an' Yak tried t'put together...'

Yak played them the tape.

No one said much.

'It sounds like a load o'pissheads,' said Micky.

Charlie frowned. Yeah, Micky was right; it certainly didn' sound as fuckin' good as it did on Saturday night – but there was still the seed o'an idea in there.

'Play it again Neil...' went Charlie in a Humphry Bogart kind of voice.

'Thaas' the task tonight,' went Charlie, '- t'see if we'n write a song with it...'

Balance looked at each other. It was goin' t'be a long night.

* * * * *

The song ended up being called 'What are you on?' – or at least, thaas' what it's title was by the time everyone was ready t'go home. The process o'putting the thing together had been awk-ward as fuck. Neil an' Charlie were pretty much agreed on what the chorus and verses should sound like. The trouble was, everyone thought they knew what it should sound like. As they were jamming, Bev put down a thudding bass line, that gave it the necessary bottom end, an' Yak started working up the beat. Once the main concept o'the song had been worked out, Micky agreed t'put in some samples an' back-beats.

'You'n put more on the remix,' he went.

The major argument was whether t'take the song in a funky direction or to slow it down – give it a more bluesy groove. In the end, they reached a kind of compromise – the verses became more bluesy whilst the chorus got funkier. The riff still kept the thing rockin' though. Micky gave the riff its own rating.

'Thaas' enough t'give me a week-long stiffy...'

Proper Job, Charlie Curnow!

Charlie reckoned it thundered along courtesy of the finest rhythm section in Cornwall today, and he hoped his semi-whispered bluesy verses worked. Then there was the eruption or vitriol as the chorus hit the listener like a sledgehammer. It didn' really have hit single written all over it. The song was too rocking for that – but Charlie reckoned on it becoming a stage classic; probably something they'd always have t'play.

As they packed away, Charlie looked 'round at Neil. The fire was back in his eyes. Ally wasn't here tonight, and the song-writing had allowed him t'forget his own troubles.

'Enjoy that?' asked Charlie.

'Yeah... it's sounding good now...'

'How's everything?'

By everything, Charlie meant Neil's universe with Ally..

'She saw the doctor today. He confirmed it...'

'It'll be a'right,' said Charlie.

'Yeah,' said Neil, as he went out the chapel door.

Micky an' Jess left soon afterwards. They'd gone for fish 'n' chips. Yak stayed around for a while, adjusting his kit an' makin' notes of the drum parts for the song. In the end, even he sensed that Charlie an' Bev wanted a bit o'time alone.

It had been a while since they'd seen each other – an' when you've had that time apart – kissing is like the first time again.

'Missed you,' Charlie said.

'You too...'

They'd spoken on the phone on Sunday night. He'd told her about the rugby, the writing session an' his da's antics.

'Has he got his shoes back yet then?'

'Not yet... When 'ee's desperate enough... he'll ask...'

Bev cudn' help but like Charlie's da. It had been that night at Centenary Chapel that had sealed it for her. There was the spark o'childhood still in him. She noticed the same thing in Charlie.

'So – are we goin' t'write some songs together Charlie Curnow?' asked Bev.

'I'd like to...'

'Come over tomorrow,' she said, 'for something to eat... Can 'ee get a lift over?'

'Yeah – no problem.'

His da owed him one or two favours.

Alan M. Kent

"Bout sixish?'

'Fine.'

Bev looked at her watch. Her da would be waiting outside.

'I got something for you over the weekend,' she said, delving into her bag. 'Open it when I'm gone...'

Bev passed Charlie a small parcel. It was wrapped up in the kind o'paper y'could only get at somewhere like *Marks and Spencer*.

They kissed goodnight. Charlie was alone in the chapel hall. He could still sense her lipstick on his lips an' Bev's perfume still mingling in the dusty, religious air. He sat down on one o'the benches and opened up the present. It was a book – a rhyming dictionary. He opened the front page.

She'd written, 'For Charlie Curnow. A book to help you re-write rock... Love Your Alanis Morissette x x x.

It took seconds for Charlie t'work out how t'use the diction-ary. A minute later, 'ee'd locked up the chapel hall, an' was heading across the road an' up t'the estate. The house was dark when he got in. His ma was doin' an early shift at *Do-It-All* an' Micky an' Jess hadn't returned home yet from the chip house.

Charlie knew what he had to do. Fuck work tomorra'. He'd survive it. He switched on the spotlight at his desk; the desk he ma had bough him for his GCSEs an' A/S Levels. The latter, o'course, 'ee never really got t'start in earnest. He grabbed a biro and some fresh A4 paper, then placed his notebook before him. The he started to write and re-write his lyrics; this time using dictionary. His soul had been waiting fur this. By six am, he had enough material to fill an album. He felt fucked, but he'd done well. 'Twas a proper job.

* * * * *

Tuesday had metamorphosised into Wednesday. The neat spine of the book at the start of the night was now creased and bat-tered. In the five hours in which he'd wrote, it had been loving-ly used; Bev there, next to 'un almost, standin' by his shoulders. He had a shower to wake himself up, and ate a good breakfast. His da's shoes were still on the table.

'What was on with you laas' night?' went his ma.

'I was up writin' lyrics...'

Proper Job, Charlie Curnow!

'Y'silly shit – I 'spect you'm knackered now...'

'I'm okay.'

His ma lit a cigarette. She told 'un the two glue-sniffers were supposed t'be out o'hospital today.

'Y'd better see this, before y'go t'work,' said his ma.

She put down an envelope before 'un.

'It's the papers t'file fur divorce...'

Charlie looked over them. There was a lot o'boxes about income an' dependencies.

His ma was waitin' t'knaw what Charlie thought. She wanted him t'ask: 'Are you sure y'want t'go through with this?' But Charlie wudn' one t'ask the obvious. He didn' want them t'split up, but it had been on the cards fur so long now that he'd learned t'live with 'ut.

'I've got t'go,' he said.

Going down into Camborne, he'd forgotten about his ma and da. His head was full o'his own songs. When he stopped at the railway crossin' t'wait for the seven-fifty t'Plymouth, he was singing one of the new songs on side two of their debut album. Inside cars, people watched the daft cunt on the bike, who looked like a goldfish.

* * * * *

'What are you on?' was goin' through his head as Charlie an' his da headed up the A30. When he'd got in the car, Charlie had handed his da his shoes an' his divorce papers.

'These are from ma...' Charlie went.

'I've been expectin' those,' said his da. 'From the solicitors 'ent 'em?'

'What did y'say t'Karen about y'shoes?'

'She didn' knaw... Dun't say anything mind... I s'pause yer moother was jumpin' wudn' she?'

'What d'y'expect?' laughed Charlie.

His da pulled over inta' a lay-by. He tore off the trainers that he was wearin' an' put his old shoes back on.

'Thaas' bedder,' he said. 'I won't do that again in a hurry...'

'Next time I reckon, they'll go out in the bins...'

His da laughed an' reached over t'the stereo.

Rainbow blasted out.

Alan M. Kent

'SINCE YOU'VE BEEN GONE, SINCE YOU'VE BEEN GONE...'

'Y'sure y'want t'get divorced?' asked Charlie. 'I mean, it's a big step...'

'I 'ebm got an option boy... Shame t'say, 'tis prob'ly fur the best...'

It prob'ly was. Charlie was fed up with being their Marriage Guidance Counsellor. They'd have t'do without 'un soon enough, when they'd hit the road, so he reckoned 'twould be better t'get it over with as quick as possible.

Bev's world in Truro seemed about as far from his own as y'could get. He found hisself in the dining room with a *nouvelle cuisine* meal in front of 'un. Everything was dribbled in some sort o'sauce an' the portions weren't big enough. Charlie seemed t'finish each o'the courses before everyone else. Bev's ma an' da were doin' the well-if-this-is-the-sort-of-yob-our-lovely-daughter-wants-to-see, we'd-best-get-to-know-him bit. Charlie brought some flowers fur Bev, in part, t'thank her for the rhyming dictionary. That impressed her ma. In fact, she thought Charlie was okay. She knew why her daughter fancied 'un. Her da was more of a problem. He'd seen where Charlie lived an', who Bev was mixin' with. There seemed no way o'communicatin' with the cunt. He was only inta' his accountancy business an' playin' golf over Carlyon Bay. His record collection wudn' no help either. Normally, Charlie could suss people instantly by lookin' at their albums. He could tell who they liked, what they'd enjoyed when they were younger, who their heroes were. He seemed t'like *Abba*, so Charlie had joked about them being on Eurovision, but that was about as far as it went.

He was doing his 'What are your intentions with my daughter bit'? Charlie looked at Bev. Surely he realised she wudn be playin' with Barbie dolls an' doin' her homework forever. Christ, she had a nose ring. Charlie hadn't even had his ears pierced.

'So you think there's money t'be made in the music business?' her da asked, when they got t'the afters.

A real question fur once. Charlie responded t'it at length between mouthfuls o'eclair an' cream.

'You'n be the band's accountant, if y'like...' tried Charlie.

Her da laughed a little. Maybe he was making contact. He wanted them t'knaw how much he thought of Bev. It was hard though. Every time he said something, it came out like the

cheesiest fuckin' thing y'could say – even worse than something his da would say, chattin' up the twenty-year-olds down
Twilight.

'I dun't want Bev t'miss any o'her studies,' Charlie went,
'because o'the band. I gave up college because I wanted t'do
this...'

What a shit thing t'say. 'This' was playin' a bunch o'west
Cornish pubs an' clubs fur fifty quid a night. He changed tack.

'We've an article in the local paper this week...'

Charlie was aiming for media respectability.

'Yes – Beverley told us. We were impressed...'

Fuck. Her da used the word 'impressed'. It had been the right
thing t'say.

'Y'must come an' see us...' offered Charlie.

Wrong thing t'say. Bev's ma asked if anyone wanted coffee.

* * * * *

After coffee, her parents left them to their own devices.

'They like you, honest...' went Bev.

Charlie wudn' bothered by now. He had tried his best. He
was more interested in tellin' her about the new songs he'd
written an' what an excellent present the book had been.

'We used them in College,' said Bev. 'I thought it'd be useful
for your lyric-writing...'

He showed her the songs he'd written.

'Think about the bass work...'

Bev fetched an acoustic guitar from her room, an' began to
play some o'the chords Charlie had sketched out. He gave her
an idea o'where the choruses came in an' what the bridge
would sound like.

'I want a sort o'sloppy bass on this,' went Charlie. 'An' that
one needs that two-guitar attack – y'knaw that classic Thin
Lizzy sort o'sound...'

The evenin' went by too quickly. Charlie was feeling tired,
but he'd never felt so creative. It was like the lode of his soul
was being mined.

'They're great songs,' went Bev. 'I mean, really emotive... I
reckon we can shape them up...'

There wudn' be much time over the next couple o'weeks

though, for Friday was the first gig o'their pub an' club tour. Only 'What are you on?' would be in the set. The rest would be the usual covers.

Charlie's da knocked on the door. He stood there rolling a fag.

'Tommy Curnow,' he went t'Bev's da, like her father should know who his da was. 'Pleased t'meet 'ee. My boy ready is a?'

Bev's da was nearnly knocked over by Charlie's da's enthusiasm.

'Nice house,' he continued.

'A'right maid,' he shouted in t'Bev.

'Hello Mr Curnow...'

Bev's da looked at the 'anging Capri parked in the drive.

'Can't beat 'um...' said his da, with pride. 'I d'like me Capris... Y'knaw – retro-like...'

Charlie stood next t'the proliferation o'stickers an' shit his da had on the rear of the car. No wonder Bev's da had more than a few concerns.

'See 'gin then,' said his da.

'See 'ee Friday,' shouted Charlie t'Bev.

Being a twat – his da sped out o'the drive like he was at Le Mans.

'You'm well in there boy... Got a bit o'money en 'um?'

'More than we have,' said Charlie.

His da had hit sixty by the time they passed the *Radio Cornwall* building.

'Nice maid though 'ent she?' went his da. 'Nice maid...'

And then, as an afterthought, 'Dunnaw 'bout that ring in her nose though...'

* * * * *

Yak's list o'top ten rock stars who died young:

1. John Lennon. Everyone agreed.
2. Freddie Mercury. Should'a been more careful where he put his cock.
3. Jimi Hendrix. What would a be doin' now? Prob'ly be like Eric Clapton.
4. Kurt Cobain. The voice o'Generation X. Yak would have done the same he reckoned, if he'd married Courtney Love.

Proper Job, Charlie Curnow!

5.   Bon Scott. A real loss.
6.   Janis Joplin. Everyone had heard o'her. No one really knew her music, apart from 'Mercedes Benz'.
7.   Tommy Bolin. Who the fuck was 'ee? Deep Purple's replacement for the departed Ritchie Blackmore.
8.   Brian Jones. Died in a swimming pool didn' a?
9.   Cliff Burton. What a waste. Original Metallica bass player – an' wearer of flared trousers.
10. Marc Bolan. Tragic. Wrapped his Mini 'round a tree.

It wudn' a bad list. Neil would've added Jim Morrison, an' then Karen Carpenter.

'Karen Carpenter?' went Yak. 'Who the fuck was she?'

'Y'knaw,' went Micky. 'She was in The Carpenters...'

'Died o'anorexia...' said Bev. 'It was really sad...'

'What about Elvis?' asked Micky. ''Ee should be in there...'

'He idn' dead,' went Neil. 'I seen 'un down *Tescos* last week...'

This was the conversation in the van on the way t'*Balance*'s first gig o'the tour – the fabulous, the infamous, the wonderful, the fuckin' mind-bogglingly awful – *London Inn*. It was a Friday nighter. It went like this: if y'went down well, you'd be asked t'come back again. If you were shite, the audience would duff y'. If y'went down really well, they might book y'for a Saturday.

'I'm fuckin' blowin' two hundred quid tonight,' went Micky, 'so this better be fuckin' good...'

He was right. Friday – he generally DJ-ed at the *Twilight*. But for the good o'the band, he'd appear here instead.

The stage at the London wudn' a stage. It was a fuckin' corner o'the room next t'the front window. Any fucker who walked in for a pint had t'walk right in front o'the band who were playin'. The times Charlie had done it, 'ee felt like a roadie. Sometimes, if y'were watchin' from the back – where the pool table was – y'could see fuck all. Upstairs, there was a kind of balcony. If y'were fuckin' clever, y'could gob on the lead singer.

Rock bands had a hard time there. If the lead singer was too much o'a wuss, the audience would reckon he was gay, an' kick the shite out of 'un, when he went fur a piss. If the lead singer reckoned he was hard, the audience would try it on an' give 'un a good kickin' anyway. It was a fine line really, between what kind o'a kickin' y'wanted.

Alan M. Kent

The good thing about *The London* was that it didn' take 'um long t'get inta' the music. It was a rock pub after all. Y'had t'do it right though, as they were a critical bunch o'fuckers. Charlie was confident though. He'd seen enough bands in there t'know how not t'be gobbed on, how not t'get kicked in – an' how t'give the audience a good time.

All 'round the pub, the landlord had stuck up *Balance* posters, an' then in the lobby, as y'came in, he'd photocopied the article from the local paper. Polglase's headline had been 'Hyperactive razor-sharp rockers from Troon'. The cunt had t'put Troon in didn' a? The rest o'the article was the usual range of shite an' misquotations that Charlie knew every rock band worth its salt had t'deal with.

'Don't believe yer own press,' he said t'them all.

Having said that though, the photo turned out good. It made 'um look mean an' moody; sussed in a good way. Respect t'Polglase as a photographer then. Y'could only just see the edges of Yak's mouth, turning upwards as he was about t'laugh at his farting.

'Me ma bought a couple o'copies,' said Neil. 'She reckons they'll be collector's items one day...'

They did a soundcheck. It felt good. Neil's hand was A1 again, even if his mindset wasn't. His eyes had that distant look, like he was really lookin' forward t'changing nappies an' luggin' a push-chair onta' the bus from Troon t'Camborne.

A few fuckers from Trelawny had made it over, an' Kelvin was there. How the fuck Mel had got in, Charlie cudn' guess, but she was chattin' up Kelvin again. Some others had come down from *Institute* t'see them. Charlie just hoped Clifford wudn' decide t'show again. The cunts in here would smack 'un from 'Druth t'Lanner.

Aside from some piss-head who decided he needed t'sing 'Come as You Are' rather than Charlie, the gig went well. The musicianship was fine. Neil was focused, an' Bev was her solid self. Micky was really into it – an' the crowd – brought up on a diet o'Faith No More, the Chili Peppers an' Rage Against the Machine, loved the hip-hop touches. The Punky kids down the front like the Green Day covers. 'What are you on?' even got a few o'they fuckers dancin' – colliding with those just entering. Yak was the only problem really. He was drinkin' like a bastard

– an' come the end of the set, he missed a few fills. The audience didn' notice – but the band did.

The landlord gave Charlie fifty quid.

'Not bad,' he said. 'Y'brought a few in... Want a Saturday do 'ee?'

They arranged a date in June.

Charlie came back an' distributed the money. Half o'Yak's was back in the till within minutes. The other half was probably being added to any other cash 'ee 'ad on 'un fur a block o'resin in the bogs. Or worse. Charlie eyed the Scouser bastards who came back out with 'un.

'Y'need t'have a word...' went Micky.

Back in the van, every cunt was onta' Yak.

'You were too fuckin' pissed...' said Neil. 'Y'can't get that drunk or stoned by the end o'the evenin'...'

Yak was drunk or stoned still. You cudn' tell which – or maybe it was both. He was givin' everyone the silent treatment 'til Charlie spoke.

'Yak, y'lost it a couple a times near the end mate. We need t'keep it tight...'

'Ah fuck off,' he went. 'I don't tell you how t'sing, s'don't tell me how t'fuckin' drum, a'right...'

After that everything went silent. Yak fucked off outside and rolled a joint.

Bev reckoned Yak had learnt his lesson. Anymore, an' Yak was goin' t'do somethun' really stupid, like he was goin' t' pack his bags an' leave.

'Enough,' she said. 'Everyone see if they can play better tomorrow...'

There was somethun' very wrong though. Charlie knawed it. Like the way the old miners could smell tin.

* * * * *

He was in bed, recording the gigs so far in his diary. He'd make the biographer's job easy.

Redruth *Miners and Mechanics Institute*: First gig. Good crowd participation. Covers only. Clifford Mellow did a striptease in the middle o'the set. Bollocked fur being too loud. 6/10.

London Inn, Redruth: Excellent crowd participation. People danced. Covers plus 'What are you on?' Positive reaction, so we've been booked again. Yak – a bit sloppy on the drums – got too pissed/stoned. 7/10.

Crown Inn, Helston: A'right, but a lot of old fuckers in. Only danced in the last set. Yak back on form. Vocals felt good. 3/10.

Plume o'Feathers, Pool: Full a ex-Crofty boys pissin' it up, an up for it. Friday night, so a lot of people in, goin' on to the *Twilight*. Altered the set 'round. 7/10.

Lanner Inn, Lanner: Shite. Like playin' in a fuckin' matchbox. No one danced. Group played well. Neil's hand givin' 'un stick. Weren't invited back. 2/10.

Heathcoat Social Club, Redruth: The kind o'audience who drives y'mad. Y'play the set – then, only when they're ready t'dance, d'they ask y't'play it all again. Danced to 'What are you on?' It was the same thing with *Hayle Conservative Club*. Both 8/10.

Charlie hoped the Hayle gig was the last one where they'd only air one o'their songs. The rehearsals between, had got four or five new songs inta' shape. He put the pen down. He could still taste the smoke o'the club in his mouth. The next job was t'get some gigs in Falmouth an' Newquay, but Charlie wudn' no ordin'ry fool. He already had it planned out. He switched off the light over his bed, an' dreamt of the future.

* * * * *

'Poor fuckers,' went Micky.

Pirate FM was reporting news of a Newlyn trawler being lost somewhere in the Western Approaches. Y'knew the scenario all too well in Cornwall. There 'ud be the initial search, scaled down after forty-eight hours. The RNAS at Culdrose would be giving their view o'conditions, an' they might find some drifting fishing equipment. Then, there was usually the waiting for the families. It was sometimes a month – sometimes three – until a body was washed up, or dragged up in some other boat's nets. Then there 'ud be the inquiry. Andrew George, the MP, would be involved – an' there'd prob'ly be something about the activity of submarines in the vicinity. This time, the trawler was the Margaritta Maria – an' five men had been lost.

Proper Job, Charlie Curnow!

What with Crofty, an' everything else, Cornwall got shat on by central government more times then the streetlights of St Ives by the resident seagull population, but there was nothun' that affected y', like a trawler goin' down. It was bad enough havin' fuckers from Europe tellin' y't'stay at home, rather than fish – or 'eave your boat in t'be scrapped, but when some boys went down t'Davey's locker, it always numbed yer brain, more so than the one pound per shot drinks at Truro's *Loft* club on Monday nights.

Y'knew no fucker from places like Trelawny ever went fishin' an' that, but it still hurt like a bastard. Come t'think o'it, no cunt did any o'the things Cornwall was s'paused t'be famous for. The fishers cudn' fish, an'the miners cudn' mine.

'We'll have t'go smugglin' again,' went Micky, with a glint in his eye.

The cunt was still livin' at Charlie's ma's. It was April now, an' he'd been there fur over a month. His sister was still in love with him. The three o'them, an' Bev had been up t'*The Loft* in Truro last night. It was a club on Calenick Street – a fuckin' cramp hovel o'a place – where the music was shite, an' the clientele full o'twenty-somethun's who thought they were fuckin hard by drinkin' fifteen shots o'Jack Daniels – an' then goin' in ta work at *Stratton an' Creber* Estate Agents in the morning – an' sayin' they didn' feel a thing. That, or fat, old fifty-year-old women looking for a squeeze of young cock. Neither Micky nor Charlie were 'zactly on top form. They'd been hittin' the *Celtic Smooth* creamflow a little too hard. It was a'right fur Micky. What with his DJ-ing an' his lock-up down Pool Market, the cunt was half-nocturnal anyway. Charlie still had t'face another day o'tackers kickin' him in the bollocks an' then wipin' their sticky hands all over his bear suit.

At seven-thirty in the mornin', the best thing t'do was t'just keep drinkin' coffee, an' listen t'the radio. His ma 'ud be up soon. She never listened t'*Pirate FM*, an' when she'd come down, she'd alter the dial t'*Radio Cornwall*. That was the fuckin' choice really. *BBC Radio Cornwall* had one o'the highest listening figures for a local radio station in the whole o'Britain. It was meant t'be down t'the fact that Cornwall had a unique distribution of population, an' that no cunt could get anywhere easily. That was bollocks in Charlie's view. The real reason they listened t'the shite was because they had nothun' better t'do than hear some cunt battle on about chibbol onions, take part in the chiropody phone-in, or listen t'someone moanin' about the public toilets being closed over Portreath. 'Bout the most radical thing they played was the fuckin' Bee Gees. It was mainly Charlie Lansborough, Bette Midler or James Last's 'Morning in Cornwall' (all pan-pipes, rugged cliffs and mist).

Pirate FM, on the other hand, played better music, but y'had t'sit through a bunch o'wankers fur DJs who all thought they were the new Chris Moyles, an' suffer every track interspersed with ads fur Redruth Market an' *Thompsons'* fuckin' plumbing an' bathroom products.

'It all comes off the satellite anyway,' said Micky.

He was right. They'd had a school visit t'the station. The DJs cudn' even choose their own music. The computer automatically choose a set fur their targeted audience. The fuckin' dive o'a shed they operated from was on an industrial estate in Pool, in the shadow o'Carn Brea.

'Y'knaw they've got a competition on, dun't 'ee?' went Micky. 'It's the *Pirate FM* Search for New Talent... Is their *Pop Idol* ennit?'

'That sounds like fuckin' Ant an' Dec or somethun'....'

'Na,' went Micky. 'Y'have t'send them a new song on a demo. The ones they like, get played on the air. The winners get their song made inta' a CD...'

'Sounds like a load o'hassle...'

'I reckon we could make a decent demo,' went Micky.

Charlie weighed it up.

'I s'pause we've nothun' t'loose,' he smiled.

This was an alteration t'Charlie's plan though. He'd always though they'd wait 'til they recorded anything. They'd wait until they had a strong enough set o'killer songs – then start puttin' it out there. But then, maybe Micky was right. Maybe thaas' what they needed t'do right now.

'I'll get the details when I go up market today,' said Micky, headin' out o'the kitchen t'the outside toilet.

Charlie looked at the clock. He had plenty o'time yet before he'd have t'leave. Over the weekend, they'd bashed out three more songs. They'd been in gestation for most o'their first tour, but *Balance* were just gettin' 'round t'perfecting them. The next few gigs would have more o'their own stuff in the set. Charlie's main aim now was t'play one o'the more major venues in Cornwall; a support gig somewhere – at *The Waterfront* up St Austell, over Newquay somewhere – or perhaps even *The Pirate* down Falmouth. As time had gone on, he was more convinced they had t'break out o'the pub an' club circuit. 'Es – it was still bread an' butter money an' that, but he didn' want t'end up being like the Great Gonzo. *Balance* were tight now – he knew that, but were they fuckin' good enough? He meant not just 'good enough', but really ready t'slay audiences, t'have them eatin' out o'their hands. His biggest fear right now, was that they weren't; that they'd disappear up their own asses thinkin' they *were* good. The next stage would have t'be carefully nego-tiated. It was about t'be as difficult as captainin' a Newlyn trawler in the Western Approaches. The band was solid an' in good shape, but Charlie was anticipating the shipping forecast – and a Force 10 gale was blawin' in from somewhere.

* * * * *

When Charlie got home from work, Ursula was there. Ursula was a fuckin' hag of a maid in her sixties – but done up like a dog's dinner (worse than the kind y'got down *The Loft*). Y'knaw the type – reckoned she still had it up the Football Club – when the only place she did, was over fuckin' *Age Concern*, in the old Mining Exchange. She was doin' his ma's hair. The kitchen smelt o'perm lotion an' Ursula's perfume. Ursula lived in No.4. She did most women's hair on the estate. That was half the rea-son most o'the women on Trelawny all looked the fuckin' same. Ursula had only two ways o' hair design – an' both o'them involved serious fuckin' perms.

Charlie's ma gettin' her hair done – not by his sister, but by Ursula – meant something was on – something important.

'Whaas' on with ma?' went Charlie t'Jess, who was already back from college, an' sitting with her tea on her lap watching *Neighbours*.

'She's on a date...' said Jess.

'Wha'?'

Jess turned at Charlie, with a look which said, 'Who-the-fuck-are-you-to-question-our-ma-when-her-fuckwit-o'-a-

Alan M. Kent

husband, is-living-with-a-girl-old-enough-t'be-his-daughter'

'Good fur her,' went Charlie. 'Who is a?'

'Some bloke from work,' Jess said, now more interested in fuckin' Ramsey Street again.

Ursula was finishin' off. As Charlie walked past, she went, 'Lovely hair 'ebm a?'

Charlie's ma nodded.

'Some thick idn' it... Could tie it back with a ribbon...' went the dolly-bird pensioner.

Fuck me, Charlie thought. He was bein' fondled by an old bird. He was meant t'have groupies an' teenage girls lust after 'un; not old bats like this.

'Yer off out I hear,' went Charlie. 'Who's the lucky fella?'

Ursula stayed fur the gossip, pretendin' t'still be packing away. Mrs Curnow wudn' tell her much.

'Can't say,' she said. 'Just a gentleman friend o'mine....'

'Like that is 'ut?' went Charlie.

'You dun't tell me much about Beverly... I dun't have t'tell you much...'

That was below the belt. He had t'hand it t'his ma. She was always good under pressure. She didn' bullshit like his da. She just went fur the bollocks an' twisted.

'Where y'goin'?' asked Charlie teasingly.

'Down Falmouth I think...'

His ma wanted Ursula t'knaw that. Women from Trelawny went out in Camborne, Redruth or Pool. Sometimes Truro. But Falmouth... that was somethin' rare.

Charlie didn' care anyway. The band had a rehearsal. He hoped Micky'd got hold o'the *Pirate FM* competition details.

'Well, you have a good time ma,' said Charlie. 'Y'deserve it...'

The back-door opened. Micky came in, back from Pool Market. Ursula said cheerio t'everyone an' left, havin' a juicy bit o'news t'spread tomorra' on her perming rounds.

Micky viewed Charlie's ma's new hairstyle.

'What're 'ee lookin' at?' said his ma.

'Very nice Mrs Curnow,' went Micky. 'Suits 'ee – very stylish...'

Charlie reckoned his ma's hair looked like a fuckin' gannet's nest, but he wudn' about t'tell her that. Micky – bein' a creep – had guaranteed his accommodation for the next month.

Proper Job, Charlie Curnow!

'Did y'get the information on the demo?' said Charlie, turnin' t'more important matters.

'Got several,' said Micky, handin' Charlie a wad o'*Pirate FM*-stamped leaflets.

'It's easy see. Y'just record the song an' send it in...'

'Shall we do it tonight then?' wondered Charlie.

''Course,' said Micky.

* * * * *

Balance were getting better. They were becoming more professional about everything. They' didn' really include Yak though. He'd stopped bein' an asshole fur the rest o'the gigs they'd done in March, but it was seven-fifteen, an' he still wudn' there.

'Sack the cunt,' went Neil.

He meant it as a joke, but Charlie knew the serious undertones o'what he said. He didn' want t'get rid o'Yak. He was a mate; one o'the boys. They'd played in the sandpit together, they'd smoked their first fag together, an' they'd got pissed together. That was part o'the problem really though – Yak was gettin' pissed an' fucked-up on blow too much.

'Sorry,' he went, when he came through the door at twenty-five t'eight. 'Fuckin' fell asleep didn' I...'

A month ago, it would've been funny. It wudn' anymore. No one laughed.

'I see you party are still miserable bastards...'

'Yak...' went Charlie.

It was too later t'stop Micky. He got out from behind his decks an' grabbed hold o'Yak by his jacket lapels.

'Get here on time y'fucker...'

Everyone moved t'separate them. Micky apologised. Yak threatened t'walk out. It wudn' the ideal circumstances t'be recordin' a demo.

'Will you lot cut it out?' went Bev. 'Stop bein' twats an' start bein' professional.'

That was all Charlie needed. A fuckin' posh maid from Truro, who everyone else reckoned he was knobbing, tellin' his mates what t'do. Yak was breathin' heavily, like he was about t'kick in the Sankey book table. Micky was rollin' a fag. No one challenged Bev though. They respected her too much. Yak could

165

walk if he wanted – but he knew he had t'get his shit together.
It was he an' Bev who provided the beat and bass. She needed
t'trust him.

'Sorry,' went Yak. He sat down behind his kit, an' adjusted
the cymbals.

So this was it, Charlie reckoned. This was really what went
on when the Press reported musical differences. Everyone
would have t'play well tonight, or fuckin' catastrophe beckoned. He explained about the demo an' why they were doin' it.
The tracks were goin' t'be 'What are you on?' and a new one
that had mutated inta' being called 'Making Faces'.

Micky had connected up mikes t'everyone – an' then he'd
mix the tracks before they'd make the final master tape t'be
sent away. When all o'that was agreed, they went fur it.
Everyone played well, because the pressure was on. No one
wanted t'cock it up. Fortunately fur Yak, he didn' put a foot or
a beat wrong.

'Thaas' the one,' went Micky. It was five past ten, an' the
fifth time they'd done 'Making Faces'. 'What are you on?' had
taken only three takes.

'The levels were better then,' went Micky. 'I'll mix 'em up
tomorra' on me laptop; an' put 'em in the post t'Pirate...'

Cunt, thought Charlie. Fuckin' traveller with a laptop. An'
the bastard had a bells an' whistle mobile. Didn' pay naw rent
though.

'I reckon we've got a good chance,' said Bev.

Charlie didn' say a lot. If they did play it, all he reckoned he
would hear, would be the sound o'tension. That evenin' everyone packed their gear away in silence. It was like one o'they
rock star strops times one thousand. Sex, drugs, rock 'n' roll –
and fuckin' aggravation.

* * * * *

Yak didn' need t'be told.

Outside the chapel gates, he said t'Charlie, 'I know... I'm
bein' a fuckin' right asshole...'

'Fame goin' t'yer head is it?' joked Charlie.

'I dunnaw,' said Yak. 'I seem t'leave you party prop'ly in the
shits... I knaw I gotta' shape up...'

166

Proper Job, Charlie Curnow!

It was like Yak was being treated at the Betty Ford clinic or something.

'You'll be a'right,' said Charlie encouragingly. Then he changed his tone. He cudn' help it.

'Yer not on anything else are 'ee?

'Fuck off...'

Charlie watched him walk back t'the estate.

'Wish me luck tomorra',' came a voice.

It was Bev.

'My driving test,' she said.

Charlie had forgotten.

''Course,' he said. 'You'll pass... I'm sure...'

But Charlie was distant. Bev noticed he wasn't as attentive. He had a lot on his mind.

'The band isn't everything you know,' she said. 'Sometimes, you have t'let other people sort it out...'

Charlie knew she was right. That wudn' stop 'un though. He had too much of himself invested in this for anything t'fuck it up.

'I knaw, I knaw,' he said, as they kissed goodnight, but his mind wudn' on Bev's pouting lips an' orgasmic body, it was on everything else.

* * * * *

There was a man sittin' in his da's chair at home.

His ma had the caffetiere out – working out how t'use it. Special occasion stuff.

'Go in, an' meet Ronnie,' said his ma. 'Go on... Jess an' Micky are in there...'

Ronnie looked like he was just recovering from meetin' Jess an' her dreadlocked boyfriend. Now he had t'deal with the son.

'A'right,' said Charlie.

'Hello,' said Ronnie. 'You must be Charles...'

His sister smirked at the formality.

'Micky tells me you've formed a band...'

The cunt was doing his 'I can relate to disaffected youth bit'. Charlie eyed 'un up. Was a good fur his ma? The fucker dressed like he'd just bought up the whole o' *Marks and Spencers* in one go. He lived up Mount Hawke. Divorced. In stock control at *Do-*

It-All. Least the cunt was Cornish. Phillipps was his last name. No relation t'Markie, thank Christ.

His ma brought in the caffetiere. She let the coffee sit for a while, then pressed the plunger, an' poured Ronnie a cup. Everyone else had t'help themselves.

'Where did y'go?' asked Jess.

'Oh well... we went down t'Falmouth, to a bistro called *Bon-ton-Roulet*... Oh, it was lovely Jess...'

His ma was talkin' cut up, like she did on the phone some-times. 'Twas as if she'd be whisked off t'Paris on a romantic weekend break.

Ronnie was on a winning ticket here. Charlie's da would never gone anywhere like that – not when a fiver would buy a solid fry-up over *Morrishs*. His ma hadn't been treated like this since the early '80s when she an' his da were first goin' out. Even then, his da prob'ly didn' have much o'a clue.

His ma an' Ronnie were spoutin' all sorts o'shit. His ma wudn' pissed or anything. She was just bein' provocative, like she kicked off her shoes an' leaned against the chair, shawin' a bit o'leg. Ronnie was a sensible man though. After coffee, he said, 'Well, it's been a lovely night. I'd best be makin' a move home...'

Charlie, Jess an' Micky left 'um to 'ut. Jess reckoned their ma wudn' be kissin' anyone yet. Charlie reckoned she might. Either way, with Ronnie 'round, it put spring back in their ma's step. Suddenly, fur Charlie's ma, life on Trelawny didn' look too bad. She'd enjoy bein' the centre o'gossip again.

* * * * *

Next mornin', there was a letter fur Charlie.

'Whaas' tha'?' went his ma.

Charlie read the letter.

'From fuckin' Gary Yelland – it's another grant application form...'

'He must reckon you've a chance...'

'Sure, like 'ee even cares...'

His ma had a letter too.

'Whaas' that then?' went Charlie.

'Nothun'. Just divorce stuff from yer faather...'

Proper Job, Charlie Curnow!

Charlie looked over the papers. So, he'd agreed to it.

He looked over at his ma. He reckoned she might have a tear in her eye, or somethin' – but there was nothun' there – oh no. He didn' blame her. In fact, he admired her – an' the way she carried on.

''Ee idn' in my life anymore,' went his ma. 'I'll take 'ut all over the solicitors this afternoon.'

She didn' alter the wireless dial that mornin', so *Pirate FM* stayed on. The search fur the trawler had been called off. He knew what his ma was on. He was on the same thing with Bev.

* * * * *

Everythin' was goin' on steady. His ma was seein' Ronnie again: he was cookin' her a meal, the fuckin' smoothie. Bev had passed her driving test: Charlie knew she would. Yak seemed t'be on task again: Charlie had thought he would shape up. He an' Micky were gettin' on. They both stayed up on Wednesday t'watch all three o'the *Star Wars* Special Edition DVDs, an' gloat over Carrie Fisher in the Jabba the Hutt slave gear, an' Micky had given Charlie a few ideas fur songs. Yeah, everythin' was goin' on steady.

Then all fuckin' hell broke lose.

Y'weren't that surprised when y'heard about it. That was the way it was on Trelawny. Everything was fine one minute; next minute, there was hell-up. The only thing was, that the hell-up this time, involved Neil. Being an ex-fuckin' con, an' part-time petrol-station robber, Markie Phillips had taken it inta' his head t'go 'round Ally's place an' have it out with her. He'd found out she was pregnant with Neil's baby, an' he was ready t'let her know how he felt. They reckoned afterwards the cunt was high on crack when he went 'round there. Thaas' why he took a fuckin' shotgun an' enough ammunition t'make UN Weapons Inspectors scared.

The way Charlie heard it told was that Markie turns up, and puts a fuckin' shot through Ally's ma's front-door. She's downstairs watchin' *Eastenders* an' Markie strolls in, lookin' fur Ally. Anyway, he dun't just find Ally. He finds her an' Neil upstairs shaggin' (well, its s'paused t'be a'right when the baby's still small). So Markie says he wants t'talk t'Ally like. 'Course, she's fuckin' screamin' an' Markie's firin' off a few rounds an' peppering the walls o'No.39, like he's in fuckin' *Pulp Fiction*.

Tidn' long o'course, before the entire estate knaws whaas' on, an' everyone's out there. You'n hear the shotgun blasts go off over Beacon you, 'tis that loud. The first coppers who get there are the normal fuckin' wankers who come up t'the estate t'deal with anything from broken windows t'graffiti, but they've no fuckin' idea. Next thing, there's a fuckin' helicopter comin' in over Carn Brea – an' a set o'rifle boys arrive – all padded up with bullet-proof vests. Honest man, 'twas like somethun' out o'a James Bond film.

An' Neil's in there – an' Markie's got the barrel aimed at his bollocks. 'Tis a whisht job when love can cause that sort o'a problem. The trained negotiators are in there next, settin' up phone links an' providin' Markie with whatever he needs. One point – he sends out fur a fuckin four pack o'Skinners an' fish n'chips – an' a copper's steppin' over the dog-shit and bits of smashed front-door, an' placin' it on Ally's ma's hallway. You can see where the gun shot t'buggery all her prized collection of velvet North American Indian pictures. The wolf shaman had been shot straight between the eyes.

Y'knaw the score. The coppers play the waitin' game an' hope Markie'll give himself up, but twelve hours soon turn inta' twenty-four. You've got the estate camped out – with deck-chairs an' barbecues an' that, t'see the action. But y'can tell the Chief Constable isn't goin' t'let it go on much longer. It made the *Ten o'clock News*, an' he was gettin' jumpy. Even Charlie's da came 'round t' 'ave a gake at what was on.

In the end, the coppers decide t'storm the house. It was the only time Charlie could remember the estate bein' really quiet. Thirty seconds later, an' they're marchin' Markie out, hand-cuffed t'fuck. His eyes are bloodshot. He's got that look – like he'd been awake fur too long. The ambulance blokes go in next, t'check on the hostages.

'Honest Charlie, 'ee had his finger that close... I thought I was goin' t'die... the stupid fucker...'

Neil was out next. Charlie had never seen anyone look so scared. He was shieldin' his bollocks like someone was still goin' ta take a pop at 'um. Then, Markie was whisked away t'be charged, an' the photographers pointed their cameras inta' the wagon. Ally's ma came out next. She was comforted by Ursula an' her other permed neighbours.

Last t'come out was Ally herself. She was stretchered out inta' an ambulance. The siege was over, an' Markie'd be locked up for a good time again. That was the story most people knew. 'Course, only a few people d'knaw the truth o'it all – how Neil had t'put his flaccid penus in he left-hand barrel, an' sweat it out, and how Ally was rushed in Tresliske. Every cunt knew the 'Love Triangle Shoot-out' headlines. What they didn' knaw was how Ally lost the baby twenty minutes after gettin' t'Treliske.

'Ah... naw,' was all y'could say.

* * * * *

Everything was goin' on steady – sort of. A siege o'that kind was enough t'keep everyone on the estate happy for a while – t'keep their ASBO fix. Ally's ma finally got the council t'come 'round an' fix up her front-door – an' replace a few o'the windows that got broken. Ally herself – understandably – was in some state after she lost the baby. They reckoned it was a boy. According to the Specialist, the trauma o' the siege actually had very little t'do with its death. The tacker had died due to a chromosomal abnormality. Neil was takin' it better than she was; leastways thaas' how it looked t'the outside world. But then, who really knew? Who really knows any cunt? Y'don't. Y'just know a bit of them.

Charlie didn' like t'think it, but in some ways, it had come as a relief for Neil. Sure, he had t'play the caring partner in it all, but he'd been shittin' himself from the start over the responsibilities o'parenthood. When Charlie looked at half o'the tackers on the estate – an' the state they were left in by mas an' das too fuckin' ignorant t'care otherwise – it wudn' such a bad thing. Maybe Ally, Neil an' the foetus had been let off lightly.

Ronnie Phillipps had been 'round their house a lot. Charlie cudn' really understand why. The way his ma told it, the cunt had some place up Mount Hawke, so why the hell was a always 'round here? His ma must've been givin' Ronnie his oats. It was either that, or the widescreen television they had, where he could watch the European Cup football on Wednesday evenings, drink a few cans o'Newcastle Brown Ale, an' get up fur work the next day. His ma doted on him. In return, he'd bought her all sorts o'tack, an' stupid cuddly toys. Each mornin' he'd send her a card from the 'Inspirations' series. There were pictures o'the rainforest, an' arctic expanses all over the fuckin' mantelpiece.

Bev an' Neil came 'round t'Charlie's a lot. The three o'them were tryin' hard t'write new songs. They had a lot of ideas, but the difficulty was sorting through them, an' really crafting material. Sometimes, songs were coming out which sounded too much like the others they'd already written. They wanted different vibes an' feelin's – but a lot of times, it wudn' happenin'. It was like there was only one kind o'way o'writing for *Balance*. Finding that out, wudn' too good. They had t'stick at 'ut though. Maybe they'd have t'write a set of fuckin' useless songs until they mastered the technique more. It was so fuckin' painful though. Charlie could see now why some bands took three or four years t'record new albums. Y'wanted it t'be perfect an' sometimes it just wasn't. They cudn' even do the punkier stuff right.

The only thing that kept them goin' was the demo they'd sent in. They didn' hear anything for a week, then the Programming Editor wrote back, an' said that one o'their songs would be aired on each o'the station's programmes during New Talent Week. Listeners then had t'vote on a set o'numbers for which band they reckoned was the best. Listeners who voted an left their address would be entered inta' the *Pirate FM* draw, t'win a fridge-fuckin'-freezer from *Homeworld*. The band who won would be called 'New Talent Winners' an' then given the money t'make a CD, an' be given a hundred copies.

They were in with a chance at least. At rehearsals, Charlie encouraged everyone t'listen in t'hear them on the radio. Once the song was on, then they had t'start votin'.

'I dun't care who votes,' went Charlie, 'just get anyone y'knaw t'phone in...'

In the event, they had t'listen t'a lot o'shite. As well as the usual blend o' middle o'the road listenin', an' sad local advertisements, there were the other entries on New Talent Week. Micky kept listenin' the most. That was prob'ly as he was home most, durin' the day. He tried phonin' t'see when it was on –

but the maid on reception didn' knaw. It got t'Thursday, an' it still hadn't been played.

* * * * *

Charlie was movin' in another musical direction. Unsatisfied with the fame that local independent radio was offerin' him, he'd finally relented t'his da's wishes, an' gone over t'see Jimmy Pengelly. The climb-down had occurred for several reasons: first of all, Charlie actually decided he wanted t'improve his singing; secondly, he had a hope Pengelly might be able t'teach 'un more about songwriting. The latter was a shot in the dark t'be honest. Pengelly prob'ly had more idea o'how t'go body-boardin' down Gwithian Sands than he did o'constructing contemporary rock, but Charlie was frustrated. He needed a mentor – a kind o'musical Yoda. Maybe the time was right t'see Jimmy Pengelly.

There were still *Balance* posters all over the area. There was one flappin' on the telegraph pole outside Pengelly's house down Treslothan. Treslothan was a fuckin' creepy place at the best o'times. It was dark there, an' the gothic-style church down the bottom looked like it was straight out o'the Hunchback o'Notre Dame. It looked like Marilyn Manson might step out from behind a gravestone an' start singin' 'bout the size of his steeple. The place was completely still, except for crows cawing. He'd walked down there before, t'see the grave o'John Harris – the cunt whose poetry 'ee was actually beginnin' t'like. He'd bought a book on 'un in Truro the other day.

'Whisht' job wudn' 'ut – that seige?' went Jimmy Pengelly. 'Knawed matey who 'ad the gun did 'ee?'

''Es – I knawed of 'un,' said Charlie. ''Ee's been like that fur years...'

'Glad y'come over anyway boy,' went the musical director of the Holman Climax male voice choir. 'I said t'faather y'should come over...'

Jesus, Charlie was thinkin'. Sometimes y'fuckin' hated Cornwall this way. It was like y'd do something, an' everyone else knew you, because o'a relative or some other cunt they'd met on the bus t'Redruth. Thaas' what y'got fur living on a near-island, Charlie s'paused. Every cunt knew everyone else.

Alan M. Kent

'Wan' a cup tea do 'ee?' went Jimmy.

Very rock 'n' rock wudn' a?

'Please,' went Charlie, waitin' fur the weaker-than-piss hot liquid.

Jimmy's place was special. The whole building was some-thing of a lash-up. Formerly, a tiny miner's cottage, it had all kinds o'tacked on extra sections for a new kitchen an' bath-room. Then there was a brand new living room; the old one was crammed with piles o'music an' records. This was where Charlie was sitting now. Above the piano was a large photo-graph of Jimmy and other musical directors taken at the Royal Albert Hall, Festival of Cornish Choirs. The walls were covered with certificates of musical proficiency from 1959 onwards – an' the regulation prints of Dolcoath. With regard t'the prints: if the Cornish cudn' have hard rock minin' fur real, they'd have it on their walls an' pretend – when they needed to.

Charlie told 'un 'bout *Pirate FM*. It took a lot o'doin' – the way it does with some people. Y'end up wishin' y'd never start-ed the fuckin' conversation. When Jimmy finally understood one o'their songs was t'be on the wireless, he went, 'Proper boy, proper. Help people hear of 'ee anyway...'

Jimmy had a mind t'tell Charlie how it was, and how he could improve his voice. They didn' do much singin'. Rather Jimmy was talkin' about the process o' learnin' t' sing.

'Ever 'ad lessons 'ave 'ee?'

'Nope – only stuff at school...'

Accordin' t'Jimmy, that was half the problem. Kids wudn' bein' taught prop'ly anymore. There wudn' enough singin' goin' on in the classroom – not like when he was a boy. The thing was t'get t' knaw yur voice, t'find out how best t'sing a particular part, an' not just launch inta' it like a long dog. Jimmy talked in 'parts' – that was, the bits o'the song the tenors, basses or baritones had t'deal with. Charlie wudn' sure if Jimmy knew he had t'cope with the whole song, but he let 'un carry on, just the same.

'Tidn' no good shoutin' either,' he went. 'I d'hear of 'um on Radio Cornwall, an' the buggers 'ent singin'... they'm shoutin'...'

Charlie wondered if he'd ever heard o'industrial or rap music. Now, he was on about stance – an' air. Charlie never

Proper Job, Charlie Curnow!

really thought about either. He just stood on stage like all rock stars did. Surely, it was more important t'look cool than end up like one o'the back-row o' the Holman Climax male voice choir.

Jimmy was up – with his chest out, like he was a fuckin' bantam.

'Y'need t'warm up as well,' he said. 'Get up an' try it...'

Jimmy was breathin' in an' out like he had severe asthma. Charlie felt a twat, but copied 'un.

'Ideal,' went Jimmy. He moved t'the piano an' dug around in a chest fur some music. It was some yellowed book with a title on it like 'Musical Exercises: Working with the Voice'. Jimmy had 'un goin' through the scales, holdin' notes – all the bollocks y'reckon Opera singers do.

'If y'don't get it right,' said Jimmy, 'you'm in the shit. You'll end up with vocal polyps – nodules on yer throat...'

Charlie had heard o'them. A lot o'rock singers got them, an' had t'get booked inta' special clinics.

There were more exercises.

'Feel stupid do 'ee?' went Jimmy, after a run o'high notes. 'See boy, 'tis like anything... if y'd'play guitar, then you have t'practise... I 'spect all the practise you d'have is listenin' t'records at home, an' singin' along t'them – or else that karaoke they d'play over Football Club...'

Jimmy wudn' far wrong, t'be honest.

'You have t'exercise your voice... Keep 'un fit see... then all they bleddy smokey clubs you do sing in, wun't affect 'un s'much...'

Charlie understood how he was mad t'think otherwise.

'You've got a good voice,' continued Jimmy, 'but a few more lessons, an' you'n have an excellent voice. It dun' matter what you'm singin' – whether 'tis choir – or whatever you do, 'tis just the same...'

'Can y'teach me anymore?' asked Charlie.

He ended up stayin' at Jimmy's 'til late on Thursday evening. The bugger was a laugh all told. Turned out once, he'd sung in a pop group – when he was a youngster.

'Wudn' no bleddy good,' Jimmy joked. 'Drummer cudn' drum an' the singer cudn' sing...'

'Who was the singer?'

'ME – y'bleddy fool!'

When Charlie got home an' was in bed, goin' through some o'the exercises Jimmy'd taught 'un, he realised the old boy had altered his approach t'music forever. The lesson had been a hard one. He wudn' playin' at 'ut anymore – and image? coolness? vibe? It didn' matter any, if y'cudn' stay in tune.

* * * * *

''Making Faces'.'

'They didn' play that did 'um?'

'Thaas' what was on,' went Micky. 'Dave James, the DJ, described us as an up-an'-coming rock band from Camborne...'

'Thaas' okay then. I s'pose we'd best get votin'...'

Charlie was at work. He hadn't even heard their song on the radio, but that didn' stop him redialling on his mobile an' votin' ten times. He just hoped everyone else would be doin' the same. He felt a right twat standin' in the middle of the holiday camp – all his bear gear on, with a phone to his ear, but it had t'be done.

If y'hit the radio, every fucker was a critic. It was like yer songs were up t'be commented on – like every other new single release. They had a point – but it was a little unfair that their's was recorded live at Troon Chapel, an'everything else had been re-recorded an' overdubbed t'fuck.

'Heard yer song,' went the woman in the ice cream kiosk. 'It wudn' bad...'

'On the radio now are ya?' went the manager of the Holiday Park. 'Sounded alright...'

'Heard it,' went a tacker on the estate, as he was cyclin' home. 'Fuckin' crap wudn' it?'

'Ah – piss off...' went Charlie.

He got in. Micky had the tape all cued.

'I know about a hundred people have phoned in,' he went.

Micky pressed play.

No one said a word.

His ma cried.

Jess held Micky like he'd just stolled off *Top of the Pops*.

Ronnie waited fur it t'end, so he could watch the *Wes'o'England News*.

Charlie was listenin' out for tension. Did the tension o'that night come across? He reckoned it was a'right. His vocals were shite though. He sounded like rock vocalist No.73 – how t'sound a complete wanker.

'When are the results out?' asked Charlie.

'Next week, I think,' replied Micky. 'What d'ya reckon to it then?'

'It's a'right,' said Charlie smiling. 'It was a good move... an' a lot more people will have heard o'*Balance*.'

Micky stopped the tape. The DJ was babblin' on about the rest o'the tossers the listeners had heard during the week.

'We were the best,' said Micky, 'by a long way...'

Bev felt the same way. Ronnie had the news on, so Charlie had t'take the phone inta' the hall.

'I got loads o'friends t'phone up fur us...' said Bev.

'Brilliant...'

'It sounded good, considering...'

'You're right...'

'Charlie – I've got us another gig – if we want it... It's a friend o'mine, who does some work booking bands down the University in Falmouth...'

'Where?'

'At *The Pirate*... support to his brother's band... Shall I say yes or not?'

Charlie considered it. He'd always wanted t'do *The Pirate* on their terms. The place was a major venue. *Balance* didn' need any fuck-ups.

'Who's headlining?'

'They're called *Break the System*...'

Charlie knawed 'um. They were a crustie/hard-core crossover Punk band, who generally brought in a good crowd. *Balance* might make some fans.

'A'right – we'll do it. When is it?'

'Same day as Trevithick Day – but in the evening...'

'We'n do that,' went Charlie. 'We'll need t'get some o'they new songs knocked inta' shape though...'

'I'll tell this bloke we'll do it then...'

''Course,' said Charlie confidently '- now we're recording artists...'

* * * * *

As it was, when *Pirate FM's* Phil James read out the winner o'the Search for New Talent competition, it wudn' *Balance*. 'Twas some maid from down Penzance who sounded like Celine Dion. Jamesie reckoned she'd had thousands o'votes.

'Like fuck,' went Micky. 'They 'ebn got that many listeners...'

They didn' say who was the runner-up, but they would be playin' this Celine Dion maid every day this week.

'What a lash-up,' went Charlie, ''an there was I hopin' t'give Gary Yelland one o'our discs...'

'Y'can still say y'featured in *Pirate FM's* New Talent competition...' offered Jess.

''Es,' went Ronnie.

'...but didn' win,' continued Micky. 'Y'might as well say '*Balance*: the band who were featured, but won bugger all...'

'Is' a'right,' said Charlie. 'Least a few more people knaw about us now...'

There wudn' really much more t'say. If you were in a band, y'had t'try stuff like that. Y'cudn' jus' give up cus' a few thousand listeners preferred the Penzance maid t'them.

'Thaas' the whole point through really ennit?' went Micky. 'I mean, maybe we should be more worried if they did vote fur us...'

''Es,' went Ronnie, like he knew fuck all. Which he didn't.

* * * * *

Nobody had heard much from Neil the laas' few days. Y'could understand why.

''Ee's prob'ly pullin' shot out a Ally's ma's wallpaper,' joked Micky, or else havin' his ball-bag checked fur any ricochet damage...'

Y'had t'laugh. Y'didn' want to – but y'had t'laugh.

When Charlie got back home that Monday evening, the Fire Brigade an' Social Services were swarmin' over the estate. Loads o'tackers were goin' inta' a caravan an' gettin' free stickers. This was the sort o''Preventative Care' y'got used to on the estate. Today, it was about the community, the fire services an' the social tryin' t'educate about the danger o'fire. Some bollocks called 'The Guardian' scheme. Y'had t'laugh: kids 'ud take all

Proper Job, Charlie Curnow!

the stickers; it wudn' stop 'um playin' with matches and petrol though. In fact, it gave them a few new ideas.

Kelvin was over Mel's place. They saw Charlie walk up the drive, avoidin' Fireman Sam an' the demonstration o'how t'put out a chip-fan fire, and both o'them came out to see 'un. Mel's ma looked out from the nets. Least she was home. Least she wudn' givin' blow-jobs t'blokes behind *Tyacks* for a fiver a time.

Kelv had an idea.

'I got an idea Charlie...'

He always had ideas – but he was useful fur all their printin', artwork an' stuff.

'The band should have a web page...'

'We 'ebn got enough stuff t'keep us amused,' went Charlie, 'let alone any other cunts out there, surfing the web...'

'Y'should have one,' went Kelv. 'I'n put yer gigs on – an' everything...'

'I think it's a good idear,' went Mel. 'We've got 'um down 'Druth school...'

'Can y'give me some biographies an' that,' said Kelv, 'an' some photos... an' any gossip...'

'Y'dun' need gossip 'round here,' went Charlie. 'They've had the fuckin' internet fur years...'

'Is' the future,' said Kelvin.

Charlie thought about it. He was right. All bands worth their while had a web-site on their singles an' albums. All the big bands like Oasis an' Metallica, they had loads o'unofficial sites as well.

'This the official *Balance* web-site then is a?' asked Charlie.

'Yeah – thaas' it...'

'A'right then – give it a go...'

Charlie reckoned he'd regret giving it the go-ahead. At least it would keep Kelv and Mel off the streets. They could now fondle each other in front of a modem and talk dirty about *html*.

'Web-site!?' Charlie said to hisself. 'Got a web-site, but we 'ebm got good enough songs...'

The chip-pan fire was out. The tackers were booing. They wanted t'see the fire again. Charlie went home smiling to hisself.

* * * * *

179

Alan M. Kent

Unadulterated drinking, drug-taking an' dancin' seemed t'Charlie t'be about the best way o'celebrating the life o'the famous Cornish inventor Richard Trevithick as y'could get. An' thaas' about the top an' bottom o'Trevithick Day for most o'the young people o'Camborne. Certainly, there were other things t'do: y'could go up Bassett Road an' fondle stream traction engines an' agricultural machinary, or y'could wander 'round the stalls in Trelowarren, which sold all kinds o'shite, or y'could even go over Rosevean where y'could be spun in a chair on some tacky fairground ride by a bloke smokin' rollies an' with tattoos on his forearms. Some people even combined all o'that with gettin' out o'their fuckin' heads, which was prob'ly by twelve o'clock at night, the reason why the police had t'clear away s'many casualties slumped on the pavements of the town centre. The fair rides, in combination with several pints o'Snakebite, were mainly the reason for the small piles o'puke y'could also discern on yer travels.

The English always championed George Stephenson as the inventor of the steam locomotive, but the Cornish knew better. Cap'n Dick was the boy. Had an engine running in 1801, but Stephenson didn' get anythin' movin' 'til four years later. 'Twas prob'ly one o'the few fuckin' elements o'Cornish history they did teach 'ee at school. Charlie remembered the story o'how Trevithick then travelled t' South America, crossin' flooded rivers an' fightin' alligators, but the fucker still died in poverty. Cornish as they come then.

Today, the people o'Camborne were tryin' t'stave off poverty by buying up any item o'value they could, from the stalls an' not s'much fightin' alligators, but fightin' one another, t'get from one end o'the town t'the other. There was gear everywhere – burger bars, candyfloss, balloons, choirs, dancin', Elvis impersonators, screamin' kids an' a sea o'black an' gold. People started early. Last year, Charlie, Neil an' Yak had tried t'cover every pub in the town centre – as well as watch the parade o'steam. That meant being in the pub at eleven in the mornin'. The key o'it was pace. Y'had t'take 'un steady – else you wudn' make 'ut...

This year wudn' that much different than normal. Y'still had the Holman Climax male voice choir performin' at midday – an' y'still had old fuckers in caps an' boiler suits checkin' piston ratios an' gettin' steam up, like most o'the twentieth century hadn' happened. Didn' matter though. 'Twas still a beauty o'a day. Y'could do as y'wanted – long as y'went up Cross Street an' paid your respects t'boy Trevithick's statue outside the library. It didn' matter that all the mines around y'could view from Camborne Hill had gone – an' the last o'Trevithick's pumps with 'um. In fact, they gave y'more reason than ever t'celebrate his achievements...

It was different in other ways though. *Balance* were doin' the lunchtime set in *Tyacks*, then they'd miss the evening's festivities as they had t'get down *The Pirate* fur the support gig. No one could afford t'get too hangin'. They were the entertainment this year. Yak had been warned about takin' it easy fur the past fortnight. Beer? Yes. Dope? No.

The *Balance* publicity-machine – such as it was – had gone inta' overdrive the past few days. It was hardly enormous, but a refined version o'their poster could be spotted on any spare piece o'architecture 'round Camborne. Kelv had even stuck their new web-site address on the thing. Everyone had t'admit it: www.balance.co.uk. looked cool. It looked like they were heading somewhere at least – even if no fucker knew where that was. Hell, such was the publicity they'd even been featured in the Chamber o'Commerce newsletter – which everyone had been given – but now littered the streets; a one-read-and-chuck-away job. *Pirate FM* had given them a push as well. Micky'd sorted that. One o'the DJs there – who also worked at the *Twilight* – owed 'un a favour or two.

Everyone said they'd come an' see them as well – even his ma an' Ronnie. Ronnie considered himself a bit o' an expert on traction engines, s'today, he'd be introducin' his ma t'the merits o' early twentieth-century plant, then takin' her out fur dinner. His ma an' him aimed t'pop in t'see 'um in *Tyacks*. She hadn' been in there since 1979. His da'd be around too – prob'-ly with Karen an' her army o'kids. Charlie reckoned the fair 'ud be a good bet. His da was always a sucker fur target shootin' or pullin' plastic ducks off a rotating' table with a stick. He was prob'ly on his second goldfish by now. Charlie just hoped the two halves o'his parents wudn' meet up – or the fuckin' Mermaid Appeal tombola Teddy Bear stand 'ud be scat over in the ruckus. His da didn' knaw 'bout Ronnie yet.

181

Most o'the estate would be down as well. 'Twas still foggy up there, but down in town, the weather was clearin' an' a bit o'sunshine was tryin' t'come out. The *Tyacks Hotel* landlord was sure t'feel the mixed emotions o'love an' hate at the same time – when a lot o'the people *Balance* knew walked in. Sure, they'd drink like fishes (he'd be changin' the barrels every whip an' wan), but with it, would come the aggravation. It turned out, 'ee was the one who'd reported Mel's ma fur the personal services she was givin' out back.

Still, y'cudn' say anything. The cunt was payin'.

The job on, was a one an' a half hour set. They'd agreed with Neil's suggestion o'splitting it inta' two three-quarter o'an hour sets. Then they could have a piss-break an' the chance o'a beer themselves. Y'cudn' get full-on at this sort o'a gig. If y'did, y'd look a complete wanker. They reckoned the best way was t'treat it as if it were MTV unplugged, like it was a specially invited audience o'record company executives, journo's an' people with the band. Only problem was – they wudn' 'zactly unplugged. Neil was heavin' his Les Paul copy over his shoulder, an' scattered around the bar were the usual crowd o' no-hopers, alcholics an' care-in-the-community cases.

'It dun' matter,' went Charlie. 'Least we'm gettin' a good whack...'

They went on at twelve-thirty. The pub was beginning t'fill with those already disaffected with steam traction an' Illogan Women's Institute's home-made produce stalls. The only way t'null the pain was t'get hammered – nothun' like drinkin' in bright sunshine t'set 'ee up for the rest o'the day.

It sounded good. The new amplifier they'd bought for Charlie's guitar kicked in nicely, an' Neil was playing like a bastard. Sometimes, 'ee could be moody as fuck beforehand, but still play a blinder. T'day he was throwin' shapes an' doin' his best Jimmy Page impersonations. Your pub audience, leastways, any o'them with a brain, likes all o'that. It means they didn' have t'travel up the line t'see some cunt twiddle up an' down the frets like there wudn' no tomorra'. They could see here, LIVE in... uh... Camborne.

Jimmy Pengelly's vocal coachin' had helped an' all. A few minutes before the gig, Charlie had gone out t'the toilets an' sat in a cubicle, aimin' t'follow Jimmy's suggested exercises. It had

Proper Job, Charlie Curnow!

made a difference – he was reaching the notes better; his voice felt more powerful, more bluesy, with more presence. Yak was on form as well – like fur a change – he was on task, not wishin' t'fuck it up. Bev was as tight as usual. A few o'the punters in, reckoned she was a bit o'a'right, an' were makin' those kind o'suggestions an' noises. She dedicated 'Making Faces' t'them. Micky meanwhile, was doin' his own thing. With the money the band had put inta' the pot, he'd bought a new synthesizer an' stand. Charlie had t'hand it to 'un – Micky worked hard at it. Some days, he'd just rehearse all day, then he'd be co-ordinatin' the publicity. Sometimes, it was like it was Micky's band in a way; he was doin' s'much o'the organisational stuff.

'Y'need t'write songs,' he had said, 'not deal with the rest o'the shit...'

An' Charlie let 'un get on with it. It worked.

They were in the middle o' 'Get it On' when his ma an' Ronnie walked in. Ronnie was holdin' a copy o'*Steam Enthusiast*, an' bought half a shandy. His ma gave him a quick wave an' then sat down with what looked like a gin 'n' tonic.

'I know it's only one o'clock,' went Charlie, 'but y'can dance if 'ee want to...'

People re-lit fags an' ate bags o'crisps. The dancefloor stayed empty.

'Anyway,' went Charlie. 'One for boy Trevithick... a song called 'What are you on?'...'

He soared in with the first verse. They'd honed it t'perfection now. Charlie reckoned it was a giant fuck-off of a song, with a killer hook. He closed his eyes as they banged inta' the chorus. When he looked forward again, two boys were out dancin'. They looked like they were students – Charlie didn' recognize them. They were goin' fur it as well – like they meant business. There were only two o'them – but this was the way it should be. Y'gave out the energy t'the audience, an' then the audience absorbed the energy and then fed it back t'the band again. This was the way real rock 'n' roll should be: a cycle o'energy between the band an' the fans.

People dancin' always upped the stakes. Y'felt y'had t'deliver better, like if y'didn', you'd let them down. They stayed fur the rest o'the first set. More people came inta' the pub. Outside, in Commercial Square, some 1950s-style rock 'n' roll singer name o' Rocky Shades was doin' a set o'Shakin' Stevens covers. Thaas' prob'ly why they'd come in.

Charlie went fur a piss. It steamed, an' he felt the relief.

'Excellent,' came a voice from behind him. It was one o'the boys who'd been dancin'. He had on surfin' gear an' a Korn t-shirt.

'I really liked that song... 'What you on' or somethun'...'

'Thanks,' went Charlie.

Charlie wanted t'sound casual about it, like who was this boy, t'say they were excellent. 'Course they were fuckin' excellent. But he didn'.

'Yeah – it rocked hard...'

'D'y'think so?' went Charlie.

'Definitely. Got any other gigs comin' up have 'ee?'

Charlie took a flyer from his pocket an' gave it to him.

'Y'playin' *The Pirate* tonight?' enthused this boy.

'Yeah, we're the support...'

'I'll be there,' he went. 'I'll bring me maates...'

'Spot on,' said Charlie.

This boy had that look in his eyes. Charlie'd seen it before. It was that look of thank-fuckin'-Christ there's someone decent around t'follow. It was a look Charlie'd seen in his own bedroom mirror. It was a look that had flourished after his da first played 'un Led Zeppelin *IV*.

'See 'ee later then...' their first fan enthused.

'A'right,' went Charlie. He put his knob away an' they shook hands – no washing – an' why should he – this was rock 'n' roll...

The second set was good, if not better than the last. The boy in the bog turned out t'be called Michael Bluett, an' 'ee was a bit o'a music head the same way Charlie was. He had tickets fur Green Day at Milton Keynes Bowl, an' he wanted t'be a doctor. In a way, he was less o'a fan, an' more o'a fanatic. His mate was on the same course over Cornwall College.

'Thaas' all we need,' went Micky. 'A fuckin' cult followin'...'

'Dun 'ee mean clot followin'...?' went Yak.

'Dun't knock it,' said Neil. 'We need fuckers like 'ee... Thaas' our audience, our real audience – not those fuckers over the bar...'

His words drifted off as he noticed Ally at the bar. It was the first time anyone – aside from Neil – had seen her since the siege an' that. He was soon over there. The rest o'them carried on packing away. Y'wanted t'say something t'Ally t'comfort her – but y'knew it would be no good. It was weird how people were like that – the stuff they wanted t'say, they never did – an' the stuff that should never be said, always did.

Charlie decided t'wander over to his ma before she came up t'the stage.

'What d'y'think?' he went, plonkin' himself down on a stool.

'Loud wudn' 'ut?' was the first thing his ma said.

She should be used t'that by now.

'Beyond tha'?' he asked.

'Oh good,' she went. 'People seemed t'like it...'

''Es,' went Ronnie. ''Twudn' bad at all...'

''Twudn' bad at all. High praise indeed from the Steam-engine-meister.

'Whaas' it like out there?' Charlie asked, pointin' t'Commercial Square.

'Heavin',' said his ma.

'Mad,' said Ronnie. 'Y'knaw what 'tis like...'

Charlie said he best get on. There was a lot t'do. Besides, Ronnie an' his ma were now headin' off t'watch the Parade o'Steam.

'That was excellent,' Bev said. 'Your singin' was really good...'

Charlie blushed. Excellent. Rocked hard. Really good. 'Twudn' bad at all... The praise was comin' thick an' fast these days. Before he'd know it, Charlie would be the new W. Axl Rose – demandin' this, an' demandin' that – as befitted his star status.

'You'll be askin' fur the fuckin' blue smarties t'be taken out next,' yipped up Yak.

'Fuck off,' said Charlie packin' away his microphone, an' givin' Yak a small shove.

* * * * *

They had a bit o'time in Camborne before *Balance* needed to load-in down *The Pirate*. Micky locked the van. It has been a hundred quid for the session. It wudn' bad money for four hours o'work.

'Meet 'ee back here at four then,' shouted Micky. He an' Jess were goin' fur some food.

Neil had gone off with Ally fur a bit. It looked like they needed t'talk.

Yak was the odd one out.

'All you fuckers are near-married these days,' he went, expectin' t'have t'go 'round on his own.

'We'n be a three-some if y'want,' joked Bev. 'We dun't mind, if you don't...'

With Bev in the middle, they linked arms an' walked up the drang t'where the main festivities were takin' place. On the stage, some boy from the Stannary Parliament was pressin' everyone t'sign a petition about minority peoples in Europe. Accordin' t' 'ee, that included the Cornish. Most people were ignorin' of 'un – an' gettin' on with manouevring push-chairs 'round *Woolworths* – or seein' what gidgees were on offer.

'I'm not ready t'settle down yet, y'see...' Yak was goin'.

'Neither are we,' went Bev, 'so don't worry...'

It was shapin' up fur a good day. In a way, everyone wished they didn' have t'do another gig. Y'wanted t'stay her an' carry on celebratin'. Bev bought some earrings off one o'the traders. They were made o'copper an' were covered in spirals. They looked cool on. She smiled at Charlie when she was tryin' on pairs. Charlie had a boner the size o'Godrevy lighthouse most o'the afternoon. There wudn' much he could do – 'cept push it towards her sometimes, so she noticed.

'Mmmm...' she said, whispering. 'Someone's happy...'

Charlie had read an *NME* interview with this Krishna-core band. The singer who was straightedge said he hadn' slept with anyone or wanked for three years. He reckoned the lack o'release gave him his energy on stage. Charlie knew what he meant. He was an intellectual, same as the next man, but his soul was tellin' him he an' Bev needed t'get it on. She wanted t'shag him as well. Y'could tell. Y'just know. It was just a matter o'time.

Trelowarren Street (with Yak watching) wasn't the place. It was goin' t'happen though. The time an' place would have t'be right though. Like the band, there'ud be no fuck-ups... he was aimin' for one long, slow fuck...

Proper Job, Charlie Curnow!

Charlie was brought back t'his senses by the crowd splitting down the middle – as if some 'Catch-me-who-can' locomotive was heading back t'wards *Tyacks Hotel*, an' takin' no prisoners. It could even have been a few nationalist boys makin' a protest – like they did when they laid down on the Tamar bridge laas' year. But no, it cudn' have been that fuckin' simple.

People were near divin' out o'the way o'whatever was comin', like 'twas goin' t'scat them over if they didn' move.

'O fuck,' went Charlie.

He recognised the pathetic chough on his da's hat bobbing above the crowd. In an instant, the stanking figure emerged, his face redder than a tourist's back on a day in August, an' eyes fierce as a buckrat.

'Wozon da?' went Charlie.

The crowd looked relieved that someone had stopped 'un. Maybe he wudn' smack at any o'they now.

'A'right Bev,' said his da, not wishin' t'offend her, an' 'avin' a soft spot fur the maid.

'Hello Mr Curnow,' she went back, tryin' t'calm 'un down. 'Whatever's happened?'

His da was snortin', makin' aggressive noises like 'I'll have the fucker' an' 'He might 'ave 'er now – but soon enough, that boy'll wish his cake dough...'

'Tell me whaas' on will 'ee?' Charlie was goin'.

His da sat down on the edge o'the pavement.

'Is' yer moother,' he went more coherently. 'I just seen her – with another bloke... Who the 'ell d'she think she is? I 'ebn been out the door five minutes an' some other bastard's in there...'

'What do 'ee expect?' went Charlie exasperated. 'You'm the one who left...'

Yak an' Bev knew all Charlie's da's sordid exploits.

'Whaas' a called?' his da asked.

'Ronnie,' said Charlie. 'Ronnie Phillipps.'

A lightbulb went on in his da's head.

'She d'work wid'un dun't she?'

Charlie nodded.

'I 'spect they was carryin' on before wudn' 'um... up there behind bleddy bits o'2 b'4... Moved in 'av a?'

'Na – tidn' like that – or anything...'

Alan M. Kent

That wudn' strictly true, but it wudn' the time nor the place t'tell 'un that Ronnie watched the football on his Satellite system in what used t'be his da's chair.

'I'll kill 'un...' he kept goin'.

'Na – that idn' sensible da... y'dun't want t'end up like Markie do 'ee?'

His da grabbed Charlie's arm t'stand up. People were makin' room fur Stithians Band t'march through. The first puke o'the day could be seen outside Barclays Bank. Charlie looked at his watch. It was ten t'four. They'd need t'head back t'the van.

'Na – 'course not,' went his da. 'I idn' that stupid...'

Charlie reckoned 'ee could be. There was more t'come though.

'See, I'm prop'ly in the shits now boy. She d'want a younger man an' that... She fuckin' 'eaved all me stuff out o'the caravan...'

So his da was homeless now. Thaas' all they needed. Good job Jessie wudn' there – or she'd be squalin' her eyes out.

'Da, I got t'go... We've got a gig down Falmouth... Where y'stayin' tonight?'

'Aw – dun't 'ee worry. Dun't 'ee worry. Clare up the *Institute*'ll put me up...'

Least that was something. Least he wudn' be camped out under boxes from *Tesco*, like many 'round Cornwall.

'How much beer's he had?' asked Bev.

'Not much,' said Charlie.' He idn' slurrin' his words yet...'

'I still want t'manage yer band mind...' said Charlie's da as they called over a taxi. 'If y'dun't want me, I got another beauty of an idea...'

'Sure da,' went Charlie.

His da was babblin' on now, makin' no sense at all.

'Can 'ee take 'un over *Institute* over 'Druth?' Charlie asked a taxi driver.

Charlie gave his da twenty quid – the money he'd earned at dinnertime.

'Get 'un in t'Clare will 'ee?'

The driver did a U-ie, an' they watched the car head down Tolcarne Street. As the car spun, his da rolled over in the back seat.

'Jesus,' went Charlie.

Proper Job, Charlie Curnow!

Bev grabbed his hand.

'Yer da should be on that American show on Sky,' said Yak.

'What show?'

'Y'knaw – where people line up on stage, an' talk about their problems...'

'Ricki Lake y'mean...?'

'Thaas' the one... or tha' Jerry Springer...'

Charlie thought about it fur a moment.

'Na, he'll be a'right. Me da can do that up *Institute* tonight...'

Y'had t'laugh. Y'had t'. If y'didn', y'd cry yer eyes out. Charlie had had enough o'his da being a beauty, an' a good old boy. 'Twas time fur a change.

As they walked back t'the van, Charlie pressed inta' Bev's ass a couple o'times. There wudn' nothun' there. His dick was softer than a Mr Whippy down St Ives on a Sunday afternoon.

* * * * *

Charlie was quieter than usual on the way t'the gig. Bev knew the reason: the tribulations o'his family were getting to him. Jess knew nothun' o'course – so both she an' Micky were in high spirits. Yak hadn't said anything either. Neil had persuaded Ally t'come along with them. She looked better, like the strain o'the last month was finally leaving her. Neil had done well t'keep her on track, an' get her back inta' the fold.

The back o'the van was an odd kind of cocoon. Y'could feel points along the way, like goin through Four Lanes, and down inta' Lanner, but that said, they'd come out o'one gig and then an hour later, they'd be in another. It was like the way all bands talked about the process o'touring: y'never saw much o'the countryside – only huge concert halls 'round Europe. 'Course, least they'd have a tour-bus, not Micky's piece o'shit.

Falmouth was always a laugh. No one really knew why. Its wide avenues were all lined with retirement bungalows an' palm trees, houses which had sea views if y'craned y'neck out o'back bedrooms, an' a lot o'posh lookin' hotels for visitors with money. It seemed like most o'the Tory population o'Cornwall lived there – y'knaw, fuckers who could afford t'

Alan M. Kent

buy their groceries from *Marks an' Spencer* an' who had cocktail parties on their yachts along the River Fal.

That said, Falmouth did have a set o'good pubs, which were always raging t'crawl around. As part o'the new Combined Universities o'Cornwall, it also had a College o'Arts which attracted anyone in Cornwall or the south-west o'England with an artistic bent – or who felt like bumming around for a few years paintin' abstracts o' seagulls an' boats. Thaas' why the streets o'Falmouth had two types – old Conservatives or else pierced scruffy bastards – as opposed t'Camborne an' Redruth – where y'had two different types – those fuckers on the dole, an' those almost on the dole.

It was an a'right place t'go though. Charlie knew the scene – a few pints in *The Grapes*, then up *t'The King's Head* – over *t'The Bosun's Locker* – then inta' *The Pirate*. On the way, y'might go down t'the harbour-front an' listen t'the flags of the yachts blowin' an' their rigging and masting, tinkling in the wind, or else look over to the shipyard where some Lithuanian-registered supertanker would be in fur a refit. Inside the houses, y'could imagine people reading *The Daily Telegraph*, an' admirin' the pictures o'Maggie Thatcher on their walls, or they'd be havin; an all-night smokin' party. Charlie had been t'one o'they about a year ago. He remembered it because one o'the blokes there arrived with a black binbag full o'grass. It was like that in Falmouth. Tory as fuck – but y'had all this subversion goin' on under their noses.

'This is goin' t'be bad,' went Neil. 'The gig's goin' t'be full o'students all discussin' post-modernism an' the merits o'Terry Frost...'

'Na,' went Charlie. 'They'll be here for a good time – t'forget all o'that bollocks... just the same as anyone else...'

'They'n still be pretentious bastards though...'

Neil was unconvinced, but Charlie an' Bev knew the scene. A lot o'them were just the same as they were. They wanted something more out o'life, wanted t'express themselves. That was one reason there were loads o'bands goin' 'round in Falmouth. Most o'them were bandwagon hoppers though – doin' whatever was the latest trend. Falmouth was that kind o'a place. It was arty-farty. It y' weren't doin' raiku pottery, y'were printin' up flyers fur raves.

Proper Job, Charlie Curnow!

'Remember boy Laity,' went Neil. 'He went College down here didn' a?'

Charlie knew of 'un. He'd been a couple o'years ahead o'them at school. He'd been brilliant at art.

'He had t'leave didn' a? Spent a couple o'years up Bodmin fur doin' too much speed. His da found 'un in his flat with all these weird pictures on the wall... He still idn' right now... He reckons he didn' sleep fur a month, he was that high...'

The first bit was true. Boy Laity had been in the mental-health care facility at Bodmin. Charlie knew it was drug-related. It was a fuckin' shame though. He'd prob'ly have done them a good album cover...

They pulled up outside *The Pirate*. It was now painted a kind o'pukey blue colour all over. Y'cudn' miss it fur miles. The place had used t'be where the sea-farers o'old had come in fur a drop o'rum before facin' the Bay of Biscay, but when most o'the docks an' shipyard went in the 1970s, the owners had t'find a new use fur it. So generally now, they had bands there most days of the week. There were two kinds – those who were climbin' up rock 'n' roll's perilous ladders – an' those who had a gake 'round up top, an' were now headin' back down. Often it was the case that the more indie y'were, the more cred y'had fur playin' somewhere like *The Pirate*. It wudn' 'zactly *The Cavern* or *The Marquee*, but it 'ud do.

Inside, it had a bar runnin' up one side, an' then a stage the other end. There were only a few tables at the shipyard end. The owners had prob'ly seen sense as the umpteenth set o'chair an' table got broken by some mosher fallin' over. All y'had now, was bare floorboards awaitin' the student hordes. The good thing about *The Pirate* was that it was a proper venue. They had a proper place for the mixing desk an' in-house lights. They even had a changin' room, which in the good tradition o' tourin', every band who'd passed through, had signed – givin' others abuse at the same time. There was that air o'sweat t'the place, which told the story o'a thousand gigs. Standin' on the stage there, was different than other pubs an' clubs, because y'knew others had trod those same boards.

Break the System wudn' there yet.

'I s'pause they're so hardcore, they only need half an hour t'set up,' went Micky.

It was a problem, because they cudn' do anything – except load in their gear. There was nothun' t'do, 'cept have a drink an' gaze at the ceiling, where dozens o' old posters had been pinned – showin' who'd played there before.

After a while, Bev's contact arrived. It turned out he was called Steve Spry. Yeah, he was a student an' that – he was repeatin' his A-Level art, havin' fucked it up the year before – but he also had fingers in other pies.

'Me an' a mate are doin' a festival down The Lizard this summer. We've got the site an' the license sorted out. I need more bands though. Y'interested?'

He moved fast this boy. He hadn' even seen them play yet. He didn' seem t'care either.

'It's goin' t'be massive...' Steve spoke like he'd just walked out o'an all-nighter.

'We've got The Levellers headlining – I hope...'

'Cool,' said Neil. 'It sounds good...'

'Whaas' the fee though?' yipped up Yak.

'We'n negotiate that,' went Steve, 'but y'have t'think o'the exposure sometimes don't ya – know what I mean like?'

That meant there was no money.

'Can we get back to 'ee?' said Charlie. 'What date is it?'

'Weekend of June 30th... a couple o'weeks after Glastonbury. We reckon a lot o' people'll come down t'Cornwall then...'

Micky came over.

'What time are we on?' he asked Steve.

'About ten-ish I reckon...'

'So – does yer brother's band want t'set up before us?'

'Yeah,' went Steve. 'They're on their way... I just spoke t'them...'

Steve was hyper. His legs were moving up an' down with energy; his hands seemingly to continuously roll a joint. He had that feel that he was permanently larging it up; his eyes full o'enthusiasm. Micky recognised the signals.

'The cunt's on speed,' he said surreptitiously. 'I can tell...'

'I appreciate you guys doing this gig. Really like... 'cause these other fuckers let me down, an' the deal here is y'got t'offer two bands. They expect it like...'

Steve took another drag of his joint an' exhaled. The smell o'dope wafted around the pub.

Proper Job, Charlie Curnow!

'Heard your stuff,' he went, 'on *Pirate*... Sounds like you fuckers know where y'going... Got any management have ya?'

They all began t'see where he was coming from.

'Yeah, we're sorted,' said Bev. 'We've got someone lined up...'

'Well, 'cause if y'haven't like, I know the very man... He's the one who got a lot o'the bands here sorted...'

It soon became clear that Steve Spry was full o'bullshit. He was perhaps the first they'd encounter; he wudn' be the last. When *Break the System* finally arrived, he went over t'help them in with some cases o'gear. Yak took the opportunity t'lighten things up.

'Steve Spry – what are you on?'

Everyone laughed. Bev apologised. She didn' realise he was such an asshole. All was well though. It was comin' up fur seven o'clock, an' soon they had another gig t'play.

* * * * *

Charlie had heard o'this sort o'thing. In most o'the interviews he'd ever read, it was t'do with the mix, the quality of the PA, or how long a band could have on-stage. This time it was about room on the stage. But then y'expected that if y'were a support band. *Break the System* were full-on wankers. Not only did they take two hours t'set up, they brought along their fuckin' full production – a load o'gear they didn' need. *Balance* had t'hang 'round fur them. Micky was doing his fuckin' nut. He looked like he was about t'rip someone's head off. Everyone else just sat an' drank – 'cept Yak an' the boy Spry who seemed t'hit it off a'right.

No one could do anything though. *Break the System* had their own merchandising stall – two types o't-shirt an' a mini-album fur sale. They'd knocked it out up the Sawmill studios near Fowey. Their lead singer – a guy called Jez – had paid fur it hisself. Their gear wudn' bad. Y'knaw, it wasn't completely fuckin' naff, but on the other hand, it wudn' great either. The artwork on the album was shite an' the production didn' do any o'their songs justice. Charlie made a mental note not t'go down that route.

'Thaas' cause they think they're hard,' went Micky. 'Y'knaw – they've got that Punk's Not Dead ethos. They prob'ly reckon

193

Alan M. Kent

havin' a production that sounds like it was recorded in a tin bucket is fuckin' right on...'

'All yours mate,' went Jez after they'd finished sound-checking.

An audience had started to arrive. They'd have t'work hard t'have everything read by ten.

'Careful!' said the *Break the System* drummer, as Yak set up his own kit stage left.

Jez and Steve Spry were socialising, kissin' an' huggin' people as they came in. The cunts seemed t'knaw everyone – like it was their own party or somethun'. A few o'the crowd had *Break the System* t-shirts on.

Micky was havin' trouble sorting out their sound. There was a dodgy connection somewhere as well. He'd noted it earlier in the day at *Tyacks*, but it seemed t'have a mind of its own down here.

'Check the leads can 'ee?' he shouted t'everyone. It was half-past nine an' he hadn' even got his own gear set up yet.

Break the System had gone inta' the changin' room t'put on make-up an' get changed inta' their stage-gear.

'Hardcore my ass-'ole,' went Micky. 'They're like Mötley-fuckin'-Crüe...'

''Es,' said Neil. 'Boy Jez reckons he's Marilyn Manson...'

Charlie tested his mike. He viewed the crowd who were in. He didn' knaw how they'd react t'their blues rock. He just hoped they'd had a listen t'Led Zep once in their life. Then he spotted a thumbs up from the back o'the room. He peered through the smoke. Fuckin' right on – it was boy Bluett from *Tyacks* with some o'this maates. Kelv an' Mel were in an' all. How the fuck she'd got past security, Charlie would never knaw.

He felt nervous. This wudn' your average pub audience who freaked out t' 'Paranoid' every Saturday after enough pints o'Skinners. People here knew their music. It 'ud have t'be cool, or they'd die a death. They'd never play there again.

'A'right lads,' went Steve. 'Everything okay like?'

'Fine,' said Charlie, even though it wasn't.

He cudn' doubt hisself – not now though. He hadn't worked this hard t'blaw it all. Besides, his voice was in good shape t'day. No fear, he told himself, as if he was about t'surf the

Proper Job, Charlie Curnow!

breakers off St Agnes in the middle o'December.

Tonight was a different set. They'd play more o'their own material. If they didn' like it, they knew where the door was.

'Y'ready?' asked Charlie.

Micky was still makin' a few adjustments.

'As we've not sound-checked, I've just left everything the same as earlier...'

Charlie found a space on the stage. There was fuck-all room. There'd be no Roger Daltry-style microphone swings. Micky being a tall bastard, had t'almost crouch, else his head would have gone through the ceiling tiles. Steve Spry did all the introductions. He was still shakin' when he took the mike an' spouted the usual bollocks.

'Good eve-ning Pir-ate. Great couple o'bands fur you tonight. Later, we've got *Break the System*...'

Pause fur wild clappin' an' whistling.

'...but first up, a new band for you – called *Balance*. Give them a big welcome...'

It was cheesy as fuck, but at least a few people clapped.

They went inta' 'Making Faces'.

'OH SO DON'T BE MAKING FACES AT ME....'

Charlie belted it out – every inch o'Jimmy Pengelly's coachin' goin' inta' it.

He'd just about got through the first verse, an' boy Bluett an' his crowd were out there, boogie-ing 'round, pogoing an rockin' their asses off. Jess an' Ally got out an' joined them. It looked good. Y'know how it is with support bands. Most o'the time, if you're havin' a pint, y'just let the sad fuckers get on with it – an' y'have a yap – only shoutin' more – above the din. Gradually though, those near the bar started turnin' t'the stage an' watchin'. A few other pissed-up boys went out. Most o'these weren't students. They were easin' off fur their minute – checkin' out *Balance's* coolness rating.

Neil's riffs were crunchin' in like Godzilla stompin' on the place, an' Yak an' Bev ere givin' the bottom end that feel-it-in-yer-breast-bone power. It was just like it should be – proud, arrogant and sweaty, like you were the only ones ever who'd the bollocks to give it a go.

'A new song for ya,' went Charlie. 'A song called 'Dons Meyn'...'

Alan M. Kent

A few puzzled expressions came over the crowd.

'It's Cornish,' he said over Neil's introductory power chords.

Yak's mate over Baripper had sorted that out fur them. It was Bev's idea – after their visit t' the Nine Maidens.

'Come on,' went Charlie. I wanna' see more people out here...'

Charlie was doin' it tonight. He had that 'rock-star aura' to 'un – that indiscernible quality that sorted the sheep from the goats in the world o'music.

Boy Bluett an' his crowd were covered in sweat by now, but lookin' as though they were lovin' every minute of it. Christ, they were even tryin' t'sing along t'the words. More people left their pints at the bar. It got so more people heard them outside, an' came in to have a gake at what was on.

He had them in his hands now. That was it with gigs. Once y'had them involved, everything was unstoppable. Everything was focused, correct, and in place.

After an hour, *The Pirate* wanted more, but they had t'get off. *Break the System* wudn' happy. This was s'paused t'be their fuckin' audience. What the fuck did they think they were doin'? It wudn' said, but it was thought. Their roadie was pulling out the leads o'their gear an' lowerin' it off the stage.

'Y'need t'give me a hand,' he moaned, 'or else I'll just chuck it onta' the floor...'

He had instructions not t'be helpful. Charlie had met the type – all fuckin' access-all-areas passes an' a hairy ass.

'Careful,' went Micky t'him.

By the time *Break the System* went on, a lot o'the energy from earlier had been dissipated. Those in *The Pirate* had already had a good work-out. They'd just watch the headliner an' have a few more beers.

'Y'were fuckin' brilliant,' went Steve. 'Sure I can't give y' the name o'that guy I know?'

'Naw – you'm a'right,' said Charlie, wiping the sweat off his face.

'You'll do The Lizard though won't ya?'

'Sure,' said Charlie. He gave Speedy Steve his number.

'I'll be in touch,' he went.

Charlie introduced Michael Bluett and his crowd t'the rest o'them.

Proper Job, Charlie Curnow!

'Excellent night,' he shouted above *Break the System*. 'Your web-site's got your gigs on it hasn't it? Kelvin was telling me about it....'

'Yeah,' went Bev. 'He's set it up fur us...'

'Listen – you interested in doin' a gig fur Surfers Against Sewage... They got this ball comin' up over Perranporth...'

'Definitely,' said Charlie.

It had been a night o'triumph all told. They'd only got fifty quid, but the manager wanted them back.

'Good band,' he had said. 'Better than some of the rubbish we get...'

It was nearnly one o'clock by the time they'd loaded up the van. Jez was havin' a word with Steve. He didn' look happy, an' kept pointin' outside, t'Micky's van.

'Got a problem have 'ee?' went Micky.

'Yeah – you cunts,' said Jez.

Micky was about t'get the first punch in, but Charlie held him back.

'Leave it...'

'Yeah – okay,' said Micky. 'They obviously can't handle being blown away...'

Charlie didn' like this kind o'aggravation. For one thing, it was so fuckin' unproductive. Every band in Cornwall – they were all in it together: there shudn' be this kind o'aggro. For another, it was too much like home.

He hoped he'd calmed Micky down, but it didn' stop Micky yellin' a final bit o'abuse at Jez as they drove away. Charlie feared the next time their paths might meet.

'They're nothun',' went Micky. 'We're in a different league...'

Charlie hoped so. He knew the game was gettin' bigger by the second.

* * * * *

Micky yanked on the handbrake. They'd stopped at *Zippy's* – a burger van y'found in a layby in Pool every Friday an' Saturday night. It catered for those lookin' fur late-night cuisine that wudn' too dear, an' had a lot o'grease. The woman who ran it was skinny as fuck, but she was hard as nails you. She was used t'dealin' with pissed-up assholes on their way home from

197

Twilight. The story went that the only reason she had a newer van was because last year, some boys decided t' 'eave the old one down a ditch by Barncoose hospital. The road was scattered with baps an' pieces o'processed cheese.

Still, work was work, an' she was throwin' out the double-cheeseburgers t' a group o'boys on a stag-night.

'Aeh? There's no BSE in these fuckers is there missus?'

''Course there fuckin' is,' she went. 'Wudn' sell anything less...'

The boy chomped down on the bun all the same.

She scraped the hot-plate for the next order.

'Seven cheeseburgers an' two veggie burgers please,' went Micky.

Jess was a veggie these days, like him.

Everyone was in high spirits. The gig had been the dog's bollocks.

'Y'want relish on these?' went the burger woman.

'Yeah – 'ave it on,' said Micky.

As the onions fried, they noticed a figure stankin' down the road. It was the stripper from up *Institute*.

'Clifford boy – whaas' on ?' went Charlie.

'Been *Twilight* 'ebn I,' said Clifford.

'Did y' pull then?' asked Neil.

Bev put her arms around Charlie, but she had no need t'worry.

'Thaas' where I'm goin' now...' said Clifford. 'I'm goin' t'see 'er...'

This was a typical fuckin' Cliff manouevre. He could be full o'shit sometimes. It was prob'ly made-up.

'You knaw her,' went Cliff t'Charlie.

'Do I?'

''Es, Karen... y'knaw... Met her down *Twilight*...'

Well, there 'twas.

That maid didn' seem t'mind what she shagged. First the three different faathers o'her kids, then his da, now Clifford.

'Make sure you'm bagged up boy!' shouted Yak.

Charlie knew that prob'ly wudn' happen. She wanted more kids. That had been the reason she'd gone lookin' fur someone else.

'I'll be a'right,' shouted back the stripper.

Proper Job, Charlie Curnow!

"Ee's prob'ly got his belt off already,' joked Yak as they bit inta' their burgers.

Charlie laughed, but he didn' find it funny t'all.

* * * * *

Back on the estate, the police were out. Someone had reported an XR3i stolen from their back-garden an' the coppers reckoned they'd gone joy-riding up the A30.

'Boy Dingle 'gain I 'spect,' went Yak.

Charlie knawed of 'un. He was fifteen, Didn' have any license of course, an' he'd already been done twice. His mind went back t'some graffiti he'd read outside the remains o'Crofty: 'Cornish lads are fishermen and Cornish lads are miners too, but when the fish and tin are gone, what are the Cornish boys to do?' The answer t'that seemed t'be t'go joyriding. Y'cudn' blame 'um. 'Twas the only thing they could do.

Micky dropped off Yak, and Steve an' Ally, then reversed the van inta' one o'the parkin' bays. It was so late, it felt early. Y'could hear the first birds reeling off their dawn chorus. It was a clear view over the Great Flat Lode. There was no fog or mist for a change.

Charlie wanted t'enjoy the moment, drink in the success o'the Trevithick Day's gigs.

'Let's walk fur a bit...'

He pulled at Bev's arm.

'Charlie – I should be gettin' back...'

She looked over at where her Fiat Uno was parked.

'Na... come on...'

Micky an' Jess let them be – an' quietly opened the back-door. Ronnie's car was still 'round the front. Jess' ma had let 'un stay over. A few bottles o'Skinners lay on the table – and they saw the remains of a couple o'gin and tonics on the mantel-piece.

Bev had relented. Sometimes Charlie was unstoppable. Tonight, it was like a film. The moon was up, an' after the smoke of *The Pirate*, the air felt wonderful in her lungs.

'You're not saying much,' she said t'Charlie.

'I dun't want to,' he said smiling an' lookin' at her.

They climbed over a stile and headed out onto the moor.

Alan M. Kent

When Charlie found the right patch o'moss an' heather, he sat down.

'Lie with me Bev,' he went. 'This won't go in the authorised biography – I promise...'

Bev lay down. The stillness was unbelievable, the force between them in complete equilibrium. There'd be no return now; no swing back or forth. In the darkness, they found each other's lips. Neither of them had much experience, but it was amazin' how good it felt t'put inta' operation everythin' you'd been fantasisin' about fur the past few months. Y'wanted it all at once somehow, like life wudn' goin' t'give 'ee enough time. Y'wanted it like this – a fumble o'fucking, an' sucking an' fondling. Charlie softly caressed each o'her tits – feelin' the nipples an' the tiny goosebumps on them which were bristling in the breeze. She'd gone fur his cock, running her fingertips 'round his bell-end – makin' it jerk an' strain. Those fingertips that put down those bass-lines were now strokin' 'un so lovingly that he forgot everything. Forgot the band. Forgot the estate. Forgot his family. Forgot his life. Forgot the fuckin' lot.

He had t'check himself as he moved t'stroke her clit. Was it for real? That she'd want t'be like this with 'ee – Charlie Curnow. It was like he'd won the lottery or somethun'. Maybe this was the way everyone felt – why people were always doin' it. All o'this goin' through his mind the way it does; the way it does when Bev asked 'un what he was thinking – an' the only thing y'can say is 'nothun''.

But she was down on him now, coatin' his knob with saliva an' runnin' her tongue along its edge, an' she was shudderin' at his hands. In a fumble, Charlie unwrapped a Durex an' pulled it on'; the wrapper blowing across the heather. She straddled him an' after a bit o'delicious sliding an 'slippin', she had him inside o'her. Neither of 'um lasted long. It didn' matter. Y'wanted it t'be like that; like two wild animals. Their panting was all 'ee could hear across the Great Flat Lode. It was funny as fuck really, an' they collapsed in laughter; their breathing still deep. Charlie wondered whether the flooded level an' adits underneath them had felt any o'that. They'd certainly churned up the moss an' crushed the heather. Bev brushed the tiny crushed flowers from his back.

As he tied a knot in the johnny, the two o'them looked back

Proper Job, Charlie Curnow!

t'the estate. Dawn was highlightin' the eastern edge, an' turnin; the white pebble-dash a kind o'orange. Y' cudn' imagine anything more beautiful. Well, y'probably could, but it had t'do.

Y'didn' want t'ask it, but y'had to.

'How was that?'

Bev looked over at the Durex laid out on the heather, an' nibbled his ear.

'That,' she said, 'was a proper job, Charlie Curnow!'

'Yeah?' asked Charlie.

'Honest.'

They walked back across the moor t'the estate. All told, it 'adn been a bad day.

* * * * *

They woke up in the middle of the afternoon. The football was on downstairs an' music was on in Jess's room.

'What are 'ee goin' t'tell yur da?' asked Charlie. 'Y'had yur mobile switched off an' all.'

'Something,' said Bev. 'I'll think of something. I'll say I had a drink an' stayed at Ally's...'

'He'll love that, t'knaw y'slept in the house where the siege took place...'

'Probably better that than here... at this point in time...'

She was right. Even so, it took 'un down a notch or two. He wanted Bev's parents t'like 'un. He'd resolved t'bare it out though. Maybe – when the money started comin' in, they might relent an' see things a bit differently.

There was a lot t'explain to his ma as well. She'd obviously seen his da; she wudn' knaw about 'ee an' Karen though – an' then, there was Bev. Could he inflict his ma an' Ronnie on her? Whatever way he thought about it, 'twas a no-win situation. Laas' night and the whole o'Trevithick Day really had been a proper job. Things could easily turn shite again though.

He scratched his bollocks; he could still feel the energy o'laas' night there. It was a good feelin'. He didn' want it t'go away. Charlie threw on some shirts an' a t-shirt an' went downstairs. Micky had gone down Pool Market as usual. His ma was watering her indoor plants. Ronnie was watching the football.

'A'right?' went Charlie.

Alan M. Kent

''Es,' said Ronnie.

'You were out late wudn' 'ee?' asked his ma.

''Es. Jess told 'ee how it went 'ave she?'

'Yes – she said you done well down Falmouth.'

Charlie followed his ma inta' the kitchen. He didn' want Ronnie t'overhear.

'Did 'ee stay here laas' night then?'

His ma blushed, like her secret was out.

'Who are you t'ask that?'

'Just wondered...'

'Well, mind yer own business...'

'Y'knaw me da's split up with Karen dun't 'ee? Y'did see 'un yes'day didn' 'ee?'

His ma assumed an air of busy-ness, like she didn' care.

'I saw the silly shit,' she said. ''Twas proper embarrassing... 'Ee all three sheets t'the wind, comin' up t'us like that... 'Ee ought t'be bleddy locked up...'

'He's stayin' with Clare...'

'Over *Institute*!? Well, thaas' the best plaace fur 'un. He d'almost live there already...'

Not an iota o'concern fur his da could be extracted from her. It looked like Ronnie was about t'be a permanent feature.

In the living-room, Ronnie had changed back the channel from the umpteenth family viewing o'*Lord of the Rings*; perhaps so 'ee could hear 'um better, instead o'orcs grunting. *Spotlight on Westminster* was on BBC1 – about more Cornish protests. Someone had thrown paint over the Government minister responsible for the South-West. Traffic had been held up on the Tamar Bridge again.

'Bev stayed laas' night,' Charlie said.

'What, here...?'

'Yeah...'

'She still here?'

'Yeah...'

'In your room?'

'Yeah...'

''Ent 'ee goin' t'bring her down then?'

His ma knew she was from Truro, from a bettermost kind o'crowd. She'd start t'talk cut-up, an' tidy up with more urgency than ever...

Proper Job, Charlie Curnow!

The good thing was, his ma cudn' say anything about Charlie's behaviour, because o'her own. In a way, it cudn' have been better timing. After Bev had had a shower, she came downstairs.

'A'right love?' went his ma, giving Bev no time t'answer. 'Treatin' of 'ee right I hope idn'a?'

His ma had a slightly tarnished view o'males, but it didn' stop Ronnie helpin' himself t'cake from the pantry.

'I'm fine Mrs Curnow... honest...'

They had t'go through the introducing the potential in-law stuff with his ma. If Jess could do it with Micky, then surely he could with Bev. She'd just need carefully steerin' off the topic o'marriage an' babies.

'I'm like you,' said his ma t'Bev. 'I wished I hadn't settled down s'soon... an' done more with me life... but thaas' the way it was back then...'

Jesus, Charlie was thinking. His ma was speaking like she'd got married in the 1880s instead o'the 1980s. But then he reckoned that actually not a lot had changed. Bev 'ud be different though. She had it written all over her.

Truth o'it was, that afternoon, they'd like t'have had another shag, t'make sure laas' night hadn' been a one-off. There wudn' time though. Her faather had already phone, an' his ma had helped them cover-up where she'd been stayin'. She was good that way. Bev had t'go though. He'd see her next on Tuesday – an' that seemed a fuckin' decade away. Least his emotions had been turned up another notch. Maybe it was time t'write.

'Hear Dingle got done laas' night,' went one o'the tackers t' Charlie.

In his hand he had a copy o'*Razzle*, an' was tearin' out pages o'naked girls fur the others widn' t' snigger over.

'Turned the car over up Scorrier... one o'the coppers crashed an' all...'

'Where's a now?' asked Charlie.

'In Camborne police station... Want one o'these slappers do 'ee?' said the tacker handin' 'un a centrefold o'a blonde.

'Na – y'a'right boys,' said Charlie. 'You enjoy her...'

The tackers went up the road, stickin' torn-out pages under the windscreen wipers o'cars. Charlie went in t'write more songs.

Alan M. Kent

'A'right?' went Ronnie.
''Es,' said Charlie.

* * * * *

It felt like Cornwall was a colony o'Australia these days; almost like y'expected a bleddy kangaroo or a koala bear t'pop up from behind a gorse bush. Y'already had Aboriginal music an' fuckin didgeridoos fur sale in all o'the New Age shops, an' then y'had cunts from over Portreath full o'shite like 'Chargin' waves man' an' 'Awesome barrel' when really the spoke just the same as the next cunt from Cornwall. It was all an act, like the way they had their hair bleached blonde, an' got the right kind o'tan t'make it look like they'd just strolled off Bondi Beach, instead o' from over Stithians. If they weren't body-boarding in the sea in mid-November, they were out servicing their VW Beetles or camper vans. And if that wudn' bad enough, every year brought in another bunch o'tossers from the South East who reckoned they were harder an' better than anyone else – an' then had t'be fuckin' rescued. Y'could find 'um wherever y'went – St Ives, Gwithian, Portreath, Newquay, Watergate Bay and Polzeath, the cunts were there with their wet suits undone, showin' off their muscles an' playing the Red Hot Chili Peppers. Charlie didn' go much on 'um.

Only thing was, y'had t'break inta' the scene. There was money there. An' it didn' matter what y'said, even though half o'Cornwall was walkin' 'round in 'Quicksilver' t-shirts an' 'Headworx' sweatshirts, an' wudn' have a clue how t'even carry a surfboard, let alone ride Atlantic waves, surf culture was fuckin' in. Y'cudn' get away from 'ut. Even the tackers on the estate wore rip-off 'O'Neil' shorts an' had surfin' style wallets on chains fur their money. It had come a long way from boys comin' home from the First World War an' comin' inta' Portreath on bits o'wood they'd pinched from up United Downs.

'They're all arrogant bastards,' went Micky. 'They all reckon they're fuckin' world champions in the makin'... Half the cunts dun't even go out. They just hang 'round t'look cool...'

It was gettin' lighter in the evenings, an on Monday at Perranporth, the usual temporary village o'campers an' vans

could be seen on the beach car park. The Perranporth Surf Life
Saving Club had lessons goin' on down on the beach, while the
more pluckier cunts were out in the evenin' water – mad bastards.

'They're rich an' all,' said Micky, as they stanked across the
beach.

The two o'them were on a mission. Boy Bluett had phoned
them up an' put 'em inta' contact with a bloke from Surfers
Against Sewage. They were the crowd who protested about too
many turds an' tampons in the sea, an' wore World War Two
gas masks while they were surfin' t'make their point. They had
regular fund-raising balls. This year's was s'paused t'be at *The
Watering Hole* on Perranporth Beach. In summer, the place sold
ice creams an' rented out boards; in winter, they catered fur the
hard-weather surfers. Between seasons, like this, they just tried
t'make a bit – same as everyone else.

'It'll be a nightmare gettin' our gear out here,' said Charlie.

Micky agreed. Y'had t'cross a stream – via a footbridge – then
walk across half a mile o'beach.

Behind them, y'could see all the shit jerry-building o'the
town; hotels 'eaved up on the cliff-side, now findin' it hard t'attract anybody besides the 'youth' market, then loads o'bungalows that looked like a serious fuckin' accident o'plannin' – the
same way Trelawny was. Then there was the town itself – fulla'
shit shops sellin' shells an' other tack fur tourists; else newer an'
better polyurethane boards at cut-prices.

Charlie felt out o'place. That was the thing: up in England,
every cunt reckoned if y'lived in Cornwall y'lived in some
quaint fuckin' thatched cottage that overlooked the beach.
That wudn' true t'all. Most o'the Cornish had been pushed in-
land – inta' the fuckin' ghettos. Only cunts from up the line
could afford t'buy anything with a sea view. Charlie reckoned
tourists had never been t'Troon. The fuckers hardly made
Camborne, let alone anywhere else. 'Twas sad you, but thaas'
the way 'twas.

Large waves were breakin' now. Fifty-odd black wetsuits
could be seen in the ocean, all waitin' t'catch that perfect ride.
'Round past Chapel Rock an' Droskyn Point, y'could see the
spray being flicked off the cliff. Why any cunt wanted t'get out
in that Charlie 'ud never understand.

Still, that wudn' stop 'um from keyin' inta' the surfin' scene.
A boy called Greg met them. He had all the lingo o'the cunts
down Portreath, plus the regulation blonde bob o'hair. He was
prob'ly from Lanner.

'Come in guys,' he went. 'Y'want a beer.'

Greg gave them a couple o'Budweisers.

'Here's the deal – we need a band for the ball. The word is,
that you guys kick butt an' we want you...'

'No problem,' went Charlie. 'Whaas' the fee?'

'Hundred an' fifty – but if we sell more than two hundred
tickets... there might be a bonus... It depends on how many
y'pack in...'

'Okay... sounds good...'

He gave them the date.

'Can you guys play from say nine to twelve? Is that cool?'

'Cool,' said Charlie, succumbing to the lingo himself.

'Y'got any posters?'

Micky handed him a newly-printed bagful of publicity.

'Do what you want with it...'

'We'll have y' in the papers an' that as well...'

Sam Polglase was still working locally. He'd fuckin' love that.

On their way back across the beach, Charlie an' Micky
reviewed the gigs coming up. Neither one said it, but things
were beginning to hot up. They'd been asked t'go back to *The
Pirate* again, then there was the chance o'supportin' some indie
fuckers down *The Waterfront*. Neil had lined them up a gig at
The Victoria Bars in Newquay, an' Charlie'd got a night at *St
Austell Band Club*. Fuck, at this rate, they'd need tour t-shirts
printed up. Kelv had received a couple o'inquiries on the net.
Christ, even Clare had said somethun' about havin' 'um back
up *Institute*.

''Ee'n whistle fur that,' went Micky, 'after the way he treated
us before...'

'Too right,' said Charlie.

Back in the car park, their van had been surrounded by a
host o'other campers an' estates. It was gettin' dark, an' many
o'the surfers were back in, dryin' their hair an' towelling
off, posin' with their girlfriends. For Charlie an' Micky, it was
like steppin' inta' another world an' yet it had t'be done.
They'd cracked the Cornish interior; now all they had t'do was

conquer the coast. It 'ud be as easy, an' as powerful as the rip comin' in off the Atlantic.

* * * * *

Neil had spent had evenin' differently. He was back on the twilight shift at *Tesco*. But that morning, he'd been in the witness stand at Truro Crown Court, t' help t'put Markie Phillips down. Ally had given most o'the evidence though. Her ma had spent most o'the session squalin' her eyes out. Markie's defence team had tried hard. Apparently, he was off the crack now and was a reformed character.

Like hell.

The jury knew the score though. They found 'un guilty on enough charges t'put 'un away for a bit. The judge said he wudn' goin' t'tolerate the likes o' 'ee terrorising the innocent people o'Troon, an' he went down fur four years. As Neil stacked the last o'the cans o'value baked beans, he checked again t'see his bollocks were safe.

Funny thing was, in the court next door, was boy Dingle, up for stealing a motor vehicle, dangerous driving, driving without a license, an' driving under the influence o'alcohol. He'd come out with his ma – wearin' his tracksuit bottoms an' a naff polyester collar an' tie off his brother.

'A'right Neil,' he had gone, like he'd just been let out o'a detention or somethun'. He wudn' be sentenced yet though. They were still working on the social worker's reports.

Mel's ma would be up there next week as well. Y' knaw the charge. Y'didn' have t'ask anymore.

Neil reckoned the clerk would be busy that afternoon. Half the letters they'd write would have t' be addressed t'Trelawny. The other half would be t' Social Services. What the fuck was on with this estate? was what the letters asked.

Ally'd prob'ly be in some state back home, but there was nothun' he could do 'bout 'ut now. He'd just get through this shift the best way he could.

* * * * *

The secret buyer who'd been interested in Crofty had pulled

Alan M. Kent

out. The thirty thousand pounds that people had raised t'keep the mine from floodin' had been wasted. The fuckers were turnin' off the pumps tomorra'. If he wudn' pissed already, Charlie reckoned his da would be cryin' his eyes out. His life was bad enough already – without that happenin'. Y'cudn' say people hadn't tried. They'd tried t'save the mine in ways that made coal miners look like softies an' lightweights. But there 'twas. The head-gear was being disassembled, an' water was risin' up through the grizzlies an' levels sure 'nough. *The Environment Agency* would be in next, checking to make sure no poisonous chemicals were leaking out. Charlie's da, an' the rest o'his shift would be at the gates makin' a kind o'last ditch protest that was more like a Methodist funeral. The word now was that the Mine Manager had bought up the last o'the shares. That cunt had been lookin' ahead all along, t'sell off the land an' walk away with a tidy profit. Come to end up, a few boys had even tied themselves t'the cages, t'make sure they wudn' be cut. It hadn't made no difference though. 'Twas goin' – an' thaas' a fact.

In fact, aside from the rugby, since the Trevithick Day gig, nothun' very positive had seemed t'happen for Cornwall. The mine was goin', an there'd be more redundancies at the Creamery down St Earth. Somehow it always felt like Cornwall got the shitty end o'the stick when it came t'any Government money – an' this crowd seemed even worse than the last fuckin' crowd – an' naw mistake. Even the weather 'ud been shite. Come end o'April, y'expected it t'brighten up a bit, an' fur the westerlies t'ease off a bit. Naw chance. Even when Camborne had a few rays o' sunshine, the estate still had a barrage o'fog an' mizzle. Still, thaas' what y'got fur buildin' it in the middle o'a moor.

'Bout the only light at the end o'the tunnel was the fact that Cornwall had beaten Yorkshire again in the County Rugby Championship up Twickenham. An' fur that, y'can read the rest o'England too – these kind o'games are internationals y'knaw. It had been a helleva' win by all accounts. 'Twas a score o'summin' like 25 points t' 7 t' Cornwall. Y'cudn' move for black an' gold rugby jerseys in Camborne an' Redruth the week after. Even the little fuckers on the estate had stopped stoning cars, an' were now wearin' black an' gold, an' chasin' the irregular bounce o'rugby balls in the park. It was a source o'pride a'right – even though there wudn' much else left t'be proud of.

Charlie an' everyone would have gone, but they had other priorities. The Friday before the match, they'd got a gig up east at *St Austell Band Club*; then the Saturday, they were over *Victoria Bars* in Newquay. They were important gigs – generally pullin' in a lot o'punters. *The Cornish Guardian* had done a feature, an' Micky had even wangled them a set on *Pirate FM* t'publicise them. Neil an' Charlie had gone in an' dun' a sort o'unplugged acoustic set. It sounded naff – like some fuckin' thing Eric Clapton would do, but in actual fact, it sounded a'right. It was the kind o'promo real bands did.

'Come on,' went Micky. 'Get yer fuckin' asses in gear – we've got t'get up St Austell yet...'

Charlie an' Neil were enjoyin' their moment o'radio fame outside the station buildin'. The session had been squeezed in between their work schedules an' Micky's ability t'co-ordinate the weekend's touring. He had a mate who lived up Bugle, so they'd be crashin' there overnight, then headin' over t'Newquay tomorra'. Bev needed t'be picked up in Truro next. Things were tight timing-wise.

'Fur fuck's sake, hurry up will 'ee?' went Micky again.

The two o'them had t'almost throw their guitars in the back. Neil was still shutting the back door as Micky spun down the road. Crofty was silent. Everyone looked up at the head-gear. All the graffiti an' posters looked pathetic now. The gates were locked, an' inside the compound nothun' moved. Even the television cameras had gone home. It wudn' a story anymore. Y'cudn' do anything though. Y'wanted to, but y' cudn'. Y'cudn' even find a Cornishman down the bottom of any hole in the world anymore. That was just a story his da said t'make 'ee feel better. Charlie reckoned they might have been quiet goin' up the A30, but they weren't. Jobs like that had long gone for their generation. Yak, Micky an' Neil knew music was the way forward. There wudn' anything else.

Bev got in. Charlie helped her load in her gear an' he saw the curtains twitchin'. It 'ud be her father checkin' up. She was tense. Her exams were comin' up an' she'd been workin' doubly hard durin' the week, so she could play the gigs. Charlie could never fault her. Sometimes, it was like she wanted it even more than he did.

'You okay?' he asked.

'Yeah – 'course,' she replied. 'Just bit tired – that's all...'

Charlie kissed her. He wished they were alone, not crammed in the back with two other farting and swearing assholes.

'How did the *Pirate FM* thing go?' she asked.

'Micky's got a tape...' said Yak.

'Put it on again...' shouted Charlie.

'Yer a fuckin' egomaniac Curnow...' went Micky. 'Here yer go...'

* * * * *

They played the tape all the way from Truro t' St Austell. *The Band Club* had the same feel as *Institute* – only y'could tell they'd spent a bit more money. The committee there wudn' hurting fur a penny or two. Fur a start, there wudn' no teak Formica – an' for another, the stage was very professional – good sockets, an' even a place for the mixing desk. The committee were as you'd expect – old cunts who wudn' knaw a decent band if it fell on their heads. Still, if it brought the 'youngsters' in, an' they drank ale – never mind – s'long as there wudn' no trouble. Charlie was gettin' used t'these types now. Every venue had its own Clare – some fuckwad who wanted t'knaw the ins and outs o'a cow's asshole, an' told 'um what they could and cudn' do.

There was a good crowd in fur them; leastways a good crowd came t'drink down there on Friday nights. There was money in St Austell still. Y' knew it had its charity shops an' problems an' that – not t'mention the fact that the town centre looked like the middle of Baghdad – but it wudn' like Camborne or Redruth. They still had the clay-mining see, an' then factories like Teddingtons out Holmbush way. Twudn' last forever though. One day, they'd be in the same shoes. Not now though, for they boys from Teddingtons drank like fish. They were givin' it stick too. If y'played the right song, they'd buy y' a pint. Christ, some o'the fuckers up there were mad enough t' even dance t'some o'their own songs. Y'had old women out on the floor an' all, dancin' like the fuckin' 1950s had never ended. Next thing, an' some bloke who was assholed had taken the mike off Charlie an' was doing his own version o' 'Stairway to Heaven'. Charlie let 'un carry on 'til he fell over.

'Any requests?'

'Thin Lizzy!'

'Know any Sepultura do 'ee?'

'No.'

'Cannibal Corpse?'

'Who?'

'Bryan Adams?'

'Na...'

'Elvis Presley!'

'Fuck off...'

They don't mind a bit o'abuse either.

Balance do their medley o'rock classics. St Austell goes nutty. The fuckers are dancin' on the tables an' fallin' over some more on the dance floor. Charlie's high-fiving the audience an' tryin' t'prevent a particularly enthusiastic fan from grabbin' the mike off him in the middle o' 'All Right Now'. In the end, he gave her a tambourine an' she's happy; boogieing off 'round the dancefloor, doing a kind of flamenco.

Charlie was even tempted t'do a David Lee Roth 'What-a-crazy-bunch-o'-fuckers-you-people-in-St-Austell-are' type rap. He didn' though. That wudn' his vision for *Balance*. Instead, he told the crowd they could see them tomorra' night, out *Vic Bars*. He hoped he'd see some of them there.

'Fuckin' right,' went one bloke. 'See 'ee tomorra'...'

* * * * *

The crowd was still in Charlie's ears as the closed the door o'the van.

'Got everything 'ave 'ee?' went the steward. 'See you lot again I s'pause...'

Micky'd already arranged another gig for early August.

'Let's head down Crinnis fur a bit,' said Charlie. 'Y'knaw – t'chill out after the gig...'

It was a good idea.

Micky drove them along the plush roads of Carlyon Bay, probably the most expensive housing in Cornwall. The cunts there, all had drives the size of the A30, an' two or three BMWs in them. Sleeping policemen slowed the van down – an' made it hellish fur anyone in the back.

'Slow down y'fucker,' went Neil.

A mike-stand crashed t'the floor.

'Fuckin' hell – you'll have me dead in a minute!'

They began the descent down to the beach. The Coliseum revealed itself as a huge concert venue built near the shore. Everyone from Page an' Plant t'the Who had played there. It was a place o'legends. The stories y'heard. The gigs y'wished you'd been at. The drumsticks y'wished you'd caught. The t-shirts you'd wished you'd bought.

'Me da saw Ritchie Blackmore's Rainbow here in '81...'

No one seemed impressed. The electronic board which had once carried the names o'the musically famous was blank now, an' the vast car parks only held a hundred an' fifty cars fur the fuckers gettin' pissed-up in *Quasar's* nightclub.

'Go 'round the back,' went Charlie.

Micky slowed the van down, an' they passed by the club door. There were the normal gorillas in dinner jackets an' squalin' maids in white dresses with visible panty lines. The back-stage area was dark. None o'the dressing room lights were on. Y'could see the route t'the stage door from the portakabins. Charlie imagined the riders, the tour-bus packed outside, the fans waiting with posters an' albums to sign.

The only lights now were from a couple o'china-clay bulk carriers in the bay – an' those from the taxis outside the club.

No one was really that impressed with it. The others all got out an' went across t'the beach. But Charlie stayed. Even the concrete here had seen the famous walk across it, an' though none o'they fuckers even knew it – or even cared – one day, one day not too distant, they'd be here – playing here. The car park 'ud be packed. They'd do two or three nights an' their world tour 'ud end here. The way they'd played at *The Band Club*, that wudn' impossible at all.

Charlie spun in a circle. In this knowledge, he windmilled his arm like he was Pete-fuckin'-Townsend.

Little did he knaw that developers were movin' in the next week. The whole lot was goin' t'be knocked down and convert-ed inta' luxurious waterside apartments known as *The Beach*.

Proper Job, Charlie Curnow!

* * * * *

They all stank of sweat. It didn' matter though. With gigs like tonight's, y'could forget every thing else. Micky started up the engine an' the van crawled out of Carlyon Bay, up t'Tregonissey Lane End. He was following his mate Trev, from Bugle. They'd be crashin' on his living room floor fur the night.

Y'cudn' see Bugle fur the fog.

'Christ,' went Yak, 'an' I thought Troon was bad...'

Boy Trev had been with Micky over United Downs, 'til he got evicted as well. He'd taken this rented place up Bugle, 'cause 'twas cheap you. He took out a tin, an' a block o'Leb, and started rollin' a large joint. Everyone watched him.

'Wha'?' he went. 'Y'have t'understand – if y'live here, the only escape's fuckin' Methodism – or this... I reckon I chose right...'

It was almost two in the mornin'. The night was still young. The fog swirled and the sweat stank. Then they understood 'zactly what Trev meant.

* * * * *

It was never foggy in Newquay. Leastways, it always seemed that way. It was always sunny. The streets were always filled with smiling children carrying buckets an' spades, and licking Mr Whippy ice creams. The kids were always smiling.

'The fuckers 'ent Cornish then,' went Yak.

'Thaas' harsh,' said Bev.

'Na – it's the truth,' replied Yak.

No one said anything. It must have been.

The road over from Bugle had been easy. Even the A30 wudn' busy. It seemed like half o'Cornwall had gone up t'Twickenham. They'd even seen a few buses go past them laas' night, as they'd packed away. The radio was givin' the usual comprehensive coverage – y'knaw – interviews with the players and the coach, interviews with nutters who'd cooked all the players pasties, an' the normal range o' pre-match shit.

Trev was in the back o'the van. He'd been hitting the Leb hard laas' night an' he'd be feeling the effects o'it for a while. Everyone else was feelin' some o'the effects o'laas night as well.

Alan M. Kent

Good as it was t'crash there, y'always felt shit the next mornin'. The crucial thing Charlie'd found was havin' a toothbrush. If y'could clean your teeth, y'were okay. He reckoned he was gettin' used t'this life-on-the-road-bit. None o'it seemed t'affect Micky at all. Maybe that was because he'd spent all that time on the road before.

In comparison t'the rest o'Newquay – all hotels with shite names like *Manderley* an' *Llawnroc* (thass' Cornwall backwards) – *Vic Bars* was an anathema. It was tucked away behind a designer pub that was *The Central Inn*. If y'were on holiday, y'd prob'ly not even want t'step past *Vic Bars*. Dun't even think 'bout it, if you'm an emmet. It looked the sort o'place where y'd be given a headbutt soon as look at anyone a bit strangely. In that way, it had a lot in common with *The London Inn* back Redruth. Inside, the walls were painted green, an' coated with pictures o'famous rock groups (mainly Motörhead and Hawkwind) an' bits o'motorcycles. The floorboards were bare, an' y'had a stage the size o'your left armpit. Funny thing was, it could get that packed in there on Saturday nights, that they had a video camera up front, relayin' the band t'the rest o'the pub on a set o'television screens.

'You *Balance* are 'ee?' said the landlord.

He was a fuckin' hairy-assed man-mountain, who was a member of the Scorpio's Motorcycle Club, the local Hell's Angels.

'There's yer plugs an' that. You'll be paid at the end. You'n crash here tonight...'

Charlie looked at the pub floor. It was temptin' an' that – but naw, they'd be headin' back tonight.

'What sort o'music do 'ee do?' asked the landlord.

'Rock,' went Charlie. 'Rock.'

'Proper,' said the landlord.

Fuck knaws what would've happened if Charlie had said dance or soul. It was that kind of a place, you.

Time they'd set up, the news had come through that Cornwall had won.

'People'll be up fur it tonight then,' went Neil.

'What 'ee mean?' joked Yak. 'There's no one Cornish left in Newquay...'

He had a point. Most o'the hotel, bunkhouse an' B&B own-

Proper Job, Charlie Curnow!

ers Charlie had ever met weren't Cornish. They'd come from up the line. They stayed in Cornwall once in 1984, an' then decided that they'd found their vocation in life. It was their sons an' daughters they'd be playin' to, tonight.

Newquay began t'wake up again this time o'year. Sometimes, y'could go there in Winter an' not see a soul. 'Twas like the place was in hibernation. Maybe it just needed a rest sometimes from the youths who frequented its streets, who visited its off-licenses, who stayed in its B&Bs, bunkhouses and caravans, who hired its surf-boards an' who danced in its clubs. The summer 'ud bring them all back again.

The usual routine in Newquay was t'do a few o'the pubs, then move on t'one o'the nightclubs – *Sailors*, *Berties* or *Tall Trees*. If y'were lucky y'd catch a decent band in *Vic Bars*. Charlie hoped tonight, that 'ud be them. Their followers were arriving. Boy Bluett was in with his mates, then there was another crowd in from over *Band Club*. These buggers were askin' for t-shirts an' recordings. Charlie had t'explain they weren't ready fur that yet. He'd send them the *Pirate FM* unplugged set though.

A few more people started t'arrive in rugby jerseys. They were the ones who'd watched it on television or heard it on the radio. They were up fur it already. 'Twas only eight o'clock, but the place was packed you. Jess, Ally, Mel an' Kelvin arrived. Ally was lookin' good – like finally, she could forget about what happened. Mel's ma was up this week fur soliciting. Y'cudn' say anything though, an' Mel knew it. She was just gettin' in the bottles of WKDs an' gettin' ready fur a good night out.

Charlie needed a dump. He found a cubicle an' sat down. There was a syringe on the floor.

'Fuckin' hell,' he said to himself, kickin' it aside.

He remembered the Community Liaison Officer at school, tellin' them how bad the drug situation was in Cornwall. Someone out there, in their crowd, was fucked-up bad. As he sat there, he tried t'warm up his voice the way Jimmy Pengelly had told 'un.

'You fuckin' Pavarotti or something?' came a voice from beyond the door.

'You takin' the piss?' asked Charlie.

'Na maate – just havin' one...'

215

Tonight, out there, in the bar, was goin' t'be wild. Just like at *The Pirate*, Charlie was feelin' nervous. What was his problem? This was what he wanted. He mustn't fuck it up – not now.

In five minutes, they were on.

'Good evening Newquay – we are *Balance...*'

Big cheer.

Charlie raised his glass.

'Here's t'the Cornish Rugby team... Cheers!'

Big cheer.

'Hope y'feel the need t'dance tonight...'

Big cheer.

Christ, he felt like Mick Jagger or some other cunt who'd said the like a thousand times. Boy Bluett an' his mates would be down the front early. Neil came in with the first chord, an' they were off; their own brand o'rock as infectious as ever. The blokes who hadn't, as yet, had enough t'drink were noddin' their heads an' the studenty maids at the back were beginning t'swing their hips. Soon, he'd have them eatin' out o'his hand. The surf dudes were arriving now, too cool t'be down the pub early. They were gettin' off on it. Yak was hittin' the drums like he was the reincarnation o'John Bonham, an y'could feel the rumble o'Bev's bass through the television screens in the distant part of the bar.

'Don't fuck it up,' Charlie was sayin' inside his head, t'hisself.

The next o'Neil's swaggerin' riffs eased out an' *Balance* had the crowd by the short an' curlies. It was one o'those kind o'riffs that are monumental, like a kind o' musical Tyrannosaurus Rex stampin' through the streets o'Newquay. Charlie could hear it stretchin' over t'Fistral an' rebounding all the way over t'Porth. The crowd were with them an' Micky's industrial samples were goin' down a treat.

Then Charlie fucked it up. He missed a cue, an' the bridge was terrible – a garbled mess o'notes and noise. Only the band noticed though. Yak made a face at him, but the crowd didn' care at all. Boy Bluett, his mates and the studenty girls were up, an' were being joined by more o'the surfer types.

Could it get any better than this? Y'could fuck-up an' no one cared. When y'could do that, in one sort o'way, y'd really made it..

Proper Job, Charlie Curnow!

'Nice one,' went the landlord. 'That was the business...'
The way he said it made it feel like he was Peter Grant. Maybe the all the NECs and Wembleys of this world were closer than Charlie thought.

* * * * *

A different kind of business awaited Charlie an' Jess when they got back home. The back-bedroom window was open, an' their ma was 'eavin' any kind o'object she could find at their da. He was staggerin' 'round the back-garden dodgin' some of the missiles bein' thrown – a bottle of Domestos, sponges an' the loo brush – an' bein' hit by others. He was kitted out in all his rugby gear, an' had got assholed on the coach up t'Twickenham an' back.
'But I still love 'ee Sally,' he was bawlin'.
'I've told 'ee Tommy – just fuck-off out o'it...'
Why dun 'ee kick out yer lover – whasisname – Ronnie idn' 'ut?'
'Fuck off Tommy, or I'll call the Police...'
'Call the cunts! I dun't care. 'Ee dun't love 'ee the way I do...'
'Thank god you pair are home,' said their ma, as she saw them step out from Micky's van. 'Do somethun' with 'un will 'ee?'
One o'his ma's shoes scat their da a beauty. He went straight down on his ass. The back-door opened. A worried Ronnie Phillips walked out, carryin' a suitcase.
'Thaas' it! Thaas' it! 'Es, 'es... I've had enough... I love 'er – but I can't stick this...'
Their ma stopped throwin' objects from upstairs.
'I'm sorry,' he shouted t'their ma, 'but I can't put up with it anymore. Yer husband's a nutter – an' I've 'ad enough...'
'No! Ronnie! Don't!' shouted his ma.
'Twas like some sort o'love scene from *Poldark* – only 'twas half-one in the fuckin' mornin'.
'Yeah – yer a'right Ronnie,' said Charlie.
'Na – 'tis a bleddy madhouse here. Yer ma's a good woman an' that, but I dun't have t'put up with this...'
'You sure?'
''Es...'

Alan M. Kent

Ronnie was in his car an' away t'go. His ma was upstairs cryin' her eyes out. Jess went up t'comfort her.

'Where y' stayin' da?' asked Charlie.

'Over Clare's... but I wanted t'see yer moother. Honest, I still love her. Y'knaw that slag Karen – she's off with Clifford Mellow. Of all the fuckin' twats... him... Did y'knaw that?'

They did, but they said they didn'.

He was singin' now.

'HOOWAY! HOOWAY! HOOWAY! CORN-WALL! CORN-WALL! CORN-WALL!'

'What shall we do with 'un?' went Micky.

Charlie looked at his caravan.

'Oh no...' said Micky.

'Sorry mate – it's the only place. Clare wun't have him now... an' he wun't be stayin' here...'

His da was on a line o'advice, the way the Cornish are, when they're pissin' their pants.

'I tell 'ee boy. Bein' in a band's the best thing y'oun do... When I seen that mine close I said t'myself, thaas' the best thing he'n do...'

Like fuck.

'If y'spew Tommy, here's a bowl,' went Micky.

'I won't,' said Charlie's da. 'I'm just happy Cornwall won fur a change...'

'Me too,' said Charlie. 'Now, get some sleep will 'ee?'

* * * * *

'What d'ee reckon?' went Micky.

He rolled up the sleeve of his sweatshirt. Underneath was a pad of cotton wool, taped with a bandage to his bicep. Carefully, he lifted the pad away.

Everyone peered at his arm.

'What is it?' went Yak.

'It's fuckin' neo-tribal 'ent it?' said Micky, admiring his beautiful new tattoo.

A perfectly executed black band of sharp spirals ran around the upper half of his arm. The skin was red and looked sore where the needle had punctured the surface again and again.

'Where did 'ee get 'ut done?' asked Charlie.

Proper Job, Charlie Curnow!

'Over Redruth...'

'How much?'

'Fifty quid...'

'Me ma'll go spare,' went Jess.

Charlie looked at it again. Actually, it looked pretty good. Looked like something the Red Hot Chili Peppers or The Prodigy might have. At least it didn' look like the fuckin' lash-up o'a rose his da had on his arm. He'd had panels put in fur the date of when he an' Charlie's ma got married – but had never got 'round t'finishin' of it off. A lot o'the boys down Crofty had tats – the usual range o'naked women, swallows an' roses. One or two had 'Made in Cornwall' inscribed on their asses – but this, this thing o'Micky's was in a different class.

'Did 'ut hurt?' asked Jess pressing the design gently.

'Na,' said Micky. 'Not really – only the first few times – then y'get used to it...'

It was the classic tattoo answer. It was what y'said. Charlie'd heard it over *Institute* many a time.

'I reckon we should all get one,' Micky went on, '- if yer in the band like, t' show sort o'unity...'

'Fuck off,' t' went Neil. 'I 'ent gettin' that done...'

Bev was more interested. Least she understood it all.

'I think it's alright... There's a renaissance going on y'know. I mean it's not on the fringe anymore is it...?'

Half the fuckers didn' knaw what renaissance meant, let alone contemplate the revival of modern primitivism, but most o'them said 'Yeah' anyway.

'Got this done as well...' announced Micky.

He pulled his sweatshirt up over his head, exposing the upper half o'his torso.

'Ah... no...' said Neil.

He put his hand in an' carefully flicked Micky's new nipple ring.

'That must've fuckin' hurt,' went Neil.

'Na – just like gettin' yer ear done.'

'You're fuckin' mad mate... Y'd'look like that twat Tommy Lee – y'know the one who shagged Pamela Anderson.'

'Well, I reckon it looks sexy...' said Jess.

No one argued with her. It must do.

'Ready are 'ee?' said Micky.

Alan M. Kent

He looked over at the van. Tonight was the Surfers Against
Sewage Ball.

'Yeah,' Charlie said. 'Let's go...'

'Can y'play a'right tonight?' said Neil t'Micky. 'I mean, is it
still hurtin'?'

''Course I can. Jus' wait 'til next week...'

'Why?'

'I'm havin' me frenum done...'

'Yer wha'?'

'Me frenum...'

'Where the fuck's that?' asked Neil innocently. 'Whaas' yer
frenum?'

'On yer knob!' everyone said.

'Really?' asked Neil.

''Course,' said Micky smiling.

The van went quiet. Neil shifted on his seat a few times, and
was pretty quiet fur the rest o'the journey. Y'could near hear of
'un contemplatin' the pain. As they pulled inta' Perranporth,
quiet-like, Neil went t'Micky, 'Where 'zactly like?'

'I'll tell 'ee later...'

* * * * *

There were still surfers out when they reached *The Watering
Hole*. It was around half-sixish, time they'd got over there. In
the end, Micky had decided t'drive the van across the beach –
an' not worry about the consequences. If the lifeguards could
do it, so could he. Y'did think about it though. Every year some
daft cunt from up the line would park up on a beach somewhere – next thing they knew, water 'ud be lappin' 'round their
bumper an' the engine wudn' start. But na, *The Watering Hole*
was far enough from the sea.

Just visible down the coast was St Agnes, where the remnants
o'thousand years o'mining littered the coast. Y'knaw the look
o'it. Wheal Coates is prob'ly the most photographed piece o'industrial paraphernalia in Western Europe. All fuckin' chimney
stacks against the copper-blue Atlantic. 'Twas on a million calendars an' postcards. Once upon a time, it 'ud been about pre-
servin' that lot. Now, 'twas the ocean itself. Y'could understand
where Surfers Against Sewage were comin' from. It was about

Proper Job, Charlie Curnow!

South West Water an' privatisation – an' all the fuckin' decent jobs goin' t'Exeter. Charlie reckoned he'd need t'make somethun' o'that at the Ball.

Ball? It made it sound like they were a violin quartet, an' anyone comin' 'ud be dressed up in gowns an' dinner jackets. Na – it wudn' nothun' like that. 'Twas just the regular surfin' crowd, plus the fifty or so tickets they'd managed t'flog t'their mates. Greg met them, an' told *Balance* where t'set up. It wudn' 'zactly huge – but y'got used t'that.

* * * * *

'What – that triangle bit where the skin moves?'

'Yeah,' said Micky.

'Really?'

'Fuckin' right… Y'never know… Ally might like it…'

'Like fuck she would…'

There was a fair-sized crowd in already. The beaus o'the surfin' world were leadin' their ladies inta' the shack, intent on partying fur the rest o'the evenin'.

Yak seemed t'be gettin hammered – though he hadn' been drinkin' a lot. Charlie cudn' understand it.

'He's a small fucker idn' a?' said Neil. 'He's always been like that?'

'Y'reckon?'

'Yeah.'

'I wish he'd lay off a bit,' said Bev.

'Y'wun't stop 'un…'

They watched Yak order another couple o'bottles, then go fur a piss. He was in there fur a long time.

'Never mind 'ee,' said Micky. ''Ave y'seen the electrics in here?'

They looked 'round t'the bottom of the wall.

The sockets looked cashed.

'I'll tell Greg…'

They did.

'Is' a'right, honest,' said Greg. 'Last night's band didn' have any problems…'

'A'right,' said Micky, but y'could tell 'ee wudn' happy.

More people arrived. They recognised a few faces.

Alan M. Kent

'Who's tha'?'

'Thas' one o'the organisers of Surfers Against Sewage... Chris Davies, I think 'ee's called...'

Greg had told them there'ud be a few speeches.

'An' him – thaas' Andrew George ennit?'

'Who's 'ee?'

'The MP fur St Ives... 'Ee used t'be in *Mebyon Kernow*...'

There was a cheer as another bloke walked in. He had on the regulation wrap-around mirrored shades.

'Who's that?' asked Bev.

'Dunnaw – must be some surfin' champion or something...'

Yak was back. His eyes looked glazed.

'Y'a'right?' asked Charlie.

''Course I am – I wish you cunts 'ud leave off...'

'Touchy...' whispered Micky.

While the speeches were goin' on inside – an' some presentations were being made, *Balance* made for a set o'tables outside. The boy in the wrap-around shades had just won the UK Student Surfing Competition, an' was dishing out some prizes t'other kids. Andrew George was talkin' about the importance o'surfin' to the Cornish economy, an' how more care should be taken over the marine environment. Chris Davies had television organised an' all. For *Balance* though, it was enough t' just sit outside an' watch the sun setting.

The only problem was that the little digs an' asides t'each other had got worse over the last few weeks. Least Charlie had been prepared. He'd warned them – that livin' on top o'each other was enough t'split some bands. It wudn' happen t'them though – not if they were careful. Y'just had t'be tolerant an' y'mustn't let it win.

He sometimes marvelled at Bev. She put up with a lot. So did Jess for that matter. Charlie knew the rest o'them – Neil, Yak, Micky – an' he included – could be proper fuckin' assholes. The least thing would set 'um off – an' someone 'ud go inta' a strop for the next couple o'hours. 'Twas silly really – they all knew one another well enough – but all the great rock 'n' roll bustups had been over somethun' trivial. It mustn't happen t'them.

Greg came out.

'You guys ready?' he asked.

''Course,' said Bev.

Proper Job, Charlie Curnow!

Everyone drank the last o'their beers, an' the sun disappeared behind Droskyn Point. 'Twas like they were makin' an album in the Caribbean somewhere – Monserrat – if the place wudn' covered in pyroclastic flows an' volcanic ash.

'This 'ud be a good place fur a video wudn' it?' went Charlie.

No one else responded, except Bev. Charlie had his dreams the others reckoned.

''Course,' she said, an' kissed him.

* * * * *

As it turned out, they played a fuckin' blinder. When it went like that, all the other crap went out the window. When it was raw, sweaty, dirty rock 'n' roll, an' everyone wanted more, you were gods. You were more than fuckin' gods. You were masters of the universe. No one could touch 'ee.

That was until the encore. Everything was goin' on proper. There were plenty up dancin'. Neil had got a radio mike an' he was wanderin' through the crowd like he was Eddie Van Halen. But what could 'ee say? They were lappin' it up. Time some o' their more funky tracks were pulled out, the place was goin' fur it big-time. Boy Bluett an' his nutters were in there as usual – more inta' the music than the surfin' babes next to 'um – the twats.

Just before the encore, Charlie did his rap. He'd developed a sort of hard-core-style attack, which ended in a pro-environment rant with a few subtle digs at the right privatised companies. Much cheering followed. He was on a roll.

Then, all hell broke loose as they went inta' 'What are you on?'. Neil had just got through the opening few chords when his amp cut out. Everything else was carryin' on – but there wudn' no guitar. The song stopped.

'Slight technical hitch up here...' went Charlie.

It wudn' slight. The fuckin' socket on the wall had frazzled. The amp didn' look much better. Back at the bar, Greg looked worried. The audience cheered the way they do when there was a hold-up like this. It was a'right. Part o'the fun up *Institute*, an' over Football Club, was how bands coped with these sort o'lash-ups.

Balance knew what t'do though. Micky fired up his decks an' shoved on one o'his dance mixes he had prepared for *Twilight*.

Neil staggered 'round like his frenum had just been pierced. Gradually, Charlie, Neil, Bev an' Yak vacated the stage.

'What is it?' asked Greg.

Micky's music began t'lock-in, an' the crowd moved inta' rave mode.

'That socket wudn' it...' said Neil.

'Shit – sorry man...'

'Can't do anything 'bout it now...'

'Sure,' went Greg. 'It dun' matter... that was a fuckin' crackin' set... here's yer money. The bonus is in there...'

They went out t'the bogs t'count it. The floor was wet with piss. Bottles o' Fosters Ice were balanced on the urinals.

'How much?' asked Bev.

'Two-hundred an' fifty.'

'Yeah... excellent,' went Yak.

They went back in an' joined the Rave. Sweat, cigarette smoke, beer an' dope all merged together. This was the good life. Was this Cornwall anymore? He cudn' tell. Everything was fusing together nicely.

* * * * *

By one o'clock, Yak was out o'it. They'd carried 'un out t'the back o'the van, an' 'eaved 'un inside. Bev moved 'un inta' the recovery position in case he spewed or anything. They didn' want a Bon Scott or a John Bonham on their hands.

'He'll be dead, time he's twenty-five,' she went on.

Charlie viewed her comment more seriously. He'd have t'pack up his kit.

'How is a?' asked Micky.

'A'right I think,' said Bev.

Micky an' Charlie knew it was a whisht job though.

'Thanks fur that set,' said Charlie. 'I never knew I'd be s'pleased t'hear some dance shit...'

'No probs,' said Micky. 'If Linkin Park can do it – so can we...'

Greg came over. Neil had the socket ready t'show him. The socket itself had near-melted.

'Sorry man – I s'pause you were right... Is yer amp alright?'

'I think a new plug'll sort it out... but I'll get back t'ya if it idn'...'

Proper Job, Charlie Curnow!

'Look,' said Greg, 'I was speakin' t'Chris – an' you're just the sort o'group we want fur the Championships...'

'The Championships?' asked Charlie.

'Up Newquay – the Headworx Pro?'

'Oh right...'

Charlie knew it – the largest surfin' competition o'the year.

'We've hopefully got *The Darkness* playin' – one of their low key warm-up dates like – but we're lookin' fur more support acts... You interested?'

''Course,' said Charlie. 'You know the number...'

'Yeah – I'll give you a ring.'

'What was that?' asked Bev.

'Another gig,' said Charlie. 'The Headworx event up Newquay – support t'*The Darkness*...'

'Really?'

'Naw!'

'Straight up...'

Now, Charlie 'ud be lying if he neglected t'mention that the lot o'them – outside the view o'Greg an' *The Watering Hole* of course – jumped for fuckin' joy. This wudn' no ordinary venue: this was a festival. This wudn' no ordinary gig: this was support t'*The Darkness*. It felt like they'd made it. It was certainly worth runnin' across Perranporth Beach for – an' jumpin' inta' the sea. This kind of collective orgasm he'd only ever felt before with boy Dean Shipton, when he had slid across Hellfire Corner an' put a try down in the last minute against Gloucestershire. You cudn' put it inta' words.

* * * * *

None o'this was really happenin' was it?

Least not t'a bunch o'cunts from Trelawny. The closest anyone had got t'this sort o'fame (excluding the court reports in *The West Briton*), was when Jimmy Pengelly had conducted the Festival o'Cornish Choirs in the Royal Albert Hall a few years back. And now, here they were, second-on-the-bill t'*The Darkness* at the largest surf festival in the world. Y'felt good. Y'felt like you'd made it. Christ, Charlie was even being interviewed by people – an' photographers wanted shots o'them next t'the right logos. Y'obliged – 'cause you didn' want t'upset anyone. All the time you were still shittin' yerself though – wishin' you were still playin' the fuckin' *Miners an' Mechanics Institute* back Redruth.

The event wudn' Glastonbury, but it was still huge. Newquay was heavin' with people – not only from the rest o'Britain, but from all corners o'the world. As y'mingled with the crowds on the beaches, it felt like Cornwall was the centre o'the world, not just some forgotten piece o'it. Even the weather seemed t'remember that; there was bright sunshine all week. Everywhere y'looked was bare flash. 'Twas terrible you. You hardly knew where t'look sometimes, but Charlie told himself t'enjoy it. There wudn' that much o'the Methodist still left in 'un.

There was a range o'surfing competitions takin' place. Charlie watched a few o'the heats in the freestyle series, but after a while, his attention wondered. From the shore of Fistral – where the waves charged in with the entrants managing what seemed t'him t'be unfeasible acts o'balance – he could see the stage. It was a temporary structure set up on the headland, but it was substantial. It was the biggest thing that *Balance* had ever walked out on. From it, y'could see over the whole festival, all the vendors, the merchandisers, the publicity tents, the food stalls, the heavin' mass o' humanity who wandered amongst it – an' then the very ocean itself. Up there, on that stage, it took your breath away an' carried it out inta' the Atlantic. As y'sung, y'd be able t'taste the salt o'the sea breeze.

The best thing about it was the access y'had. The Promoter had sent them a set o'passes t'get through even the most stringent security, so at the drive out t'the Headland Hotel, most people were gettin' turned back. Not them though. It was brilliant watchin' all the campers an' Beetles gettin' turned 'round, an' Micky's battered heap ploughing straight through.

'Fuckin' surfin' bastards,' Micky was goin', as he had t'stop every ten seconds or so, t'let people cross – or simply walk back up the drive inta' the town centre.

'Dun't knock 'em,' Neil had said. 'They're the reason we're here…'

'I know… I know…' went Micky. 'They're still bastards though…'

Proper Job, Charlie Curnow!

The other good thing about playin' here was tellin' everyone that y'were doin' it – especially anyone y'didn' like – anyone who didn' believe – or thought y'were playin' at it – or thought no cunts from Cornwall are ever goin' t'make it in the music business. Thaas' why when Charlie jacked in the Freddy Bear job, he made sure the manager knew. An' why earlier that week, he'd strolled inta' the Job Centre t'see Gary Yelland. 'Twas all different now – boy Yelland was near fallin' over himself t'help 'um. Headworx Pro World Championship? Yes, the cunt had heard o'that. Didn' want t'knaw about any band before, from that crowd o'layabouts. But now, well, things were different now. He might even be able t'arrange for that grant application t'be reconsidered. Charlie told 'un 'ee was a'right. They didn' need it now. Micky made sure a *Balance* sticker went on their new employment service logo on the entrance door to the Job Centre though. Fur him, it was sweet revenge.

Then there was every other fucker on the estate. Whereas before, they reckoned formin' a band was a waste o'time an' money, now they were queuing up t'congratulate 'um on this gig. His ma was tellin' everyone. Even the tackers had heard about it. Maybe the boy Curnow wudn' such a cunt after all. Maybe the other wasters he hung out with wudn' that bad either. Maybe there was a bit o'fuckin' hope.

'Course, his da had knawed it all along. 'Twas in his fuckin' genes. He knawed they'd had their disagreements an' that, but he told 'un thaas' what he should do – an' they only had t'remember, 'ee could step in as their manager at a moment's notice...'

'What time do we go on?' asked Bev.

'Matey told me we go on at eight. We've got about an hour. Then its changeover – an' then it's *The Darkness*...' answered Charlie. 'Obviously, they've got the full rig an' that – but we'll have some lights...'

''Es – a couple o'spots I 'spect,' went Micky. 'No more than that...'

'It's a cool time though isn't it?' Bev offered. 'I mean, we're on when its twilight. The light's good then...'

'They say that dun't they?' said Charlie, ' – that second-on-the-bill bands go down well... I've read it loads a times...'

'Yeah,' said Yak, 'but remember, this idn' *The fuckin' Pirate* – an we're up against *The Darkness*...'

'Not up against,' said Charlie. 'Just supportin'. Remember, they had t'do it too...'

'I just hope we dun't get canned off...' went Yak.

'We wun't,' said everyone else.

There was security in numbers.

'If any cunt 'eaves anything at me,' said Yak, 'I'll have 'um. I'll be inta' the crowd, t'sort out the bastard...'

'There's bound t'be some stuff thrown up,' went Charlie.

Everyone looked at him like it wasn't the thing t'say.

'I mean, people do, dun't they?'

''Es – fuckin' bottles o'piss an' that...' went Yak. 'One o'they caught me 'round the head at Reading laas' year...'

'Just keep an eye out,' went Micky as the voice o'reason. 'But dun't rely on security. Those fat fuckers are clueless at the best o'times...'

They looked over at the Showsec men in their yellow t-shirts who seemed t'be permanently talkin' inta' walkie-talkies 'round the back-stage area.

'Anyway, it's all on the frontman, I reckon,' said Neil. 'If they like you, we'll be a'right... Depends what sort o'day people have had...'

So it mattered nothun' about songs, or musicianship, or talent, or fuckin' originality – none o'that. It mattered what sort o'day people had had. That was it.

Charlie thought about it. He knew lots o'musicians who had all o'that – an' they hadn' made it. Maybe Neil was right. Maybe rock 'n' roll was like that – a toss of a coin. Heads y'win. Tails y'lose. Maybe some just got lucky – an' some didn'.

The Darkness, were definitely lucky. There were hundreds o'maids waitin' fur them at the entrance t'the back-stage area. They were flyin' inta' Newquay airport – straight from recordin' sessions in London on their new album. They liked playin' Cornwall though – thaas' why they'd interrupted their new recording t'play the gig. Accordin' t'their press release, it was a last minute thing. Back near Christmas, Charlie would've given a lot t'meet Justin or Dan Hawkins – but now, well, he was less interested. They were peers now after all. He wudn' be kow-towin' t' no one.

Even that wankstain Sam Polglase had phoned up fur another interview before this. So a'right – he'd finally realised the

Proper Job, Charlie Curnow!

buzz about *Balance* – that didn' mean they had t'like 'un. The thing was y'needed the press. Y'needed 'um t'help define who you were. Perhaps Polglase realised it might be good t'promote *Balance* as well. He'd given up applyin' fur jobs at *NME*. He was happier in Cornwall – or so he reckoned.

Bluett an' his boys were out on Fistral already, handin' out a set o'flyers advertising future *Balance* dates an' where t'check out their website. The flyers looked classy n'all – with colour printing. Kelvin had redesigned their logo t'help appeal t'the surfin' clientele. They just hoped the fuckers still out there on Fistral could be bothered t'check them out. The other hope was that enough people from the Surfers Against Sewage Ball would be at the World Championships – an' have enjoyed *Balance* enough the last time 'round t'stay an' see them again.

None o'this was really happenin' was it? This meteoric rise...?

They had t'soundcheck in the late afternoon. The day's competitions were just finishin' an' you could sense the tension around, as the judges made their final decisions as t'who would go through t'Saturday's finals. *Balance's* entry onto the stage would end some o'that silence. It also caused three scavenging seagulls t'cawk at them, then fly off towards the Atlantic Hotel. It felt big up there. Like normally, Charlie could lean over an' touch Bev if he needed to. Now it seemed she was a mile away. He could jump an' not be worried about banging his head on the ceilin' of the venue. As he looked across at Neil, the light came in from the West, an' he could only catch his silhouette – the machine head of his Gibson falling onto the monitor before him. Micky was back there sortin' out his samples an' keyboards, an Yak, well, just looked like Yak – only here – live at Newquay.

In the temporary arena, a few bodies had started t'gather – but in the centre, there lay a few o'the previous night's casualties, still wrapped in sleeping bags an' bits o'cardboard. 'Round the edges, those tired o'watchin' the surfin' action sat down an' smoked, or just tried t'catch the last o'the day's sunshine.

Charlie looked over the edge o'the stage. Fuck, he said t'hisself. It was a long way down t'where the bouncers would later stand for *The Darkness*. He curled his toes 'round the wiring that ran past the monitors. The chasm yawned before him. He

Alan M. Kent

could tell it was serious. *Clear Channel* were one of the biggest rock promoters in the world and their posters were draped over everything.

'Are y'ready?' came a voice through the monitors.

Beyond the chasm, out in the arena, a structure housed the sound engineer. He had a tight schedule, an' would want t'sort out this lot as quickly as possible. Behind him, a roadie ran on, an' checked some of the connections. Charlie dodged out o'his way.

'Yeah – whatever...' came the voice of the tired sound engineer.

They ran through 'Making Faces'. It wasn't comfortable. Everyone reckoned y'were so far away from each other, that it felt like you were playin' on yer own. Still, 'round the edge of the arena, a few people clapped. Something must've sounded right.

'How was that?' went Charlie t'the engineer.

'Oh, alright. I'll put yer vocals up a bit. We reckon we need t're-mike some o' the drums...'

Y'felt a complete fuckin' twat talkin' t'someone through a mike – with everyone watchin'.

While the roadie on stage re-miked Yak's drums, the judges were announcing those who'd made it through t'the freestyle finals. One who'd made it through was a Newquay boy; the other two were Aussies. The end o'the competitions meant that any fucker could now go out, so there was a mass dash t'catch the laas' o'the light. Y'could see the surf life-saving teams preparin' for a night o'it. They'd be there 'til four in the mornin' advising drunk fuckers it wudn' 'zactly the time t'go out. Y'could feel anyone over thirty-five 'round Newquay start t'prepare for the night's festivities – the first o'this year's youth culture events. There were still other surfing competitions yet, an' then Run t'the Sun. Would it be the pile o'sick or the half-drunk cans o' Special Brew they'd find in the azaleas? On the beach itself, barbecues started up, an' the first o'the night's rave music began t'travel across the dunes. The old fuckers would have their pens at the ready t'complain t'the council and local newspapers.

Once Yak had his drums sorted out, that was it. The sound engineer crossed his arms an' tapped his watch. They'd have t'make do with that.

Proper Job, Charlie Curnow!

'It 'ull prob'ly sound like fuckin' *Institute*'s jukebox,' went Micky.

He hated it when the control over *Balance's* sound passed into somebody else's hands. He knew what *Balance* should sound like.

'I know what *Balance* should sound like,' he was goin'.

The arena started to fill.

Fuck.

None o'this was really happenin' was it?

In the backstage area, Bev had managed t'encounter Steve Spry.

'Who's that tosser again?' went Neil.

'Y'knaw – that fuckin' speed-king we met down *The Pirate*...' said Micky.

'Oh shite – he's comin' over...' said Charlie.

'Hi guys – I knew we'd meet again,' went Spryer. 'Glad y'got on this bill...'

Least the cunt didn' look like he was on speed now.

'So why are you here then Steve?' asked Bev.

'Oh – you know – chasin' a few contacts. I know the Promotor here y'see. He's a good bloke an' that... The boys are here – y'knaw... *Break the System*...'

'Right...'

Thaas' all they needed was they cunts showin' up an' wreckin' it all.

'Got t'see who's doin' the business an' that. Anyway – I'm still interested in representing you...'

He handed Bev a card.

'...an' that gig down The Lizard is on for definite. Got the license an' everything. Hope you're up for it... Anyway – must dash...'

Spryer flipped open his mobile phone, an' went over towards some of the Security boys.

'We'll do the gig,' went Micky, 'but there's no fuckin' way he's goin' t'be our manager...'

No one confirmed it. They didn' need to. No one wanted the cunt.

The food passes worked. There was a lot on offer in the Hospitality tent. A lot o'the crew were in there, stuffing down the salad and gateaus on offer. None o' *Balance* were really

231

hungry though. Afterwards – maybe they could eat, but not now. The wine helped though. It made Charlie more relaxed. They were on in fifteen minutes. Yak had been knockin' it back as well. The two o'them went for a piss.

Y'could feel the arena filling. Y'could sense the anticipation. *Balance* had t'deliver.

Yak entered a cubicle an' Charlie found a urinal. Charlie heard the seat go down – but nothun' else. He zipped up an' went t'the sink t'wash his hands.

'How long y'goin' t'be Yak?' he asked.

'A – you go on Charlie. I'll be there in a minute...'

Something fell on the floor inside the cubicle. It wasn't a fuckin' bog roll.

'Na – yer a'right,' said Charlie. 'I'll hang on for 'ee...'

Charlie bent down.

He just caught Yak's arm pickin' up the object from the floor. There was still no splosh inta' the pan.

'What the fuck's on with you?'

'Nothun' – I'm 'aving a dump fur Chrissakes...'

But Charlie cudn' leave it. He had t'see what was on. Was the cunt feeling a'right? He was prob'ly nervous too.

He went inta' the cubicle next door, an' climbed up onta the pan. He looked over. He didn' want t'see what 'ee saw. Of all the fuckin' things, o'all the fuckin' fuck-ups, he had t'see this.

There was a brown-stained hot spoon and a lighter on the floor. Yak had a needle stuck in his lower arm – a tourniquet 'round the upper part. The vein he had the syringe yanked inta', looked like it might collapse at any moment; it was that rancid. The cunt looked like 'ee was about t'die , yet at the same time 'ee gaked up t'Charlie like he'd been caught smokin' on the school bus. Like it was the same Yak he'd always known – only the cunt wasn't.

None o'this was really happenin' was it?

Yeah – it fuckin' was.

Balance's drummer was fuckin' hisself up, good an' proper.

'It's not like it looks Charlie...' went Yak, the cunt, pulling the syringe outta' his arm.

'What is it then?'

'Bit o'smack thaas' all...'

It didn' look like that t'Charlie. It was prob'ly from the the

Proper Job, Charlie Curnow!

same fuckin' crowd that had taken Chrissie Willaims out – bad shit. Heroin, Smack, Junk, Brown, H, whatever – 'twas all the fuckin' same..

'Why?'

'Gives me confidence like...'

'Yeah – an' fucks things up. How long 'ave 'ee been on this?'

Yak didn' answer.

For a while then.

'All those times when...'

'Yeah...'

No wonder the fucker lost it sometimes.

'I'm a cunt 'ent I Charlie?'

'Fuckin' right you are...'

'Dun't tell the rest o'them...'

'I wun't. Just open the fuckin' door...'

Na – this was really happenin'.

Yak leant forward an' released the latch.

'You fucker... you fucker... you fucker...' Charlie was goin'.

He wanted t'beat seven shades o'shit out o' the cunt.

'I'n still drum...'

Six would do.

'If you fuck up Yak – I'll fuckin' kill you... before this fuckin' gear...'

There was about a minute where neither ov 'um spoke. Then Charlie had t'ask 'ut.

'This your needle or some other cunts?

Yak didn' answer, but 'ee didn' need to.

'Ah – y'stupid fucker...' went Charlie.

He stamped down on the syringe. Splinters o'glass spun across the cubicle floor. He went through his pockets and found a plastic bag of more heroin. Charlie instantly flushed it down the bog.

Yak was cryin' like a baby.

'I've let y'down Charlie...'

'Na – come on... Every groups needs a fuckin' wild drummer dun't 'um?'

Yak didn' smile. He'd heard o'Keith Moon an' John Bonham. He was putting them in the same category as Chrissie Williams. Maybe it was the wrong thing t'say.

'Come on – get up y'bastard!'

Charlie got him outside. From thereon, he was on his own.

'Now – fuckin' do it!'

'A'right Charlie boy – I wun't let 'ee down...'

They walked over t'the others.

'Where the fuck y'been?' went Micky.

'Had the shits didn' us...' said Charlie. It was the only thing y'could say.

'We're on in five minutes... I've given the roadie the set lists t'tape down...' said Bev.

'Y'ready?' asked Micky t'Charlie, like they were about t'leap out over enemy territory or somethun'.

''Course,' went Charlie. 'Been ready fur this all me life?'

They moved t'the side of the stage. The roadies were doin' a few last minute checks. Through the PA stack, y'could see a decent-sized crowd in the arena. A roadie beckoned them forward.

'You a'right?' Charlie asked Yak.

'Proper,' was the drummer's response. The cunt was goin' t'do it despite being up t'the eyeballs in skag.

They hugged each other. It was naff an' wonderful at the same time. Then they walked out onstage – first Neil, then Yak, then Micky, then Bev, then Charlie. It was *Balance*, live at Newquay. Neil's first riff echoed 'round the arena as a couple o' thousand people watched. Charlie nervously looked down the front row. The singer an' drummer o' *Break the System* were down there, makin' wanker signs at 'un. But then, *Balance* had the songs – hook-peppered rock which punched them right in the guts. The chasm closed, an' Charlie felt he could touch everyone. *Balance* were on top form, their infectious pop genius coupled with taut, tight and turbo-charged razor-riffing. It was thrilling an' edgy, the adrenaline crackling in the air. Charlie was the consummate showman, whipping the crowd inta' a frenzy – all focused anger an' inspired escapism. Within minutes, the crowd and band took on the communal vibe of rock. In short, *Balance* gave Newquay a good seein' to.

'Who are they?' someone in the audience mouthed.

'Dun't knaw – but they'm fuckin good though...'

* * * * *

Proper Job, Charlie Curnow!

None o'this was really happenin' was it? Five fuckers, straight outta' Camborne, comin' off from a stormer of a gig.

'Nice one man!' said Justin Hawkins from *The Darkness*, as they came off stage.

'Cheers,' said Charlie.

'That was him wudn' it?' asked Neil.

''Course,' said Charlie.

'What, come t'watch us?'

''Course.'

The others walked on back t'the Hospitality tent.

'Y'did well Yak,' said Charlie.

'Cheers. I won't fuck it up again...'

'Sure boy... we'll have t'sort out yer problem like...'

'Na – I mean it Charlie. I mean, it's been good n' that, but I 'ent cut out fur it... Thaas' part o'the problem like... an' then there's me medicinal needs t'deal with...'

'We'll sort it out Yak.'

'Na Charlie – sorry boy, but I'm leavin'... I mean, I need t'sort meself out... an' well, you fuckers need someone who's not fuckin' wasted all the time...'

'No! Y'can't Yak... We fuckin' need 'ee...'

'Look, I was thinkin' about it just now. I mean, I was okay. I kept time an' stuff... but I dun't want t'carry on... I'm through with it...'

'Wha', an' go an' pick fuckin' daffodils fur a hundred quid a week?'

That was harsh. Charlie knew it.

'Yeah – if I fuckin' have to...'

'Yak, all I'm sayin' is think about it... think about it just now...'

'I have done. I'm sorry. I'm really fuckin' sorry...'

Yak started t'walk away an' sat down where Micky's van was parked.

'You'll change yer mind...' Charlie shouted.

'Na...'

Charlie thought he was kiddin'; he thought it was a joke t'make up fur what he'd discovered earlier. But it wasn't. You could see it. Yak was goin' the way o' others he knew back home. He didn' want it enough. The only thing he wanted was t'get fucked up. Charlie nor anyone else could change the cunt.

Alan M. Kent

What a fuckin' lash-up.

Yak leavin', had really fuckin' happened, an' it was somethun' y'cudn' file under musical differences.

* * * * *

The joy, the rush, the kick he'd felt comin' off-stage seemed short-lived. In fact, it seemed fuckin' non-existent; that was until 'ee got back inside the Hospitality tent.

'Where's Yak?' asked Neil.

He cudn' tell them – not now – not after that gig.

'Gone fur a piss n' that…' was what Charlie said.

Everything now was a bit o'a blur t'be honest with 'ee. The rest o'*Balance* were sittin' down – havin' a celebratory drink, an' Charlie found hisself standin' up. Everybody an' their uncle seemed t'be comin' up an' shakin' his hand, or givin' 'un a part on the back. There was a stream o' 'Nice ones!' an' 'Great gig man!' which all merged inta' one. For a few minutes, he almost forgot about Yak. Bev was up kissing 'un – whisperin' in his ear what she wanted t'do later. So this was it? This was what it was really like.

Y'had all yer hangers-on comin' up an' sayin' how they knew you'd do it. Spryer was in there too; gettin' in on the celebration. Charlie grabbed a bottle of Fosters Ice an' sat down t'drink it.

'You should meet him over there…' said Bev to 'un.

'Who?'

'That bloke there…'

She pointed to a man who was talkin' to another guy who looked like he might be *The Darkness'* tour manager.

'Why?'

'Well, when we came back – he wanted t'know where you were…'

'What, like Spryer is a?'

'No Charlie – he's different. In a different league. You need to speak to him…'

Charlie looked over at this bloke. He was prob'ly another bullshitter; someone who knew everything an' knew nothun'. Another distraction from *Balance's* rise. He looked at him again as he downed the rest of the beer. The bloke had money. You could see it. There was the tanned skin. No fucker in Cornwall had that – not least in places south o'Camborne. Then there was his hair. He was about his da's age – but the way his hair was styled allowed 'un t' keep a bit of his youth. Like he knew he'd lost it, but wanted t' at least stay someone close to 'ut. Not like his da – fuckin' clueless – a couple o'quid cut down Bert Brewer's barber shed.

Fuck. He was comin' over. Charlie 'ud need t'put inta' action every survival skill he'd ever learnt. Charlie looked over at Neil an' Micky. They nodded, like whatever this bloke wanted, Charlie need t'deal with it. He was the one who formed the band; he was the one who should deal with this.

'Hi,' said the bloke. 'Charlie isn't it?'

'Hi,' went Charlie. 'Yeah... I'm Charlie...'

'My name's Pete Thomas... I'm a producer. I used t'work for *Virgin* – and now I'm working on my own. I'm setting up my own label... and I saw your set just now. I've been talking to a few people about the scene in Cornwall... Put it this way, I'm interested.'

'Interested?'

'Yeah – I mean, you guys *had* that audience just now – and that's no pub gig. And the songs – you've got some great songs. Do you have any management?'

Fuck. What should Charlie say?

'We've got some people interested... y'know...'

A few? Some asshole called Spryer an' his faather. Charlie looked over at Neil an' Micky again. Good job they weren't laughing.

'Sure. So it's okay to talk to you then?' went Pete Thomas. 'I mean I don't want t'tred on anybody's shoes...'

''Course,' said Charlie.

'Well, like I say, I'm interested. Your stuff's got that classic feel... y'know, kind o'retro, but kind o'contemporary as well. Have you got a demo?'

'Na,' said Charlie. 'We decided not t'make one. I mean these days, y'just get lost in the void really. I reckon the bigger labels are lookin' for a CD now – an' well, by the end o'the summer, we might have the money t'cut one...'

'You're right,' went Pete Thomas. 'I mean a lot o'bands do, but you lot waiting, seems t'have paid off...'

'How d'y'mean?' went Charlie.

What the fuck was a goin' t'say next?

'I'm serious – I'd like t'see you lot on the label. Either way you win – y'carry on with me – or we try t'sell you to a biggie...'

'Biggie?'

'Y'know. I've got a lot of contacts at *Virgin* and *Atlantic*...'

Fuck. *Atlantic*. *The Darkness* were on them. *Led Zeppelin* too.

Charlie could feel his eyes gettin' bigger. Like he was six again, an' had just been handed a double Mr Whippy with a flake, on the beach down Portreath.

'You need to know I'm genuine an' that, so if you're interested, you'll need a solicitor... Anyway, are you lot hanging out here tonight? Oh, and make sure I've got your phone number...'

''Course they were hanging out. Besides *The Darkness* were on in twenty minutes.

'Can I buy you all a beer?'

'Sure,' went Micky holding up his glass. Charlie knew what he was thinking. This was all a long way from United Downs.

'Another Fosters Ice,' went Neil. This was the other side o'the world from Camborne *Tescos*.

'A diet coke please,' said Bev. Maybe Charlie was right. Maybe one day, they'd be playing the NECs and the Wembleys.

'Please,' said Charlie. 'Another Fosters would be proper...'

'Back in a minute... then I can get to know the rest of you a bit better...'

'Fuckin' hell Charlie,' went Micky. 'Is 'ee fur real?'

Charlie didn' knaw.

'Is he being straight up?' asked Neil.

Charlie reckoned so.

'Is he offerin' us some sort o'record deal?' said Bev.

Yeah, that was what was on offer.

'Proper job then,' went Neil.

Pete Thomas came back with a trayful of drinks and was proposin' a toast to *Balance*. Charlie raised his bottle, but he cudn' stop thinkin' about Yak. No one else seemed t'give a toss about 'un.

* * * * *

Proper Job, Charlie Curnow!

They found Yak. He'd been watchin' *The Darkness* from the side o'the stage. He'd come down a bit from his opiate rush. Scouser fuckin' skag – that was what the cunt was on.

'Where the fuck were you?' asked Neil.

He told 'un about the offer. Yak didn' have much t'say – even less t'Charlie. Neil cudn' fuckin' believe it. No one cudn'. Some record producer had just been kissin' their ass, an' here was Yak, actin' like a right cunt. He'd known him all his life, an' he was being a right tosser.

'You're a stupid cunt,' went Neil.

Yak didn' respond t'his bait.

Charlie advised Neil t'leave it.

No one said very much more. *The Darkness* had been fuckin' brilliant, an' they'd been offered a deal, but the van was silent. It was late, an' the warmer air o'summer made the vehicle feel claustrophobic. Charlie wound down the window. They passed the hordes of camper vans that lined the Newquay streets, an' then headed homewards past windfarms and parked caravans into Truro, to drop off Bev, then back down the A30 t'Camborne. Then there was the final smeech of diesel as the van headed up towards Troon. All the time Charlie had been watchin' Yak – makin' sure he was okay. The last thing he needed was a Treliske job.

Micky rounded the corner o'the estate an' stopped so Yak could get out.

'Take 'un easy boy,' said Charlie.

Yak barely turned 'round.

His leaving allowed the real question t'be asked.

'What's up with that fucker?' went Neil.

'Nothun',' said Charlie. 'He just told me he wants t'leave the band...'

'Wants t'leave?'

'Well... no... he has left...'

'The twat,' mouthed Micky.

'I'll kill the cunt,' said Neil.

Charlie didn' say much more. He was just glad Yak was still alive.

* * * * *

Alan M. Kent

Yak's leavin' put things inta' perspective fur a bit. Charlie had Pete Thomas' number in his wallet, but now they were shafted. The next set o'gigs had t'be cancelled. Before anything else, they'd need a new drummer. That was never goin' t'be easy. Neil an' Micky had gone 'round t' try t'change his mind. They cudn' even get t'see the cunt. His ma said he was in hospital. Hospital? Well, thaas' when Charlie had t'tell 'um all what he found, an' what had been goin' on for a while now. Smack was gettin' big around the estate. Well, it was so fuckin' cheap now wudn' it? First of all, they all laid inta' Charlie fur givin' 'un shit – an' forcin' 'un out. Even Bev thought that's what had gone on – but 'twudn' ever like that. He'd never do that to a mate – not Charlie. He'd even promised not t'tell the rest o'them, but they needed t'know. Yak hadn't even bothered t'pick up his kit. It was weird without 'un.

Charlie had t'tell Pete Thomas about it. He'd sussed it before Charlie even said anything.

'Your drummer is it?' he'd gone. 'Thought so – that's why he wasn't there afterwards...'

'Yeah – y'know how it is...'

'Of course,' said Pete. 'It happens all the time... You auditioning?'

'Yeah...'

'Couse they were auditioning. They'd put ads in the local papers; even in some of the music magazines. It had worked with Bev – why not with a new drummer? They were all tossers though – who turned up. Y'know – they could play an' that – but they didn' have it – what they were lookin' for. Ten gigs had t'be cancelled afterwards. They reckoned they'd find someone over the summer. Then, the rest o'June got written off. Bev was doin' her A-Levels. Charlie barely got t'see her at all. He an' Neil decided the best thing t'do was t'write a new set o'songs. Micky was back up Pool Market with his bootlegs, doin' up his caravan an' then back DJ-ing down *Twilight*.

Charlie had tried askin' fur his Freddy Bear job back. Well, he needed the cash. He expected the fuckers t'say no – an' they did. Wudn' a s'pause t'be a big rock star now anyway? Still, who needs a bunch o'tackers from the up the line kickin' 'ee in the bollocks anyway? Y'could get that just walkin' across the estate most evenings. So he was back – for a temporary basis at least –

Proper Job, Charlie Curnow!

down the Job Centre. Yelland gave him the forms. Accordin' t'him, they had a new set o'programmes lined up fur the unemployed in west Cornwall – millions o'pounds worth o'Government and European money: Objective One an' that. There was a special scheme fur they who'd been laid off up Crofty. No proper jobs, just fuckin' real miners dressin' up t'show visitors what it used t'be like.

Yelland always liked it when Charlie walked in. Fuckers like Charlie Curnow were always good fur a laugh. He'd some notion o'puttin' a band together. If he was that fuckin' good, why was a down here on forty-nine quid a week?

There were other fuckin' nightmares as well. His da had gone on a course about runnin' yer own business. He'd been pleased as punch when he heard about the record deal.

'Told 'ee boy. Told 'ee see... all that with Jimmy paid off didn' 'ut?'

His da was keepin' his spirits up. *The West Briton* that week, had a photo o' Clifford Mellow an' his da's ex-lover, Karen, gettin' married.

'You knawed about that did 'ee?' asked Charlie.

''Course,' said his da matter-of-factly. 'They had the do over *Institute...*'

'Go, did 'ee?'

'Na, I was on a Business Start-Up dayschool... Anyway, 'twunt last t'all... The moment 'ee has his cacks off up *Institute*, she'll thraw 'un out...'

His da should knaw. Karen had 'eaved him out enough times.

'How's yer mother?' he asked secretively.

'A'right,' went Charlie. 'You should talk t'her – thaas' all – preferably when you 'ent assholed...'

'I knaw boy... I knaw...'

So thaas' how 'twas.

An' fur the early half o'the summer, *Balance* was in balance. 'Twas swinging on the scales you. Charlie'd met with Pete Thomas again. He was all up fur gettin' in a session over August. Studio time was cheap then – everyone else was on holiday. He'd had a design team work on their name, an' on an image an' that, puttin' Kelvin out of business. Charlie had t'be straight with Pete an' tell 'un the situation. But it was a'right.

Alan M. Kent

Pete was cool about 'ut. Christ, Def Leppard took fuckin' four years t'make an album that went on t'sell millions. He needn't worry.

Need he?

Things were going' the right way until the start o'August. Even the weather was shapin' up, like Troon might see a bit o'summer. 'Ee'd had a couple o'drummers phone up who both sounded a'right, like they might fit the bill. They had the same influences as he did. An' then people were phonin' up, seeing if they were into doing anything in the autumn. Provisionally, Charlie said yes.

Then every-fuckin'-thing went wrong.

The first thing was that Micky'd been on about how he need-ed a holiday, how he need t'get out on the road again. Ever since the band had started, there'ud always been that bit o'ten-sion between 'ee an' Charlie – an' all the time, they'd dealt with it; not let it get in the way. But the lay-off from gigs an' that, had made things difficult. There'd been some tough-talking. What the fuck was Charlie goin' t'do about it? Next thing Charlie knew – Micky wasn't there anymore. Neither was Jess. He'd ended the lease on his stall an' lock-up down Pool Market. The van an' the caravan were gone from out back.

Then Neil announced Ally was pregnant again. He was makin' enough down *Tesco* fur them t'get a flat together. They'd be gettin' married in the autumn.

'What about the deal?' Charlie had asked.

'Pie in the sky wudn' it?' said Neil. 'Wudn' never goin' t'come to we... not fur real like. I reckon that Pete Thomas was bullshittin' anyway...'

'Twudn' no use arguing with the cunt. He wanted t'be changin' nappies an' livin' in a semi-detached up Lanner. All that, despite the fact he'd written some o'the coolest fuckin' guitar riffs t'ever walk the earth. Laas' time Charlie saw his Gibson that summer, it had s'much dust on it, you could write yer name on the machine head. 'Twas a sad fuckin' waste – but what could 'ee do? They were off up *Mothercare* over Truro.

Charlie wanted t'say a lot. He wanted t'say, 'Wake up fur Chrissakes an' see what yer givin' up...' but he didn'. Sometimes, he was a total fuckin' waste o'space. Maybe *Balance* 'ud still be there, if he'd spoke up a bit. He wished t'fuck he

Proper Job, Charlie Curnow!

wudn' s'Cornish – better he'd dealt with shit, instead of leavin' it fur dreckly.

The only thing he had tried t'deal with, was the situation with Bev. Y'knaw there were always times when you thought it was goin' t'last forever. Y'tell yourself that – but inside, there's a voice tellin' y' it idn'. Her exams had gone really well – an' Charlie knew she'd be getting decent A Levels later on in the month. Somehow music got lower on her list o'priorities. And he with it. They still made love – but it wudn' like it was before. Charlie cudn' tell which one o'them had changed. In the end, he reckoned it was 'ee.

She had a job fur the summer – in *The Body Shop* in Truro. He'd go in – if he was in *WH Smith* lookin' at *Kerrang!* or *Classic Rock*, or up *Solo* Records or down *HMV* chasin' a bargain. He still loved her, the way y'do. Fuck, her parents even started t'like 'un.

Maybe that was the problem… Maybe thaas' when all rock 'n' roll was worthless – when yer parents start t'like it.

* * * * *

So, there 'twas.

A right fuckin' lash-up all told.

The whole thing scat t'lerraps like. *Balance* were on auto-destruct.

An' what could y'say? Nothun'.

Y'cudn' say nothun'.

Balance was there in spirit. It 'ud be there forever, like a sort of motto, like One and All, like that one game o'rugby you'd never forget, or that one fuckin' brilliant guitar riff that 'ud make yer dick go hard.

An' then when they were pushin' the age o'his da, or approachin' the sort of senility o'Jimmy Pengelly, then they could sit around over *Institute*, an reminisce over the band, all the gigs they played an' all the songs they'd wrote – the way the old buggers did now, about South Crofty. An' as time went on, small stories 'ud be larger stories, an' y'wudn' mind that it didn' happen the way it was meant t'happen, the way it could've happened. You were just happy every fucker who was around then, was still around now – an' wudn' no different.

Alan M. Kent

So, you'm prob'ly wond'ring what happened t'everyone. One day, it might even be written up somewhere in one o'they Pete Frame rock family-trees, but fur the record, here 'tis:

Troon stayed the same as it always was. Every fucker knew every other fucker, an' from the chapel, the ghost o'Wesley kept an eye on anyone procreatin' or breakin' the rules o'temperance.

Camborne an' Redruth stayed much the same as well. Boys from both towns still fought each other on Saturday nights down *The Twilight Zone*, an' the two Job Centres moved t'bigger premises. Everyone still got 'anging on Trevithick Day.

Boy Bluett kept a bunch o'flyers an' posters he'd 'rescued' from every venue *Balance* had played, vainly hoping that one day, they'd be sold off at one o'*Sothebys* auctions o'rock 'n' roll memorabilia.

Kelvin carried on at the bank in town an' updated his PC with Windows Version umpteenth. He carried on seein' Mel. He'd forgotten how old she was by now.

No one saw much o'Markie Phillips. An' as good as his word, Neil an' Ally got married. The stupid bastard was only nineteen, an' Ally was expectin' again. Someone said they'd seen 'un playin' guitar in a covers band down Portreath. In the day, 'ee still stacked value beans at *Tescos*.

An' what of Yak? Well, things got worse fur 'ee before they got better. See, no one in the band really knew how bad the drinkin' an' the smack had got. The needles out *Vic Bars* – then at the festival – well, that was the last straw. Still, Neil said he'd gone in fur some cou세llin' an' was doin' better now. He was still drumming too. Least they wudn' find 'un over Trelawny Shaft dead t'the world with his eyes wide open.

An' Micky an' Jess? Well, that had been hard fur his ma. She'd woken up one mornin' an' Micky's caravan an' van had gone. They'd gone off travellin' fur the summer 'round Britain an' Europe. An' all that after his ma had fixed up Jess with a summer holiday job hairdessin' with Ursula – the cheek o'the maid. An' that Micky – she'd no sooner turned her back, an' he'd moved in – 'ee with the tattoo – an' the pierced frenum – whatever that was.

Talkin' o'movin' in, well, 'twas only temporary-like, an' only on a trial basis, but Tommy had moved back home. An' there

wudn' nothun' like that goin'on yet mind – he was consigned
t'what was Jess's room. An' his ma was sure – if 'ee was t'stay,
they had t'work at it. She knew. She'd seen it on Ricki Lake in
the afternoons. And beer? He only had t'put one step out o'line
an' his fat ass would be out o'the house quicker than a duck can
shit. An' his womanisin' would have t'stop too – 'cept when
'twas on her.

Then there was Bev. Well, when she dropped that final
bombshell about actually goin' t'University on 'un, he knew
there wudn' much point in carryin' on. T'be honest, he'd
expected it fur a while. It wudn' like 'ee stopped loving her
either. It wudn' like that. It was just fur the best. She'd invite
'un up t'Bristol an' that. They had decent bands play up there.
An' she'd write. He'd always be special. They'd always meet up
when she was back down in Cornwall. But na – she was headin'
other places, an' Charlie, well, Charlie was headin' back
t'Trelawny.

The estate? Well, that was a beauty. Followin' a comprehensive study by Kerrier District Council, Cornwall County
Council an' Social Services, the summer would see the start
o'an environmental enhancement scheme. Y'knaw – paint
jobs, trees an' little mulched-in bushes, more seats an' a general face-lift. First off, was the Mayor of Camborne rededicating a
new sign with 'Welcome to Trelawny Gardens' on it. That was
it. Everything was Trelawny Gardens from now on. 'Spect the
sign was in a week before someone had put in the regulation
'You're' before the rest o'it. You really were welcome to it. At
least they'd spelt it right this time.

An' Charlie? What of Charlie? Well, he still saw everyone.
Still drank the same places. Still teased the tackers around the
'Gardens'. Still wished things had been different. You could still
see 'un most Saturdays comin' home from *John Olivers* with a
new CD or two in his hand. He still had a mind t'form another band, but fur now, he was happy enough t'think *Balance* had-
n't been a total lash-up. In some ways, it had been the best
o'times. He knew that, when he stepped on the *First* bus t'go t'
Trelawny Gardens. He knew his legendary status had been guaranteed.

'Eh? You'm Charlie Curnow 'ent 'ee? You used t'be in that
band...'

Alan M. Kent

It wudn' MTV, an' it certainly wudn' the Brit Awards. There wudn' no platinum discs on the wall at home. But it didn' matter. If the bus driver t'Trelawny knew of 'un, he'd made it. He knew it had been a proper bleddy job.

ACKNOWLEDGMENTS

'Lyin' Eyes', words and music by D. Henley/G.Frey. ©1975, Elektra/Asylum, Warner Communications Ltd.

'Paranoid', words and music by Tony Iommi/Bill Ward/Geezer Butler/Ozzy Osbourne. ©1970, Essex Music International Limited.

'Smoke on the Water', words and music by Ian Paice/Jon Lord/Ian Gillan/ Ritchie Blackmore/Roger Glover. ©1972, B. Feldman and Co., Ltd, trading as Hec Music, EMI Music Publishing Ltd.

'Eye of the Tiger', words and music by Frankie Sullivan III and Jim Peterik. ©1982 WB Music Corp., Easy Action Music, Holy Moley Music and Rude Musi©

'Tarot Woman', words and music by Ritchie Blackmore/Ronnie James Dio. ©1976, Eule Music Inc/Armchair Music, BMI.

'All Right Now', words and music by A.Fraser/P. Rodgers. ©1970, Blue Mountain Music Ltd.

'NIB', words and music by Tony Iommi/Geezer Butler/Bill Ward/Ozzy Osbourne. ©1971, Essex Music International Inc.

'Rock and Roll', words and music by Jimmy Page/Robert Plant/John Paul Jones/John Bonham. ©1971, WEA International In©

'Get it on (Bang a Gong)', words and music by Marc Bolan. ©1971, Westminster Music Ltd.

'Since You've Been Gone', words and music by Russ Ballard. ©1979, Island Music Ltd.